George MacDonald

Adela Catheart

George MacDonald

Adela Catheart

ISBN/EAN: 9783337007553

Printed in Europe, USA, Canada, Australia, Japan

Cover: Foto ©Andreas Hilbeck / pixelio.de

More available books at **www.hansebooks.com**

BY

GEORGE MACDONALD

AUTHOR OF "DAVID ELGINBROD," "ROBERT FALCONER," "PHANTASTES," ETC,

> " Me list not of the chaf ne of the stre
> Maken so long a tale as of the corn."
> —CHAUCER.—*Man of Lawes Tale,*

GEORGE ROUTLEDGE AND SONS, LIMITED
NEW YORK: 9 LAFAYETTE PLACE
LONDON, GLASGOW AND MANCHESTER

ADELA CATHCART.

CHAPTER I

CHRISTMAS EVE.

IT was the afternoon of Christmas Eve, sinking towards the night. All day long the wintry light had been diluted with fog, and now the vanguard of the darkness coming to aid the mist, the dying day was well-nigh smothered between them. When I looked through the window, it was into a vague and dim solidification of space, a mysterious region in which awful things might be going on, and out of which anything might come; but out of which nothing came in the mean time, except small sparkles of snow, or rather ice, which, as we swept rapidly onwards, and the darkness deepened, struck faster and faster against the weather-windows. For we, that is, myself and a fellow-passenger, of whom I knew nothing yet but the waistcoat and neckcloth, having caught a glimpse of them as he searched for an obstinate railway-ticket, were in a railway-carriage, darting along, at an all but frightful rate, northwards from London.

Being the sole occupants of the carriage, we had made the most of it, like Englishmen, by taking seats diagonally opposite to each other, laying our heads in the corners, and trying to go to sleep. But for me it was of no use to try any longer. Not that I had anything particular on my mind or spirits; but a man cannot always go to sleep at spare moments. If any-one can, let him consider it a great gift, and make good use of it accordingly; that is, by going to sleep on every such opportunity.

As I, however, could not sleep, much as I should have enjoyed it, I proceeded to occupy my very spare time with building up what I may call a conjectural mould, into which the face, dress, carriage, etc., of my companion would fit. I had already discovered that he was a clergyman; but this added to my difficulties in constructing the said mould. For, theoretically, I had a great dislike to clergymen; having, hitherto, always found that the *clergy* absorbed the *man;* and that the *cloth*, as they called it even themselves, would be no bad epithet for the individual as well as the class. For all clergymen whom I had yet met regarded mankind and their interests solely from the clerical point of view, seeming far more desirous that a man should be a good churchman, as they called it, than that he should love God. Hence there was always an indescribable and, to me, unpleasant odor of their profession about them. If they knew more concerning the *life* of the world than other men, why should everything they said remind one of mustiness and mildew? In a word, why were they not men at worst, when at best they ought to be more of men than other men? And here lay the difficulty: by no effort could I get the face before me to fit into the clerical mould which I had all ready in my own mind for it. That was, at all events, the face of a man, in spite of waistcoat and depilation. I was not even surprised when, all at once, he sat upright in his seat, and asked me if I would join him in a cigar. I gladly consented. And here let me state a fact, which added then to my interest in my fellow-passenger, and will serve now to excuse the enormity of smoking in a railway carriage. We were going to the same place — we must be; and nobody would enter that carriage to-night but the man who had to clean it. For, although we were shooting along at a terrible rate, the train would not stop to set us down, but would cast us loose a mile from our station; and some minutes after it had shot by like an infernal comet of darkness, our carriage would trot gently up to the platform, as if it had come from London all on its own hook — and thought nothing of it.

We were a long way yet, however, from our destination.

The night grew darker and colder, and after the necessary un-muffling occasioned by the cigar process, we drew our wraps closer about us, leaned back in our corners, and smoked away in silence; the red glow of our cigars serving to light the carriage nearly as well as the red nose of the neglected and half-extinguished lamp. For we were in a second-class carriage, a fact for which I leave the clergyman to apologize: it is nothing to me, for I am nobody.

But, after all, I fear I am unjust to the Railway Company, for there was light enough for me to see, and in some measure scrutinize. the face of my fellow-passenger. I could discern a strong chin, and good, useful jaws; with a firm-lipped mouth, and a nose more remarkable for quantity than disposition of mass, being rather low, and very thick. It was surmounted by two brilliant, kindly, black eyes. I lay in wait for his forehead, as if I had been a hunter, and he some peculiar animal that wanted killing right in the middle of it. But it was some time before I was gratified with a sight of it. I did see it, however, and I *was* gratified. For when he wanted to throw away the end of his cigar, finding his window immovable (the frosty wind that bore the snow-flakes blowing from that side), and seeing that I opened mine to accommodate him, he moved across, and, in so doing, knocked his hat against the roof. As he displaced, to replace it, I had my opportunity. It was a splendid forehead for size every way, but chiefly for breadth. A kind of rugged calm rested upon it, — a suggestion of slumbering power, which it delighted me to contemplate. I felt that that was the sort of man to make a friend of, if one had the good luck to be able. But I did not yet make any advance towards further acquaintance.

My reader may, however, be desirous of knowing what kind of person is making so much use of the pronoun *I*. He may have the same curiosity to know his fellow-traveller over the region of these pages, that I had to see the forehead of the clergyman. I can at least prevent any further inconvenience from this possible curiosity, by telling him enough to destroy his interest in me.

I am an —; well, I suppose I *am* an old bachelor; not very far from fifty, in fact; old enough, at all events, to be able to take pleasure in watching without sharing; yet ready, notwithstanding, when occasion offers, to take any necessary part in what may be going on. I am able, as it were, to sit quietly alone, and look down upon life from a second-floor window, delighting myself with my own speculations, and weaving the various threads I gather, into webs of varying kind and quality. Yet, as I have already said, in another form, I am not the last to rush downstairs and into the street, upon occasion of an accident or a row in it, or a conflagration next door. I may just mention, too, that having many years ago formed the Swedenborgian resolution of never growing old, I am as yet able to flatter myself that I am likely to keep it.

In proof of this, if further garrulity about myself can be pardoned, I may state that every year, as Christmas approaches, I begin to grow young again. At least I judge so from the fact that a strange, mysterious pleasure, well known to me by this time, though little understood and very varied, begins to glow in my mind with the first hint, come from what quarter it may, whether from the church-service, or a bookseller's window, that the day of all the year is at hand, — is climbing up from the under-world. I enjoy it like a child. I buy the Christmas number of every periodical I can lay my hands on, especially those that have pictures in them; and, although I am not very fond of plum-pudding, I anticipate with satisfaction the roast beef and the old port that ought always to accompany it. And, above all things, I delight in listening to stories, and sometimes in telling them.

It amuses me to find what a welcome nobody I am amongst young people; for they think I take no heed of them, and don't know what they are doing; when, all the time, I even know what they are thinking. They would wonder to know how often I feel exactly as they do; only I think the feeling is a more earnest and beautiful thing to me than it can be to them yet. If I see a child crowing in his mother's arms, I seem to myself to remember making precisely the same noise in my mother's arms. If I see a youth and a maiden looking into each other's eyes, I know what it means perhaps better than they do. But I say nothing. I do not even smile; for my face is puckered, and I have a weakness about the eyes. But all this will be proof enough that I have not grown very old, in any bad and to-be-avoided sense, at least.

And now all the glow of the Christmas-time was at its height in my heart. For I was going to spend the Day, and a few weeks besides, with a very old friend of mine, who lived near the town at which we were about to arrive like a postscript. Where could my companion be going? I wanted to know, because I hoped to meet him again somehow or other.

I ought to have told you, kind reader, that my name is Smith, — actually *John* Smith; but I'm none the worse for that; and as I do not want to be distinguished much from other people, I do not feel it a hardship.

But where was my companion going? It could not be to my friend's; else I should have known something about him. It could hardly be to the clergyman's, because the vicarage was small, and there was a new curate coming with his wife, whom it would probably have to accommodate until their own house was ready. It could not be to the lawyer's on the hill, because there all were from home on a visit to their relations. It might be to Squire Vernon's, but he was the last man likely to ask a clergyman to visit him; nor would a clergyman be likely to find himself comfortable with the swearing old fox-hunter. The question must, then, for the present, remain unsettled. So I left it, and, looking out of the window once more, buried myself in Christmas fancies.

It was now dark. We were the under half of the world. The sun was scorching and glowing on the other side, leaving us to night and frost. But the night and the frost wake the sunshine of a higher world in our hearts; and who cares for winter weather at Christmas? I believe in the proximate correctness of the date of our Saviour's birth. I believe he always comes in winter. And then let Winter reign without; Love is king within; and Love is lord of the Winter.

How the happy fires were glowing everywhere! We shot past many a lighted cottage, and now and then a brilliant mansion. Inside both were hearts like our own, and faces like ours, with the red coming out on them, the red of joy, because it was Christmas. And most of them had some little feast *toward*. Is it vulgar, this feasting at Christmas? No. It is the Christmas feast that justifies all feasts, as the bread and wine of the communion are the essence of all bread and wine, of all strength and rejoicing. If the Christianity of eating is lost, — I will not say *forgotten*, — the true type of eating is to be found at the dinner-hour in the Zoological Gardens. Certain I am, that but for the love which, ever revealing itself, came out brightest at that first Christmas-time, there would be no feasting, — nay, no smiling; no world to go careering in joy about its central fire ; no men and women upon it, to look up and rejoice.

"But you always look on the bright side of things."

No one spoke aloud; I heard the objection in my mind. Could it come from the mind of my friend, —· for so I already counted him, — opposite to me ? There was no need for that supposition; I had heard the objection too often in my ears. And now I answered it in set, though unspoken form.

"Yes," I said, "I do; for I keep in the light as much as I can. Let the old heathens count Darkness the womb of all things. I count Light the older, from the tread of whose feet fell the first shadow, — and that was Darkness. Darkness exists but by the light, and for the light."

"But that is all mysticism. Look about you. The dark places of the earth are the habitations of cruelty. Men and women blaspheme God and die. How can this, then, be an hour for rejoicing ? "

"They are in God's hands. Take from me my rejoicing, and I am powerless to help them. It shall not destroy the whole bright holiday to me, that my father has given my brother a beating. It will do him good. He needed it somehow. He is looking after them."

Could I have spoken some of these words aloud ? For the eyes of the clergyman were fixed upon me from his corner, as if he were trying to put off his curiosity with the sop of a probable conjecture about me.

"I fear he would think me a heathen," I said to myself. "But if ever there was humanity in a countenance, there it is."

It grew more and more pleasant to think of the bright fire and the cheerful room that awaited me. Nor was the idea of the table, perhaps already beginning to glitter with crystal and silver, altogether uninteresting to me. For I was growing hungry.

But the speed at which we were now going was quite com-

forting. I dropped into a reverie. I was roused from it by
the sudden ceasing of the fierce oscillation, which had for
some time been threatening to make a jelly of us. We were
loose. In three minutes more we should be at Purleybridge.

And, in three minutes more, we were at Purleybridge, —
the only passengers but one who arrived at the station that
night. A servant was waiting for me, and I followed him
through the booking-office to the carriage destined to bear me
to "The Swanspond," as my friend Colonel Cathcart's house
was called.

As I stepped into the carriage, I saw the clergyman walk
by, with his carpet-bag in his hand.

Now I knew Colonel Cathcart intimately enough to offer
the use of his carriage to my late companion; but, at the
moment I was about to address him, the third passenger, of
whom I had taken no particular notice, came between us, and
followed me into the carriage. This occasioned a certain hesitation, with which I am only too easily affected; the footman
shut the door; I caught one glimpse of the clergyman turning the corner of the station into a field path; the horses
made a scramble; and away I rode to the Swanspond, feeling
as selfish as ten Pharisees. It is true, I had not spoken a
word to him beyond accepting his invitation to smoke with
him; and yet I felt almost sure that we should meet again,
and that, when we did, we should both be glad of it. And
now he was carrying a carpet-bag, and I was seated in a carriage and pair!

It was far too dark for me to see what my new companion
was like; but when the light from the colonel's hall-door
flashed upon us as we drew up, I saw that he was a young
man, with a certain expression in his face which a first glance
might have taken for fearlessness and power of some sort, but
which, notwithstanding, I felt to be rather repellant than
otherwise. The moment the carriage-door was opened, he
called the servant by his name, saying: —

"When the cart comes with the luggage, send mine up
directly. Take that now."

And he handed him his dressing-bag.

He spoke in a self-approving tone, and with a drawl which
I will not attempt to imitate, because I find all such imitation

tends to caricature; and I want to be believed. Besides, I find the production of caricature has unfailingly a bad moral reaction upon myself. I dare say it is not so with others, but with that I have nothing to do: it is one of my weaknesses.

My worthy old friend, the colonel, met us in the hall, — straight, broad-shouldered, and tall, with a severe military expression underlying the genuine hospitality of his countenance, as if he could not get rid of a sense of duty, even when doing what he liked best. The door of the dining-room was partly open, and from it came the red glow of a splendid fire, the chink of encountering glass and metal, and, best of all, the pop of a cork.

"Would you like to go upstairs, Smith, or will you have a glass of wine first? How do you do, Percy?"

"Thank you; I'll go to my room at once," I said.

"You'll find a fire there, I know. Having no regiment now, I look after my servants. Mind you make use of them. I can't find enough of work for them."

He left me, and again addressed the youth, who had by this time got out of his great-coat, and, cold as it was, stood looking at his hands by the hall-lamp. As I moved away, I heard him say, in a careless tone: —

"And how's Adela, uncle?"

The reply did not reach me, but I knew now who the young fellow was.

Hearing a kind of human grunt behind me, I turned and saw that I was followed by the butler; and, by a kind of intuition, I knew that this grunt was a remark, — an inarticulate one, true, but not the less to the point on that account. I knew that he had been in the dining-room by the pop I had heard; and I knew by the grunt that he had heard his master's observation about his servants.

"Come, Beeves," I said, "I don't want your help. You've got plenty to do, you know, at dinner-time; and your master is rather hard upon you, — isn't he?"

I knew the man, of course.

"Well, Mr. Smith, master is the best master in the country, *he is*. But he don't know what work is, *he don't*."

"Well, go to your work, and never mind me. I know every turn in the house as well as yourself, Beeves."

"No, Mr. Smith; I'll attend to you, if *you* please. Mr. Percy will take care of *his*-self. There's no fear of him. But you're my business. You are sure to give a man a kind word who does his best to please you."

"Why, Beeves, I think that is the least a man can do."

"It's the most too, sir; and some people think it's too much."

I saw that the man was hurt, and sought to soothe him.

"You and I are old friends, at least, Beeves."

"Yes, Mr. Smith. Money won't do't, sir. My master gives good wages, and I'm quite independing of visitors. But when a gentleman says to me, 'Beeves, I'm obliged to you,' why, then, Mr. Smith, you feels at one *and* the same time, that he's a gentleman, and that you aint a boot-jack or a coal-scuttle. It's the sentiman, Mr. Smith. If he despises us, why, we despises him. And we don't like waiting on a gentleman as aint a gentleman. Ring the bell, Mr. Smith, when you want anythink, and *I'll* attend to you."

He had been twenty years in the colonel's service. He was not an old soldier, yet had a thorough *esprit de corps*, looking upon service as an honorable profession. In this he was not only right, but had a vast advantage over everybody whose profession is not sufficiently honorable for his ambition. All such must *feel* degraded. Beeves was fifty; and, happily for his opinion of his profession, had never been to London.

And the colonel was the best of masters; for, because he ruled well, every word of kindness told. It is with servants as with children and with horses, — it is of no use caressing them unless they know that you mean them to go.

When the dinner-bell rang, I proceeded to the drawing-room. The colonel was there, and I thought for a moment that he was alone. But I soon saw that a couch by the fire was occupied by his daughter, the Adela after whose health I had heard young Percy Cathcart inquiring. She was our hostess, for Mrs. Cathcart had been dead for many years, and Adela had been her only child. I approached to pay my respects; but as soon as I got near enough to see her face, I turned involuntarily to her father, and said: —

"Cathcart, you never told me of this!"

He made me no reply; but I saw the long, stern upper lip

twitching convulsively. I turned again to Adela, who tried
to smile — with precisely the effect of a momentary gleam of
sunshine upon a cold, leafless, and wet landscape.

" Adela, my dear, what is the matter ? "

" I don't know, uncle."

She had called me unc.e since ever she had begun to speak,
which must have been nearly twenty years ago.

I stood and looked at her. Her face was pale and thin, and
her eyes were large, and yet sleepy. I may say at once that
she had dark eyes and a sweet face ; and that is all the description I mean to give of her. I had been accustomed to see
that face, if not rosy, yet plump and healthy ; and those eyes
with plenty of light for themselves, and some to spare for other
people. But it was neither her wan look nor her dull eyes
that distressed me ; it was the expression of her face. It was
very sad to look at ; but it was not so much sadness as utter
and careless hopelessness that it expressed.

" Have you any pain, Adela ? " I asked.

" No," she answered.

" But you feel ill ? "

" Yes."

" How ? "

" I don't know."

And as she spoke, she tapped with one finger on the edge
of the *couvre-pied* which was thrown over her, and gave a
sigh as if her very heart was weary of everything.

" Shall you come down to dinner with us ? "

" Yes, uncle ; I suppose I must."

" If you would rather have your dinner sent up, my love
— " began her father.

" Oh ! no. It is all the same to me. I may as well go
down."

My young companion of the carriage now entered, got up
expensively. He, too, looked shocked when he saw her.

" Why, Addie ! " he said.

But she received him with perfect indifference, just lifting
one cold hand towards his, and then letting it fall again where
it had lain before. Percy looked a little mortified ; in fact,
more mortified now than sorry ; turned away, and stared at
the fire.

Every time I open my mouth in a drawing-room before dinner, I am aware of an amount of self-denial worthy of a forlorn hope. Yet the silence was so awkward now, that I felt I must make an effort to say something; and the more original the remark the better I felt it would be for us all. But, with the best intentions, all I could effect was to turn towards Mr. Percy and say :—

"Rather cold for travelling, is it not?"

"Those foot-warmers are capital things, though," he answered. "Mine was jolly hot. Might have roasted a potato on it, by Jove!"

"I came in a second-class carriage," I replied; "and they are too cold to need a foot-warmer."

He gave a shrug with his shoulders, as if he had suddenly found himself in low company, and must make the best of it. But he offered no further remark.

Beeves announced dinner.

"Will you take Adela, Mr. Smith?" said the colonel.

"I think I won't go, after all, papa, if you don't mind. I don't want any dinner."

"Very well, my dear," began her father, but could not help showing his distress; perceiving which, Adela rose instantly from her couch, put her arm in his, and led the way to the dining-room. Percy and I followed.

"What can be the matter with the girl?" thought I. "She used to be merry enough. Some love affair, I shouldn't wonder. I've never heard of any. I know her father favors that puppy Percy; but I don't think she is dying for *him*."

It was the dreariest Christmas Eve I had ever spent. The fire was bright; the dishes were excellent; the wine was thorough; the host was hospitable; the servants were attentive; and yet the dinner was as gloomy as if we had all known it to be the last we should ever eat together. If a ghost had been sitting in its shroud at the head of the table, instead of Adela, it could hardly have cast a greater chill over the guests. She did her duty well enough; but she did not look it; and the charities which occasioned her no pleasure in the administration could hardly occasion us much in the reception.

As soon as she had left the room, Percy broke out, with more emphasis than politeness: —

"What the devil's the matter with Adela, uncle?"

"Indeed, I can't tell, my boy," answered the colonel, with more kindness than the form of the question deserved.

"Have you no conjecture on the subject?" I asked.

"None. I have tried hard to find out; but I have altogether failed. She tells me there is nothing the matter with her, only she is so tired. What has she to tire her?"

"If she is tired inside first, everything will tire her."

"I wish you would try to find out, Smith."

"I will."

"Her mother died of a decline."

"I know. Have you had no advice?"

"Oh, yes! Dr. Wade is giving her steel-wine, and quinine, and all that sort of thing. For my part, I don't believe in their medicines. Certainly they don't do her any good."

"Is her chest affected, — does he say?"

"He says not; but I believe he knows no more about the state of her chest than he does about the other side of the moon. He's a stupid old fool. He comes here for his fees, and he has them."

"Why don't you call in another, if you are not satisfied?"

"Why, my dear fellow, they're all the same in this infernal old place. I believe they've all embalmed themselves, and are going by clock-work. They and the clergy make sad fools of us. But we make worse fools of ourselves to have them about us. To be sure, they see that everything is proper. The doctor makes sure that we are dead before we are buried, and the parson that we are buried after we are dead. About the resurrection I suspect he knows as much as we do. He goes by book."

In his perplexity and sorrow, the poor colonel was irritable and unjust. I saw that it would be better to suggest than to reason. And I partly took the homœopathic system, — the only one on which mental distress, at least, can be treated with any advantage.

"Certainly," I said, "the medical profession has plenty of men in it who live on humanity, like the very diseases they attempt to cure. And plenty of the clergy find the Church a tolerably profitable investment. The reading of the absolution is as productive to them now, as it was to the pardon-sellers of old. But surely, colonel, you won't huddle them all up together in one shapeless mass of condemnation?"

"You always were right, Smith, and I'm a fool, as usual. Percy, my boy, what's going on at Somerset House?"

"The river, uncle."

"Nothing else?"

"Well — I don't know. Nothing much. It's horribly slow!"

"I'm afraid you won't find this much better. But you must take care of yourself."

"I've made that a branch of special study, uncle. I flatter myself I *can* do that."

Colonel Cathcart laughed. Percy was the son of his only brother, who had died young, and he had an especial affection for him. And where the honest old man loved, he could see no harm; for he reasoned something in this way: "He must be all right, or how could I like him as I do?" But Percy was a commonplace, selfish fellow, — of that I was convinced, — whatever his other qualities, good or bad, might be; and I sincerely hoped that any designs he might have of marrying his cousin might prove as vain as his late infantile passion for the moon. For I beg to assure my readers that the circumstances in which I have introduced Adela Cathcart are no more fair to her real character than my lady readers would consider the effect of a lamp-shade of bottle-green true in its presentation of their complexion.

We did not sit long over our wine. When we went up to the drawing-room, Adela was not there, nor did she make her appearance again that evening. For a little while we tried to talk; but, after many failures, I yielded and withdrew on the score of fatigue; no doubt relieving the mind of my old friend by doing so, for he had severe ideas of the duty of a host as well as of a soldier, and to these ideas he found it at present impossible to elevate the tone of his behavior.

When I reached my own room, I threw myself into the easiest of arm-chairs, and began to reflect.

"John Smith," I said, "this is likely to be as uncomfortable a Christmas-tide, as you, with your all but ubiquity, have ever had the opportunity of passing. Nevertheless, please to remember a resolution you came to once upon a time, — that, as you were nobody, so you would be nobody, — and see if you can make yourself useful. — What can be the matter with Adela?"

I sat and reflected for a long time; for during my life I had had many opportunities of observation, and amongst other cases that had interested me I had seen some not unlike the present. The fact was, that as everybody counted me nobody, I had taken full advantage of my conceded nonentity, which, like Jack the Giant-killer's coat of darkness, enabled me to learn much that would otherwise have escaped me. My reflections on my observations, however, did not lead me to any further or more practical conclusion, just yet, than that other and better advice ought to be called in.

Having administered this sedative sop to my restless practicalness, I went to bed and to sleep.

CHAPTER II.

CHURCH.

ADELA did not make her appearance at the breakfast-table next morning, although it was the morning of Christmas day. And no one who had seen her at dinner on Christmas eve, would have expected to see her at breakfast on Christmas morn. Yet although her absence was rather a relief, such a gloom occupied her place that our party was anything but cheerful. But the world about us was happy enough, not merely at its unseen heart of fire, but on its wintered countenance, — evidently to all men. It was not "to hide her guilty front," as Milton says, in the first two — and the least worthy — stanzas on the Nativity, that the earth wooed the gentle air for innocent snow, but to put on the best smile and the loveliest dress that the cold time and her suffering state would allow, in welcome of the Lord of the snow and the summer. I thought of the lines from Crashaw's "Hymn of the Nativity," — Crashaw, who always suggested to me Shelley turned a Catholic Priest:

> • I saw the curled drops, soft and slow,
>   Come hovering o'er the place's **head,**
> Offering their whitest sheets of snow,
>   To furnish the fair infant's bed.
> Forbear, said I, be not too bold:
> Your fleece is white, but 'tis too cold.".

And as the sun shone rosy with mist, I naturally thought of the next following stanza of the same hymn: —

> "I saw the obsequious seraphim
>   Their rosy fleece of fire bestow;
> For well they now can spare their wings,
>   Since heaven itself lies here below.
> Well done! said I; but are you sure
> Your down, so warm, will pass for pure?"

Adela, pale face and all, was down in time for church; and she and the colonel and I walked to it together by the meadow path, where, on each side, the green grass was peeping up through the glittering frost. For the colonel, notwithstanding his last night's outbreak upon the clergy, had a profound respect for them, and considered church-going one of those military duties which belonged to every honest soldier and gentleman. Percy had found employment elsewhere.

It was a blessed little church that, standing in a little meadow, church-yard, with a low, strong ancient tower, and great buttresses that put one in mind of the rock of ages, and a mighty still river that flowed past the tower end, and a picturesque, straggling, well-to-do parsonage at the chancel end. The church was nearly covered with ivy, and looked as if it had grown out of the church-yard, to be ready for the poor folks, as soon as they got up again, to praise God in. But it had stood a long time, and none of them came; and the praise of the living must be a poor thing to the praise of the dead, notwithstanding all that the Psalmist says. So the church got disheartened, and drooped, and now looked very old and gray-headed. It could not get itself filled with praise enough. And into this old, and quaint, and weary but stout-hearted church, we went that bright winter morning, to hear about a baby. My heart was full enough before I left it.

Old Mr. Venables read the service with a voice and manner far more memorial of departed dinners than of joys to come:

but I sat, — little heeding the service, I confess, — with my mind full of thoughts that made me glad.

Now all my glad thoughts came to me through a hole in the tower-door. For the door was far in a shadowy retreat, and in the irregular, lozenge-shaped hole in it there was a piece of coarse thick glass of a deep yellow. And through this yellow glass the sun shone. And the cold shine of the winter sun was changed into the warm glory of summer by the magic of that bit of glass.

Now, when I saw the glow first, I thought, without thinking, that it came from some inner place, some shrine of old, or some ancient tomb in the chancel of the church, — forgetting the points of the compass, — where one might pray as in the *penetralia* of the temple; and I gazed on it as the pilgrim might gaze upon the lamp-light oozing from the cavern of the Holy Sepulchre. But some one opened the door, and the clear light of the Christmas morn broke upon the pavement, and swept away the summer splendor. The door was to the outside. And I said to myself: All the doors that lead inwards to the secret place of the Most High are doors outwards, — out of self, — out of smallness, — out of wrong. And these were some of the thoughts that came to me through the hole in the door, and made me forget the service, which Mr. Venables mumbled like a nicely cooked sweetbread.

But another voice broke the film that shrouded the ears of my brain, and the words became inspired and alive, and I forgot my own thoughts in listening to the Holy Book. For is not the voice of every loving spirit a fresh inspiration to the dead letter? With a voice other than this, does it not kill? And I thought I had heard the voice before, but where I sat I could not see the Communion Table. At length the preacher ascended the pulpit stairs, and, to my delight and the rousing of an altogether unwonted expectation, who should it be but my fellow-traveller of last night!

He had a look of having something to say; and I immediately felt that I had something to hear. Having read his text, which I forget, the broad-browed man began with something like this : —

"It is not the high summer alone that is God's. The winter also is his. And into his winter he came to visit us.

And all man's winters are his, — the winter of our poverty, the winter of our sorrow, the winter of our unhappiness — even the 'winter of our discontent.' ''

I stole a glance at Adela. Her large eyes were fixed on the preacher.

"Winter," he went on, "does not belong to death, although the outside of it looks like death. Beneath the snow the grass is growing. Below the frost the roots are warm and alive. Winter is only a spring too weak and feeble for us to see that it is living. The cold does for all things what the gardener has sometimes to do for valuable trees, — he must half kill them before they will bear any fruit. Winter is in truth the small beginnings of the spring."

I glanced at Adela again; and still her eyes were fastened on the speaker.

"The winter is the childhood of the year. Into this childhood of the year came the child Jesus; and into this childhood of the year must we all descend. It is as if God spoke to each of us according to our need: My son, my daughter, you are growing old and cunning; you must grow a child again, with my Son, this blessed birth-time. You are growing old and selfish; you must become a child. You are growing old and careful; you must become a child. You are growing old and distrustful; you must become a child. You are growing old, and petty, and weak, and foolish; you must become a child, — my child, like the baby there, that strong sunrise of faith and hope and love, lying in his mother's arms in the stable.

"But one may say to me: 'You are talking in a dream. The Son of God is a child no longer. He is the King of Heaven.' True, my friends. But He who is the Unchangeable could never become anything that He was not always, for that would be to change. He is as much a child now as ever he was. When he became a child, it was only to show us by itself, that we might understand it better, what he was always in his deepest nature. And when he was a child, he was not less the King of Heaven; for it is in virtue of his childhood, of his sonship, that he is Lord of Heaven and of Earth, — 'for of such' — namely, of children — 'is the kingdom of heaven.' And, therefore, when we think of the baby now, it is still of the Son of man, of the King of men, that we think. And all the feelings that the thought of that babe can wake in us are as true now as they were on that first Christmas day, when Mary covered from the cold his little naked feet, ere long to be washed with the tears of repentant women, and nailed by the hands of thoughtless men, who know not what they did, to the cross of fainting, and desolation, and death."

Adela was hiding her face now.

"So, my friends, let us be children this Christmas. Of course, when I say to any one, 'You must be like a child,' I mean a good child. A naughty child is not a child as long as his naughtiness lasts. He is not what God meant when he said, 'I will make a child.' Think of the best child you know, — the one who has filled you with most admiration. It is his child-likeness that has so delighted you. It is because he is so true to the child-nature that you admire him. Jesus is like that child. You must be like that child. But you cannot help knowing some faults in him, — some things that are like ill-grown men and women. Jesus is not like him, there. Think of the best child you can imagine ; nay, think of a better than you can imagine, — of the one that God thinks of when he invents a child in the depths of his fatherhood : such childlike men and women must you one day become ; and what day better to begin, than this blessed Christmas morn ? Let such a child be born in your hearts this day. Take the child Jesus to your bosoms, into your very souls, and let him grow there till he is one with your every thought, and purpose, and hope. As a good child born in a family will make the family good ; so Jesus, born into the world, will make the world good at last. And this perfect child, born in your hearts, will make your hearts good ; and that is God's best gift to you.

"Then be happy this Christmas day ; for to you a child is born. Childless women, this infant is yours — wives or maidens. Fathers and mothers, he is your first-born, and he will save his brethren. Eat and drink, and be merry and kind, for the love of God is the source of all joy and all good things, and this love is present in the child Jesus. Now, to God the Father, etc "

"O my baby Lord!" I said in my heart; for the clergyman had forgotten me, and said nothing about us old bachelors.

Of course this is but the substance of the sermon; and as, although I came to know him well before many days were over, he never lent me his manuscript, — indeed, I doubt if he had any, — my report must have lost something of his nervous strength, and be diluted with the weakness of my style.

Although I had been attending so well to the sermon, however, my eyes had now and then wandered, not only to Adela's face, but all over the church as well; and I could not help observing, a few pillars off, and partly round a corner, the face of a young man, — well, he was about thirty, I should guess, — out of which looked a pair of well-opened hazel eyes, with rather notable eyelashes. Not that I, with my own weak pair of washed-out gray, could see the eyelashes at that distance, but I judged it must be their length that gave a kind of feminine cast to the outline of the eyes. Nor should I have noticed the face itself much, had it not seemed to me that those eyes were pursuing a very thievish course; for, by the fact that, as often as I looked their way, I saw the motion of their withdrawal, I concluded that they were stealing glances at, certainly not from, my adopted niece, Adela. This made me look at the face more attentively. I found it a fine, frank, brown, country-looking face. Could it have anything to do with Adela's condition? Absurd! How could such health and ruddy life have anything to do with the worn pallor of her countenance? Nor did a single glance on the part of Adela reveal that she was aware of the existence of the neighboring observatory. I dismissed the idea. And I was right, as time showed.

We remained to the Communion. When that was over, we walked out of the old dark-roofed church, Adela looking as sad as ever, into the bright, cold sunshine, which wrought no change on her demeanor. How could it, if the sun of righteousness, even, had failed for the time? And there, in the church-yard, we found Percy, standing astride of an infant's grave, with his hands in his trowser-pockets, and an air of condescending satisfaction on his countenance, which seemed to say to the dead beneath him: "Pray, don't apologize. I know you are disagreeable; but you can't help it, you know;" and to the living coming out of church : " Well, have you had your little whim out ? "

But what he did say was to Adela : —

" A merry Christmas to you, Addie! Won't you lean on me ? You don't look very stunning."

But her sole answer was to take my arm ; and so we walked towards the Swanspond.

" I suppose that's what they call 'Broad Church,' " said the colonel.

" Generally speaking, I prefer breadth," I answered, vaguely. " Do you think that's 'Broad Church' ? "

" Oh ! I don't know. I suppose it's all right. He ran me through, anyhow."

" I hope it *is* all right," I answered. " It suits me."

" Well, I'm sure you know ten times better than I do. He seems a right sort of man, whatever sort of clergyman he may be."

" Who is he, — can you tell me ? "

" Why, don't you know? That's our new curate, Mr. Armstrong."

" Curate! " I exclaimed. " A man like that ! And at his years too ! He must be forty. You astonish me ! "

" Well, I don't know. He may be forty. He is our curate; that is all I can answer for."

" He was my companion in the train last night."

" Ah, that accounts for it. You had some talk with him, and found him out? I believe he is a superior sort of man, too. Old Mr. Venables seems to like him."

" All the talk I have had with him passed between pulpit and pew this morning," I replied; " for the only words that we exchanged last night were, ' Will you join me in a cigar ? ' from him, and ' With much pleasure,' from me."

" Then, upon my life, I can't see what you think remarkable in his being a curate. Though I confess, as I said before, he ran me through the body. I'm rather soft-hearted, I believe, since Addie's illness."

He gave her a hasty glance. But she took no notice of what he had said; and, indeed, seemed to have taken no notice of the conversation, — to which Percy had shown an equal amount of indifference. A very different indifference seemed the only bond between them.

When we reached home, we found lunch ready for us, and after waiting a few minutes for Adela, but in vain, we seated ourselves at the table.

"Awfully like Sunday, and a cold dinner, uncle!" remarked Percy.

"We'll make up for that, my boy, when dinner-time comes."

"You don't like Sunday, then, Mr. Percy?" I said.

"A horrid bore," he answered. "My old mother made me hate it. We had to go to church twice; and that was even worse than her veal-broth. But the worst of it is, I can't get it out of my head that I ought to be there, even when I'm driving tandem to Richmond."

"Ah! your mother will be with us on Sunday, I hope, Percy."

"Good heavens, uncle! Do you know what you are about? My mother here! I'll just ring the bell, and tell James to pack my traps. I won't stand it. I can't. Indeed I can't."

He rose as he spoke. His uncle caught him by the arm, laughing, and made him sit down again; which he did with real or pretended reluctance.

"We'll take care of you, Percy. Never mind. Don't be a fool," he added, seeing the evident annoyance of the young fellow.

"Well, uncle, you ought to have known better," said Percy, sulkily, as, yielding, he resumed his seat, and poured himself out a bumper of claret, by way of consolation.

He had not been much of a companion before; now he made himself almost as unpleasant as a young man could be, and that is saying a great deal. One, certainly, had need to have found something beautiful at church, for here was the prospect of as wretched a Christmas dinner as one could ever wish to avoid.

When Percy had drunk another bumper of claret, he rose and left the room, and my host, turning to me, said: —

"I fear, Smith, you will have anything but a merry Christmas, this year. I hoped the sight of you would cheer up poor Adela, and set us all right. And now Percy's out of humor at the thought of his mother coming, and I'm sure I don't know what's to be done. We shall sit over our dinner to-day like four crows over a carcass. It's very good of you to stop."

"Oh! never mind me," I said. "I, too, can take care of myself. But has Adela no companions of her own age?"

"None but Percy. And I am afraid she has got tired of him. He's a good fellow, though a bit of a puppy. That'll wear off. I wish he would take a fancy to the army, now."

I made no reply, but I thought the more. It seemed to me that to get tired of Percy was the most natural proceeding that could be adopted with regard to him and all about him.

But men judge men — and women, women — hardly.

"I'll tell you what I will do," said the colonel. "I will ask Mr. Bloomfield, the school-master, and his wife, to dine with us. It's no use asking anybody else that I can think of. But they have no family, and I dare say they can put off their own Christmas dinner till to-morrow. They have but one maid, and she can dine with our servants. They are very respectable people, I assure you."

The colonel always considered his plans thoroughly, and then acted on them at once. He rose.

"A capital idea!" I said, as he disappeared. I went up to look for Adela. She was not in the drawing-room. I went up again, and tapped at the door of her room.

"Come in," she said, in a listless voice.

I entered.

"How are you now, Adela?" I asked.

"Thank you, uncle," was all her reply.

"What is the matter with you, my child?" I said, and drew a chair near hers. She was half reclining, with a book lying upside down on her knee.

"I would tell you at once, uncle, if I knew," she answered very sweetly, but as sadly. "I believe I am dying; but of what I have not the smallest idea."

"Nonsense!" I said. "You're not dying."

"You need not think to comfort me that way, uncle; for I think I would rather die than not."

"Is there anything you would like?"

"Nothing. There is nothing worth liking, but sleep."

"Don't you sleep at night?"

"Not well. I will tell you all I know about it. Some six

weeks ago, I woke suddenly one morning, very early, — I think about three o'clock, —with an overpowering sense of blackness and misery. Everything I thought of seemed to have a core of wretchedness in it. I fought with the feeling as well as I could, and got to sleep again. But the effect of it did not leave me next day. I said to myself: 'They say " morning thoughts are true." What if this should be the true way of looking at things?' And everything became gray and dismal about me. Next morning it was just the same. It was as if I had waked in the middle of some chaos over which God had never said : 'Let there be light.' And the next day was worse. I began to see the bad in everything, — wrong motives, and self-love, and pretence, and everything mean and low. And so it has gone on ever since. I wake wretched every morning. I am crowded with wretched, if not wicked, thoughts, all day. Nothing seems worth anything. I don't care for anything."

"But you love somebody?"

" I hope I love my father. I don't know. I don't feel as if I did."

"And there's your cousin Percy." I confess this was a feeler I put out.

" Percy's a fool!" she said, with some show of indignation, which I hailed, for more reasons than one.

" But you enjoyed the sermon this morning, did you not?"

" I don't know. I thought it very poetical and very pretty; but whether it was true, — how could I tell? I didn't care. The baby he spoke about was nothing to me. I didn't love him, or want to hear about him. Don't you think me a brute, uncle?"

" No, I don't. I think you are ill. And I think we shall find something that will do you good; but I can't tell yet what. You will dine with us, won't you?"

" Oh! yes, if you and papa wish it."

" Of course we do. He is just gone to ask Mr. and Mrs. Bloomfield to dine with us."

" Oh!"

" You don't mind, do you?"

" Oh, no! They are nice people. I like them both."

" Well, I will leave you, my child. Sleep if you can

will go and walk in the garden, and think what can be done for my little girl."

"Thank you, uncle. But you can't do me any good. What if this should be the true way of things? It is better to know it, if it is."

"Disease couldn't make a sun in the heavens. But it could make a man blind, that he could not see it."

"I don't understand you."

"Never mind. It's of no consequence whether you do or not. When you see light again, you will believe in it. For light compels faith."

"I believe in you, uncle; I do."

"Thank you, my dear. Good-by."

I went round by the stables, and there found the colonel, talking to his groom. He had returned already from his call, and the Bloomfields were coming. I met Percy next, sauntering about, with a huge cigar in his mouth.

"The Bloomfields are coming to dinner, Mr. Percy," I said.

"Who are they?"

"The school-master and his wife."

"Just like that precious old uncle of mine! Why the deuce did he ask *me* this Christmas? I tell you what, Mr. Smith, — I can't stand it. There's nothing, not even cards, to amuse a fellow. And when my mother comes, it will be ten times worse. I'll cut and run for it."

"Oh, no, you won't," I said. But I heartily wished he would. I confess the insincerity, and am sorry for it.

"But what the devil does my mother want, coming here?"

"I haven't the pleasure of knowing your mother, so I cannot tell what the devil she can want, coming here."

"Humph!"

He walked away.

CHAPTER III.

THE CHRISTMAS DINNER.

MR. AND MRS. BLOOMFIELD arrived; the former a benevolent, gray-haired man, with a large nose and small mouth, yet with nothing of the foolish look which often accompanies such a malconformation; and the latter a nice-looking little body, middle-aged, rather more; with half-gray curls, and a cap with black ribbons. Indeed, they were both in mourning. Mr. Bloomfield bore himself with a kind of unworldly grace, and Mrs. Bloomfield with a kind of sweet primness. The school-master was inclined to be talkative; nor was his wife behind him; and that was just what we wanted.

"I am sorry to see you in mourning," said the colonel to Mr. Bloomfield, during dessert. "I trust it is for no near relative."

"No relative at all, sir. But a boy of mine, to whom, through God's grace, I did a good turn once, and whom, as a consequence, I loved ever after."

"Tell Colonel Cathcart the story, James," said his wife. "It can do no harm to anybody now; and you needn't mention names, you know. You would like to hear it, wouldn't you, sir?"

"Very much indeed," answered the colonel.

"Well, sir," began the school-master, there's "not much in it to you, I fear; though there was a good deal to him and me. I was usher in a school at Peckham once. I was but a lad, but I tried to do my duty; and the first part of my duty seemed to me to take care of the characters of the boys. So I tried to understand them all, and their ways of looking at things, and thinking about them.

"One day, to the horror of the masters, it was discovered that a watch belonging to one of the boys had been stolen.

The boy who had lost it was making a dreadful fuss about it, and declaring he would tell the police, and set them to find it.   The moment I heard of it, my suspicion fell, half by knowledge, half by instinct, upon a certain boy.   He was one of the most gentlemanly boys in the school; but there was a look of cunning in the corner of his eye, and a look of greed in the corner of his mouth, which now and then came out clear enough to me.   Well, sir, I pondered for a few moments what I should do.   I wanted to avoid calling any attention to him; so I contrived to make the worst of him in the Latin class, — he was not a bad scholar, — and so keep him in when the rest went to play.   As soon as they were gone, I took him into my own room, and said to him, 'Fred, my boy, you knew your lesson well enough; but I wanted you here.   You stole Simmons' watch.' "

" You had better mention no names, Mr Bloomfield," interrupted his wife.

" I beg your pardon, my dear.   But it doesn't matter. Simmons was eaten by a tiger, ten years ago.   And I hope he agreed with him, for he never did with anybody else I ever heard of.   He was the worst boy I ever knew.   'You stole Simmons' watch.   Where is it?'   He fell on his knees, as white as a sheet.   'I sold it,' he said, in a voice choked with terror.   'God help you, my boy !'   I exclaimed.   He burst out crying.   'Where did you sell it?'   He told me.   'Where's the money you got for it?' — 'That's all I have left,' he answered, pulling out a small handful of shillings and half-crowns.   'Give it me,' I said.   He gave it me at once.   'Now you go to your lesson, and hold your tongue.'   I got a sovereign of my own to make up the sum, — I could ill spare it, sir, but the boy could worse spare his character, — and I hurried off to the place where he had sold the watch.   To avoid scandal, I was forced to pay the man the whole price, though I dare say an older man would have managed better.   At all events, I brought it home.   I contrived to put it in the boy's own box, so that the whole affair should appear to have been only a trick, and then I gave the culprit a very serious talking-to.   He never did anything of the sort again, and died an honorable man and a good officer, only three months ago, in India.   A thousand times over did he repay me the money I had spent for him, and he left me this gold watch in his will, — a memorial, not so much of his fault as of his deliverance from some of its natural consequences."

The school-master pulled out the watch as he spoke, and we all looked at it with respect.

It was a simple story and simply told. But I was pleased to see that Adela took some interest in it. I remembered that, as a child, she had always liked better to be told a story than to have any other amusement whatever. And many a story I had had to coin on the spur of the moment for the satisfaction of her childish avidity for that kind of mental bull's eye.

When we gentlemen were left alone, and the servants had withdrawn. Mr. Bloomfield said to our host : —

"I am sorry to see Miss Cathcart looking so far from well, colonel. I hope you have good advice for her."

"Dr. Wade has been attending her for some time, but I don't think he's doing her any good."

"Don't you think it might be well to get the new doctor to see her? He's quite a remarkable man, I assure you."

"What! The young fellow that goes flying about the country in boots and breeches?"

"Well, I suppose that is the man I mean. He's not so very young though, — he's thirty at least. And for the boots and breeches, — I asked him once, in a joking way, whether he did not think them rather unprofessional. But he told me he saved ever so much time in open weather by going across the country. 'And,' said he, 'if I can see patients sooner, and more of them, in that way, I think it is quite professional. The other day,' he said, 'I was sent for, and I went straight as the crow flies, and I beat a little baby only by five minutes after all.' Of course after that there was nothing more to say."

"He has very queer notions, hasn't he?"

"Yes, he has, for a medical man. He goes to church, for instance."

"I don't count that a fault."

"Well, neither do I. Rather the contrary. But one of the profession here says it is for the sake of being called out in the middle of the service."

"Oh! that is stale. I don't think he would find that answer. But it is a pity he is not married."

"So it is. I wish he were. But that is a fault that may be remedied some day. One thing I know about him is, that when I called him in to see one of my boarders, he sat by his bedside half an hour, watching him, and then went away without giving him any medicine."

"I don't see the good of that. What do you make of that? I call it very odd."

"He said to me: 'I am not sure what is the matter with him. A wrong medicine would do him more harm than the right one would do him good. Meantime he is in no danger. I will come and see him to-morrow morning.' Now I liked that, because it showed me that he was thinking over the case. The boy was well in two days. Not that that indicates much. All I say is, he is not a common man."

"I don't like to dismiss Dr. Wade."

"No; but you must not stand on ceremony, if he is doing her no good. You are judge enough of that."

I thought it best to say nothing; but I heartily approved of all the honest gentleman said; and I meant to use my persuasion afterwards, if necessary, to the same end; for I liked all he told about the new doctor. I asked his name.

"Mr. Armstrong," answered the school-master.

"Armstrong?" I repeated. "Is not that the name of the new curate?"

"To be sure. They are brothers. Henry, the doctor, is considerably younger than the curate."

"Did the curate seek the appointment because the doctor was here before him?"

"I suppose so. They are much attached to each other."

"If he is at all equal as a doctor to what I think his brother is as a preacher, Purleybridge is a happy place to possess two such healers," I said.

"Well, time will show," returned Mr. Bloomfield.

All this time Percy sat yawning and drinking claret. When we joined the ladies, we found them engaged in a little gentle chat. There was something about Mrs. Bloomfield that was very pleasing. The chief ingredient in it was a certain quaint repose. She looked as if her heart were at rest; as if for her everything was right; as if she had a little room of her own, just to her mind, and there her soul sat, looking out, through the muslin curtains of modest charity, upon the world that went hurrying and seething past her windows. When we entered —

"I was just beginning to tell Miss Cathcart," she said, "a curious history that came under my notice once. I don't know if I ought though, for it is rather sad."

"Oh! I like sad stories," said Adela.

"Well, there isn't much of romance in it either, but I will cut it short now the gentlemen are come. I knew the lady. She had been married some years. And report said her husband was not over-kind to her. All at once she disappeared, and her husband thought the worst of her. Knowing her as well as I did, I did not believe a word of it. Yet it was strange that she had left her baby, her only child, of a few months, as well as her husband. I went to see her mother directly I heard of it, and together we went to the police; and such a search as we had! We traced her to a wretched lodging, where she had been for two nights, but they did not know what had become of her. In fact, they had turned her out because she had no money. Some information that we had, made us go to a house near Hyde Park. We rang the bell. Who should open the door, in a neat cap and print-gown, but the poor lady herself! She fainted when she saw her mother. And then the whole story came out. Her husband was stingy, and only allowed her a very small sum for house-keeping; and perhaps she was not a very good manager, for good management is a gift, and everybody has not got it. So she found that she could not clear off the butcher's bills on the sum allowed her; and she had let the debt gather and gather, till the thought of it, I believe, actually drove her out of her mind for the time. She dared not tell her husband; but she knew it must come out some day, and so at last, quite frantic with the thought of it, she ran away, and left her baby behind her."

"And what became of her?" asked Adela.

"Her husband would never hear a word in her favor. He laughed at her story in the most scornful way, and said he was too old a bird for that. In fact, I believe he never saw her again. She went to her mother's. She will have her child now, I suppose; for I hear that the wretch of a husband, who would not let her have him, is dead. I dare say she is happy at last. Poor thing! Some people would need stout hearts, and have not got them."

Adela sighed. This story, too, seemed to interest her.

"What a miserable life!" she said.

"Well, Miss Cathcart," said the school-master, "no doubt it was. But every life that has to be lived, can be lived; and however impossible it may seem to the onlookers, it has its own consolations, or at least, interests. And I always fancy the most indispensable thing to a life is, that it should be interesting to those who have it to live. My wife and I have come through a good deal, but the time when the life looked hardest to others was not, probably, the least interesting to us. It is just like reading a book, — anything will do if you are taken up with it."

"Very good philosophy! Isn't it, Adela?" said the colonel.

Adela cast her eyes down, as if with a despairing sense of rebuke, and did not reply.

"I wish you would tell Miss Cathcart," resumed the school-master to his wife, "that little story about the foolish lad you met once. And you need not keep back the little of your own history that belongs to it. I am sure the colonel will excuse you."

"I insist on hearing the whole of it," said the colonel, with a smile.

And Mrs. Bloomfield began.

Let me say here once for all, that I cannot keep the tales I tell in this volume from partaking of my own peculiarities of style, any more than I could keep the sermon free of such; for of course I give them all at second-hand; and sometimes, where a joint was missing, I have had to supply facts as well as words. But I have kept as near to the originals as these necessities and a certain preparation for the press would permit me.

Mrs. Bloomfield, I say, began: —

"A good many years ago, now, on a warm summer evening, a friend whom I was visiting asked me to take a drive with her through one of the London parks. I agreed to go, though I did not care much about it. I had not breathed the fresh air for some weeks; yet I felt it a great trouble to go. I had been ill, and my husband was ill, and we had nothing to do, and we did not know what would become of us. So I was anything but cheerful. I *knew* that all was for the best, as my good husband was always telling me; but my eyes were dim and my heart was troubled, and I could not feel sure that God cared quite so much for us as he did for the lilies.

"My friend was very cheerful, and seemed to enjoy everything; but a kind of dreariness came over me, and I began comparing the loveliness of the summer evening with the cold, misty blank that seemed to make up my future. My wretchedness grew greater and greater. The very colors of the flowers, the blue of the sky, the sleep of the water, seemed to push us out of the happy world that God had made. And yet the children seemed as happy as if God were busy making the things before their eyes, and holding out each thing, as he made it, for them to look at.

"I should have told you that we had two children then."

"I did not know you had any family," interposed the colonel.

"Yes, we had two then. One of them is now in India, and the other was not long out of heaven. Well, I was glad when my friend stopped the carriage, and got out with the children, to take them close to the water's edge, and let them feed the swans. I liked better to sit in the carriage alone, —an ungrateful creature, in the midst of causes for thankfulness. I did not care for the beautiful things about me; and I was not even pleased that other people should enjoy them. I listlessly watched the well-dressed ladies that passed, and hearkened contemptuously to the drawling way in which they spoke. So bad and proud was I, that I said in my heart, 'Thank God! I am not like them yet!' Then came nursemaids and children; and I did envy the servants, because they had work to do, and health to do it, and wages for it when it was done. The carriage was standing still all this time, you know. Then sickly looking men passed, with still more sickly looking wives, some of them leading a child between them. But even their faces told of wages, and the pleasure of an evening's walk in the park. And now I was able to thank God that they had the parks to walk in. Then came tottering by, an old man, apparently of eighty years, leaning on the arm of his grand-daughter, I supposed, — a tidy, gentle-looking maiden. As they passed, I heard the old man say: 'He maketh me to lie down in green pastures; he leadeth me beside the still waters.' And his quiet face looked as if the fields were yet green to his eyes, and the still waters as pleasant as when he was a little child.

"At last I caught sight of a poor lad, who was walking along very slowly, looking at a gay-colored handkerchief which he had spread out before him. His clothes were rather ragged, but not so ragged as old. On his head was what we now call a wide-awake. It was very limp and shapeless; but some one that loved him had trimmed it with a bit of blue ribbon, the ends of which hung down on his shoulder. This gave him an odd appearance even at a distance. When he came up and I could see his face, it explained everything. There was a constant smile about his mouth, which in itself was very sweet; but as it had nothing to do with the rest of the countenance, the chief impression it conveyed was of idiotcy. He came near the carriage, and stood there, watching some men who were repairing the fence which divided the road from the footpath. His hair was almost golden, and went waving about in the wind. His eye was very large and clear, and of a bright blue. But it had no meaning in it. He would have been very handsome, had there been mind in his face; but, as it was, the very regularity of his unlighted features made the sight a sadder one. His figure was young; but his face might have belonged to a man of sixty.

"He opened his mouth, stuck out his under jaw, and stood staring and grinning at the men. At last one of them stopped to take breath, and, catching sight of the lad, called out: —

"'Why, Davy! is that you?'

"'Ya-as, it be,' replied Davy, nodding his head.

"'Why, Davy, it's ever so long since I clapped eyes on yo!' said the man. 'Where ha' ye been?'

"'I 'aint been nowheres, as I knows on.'

"'Well, if ye 'aint been nowheres, what have ye been doing? Flying your kite?'

"Davy shook his head sorrowfully, and at the same time kept on grinning foolishly.

"'I 'aint got no kite; so I can't fly it.'

"'But you likes flyin' kites, don't ye?' said his friend, kindly.

"'Ya-as,' answered Davy, nodding his head, and rubbing his hands, and laughing out. 'Kites is such fun! I wish I'd got un.'

"Then he looked thoughtfully, almost moodily, at the man, and said : —

"'Where's *your* kite? I likes kites. Kites is friends to me.'

"But by this time the man had turned again to his work, and was busy driving a post into the ground; so he paid no attention to the lad's question."

"Why, Mrs. Bloomfield," interrupted the colonel, "I should just like you to send out with a reconnoitring party, for you seem to see everything and forget nothing."

"You see best and remember best what most interests you, colonel; and, besides that, I got a good rebuke to my ingratitude from that poor fellow. So you see I had reason to remember him. I hope I don't tire you, Miss Cathcart."

"Quite the contrary," answered our hostess.

"By this time," resumed Mrs. Bloomfield, "another man had come up. He had a coarse, hard-featured face; and he tried, or pretended to try, to wheel his barrow, which was full of gravel, over Davy's toes. The said toes were sticking quite bare through great holes in an old pair of woman's boots. Then he began to tease him rather roughly. But Davy took all his banter with just the same complacency and mirth with which he had received the kindliness of the other man.

"'How's yer sweetheart, Davy?' he said.

"'Quite well, thank ye,' answered Davy.

"'What's her name?'

"'Ha! ha! ha! I won't tell ye that.'

"'Come now, Davy, tell us her name.'

"'Noa.'

"'Don't be a fool.'

"'I aint a fool. But I won't tell you her name.'

"'I don't believe ye've got e'er a sweetheart. Come now.'

" 'I have though.'

" 'I don't believe ye.'

" 'I have though. I was at church with her last Sunday.'

"Suddenly the man, looking hard at Davy, changed his tone to one of surprise, and exclaimed : —

" 'Why, boy, ye've got whiskers ! Ye hadn't *them* the last time I see'd ye. Why, ye *are* set up now ! When are ye going to begin to shave ? Where's your razors ? '

" ' 'Aint begun yet,' replied Davy. ' Shall shave some day, but I 'aint got too much yet.'

"As he said this, he fondled away at his whiskers. They were few in number, but evidently of great value in his eyes. Then he began to stroke his chin, on which there was a little down visible, — more like mould in its association with his curious face than anything of more healthy significance. After a few moments' pause, his tormentor began again : —

" 'Well, I can't think where ye got them whiskers as ye're so fond of. Do ye know where ye got them ? '

" Davy took out his pocket-handkerchief, spread it out before him, and stopped grinning.

" 'Yaas ; to be sure I do,' he said at last.

" 'Ye do ? ' growled the man, half humorously, half scorn-fully.

" 'Yaas,' said Davy, nodding his head again and again.

" 'Did ye buy 'em ? '

" 'Noa,' answered Davy ; and the sweetness of the smile which he now smiled was not confined to his mouth, but broke like light, the light of intelligence, over his whole face.

" 'Were they gave to ye ? ' pursued the man, now really curious to hear what he would say.

" 'Yaas,' said the poor fellow ; and he clapped his hands in a kind of suppressed glee.

" 'Why, who gave 'em to ye ? '

" Davy looked up in a way I shall never forget, and, point-ing up with his finger too, said nothing.

" 'What do ye mean ? ' said the man. ' Who gave ye yer whiskers ? '

" Davy pointed up to the sky again ; and then, looking up with an earnest expression, which, before you saw it, you would not have thought possible to his face, said : —

" ' Blessed Father.'

" ' Who?' shouted the man.

" ' Blessed Father,' Davy repeated, once more pointing upwards.

" ' Blessed Father!' returned the man, in a contemptuous tone. 'Blessed Father! — I don't know who *that* is. Where does he live? I never heerd on *him*.'

" Davy looked at him as if he were sorry for him. Then going closer up to him, he said : —

" ' Didn't you though? He lives up there,' — again pointing to the sky. 'And he is so kind! He gives me lots o' things.'

" ' Well!' said the man, 'I wish he'd give me things. But you don't look so very rich nayther.'

" 'Oh! but he gives me lots o' things; and he's up there, and he gives everybody lots o' things as likes to have 'em.'

" ' Well, what's he gave you?'

" ' Why, he's gave me some bread this mornin', and a tart last night, — he did.'

" And the boy nodded his head, as was his custom, to make his assertion still stronger.

" ' But you was sayin' just now, you hadn't got a kite. Why don't he give you one?'

" ' *He'll* give me one fast 'nuff,' said Davy, grinning again, and rubbing his hands.

" Miss Cathcart, I assure you I could have kissed the boy. And I hope I felt some gratitude to God for giving the poor lad such trust in him, which, it seemed to me, was better than trusting in the three-per-cents, colonel; for you can draw upon him to no end o' good things. So Davy thought, anyhow; and he had got the very thing for the want of which my life was cold, and sad, and discontented. Those words, *Blessed Father*, and that look that turned his vacant face, like Stephen's, into the face of an angel, because he was looking up to the same glory, were in my ears and eyes for days. And they taught me, and comforted me. He was the minister of God's best gifts to me. And to how many more, who can tell? For Davy believed that God did care for his own children.

" Davy sauntered away, and before my friend came back

with the children I had lost sight of him; but at my request
we moved on slowly till we should find him again. Nor had
we gone far, before I saw him sitting in the middle of a group
of little children. He was showing them the pictures on his
pocket-handkerchief. I had one sixpence in my purse, — it
was the last I had, Mr. Smith."

Here, from some impulse or other, Mrs. Bloomfield addressed me.

"But I wasn't so poor but I could borrow, and it was a
small price to give for what I had got; and so, as I was not
able to leave the carriage, I asked my friend to take it to him,
and tell him that Blessed Father had sent him that to buy a
kite. The expression of childish glee upon his face, and the
devout *God bless you, lady!* upon his tongue, were strangely
but not incongruously mingled.

"Well, it was my last sixpence then; but here I and my husband are, owing no man anything, and spending a happy
Christmas day, with many thanks to Colonel and Miss Cathcart."

"No, my good madam," said the colonel; "it is we who owe
you the happiest part of our Christmas day. Is it not, Adela?"

"Yes, papa, it is indeed," answered Adela.

Then, with some hesitation, she added: —

"But do you think it was quite fair? It was *you*, Mrs.
Bloomfield, who gave the boy the sixpence."

"I only said God sent it," said Mrs. Bloomfield.

"Besides," I interposed, "the boy never doubted it; and I
think, after all, with due submission to my niece, he was the
best judge."

"I should be only too happy to grant it," she answered with
a sigh. "Things might be all right if one could believe that,
— thoroughly, I mean."

"At least you will allow," I said, "that this boy was not
by any means so miserable as he looked."

"Certainly," she answered, with hearty emphasis. "I
think he was much to be envied."

Here I discovered that Percy was asleep on a sofa.

Other talk followed, and the colonel was looking very
thoughtful. Tea was brought in, and, soon after, our visitors
rose to take their leave.

" You are not going already ? " said the colonel.

" If you will excuse us," answered the school-master. " We
are early birds."

" Well, will you dine with us this day week ? "

" With much pleasure," answered both in a breath.

It was clear both that the colonel liked their simple, honest
company, and that he saw they might do his daughter good ;
for her face looked very earnest and sweet, and the clearness
that precedes rain was evident in the atmosphere of her eyes.

After their departure we soon separated ; and I retired to
my room full of a new idea, which I thought, if well carried
out, might be of still further benefit to the invalid.

But before I went to bed, I had made a rough translation
of the following hymn of Luther's, which I have since completed, — so far at least as the following is complete. I often
find that it helps to keep good thoughts before the mind, to
turn them into another shape of words : —

> From heaven above I come to you,
> To bring a story good and new :
> Of goodly news so much I bring, —
> I cannot help it, I must sing.
>
> To you a child is come this morn,
> A child of holy maiden born,
> A little babe, so sweet and mild, —
> It is a joy to see the child.
>
> 'Tis little Jesus, whom we need
> Us out of sadness all to lead :
> He will himself our Saviour be,
> And from all sinning set us free.
>
> Here come the shepherds, whom we know;
> Let all of us right gladsome go,
> To see what God to us hath given, —
> A gift that makes a stable heaven.
>
> Take heed, my heart ! Be lowly. So
> Thou seest him lie in manger low :
> That is the baby sweet and mild,
> That is the little Jesus-child.
>
> Ah, Lord ! the maker of us all,
> How hast thou grown so poor and small,
> That there thou liest on withered grass, —
> The supper of the ox and ass?

Were the world wider many-fold,
And decked with gems and cloth of gold,
'Twere far too mean and narrow all,
To make for thee a cradle small.

Rough hay, and linen not too fine,
The silk and velvet that are thine;
Yet as they were thy kingdom great,
Thou liest in them in royal state.

And this, all this, hath pleased thee,
That thou mightst bring this truth to me;
That all earth's good, in one combined,
Is nothing to thy mighty mind.

Ah, little Jesus, lay thy head
Down in a soft, white, little bed,
That waits thee in this heart of mine,
And then this heart is always thine.

Such gladness in my heart would make
Me dance and sing for thy sweet sake.
Glory to God in highest heaven,
For he his Son to us hath given!

CHAPTER IV.

THE NEW DOCTOR.

Next forenoon, wishing to have a little private talk with my friend, I went to his room, and found him busy writing to Dr. Wade. He consulted me on the contents of the letter, and I was heartily pleased with the kind way in which he communicated to the old gentleman the resolution he had come to, of trying whether another medical man might not be more fortunate in his attempt to treat the illness of his daughter.

"I fear Dr. Wade will be offended, say what I like," said he.

"It is quite possible to be too much afraid of giving offence," I said; "but nothing can be more gentle and friendly than the way in which you have communicated the necessity."

"Well, it is a great comfort you think so. Will you go with me to call on Mr. Armstrong?"

"With much pleasure," I answered; and we set out at once.

Shown into the doctor's dining-room, I took a glance at the books lying about. I always take advantage of such an opportunity of gaining immediate insight into character. Let me see a man's book-shelves, especially if they are not extensive, and I fancy I know at once, in some measure, what sort of a man the owner is. One small bookcase in a recess of the room seemed to contain all the non-professional library of Mr. Armstrong. I am not going to say here what books they were, or what books I like to see; but I was greatly encouraged by the consultation of the auguries afforded by the backs of these. I was still busy with them, when the door opened, and the doctor entered. He was the same man whom I had seen in church looking at Adela. He advanced in a frank, manly way to the colonel, and welcomed him by name, though I believe no introduction had ever passed between them. Then the colonel introduced me, and we were soon chatting very comfortably. In his manner, I was glad to find that there was nothing of the professional. I hate the professional. I was delighted to observe, too, that what showed at a distance as a broad, honest country face, revealed, on a nearer view, lines of remarkable strength and purity.

"My daughter is very far from well," said the colonel, in answer to a general inquiry.

"So I have been sorry to understand," the doctor rejoined. "Indeed, it is only too clear from her countenance."

"I want you to come and see if you can do her any good."

"Is not Dr. Wade attending her?"

"I have already informed him that I meant to request your advice."

"I shall be most happy to be of any service; but — might I suggest the most likely means of enabling me to judge whether I can be useful or not?"

"Most certainly."

"Then will you give me the opportunity of seeing her in a non-professional way first? I presume, from the fact that she is able to go to church, that she can be seen at home without the formality of an express visit?"

"Certainly," replied the colonel, heartily. "Do me the

favor to dine with us this evening, and, as far as that can go, you will see her, — to considerable disadvantage, I fear," he concluded, smiling sadly.

'Thank you; thank you. If in my power I shall not fail you. But you must leave a margin for professional contingencies."

"Of course. That is understood."

I had been watching Mr. Armstrong during this brief conversation, and the favorable impressions I had already received of him were deepened. His fine manly vigor, and the simple honesty of his countenance, were such as became a healer of men. It seemed altogether more likely that health might flow from such a source, than from the *pudgey*, flabby figure of snuff-taking Dr. Wade, whose face had no expression except a professional one. Mr. Armstrong's eyes looked you full in the face, as if he was determined to understand you if he could; and there seemed to me, with my foolish way of seeing signs everywhere, something of tenderness about the droop of those long eyelashes, so that his interpretation was not likely to fail from lack of sympathy. Then there was the firm-set mouth of his brother the curate, and a forehead as broad as his, if not so high or so full of modelling. When we had taken our leave, I said to the colonel: —

"If that man's opportunity has been equal to his qualification, I think we may have great hopes of his success in encountering this unknown disease of poor Adela."

" God grant it ! " was all my friend's reply.

When he informed Adela that he expected Mr. Henry Armstrong to dinner, she looked at him with a surprised expression, as much as to say, "Surely you do not mean to give me into his hands ! " but she only said : —

" Very well, papa."

So Mr. Armstrong came, and made himself very agreeable at dinner, talking upon all sorts of subjects, and never letting drop a single word to remind Adela that she was in the presence of a medical man. Nor did he seem to take any notice of her more than was required by ordinary politeness; but, behaving without speciality of any sort, he drew his judgments from her general manner, and such glances as fell naturally to his share, of those that must pass between all the persons

making up a small dinner company. This enabled him to see
her as she really was, for she remained quite at such ease as
her indisposition would permit. He drank no wine at dinner,
and only one glass after; and then asked the host if he might
go to the drawing-room.

"And will you oblige me by coming with me, Mr. Smith?
I can see that you are at home here."

Of course the colonel consented, and I was at his service.
Adela rose from her couch when we entered the room. Mr.
Armstrong went up to her gently, and said : —

"Are you able to sing something, Miss Cathcart? I have
heard of your singing."

"I fear not," she answered ; "I have not sung for
months."

"That is a pity. You must lose something by letting
yourself get out of practice. May I play something to you,
then ? "

She gave him a quick glance that indicated some surprise,
and said : —

"If you please. It will give me pleasure."

"May I look at your music first ? "

"Certainly."

He turned over all her loose music from beginning to end.
Then without a word seated himself at the grand piano.

Whether he extemporized or played from memory, I, as
ignorant of music as of all other accomplishments, could not
tell, but even to stupid me, what he did play spoke. I assure
my readers that I hardly know a term in the whole musical
vocabulary; and yet I am tempted to try to describe what this
music was like.

In the beginning, I heard nothing but a slow sameness, of
which I was soon weary. There was nothing like an air of
any kind in it. It seemed as if only his fingers were playing,
and his mind had nothing to do with it. It oppressed me with
a sense of the commonplace, which, of all things, I hate. At
length, into the midst of it, came a few notes, like the first
chirp of a sleepy bird trying to sing; only the attempt was
half a wail, which died away, and came again. Over and over
again came these few sad notes, increasing in number, fainting,
despairing, and reviving again; till at last, with a fluttering

of agonized wings, as of a soul struggling up out of the purgatorial smoke, the music-bird sprang aloft, and broke into a wild but unsure jubilation. Then, as if in the exuberance of its rejoicing it had broken some law of the kingdom of harmony, it sank, plumb-down, into the purifying fires again; where the old wailing and the old struggle began, but with increased vehemence and aspiration. By degrees, the surrounding confusion and distress melted away into forms of harmony, which sustained the mounting cry of longing and prayer. Then all the cry vanished in a jubilant praise. Stronger and broader grew the fundamental harmony, and bore aloft the thanksgiving; which, at length, exhausted by its own utterance, sank peacefully, like a summer sunset, into a gray twilight of calm, with the songs of the summer birds dropping asleep one by one; till, at last, only one was left to sing the sweetest prayer for all, before he, too, tucked his head under his wing, and yielded to the restoring silence.

Then followed a pause. I glanced at Adela. She was quietly weeping.

But he did not leave the instrument yet. A few notes, as of the first distress, awoke; and then a fine manly voice arose, singing the following song, accompanied by something like the same music he had already played. It was the same feelings put into words; or, at least, something like the same feelings, for I am a poor interpreter of music : —

Rejoice, said the sun, I will make thee gay
With glory, and gladness, and holiday;
I am dumb, O man, and I need thy voice;
But man would not rejoice.

Rejoice in thyself, said he, O sun;
For thou thy daily course dost run.
In thy lofty place, rejoice if thou can:
For me, I am only a man.

Rejoice, said the wind, I am free and strong;
I will wake in thy heart an ancient song.
In the bowing woods — hark! hear my voice!
But man would not rejoice.

Rejoice, O wind, in thy strength, said he,
For thou fulfillest thy destiny.
Shake the trees, and the faint flowers fan:
For me, I am only a man.

I am here, said the night, with moon and star;
The sun and the wind are gone afar;
I am here with rest and dreams of choice;
But man would not rejoice.

For he said, What is rest to me, I pray,
Who have done no labor all the day?
He only should dream who has truth behind.
Alas for me and my kind!

   Then a voice that came not from moon nor star,
From the sun, nor the roving wind afar,
Said, Man, I am with thee, — rejoice, rejoice!
And man said, I will rejoice!

" A wonderful physician this!" thought I to myself. " He must be a follower of some of the old mystics of the profession, counting harmony and health all one."

He sat still, for a few moments, before the instrument, perhaps to compose his countenance, and then rose and turned to the company.

The colonel and Percy had entered by this time. The traces of tears were evident on Adela's face, and Percy was eying first her and then Armstrong, with some signs of disquietude. Even during dinner it had been clear to me that Percy did not like the doctor, and now he was as evidently jealous of him.

A little general conversation ensued, and the doctor took his leave. The colonel followed him to the door. I would gladly have done so too, but I remained in the drawing-room. All that passed between them was : —

" Will you oblige me by calling on Sunday morning, half an hour before church-time, colonel?"

" With pleasure."

" Will you come with me, Smith?" asked my friend after informing me of the arrangement.

" Don't you think I might be in the way?"

" Not at all. I am getting old and stupid. I should like you to come and take care of me. He won't do Adela any good, I fear."

" Why do you think so?"

" He has a depressing effect on her already. She is sure

not to like him. She was crying when I came into the room after dinner."

"Tears are not grief," I answered; "nor only the signs of grief, when they do indicate its presence. They are a relief to it as well. But I cannot help thinking there was some pleasure mingled with those tears, for he had been playing very delightfully. He must be a very gifted man."

"I don't know anything about that. You know I have no ear for music. That won't cure my child anyhow."

"I don't know," I answered. "It may help."

"Do you mean to say he thinks to cure her by playing the piano to her? If he thinks to come here and do that, he is mistaken."

"You forget, Cathcart, that I have had no more conversation with him than yourself. But surely you have seen no reason to quarrel with him already."

"No, no, my dear fellow. I do believe I am getting a crusty old curmudgeon. I can't bear to see Adela like this."

"Well, I confess, I have hopes from the new doctor; but we will see what he says on Sunday."

"Why should we not have called to-morrow?"

"I can't answer that. I presume he wants time to think about the case."

"And meantime he may break his neck over some gate that he can't or won't open."

"Well, I should be sorry."

"But what's to become of us then?"

"Ah! you allow that? Then you do expect something of him?"

"To be sure I do, only I am afraid of making a fool of myself, and that sets me grumbling at him, I suppose."

Next day was Saturday; and Mrs. Cathcart, Percy's mother, was expected in the evening. I had a long walk in the morning, and after that remained in my own room till dinner time. I confess I was prejudiced against her; and just because I was prejudiced I resolved to do all I could to like her, especially as it was Christmas-tide. Not that one time is not as good as another for loving your neighbor, but if ever one is reminded of the duty, it is then. I schooled myself all I could, and went into the drawing-room like a boy trying to be good; as a means to which end I put on as pleasant a face as would come. But my good resolutions were sorely tried.

.   .   .   .

These points indicate the obliteration of the personal description which I had given of her. Though true, it was ill-natured. And, besides, so indefinite is all description of this kind, that it is quite possible it might be exactly like some woman to whom I am utterly unworthy to hold a candle. So I won't tell what her features were like. I will only say, that I am certain her late husband must have considered her a very fine woman; and that I had an indescribable sensation in the calves of my legs when I came near her. But then, although I believe I am considered a good-natured man, I confess to prejudices (which I commonly refuse to act upon) and to profound dislikes, especially to certain sorts of women, which I can no more help feeling than I can help feeling the misery that permeates the joints of my jaws when I chance to bite into a sour apple. So my opinions about such women go for little or nothing.

When I entered the drawing-room, I saw at once that she had established herself as protectress of Adela, and possibly as mistress of the house. She leaned back in her chair at a considerable angle, but without bending her spine, and her hands lay folded in her lap. She made me a bow with her neck, without in the least altering the angle of her position, while I made her one of my most profound obeisances. A few commonplaces passed between us, and then her brother-in-law leading her down to dinner, the evening passed by with politeness on both sides. Adela did not appear to heed her presence one way or the other. But then of late she had been very inexpressive.

Percy seemed to keep out of his mother's way as much as possible. How he amused himself, I cannot imagine.

Next morning we went to call on the doctor, on our way to church.

" Well, Mr. Armstrong, what do you think of my daughter ? " asked the colonel.

" I do not think she is in a very bad way. Has she had any disappointment that you know of ? "

"None whatever."

"Ah! I have seen such a case before. There are a good many of them amongst girls at her age. It is as if, without any disease, life were gradually withdrawing itself, — ebbing back as it were to its source. Whether this has a physical or a psychological cause, it is impossible to tell. In her case, I think the latter, if indeed it have not a deeper cause; that is, if I am right in my hypothesis. A few days will show me this; and, if I am wrong, I will then make a closer examination of her case. At present it is desirable that I should not annoy her in any such way. Now for the practical: my conviction is that the best thing that can be done for her is, to interest her in something, if possible, — no matter what it is. Does she take pleasure in anything?"

"She used to be very fond of music. But of late I have not heard her touch the piano."

"May I be allowed to speak?" I asked.

"Most certainly," said both at once.

"I have had a little talk with Miss Cathcart, and I am entirely of Mr. Armstrong's opinion," I said. "And with his permission, — I am pretty sure of my old friend's concurrence, — I will tell you a plan I have been thinking of. You remember, colonel, how she was more interested in the anecdotes our friends the Bloomfields told the other evening, than she has been in anything else since I came. It seems to me that the interest she cannot find for herself we might be able to provide for her, by telling her stories; the course of which every one should be at liberty to interrupt, for the introduction of any remark whatever. If we once got her interested in anything, it seems to me, as Mr. Armstrong has already hinted, that the tide of life would begin to flow again. She would eat better, and sleep better, and speculate less, and think less about herself, — not of herself, — I don't mean that, colonel, for no one could well think less *of* herself than she does. And if we could amuse her in that way for a week or two, I think it would give a fair chance to any physical remedies Mr. Armstrong might think proper to try, for they act most rapidly on a system in movement. It would be beginning from the inside, would it not?"

"A capital plan," said the doctor, who had been listening

with marked approbation; "and I know one who I am sure would help us. For my part, I never told a story in my life, but I am willing to try, — after a while, that is. My brother, however, would, I know, be delighted to lend his aid to such a scheme, if Colonel Cathcart would be so good as to include him in the conspiracy. It is his duty as well as mine, for she is one of his flock. And he can tell a tale, real or fictitious, better than any one I know."

"There can be no harm in trying it, gentlemen, — with kindest thanks to you for your interest in my poor child," said the colonel. "I confess I have not much hope from such a plan, but —"

"You must not let her know that the thing is got up for her," interrupted the doctor.

"Certainly not. You must all come and dine with us, any day you like. I will call on your brother to-morrow."

"This Christmas-tide gives good opportunity for such a scheme," I said. "It will fall in well with all the festivities; and I am quite willing to open the entertainment with a funny kind of fairy-tale, which has been growing in my brain for some time."

"Capital!" said Mr. Armstrong. "We must have all sorts."

"Then shall it be Monday at six, — that is, to-morrow?" asked the colonel. "Your brother won't mind a short invitation?"

"Certainly not. Ask him to-day. But I would suggest five, if I might, to give us more time afterwards."

"Very well. Let it be five. And now we will go to church."

The ends of the old oak pews next the chancel were curiously-carved. One had a ladder and a hammer and nails on it. Another a number of round flat things, and when you counted them you found that there were thirty. Another had a curious thing, — I could not tell what, till one day I met an old woman carrying just such a bag. On another was a sponge on the point of a spear. There were more of such carvings, but these I could see from where I sat. And all the sermon was a persuading of the people that God really loved them, without any *if* or *but*.

Adela was very attentive to the clergyman, but I could see her glance wander now and then from his face to that of his brother, who was in the same place he had occupied on Christmas day. The expression of her aunt's face was judicial.

When we came out of church, the doctor shook hands with me and said : —

" Can I have a word with you, Mr. Smith ? "

" Most gladly," I answered. " Your time is precious; I will walk your way."

" Thank you. I like your plan heartily. But, to tell the truth, I fancy it is more a case for my brother than for me. But that may come about all in good time, especially as she will now have an opportunity of knowing him. He is the best fellow in the world. And his wife is as good as he is. But — I feel I may say to you what I could not well say to the colonel — I suspect the cause of her illness is rather a spiritual one. She has evidently a strong mental constitution, and this strong frame, so to speak, has been fed upon slops, and an atrophy is the consequence. My hope in your plan is, partly, that it may furnish a better mental table for her for the time, and set her foraging in new directions for the future."

" But how could you tell that from the very little conversation you had with her ? "

" It was not the conversation only, — I watched everything about her; and interpreted it by what I know about women. I believe that many of them go into a consumption just from discontent, — the righteous discontent of a soul which is meant to sit at the Father's table, and so cannot content itself with the husks which the swine eat. The theological nourishment which is offered them is generally no better than husks. They cannot live upon it, and so die and go home to their Father. And without good spiritual food to keep the spiritual senses healthy and true, they cannot see the things about them as they really are. They cannot find interest in them, because they cannot find their *own* place amongst them. There was one thing, though, that confirmed me in this idea about Miss Cathcart. I looked over her music on purpose, and I did not find one song that rose above the level of the drawing-room, or one piece of music that had any deep feeling or any thought in it Of course I judged by the composers."

"You astonish me by the truth and rapidity of your judgments. But how did you, who like myself are a bachelor, come to know so much about the minds of women?"

"I believe in part by reading Milton, and learning from him a certain high notion about myself and my own duty. None but a pure man can understand women, — I mean the true womanhood that is in them. But more than to Milton am I indebted to that brother of mine you heard preach to-day. If ever God made a good man, he is one. He will tell you himself that he knows what evil is. He drank of the cup, found it full of thirst and bitterness; cast it from him, and, turning to the fountain of life, kneeled and drank, and rose up a gracious giant. I say the last, — not he. But this brother kept me out of the mire in which he soiled his own garments, though, thank God! they are clean enough now. Forgive my enthusiasm, Mr. Smith, about my brother. He is worthy of it."

I felt the wind cold to my weak eyes, and did not answer for some time, lest he should draw unfair conclusions.

"You should get him to tell you his story. It is well worth hearing; and, as I see we shall be friends all, I would rather you heard it from his own mouth."

"I sincerely hope I may call that man my friend, some day."

"You may do so already. He was greatly taken with you on the journey down."

"A mutual attraction then, I am happy to think. Goodby, I am glad you like my plan."

"I think it excellent. Anything hearty will do her good. Isn't there any young man to fall in love with her?"

"I don't know of any at present."

"Only the *best* thing will make her well; but all true things tend to healing."

"But how is it that you have such notions, — so different from those of the mass of your professional brethren?"

"Oh!" said he, laughing, "if you really want an answer, be it known to all men that I am a student of Van Helmont."

He turned away, laughing; and I, knowing nothing of Van Helmont, could not tell whether he was in jest or in earnest.

At dinner some remark was made about the sermon, I think by our host.

" You don't call that the gospel ! " said Mrs. Cathcart, with a smile.

" Why, what do you call it, Jane ? "

" I don't know that I am bound to put a name upon it.   I should, however, call it pantheism."

" Might I ask you, madam, what you understand by *pantheism ?* "

" Oh ! neology, and all that sort of thing."

" And neology is — ? "

" Really, Mr. Smith, a dinner-table is not the most suitable place in the world for theological discussion."

" I quite agree with you, madam," I responded, astonished at my own boldness.   I was not quite so much afraid of her after this, although I had an instinctive sense that she did not at all like me.   But Percy was delighted to see his mother discomfited, and laughed into his plate.   She regarded him with lurid eyes for a moment, and then took refuge in her plate in turn.   The colonel was too polite to make any remark at the time, but when he and I were alone, he said : —

" Smith, I didn't expect it of you.   Bravo, my boy ! "

And I, John Smith, felt myself a hero.

CHAPTER V.

THE LIGHT PRINCESS.

FIVE o'clock, anxiously expected by me, came, and with it the announcement of dinner.   I think those of us who were in the secret would have hurried over it, but, with Beeves hanging upon our wheels, we could not.   However, at length we were all in the drawing-room, the ladies of the house evidently surprised that we had come upstairs so soon.   Besides the curate, with his wife and brother, our party comprised our old friends, Mr. and Mrs. Bloomfield, whose previous engagement had been advanced by a few days.

When we were all seated, I began, as if it were quite a private suggestion of my own : —

"Adela, if you and our friends have no objection, I will read you a story I have just scribbled off."

"I shall be delighted, uncle."

This was a stronger expression of content than I had yet heard her use, and I felt flattered accordingly.

"This is Christmas-time, you know, and that is just the time for story-telling," I added.

"I trust it is a story suitable to the season," said Mrs. Cathcart, smiling.

"Yes, very," I said; "for it is a child's story, — a fairy-tale, namely; though I confess I think it fitter for grown than for young children. I hope it is funny, though. I think it is."

"So you approve of fairy-tales for children, Mr. Smith?"

"Not for children alone, madam; for everybody that can relish them."

"But not at a sacred time like this?"

And again she smiled an insinuating smile.

"If I thought God did not approve of fairy-tales, I would never read, not to say write, one, Sunday or Saturday. Would you, madam?"

"I never do."

"I feared not. But I must begin, notwithstanding."

The story, as I now give it, is not exactly as I read it then, because, of course, I was more anxious that it should be correct when I prepared it for the press, than when I merely read it before a few friends.

"Once upon a time," I began; but I was unexpectedly interrupted by the clergyman, who said, addressing our host : —

"Will you allow me, Colonel Cathcart, to be Master of the Ceremonies for the evening?"

"Certainly, Mr. Armstrong."

"Then I will alter the arrangement of the party. Here, Henry, — don't get up, Miss Cathcart, — we'll just lift Miss Cathcart's couch to this corner by the fire. Lie still, please. Now, Mr. Smith, you sit here in the middle. Now, Mrs. Cathcart, here is an easy-chair for you. With my commanding officer I will not interfere. But having such a jolly fire

it was a pity not to get the good of it.   Mr. Bloomfield, here
is room for you and Mrs. Bloomfield."

"Excellently arranged," said our host.   "I will sit by
you, Mr. Armstrong.   Percy, won't you come and join the
circle ? "

"No, thank you, uncle," answered Percy, from a couch;
"I am more comfortable here."

"Now, Lizzie," said the curate to his wife, "you sit on
this stool by me.   Too near the fire ?   No ?   Very well.
Harry, put the bottle of water near Mr. Smith.   A fellow-
feeling for another fellow, — you see, Mr. Smith.   Now
we're all right, I think; that is, if Mrs. Cathcart is comfortable."

"Thanks.   Quite."

"Then we may begin.   Now, Mr. Smith.   One word more:
anybody may speak that likes.   Now, then."

So I did begin : —

"Title: THE LIGHT PRINCESS.

"Second Title: A FAIRY–TALE WITHOUT FAIRIES.

"Author: JOHN SMITH, Gentleman.

"Motto : — ' *Your Servant, Goody Gravity.*'

"From — SIR CHARLES GRANDISON."

"I must be very stupid, I fear, Mr. Smith; but, to tell the
truth, *I* can't make head or tail of it," said Mrs. Cathcart.

"Give me leave, madam," said I; "that is my office.
Allow me, and I hope to make both head and tail of it for
you.   But let me give you first a more general, and indeed a
more applicable, motto for my story.   It is this, — from no
worse authority than John Milton : —

> "' Great bards besides
> In sage and solemn times have sung
> Of turneys and of trophies hung;
> Of forests and enchantments drear,
> Where more is meant than meets the ear.'

"Milton here refers to Spenser in particular, most likely. But what distinguishes the true bard in such work is, that *more is meant than meets the ear;* and, although I am no bard, I should scorn to write anything that only spoke to the *ear,* which signifies the surface understanding."

General silence followed, and I went on.

"THE LIGHT PRINCESS.

"Chapter I. — What! no children?

"Once upon a time, so long ago that I have quite forgotten the date, their lived a king and queen who had no children.

"And the king said to himself: 'All the queens of my acquaintance have children, some three, some seven, and some as many as twelve; and my queen has not one. I feel ill-used.' So he made up his mind to be cross with his wife about it. But she bore it all like a good, patient queen, as she was. Then the king grew very cross indeed. But the queen pretended to take it all as a joke, and a very good one too.

"'Why don't you have any daughters, at least?' said he, 'I don't say *sons;* that might be too much to expect.'

"'I am sure, dear king, I am very sorry,' said the queen.

"'So you ought to be,' retorted the king; 'you are not going to make a virtue of *that,* surely.'

"But he was not an ill-tempered king; and, in any matter of less moment, he would have let the queen have her own way, with all his heart. This, however, was an affair of state.

"The queen smiled.

"'You must have patience with a lady, you know, dear king,' said she.

"She was, indeed, a very nice queen, and heartily sorry that she could not oblige the king immediately.

"The king tried to have patience, but he succeeded very badly. It was more than he deserved, therefore, when, at last, the queen gave him a daughter, — as lovely a little princess as ever cried.

" The day drew near when the infant must be christened
The king wrote all the invitations with his own hand. Of
course somebody was forgotten.

" Now, it does not generally matter if somebody *is* forgotten; but you must mind who. Unfortunately, the king
forgot without intending it; and the chance fell upon the
Princess Makemnoit, which was awkward; for the princess
was the king's own sister, and he ought not to have forgotten
her. But she had made herself so disagreeable to the old
king, their father, that he had forgotten her in making his
will; and so it was no wonder that her brother forgot her in
writing his invitations. But poor relations don't do anything
to keep you in mind of them. Why don't they? The king
could not see into the garret she lived in, could he? She was
a sour, spiteful creature. The wrinkles of contempt crossed
the wrinkles of peevishness, and made her face as full of
wrinkles as a pat of butter. If ever a king could be justified
in forgetting anybody, this king was justified in forgetting his
sister, even at a christening. And then she was so disgrace-
fully poor! She looked very odd, too. Her forehead was as
large as all the rest of her face, and projected over it like a
precipice. When she was angry, her little eyes flashed blue.
When she hated anybody, they shone yellow and green.
What they looked like when she loved anybody, I do not
know; for I never heard of her loving anybody but herself,
and I do not think she could have managed that, if she had
not somehow got used to herself. But what made it highly
imprudent in the king to forget her, was — that she was
awfully clever. In fact, she was a witch; and when she
bewitched anybody, he very soon had enough of it; for she
beat all the wicked fairies in wickedness, and all the clever
ones in cleverness. She despised all the modes we read of in
history, in which offended fairies and witches have taken their
revenges; and therefore, after waiting and waiting in vain for
an invitation, she made up her mind at last to go without one,
and make the whole family miserable, like a princess and a
philosopher

"She put on her best gown, went to the palace, was kindly received by the happy monarch, who forgot that he had forgotten her, and took her place in the procession to the royal chapel. When they were all gathered about the font, she contrived to get next to it, and throw something into the water. She maintained then a very respectful demeanor till the water was applied to the child's face. But at that moment she turned round in her place three times, and muttered the following words, loud enough for those beside her to hear: —

> " 'Light of spirit, by my charms,
> Light of body, every part,
> Never weary human arms —
> Only crush thy parents' heart!'

"They all thought she had lost her wits, and was repeating some foolish nursery rhyme; but a shudder went through the whole of them. The baby, on the contrary, began to laugh and crow; while the nurse gave a start and a smothered cry, for she thought she was struck with paralysis: she could not feel the baby in her arms. But she clasped it tight, and said nothing.

"The mischief was done."

Here I came to a pause, for I found the reading somewhat nervous work, and had to make application to the water-bottle.

"Bravo! Mr. Smith," cried the clergyman. "A good beginning, I am sure; for I cannot see what you are driving at."

"I think I do," said Henry. "Don't you, Lizzie?"

"No, I don't," answered Mrs. Armstrong.

"One thing," said Mrs. Cathcart, with a smile, not a very sweet one, but still a smile, — "one thing I must object to. That is, introducing church ceremonies into a fairy-tale."

"Why, Mrs. Cathcart," answered the clergyman, taking up the cudgels for me, "do you suppose the church to be such a cross-grained old lady that she will not allow her children to take a few gentle liberties with their mother? She's able to stand that surely. They won't love her the less for that."

"Besides," I ventured to say, "if both church and fairy-tale belong to humanity, they may occasionally cross circles without injury to either. They must have something in common. There is the 'Fairy Queen,' and the 'Pilgrim's Progress,' you know, Mrs. Cathcart. I can fancy the pope even telling his nephews a fairy-tale."

"Ah, the pope. I dare say."

"And not the arch-bishop?"

"I don't think your reasoning quite correct, Mr. Smith," said the clergyman; "and I think, moreover, there is a real objection to that scene. It is, that no such charm could have had any effect where holy water was employed as the medium. In fact, I doubt if the wickedness could have been wrought in a chapel at all."

"I submit," I said. "You are right. I hold up the four paws of my mind, and crave indulgence."

"In the name of the church, having vindicated her power over evil incantations, I permit you to proceed," said Mr. Armstrong, his black eyes twinkling with fun.

Mrs. Cathcart smiled, and shook her head.

———

"Chapter III. — She can't be ours.

"Her atrocious aunt had deprived the child of all her gravity. If you ask me how this was effected, I answer: In the easiest way in the world. She had only to destroy gravitation. And the princess was a philosopher, and knew all the *ins* and *outs* of the laws of gravitation as well as the *ins* and *outs* of her boot-lace. And being a witch as well, she could abrogate those laws in a moment, or at least so clog their wheels and rust their bearings, that they would not work at all. But we have more to do with what followed than with how it was done.

"The first awkwardness that resulted from this unhappy privation was, that the moment the nurse began to float the baby up and down, she flew from her arms towards the ceiling. Happily, the resistance of the air brought her ascending career to a close within a foot of it. There she remained, horizontal as when she left her nurse's arms, kicking and laughing amazingly. The nurse in terror flew to the bell, and begged the footman, who answered it, to bring up the house-steps directly. Trembling in every limb, she climbed upon the steps, and had to stand upon the very top, and reach up, before she could catch the floating tail of the baby's long clothes.

"When the strange fact came to be known, there was a terrible commotion in the palace. The occasion of its discovery by the king was naturally a repetition of the nurse's experience. Astonished that he felt no weight when the child was laid in his arms, he began to wave her up and — not down, for she slowly ascended to the ceiling as before, and there remained floating in perfect comfort and satisfaction, as was testified by her peals of tiny laughter. The king stood staring up in speechless amazement, and trembled so that his beard shook like grass in the wind. At last, turning to the queen, who was just as horror-struck as himself, he said, gasping, staring, and stammering : —

" ' She *can't* be ours, queen.'

" Now the queen was much cleverer than the king, and had begun already to suspect that ' this effect defective came by cause.'

" ' I am sure she is ours,' answered she. ' But we ought to have taken better care of her at the christening. People who were never invited ought not to have been present.'

" ' Oh, ho ! ' said the king, tapping his forehead with his forefinger, ' I have it all. I've found her out. Don't you see it, queen ? Princess Makemnoit has bewitched her.'

" ' That's just what I say,' answered the queen.

" ' I beg your pardon, my love, I did not hear you. John, bring the steps I get on my throne with.'

" For he was a little king with a great throne, like many other kings.

" The throne-steps were brought, and set upon the dining table, and John got upon the top of them. But he could not reach the little princess, who lay like a baby-laughter-cloud in the air, exploding continuously.

" ' Take the tongs, John,' said his majesty, and, getting up on the table, he handed them to him.

" John could reach the baby now, and the little princess was handed down by the tongs.

CHAPTER IV. — WHERE IS SHE?

"One fine summer day, a month after these her first adventures, during which time she had been very carefully watched, the princess was lying on the bed in the queen's own chamber, fast asleep. One of the windows was open, for it was noon, and the day so sultry that the little girl was wrapped in nothing less ethereal than slumber itself. The queen came into the room, and, not observing that the baby was on the bed, opened another window. A frolicsome fairy wind, which had been watching for a chance of mischief, rushed in at the one window, and, taking its way over the bed where the child was lying, caught her up, and rolling and floating her along like a piece of flue, or a dandelion-seed, carried her with it through the opposite window, and away. The queen went downstairs, quite ignorant of the loss she had herself occasioned. When the nurse returned, she supposed that her majesty had carried her off, and, dreading a scolding, delayed making inquiry about her. But, hearing nothing, she grew uneasy, and went at length to the queen's boudoir, where she found her majesty.

"'Please your majesty, shall I take the baby?' said she.

"'Where is she?' asked the queen.

"'Please forgive me. I know it was wrong.'

"'What do you mean?' said the queen, looking grave.

"'Oh! don't frighten me, your majesty!' exclaimed the nurse, clasping her hands.

"The queen saw that something was amiss, and fell down in a faint. The nurse rushed about the palace, screaming, 'My baby! my baby!'

"Every one ran to the queen's room. But the queen could give no orders. They soon found out, however, that the princess was missing, and in a moment the palace was like a beehive in a garden. But in a minute more the queen was brought to herself by a great shout and a clapping of hands. They had found the princess fast asleep under a rosebush, to which the elvish little wind-puff had carried her, finishing its mischief by shaking a shower of red rose-leaves all over the little white sleeper. Startled by the noise the servants made, she woke ; and, furious with glee, scattered the rose-leaves in all directions, like a shower of spray in the sunset.

" She was watched more carefully after this, no doubt; yet it would be endless to relate all the odd incidents resulting from this peculiarity of the young princess. But there never was a baby in a house, not to say a palace, that kept a household in such constant good-humor, at least below stairs. If it was not easy for her nurses to hold her, certainly she did not make their arms ache. And she was so nice to play at ball with ! There was positively no danger of letting her fall. You might throw her down, or knock her down, or push her down, but you couldn't *let* her down. It is true, you might let her fly into the fire or the coal-hole, or through the window ; but none of these accidents had happened as yet. If you heard peals of laughter resounding from some unknown region, you might be sure enough of the cause. Going down into the kitchen, or *the room*, you would find Jane and Thomas, and Robert and Susan, all and sum, playing at ball with the little princess. She was the ball herself, and did not enjoy it the less for that. Away she went, flying from one to another, screeching with laughter. And the servants loved the ball itself better even than the game. But they had to take care how they threw her, for, if she received an upward direction, she would never come down without being fetched.

" Chapter V. — What is to be done?

" But above stairs it was different. One day, for instance, after breakfast, the king went into his counting-house, and counted out his money. The operation gave him no pleasure.

" ' To think,' said he to himself, ' that every one of these gold sovereigns weighs a quarter of an ounce, and my real, live flesh-and-blood princess weighs nothing at all ! '

" And he hated his gold sovereigns, as they lay with a broad smile of self-satisfaction all over their yellow faces.

" The queen was in the parlor, eating bread and honey. But at the second mouthful, she burst out crying, and could not swallow it. The king heard her sobbing. Glad of anybody, but especially of his queen, to quarrel with, he clashed his gold sovereigns into his money-box, clapped his crown on his head, and rushed into the parlor.

"'What is all this about?' exclaimed he. 'What are you crying for, queen?'

"'I can't eat it,' said the queen, looking ruefully at the honey-pot.

"'No wonder!' retorted the king. 'You've just eaten your breakfast, — two turkey eggs, and three anchovies.'

"'Oh! that's not it!' sobbed her majesty. It's my child, my child!'

"'Well, what's the matter with your child? She's neither up the chimney nor down the draw-well. Just hear her laughing. Yet the king could not help a sigh, which he tried to turn into a cough, saying: —

"'It is a good thing to be light-hearted, I am sure, whether she be ours or not.'

"'It is a bad thing to be light-headed,' answered the queen, looking, with prophetic soul, far into the future.

"''Tis a good thing to be light-handed,' said the king.

"''Tis a bad thing to be light-fingered,' answered the queen.

"''Tis a good thing to be light-footed,' said the king.

"''Tis a bad thing,' began the queen; but the king interrupted her.

"'In fact,' said he, with the tone of one who concludes an argument in which he has had only imaginary opponents, and in which, therefore, he has come off triumphant, — 'in fact, it is a good thing altogether to be light-bodied.'

"'But it is a bad thing altogether to be light-minded,' retorted the queen, who was beginning to lose her temper.

This last answer quite discomfited his majesty, who turned on his heel, and betook himself to his counting-house again. But he was not half-way towards it, when the voice of his queen overtook him: —

"'And it's a bad thing to be light-haired,' screamed she, determined to have more last words, now that her spirit was roused.

"The queen's hair was black as night; and the king's had been, and his daughter's was golden as morning. But it was not this reflection on his hair that troubled him; it was the double use of the word *light*. For the king hated all witticisms, and punning especially. And besides he could not tell whether the queen meant light-*haired* or light-*heired*; for why might she not aspirate her vowels when she was ex-as-perated herself?"

"Now, really," interrupted the clergyman, "I must protest. Mr. Smith, you bury us under an avalanche of puns, and, I must say, not very good ones. Now, the story, though humorous, is not of the kind to admit of such fanciful embellishment. It reminds one rather of a burlesque at a theatre, — the lowest thing, from a literary point of view, to be found."

"I submit," was all I could answer; for I feared that he was right. The passage, as it now stands, is not nearly so bad as it was then, though, I confess, it is still bad enough.

"I think," said Mrs. Armstrong, "since criticism is the order of the evening, and Mr. Smith is so kind as not to mind it, that he makes the king and queen too silly. It takes away from the reality."

"Right, too, my dear madam," I answered.

"The reality of a fairy-tale?" said Mrs. Cathcart, as if asking a question of herself.

"But will you grant me the justice," said I, "to temper your judgments of me, if not of my story, by remembering that this is the first thing of the sort I ever attempted?"

"I tell you what," said the doctor, "it's very easy to criticise, but none of you could have written it yourselves."

"Of course not, for my part," said the clergyman.

Silence followed; and I resumed.

"He turned upon his other heel, and rejoined her. She looked angry still, because she knew that she was guilty, or, what was much the same, knew that he thought so.

"'My dear queen,' said he, 'duplicity of any sort is exceedingly objectionable between married people, of any rank, not to say kings and queens; and the most objectionable form it can assume is that of punning.'

"'There!' said the queen, 'I never made a jest, but I broke it in the making. I am the most unfortunate woman in the world!'

" She looked so rueful, that the king took her in his arms; and they sat down to consult.

" ' Can you bear this ? ' said the king.

" ' No, I can't,' said the queen.

" ' Well, what's to be done ? ' said the king.

" ' I'm sure I don't know,' said the queen. ' But might you not try an apology ? '

" ' To my old sister, I suppose you mean ? ' said the king.

" ' Yes,' said the queen.

" ' Well, I don't mind,' said the king.

" So he went the next morning to the garret of the princess, and, making a very humble apology, begged her to undo the spell. But the princess declared, with a very grave face, that she knew nothing at all about it. Her eyes, however, shone pink, which was a sign that she was happy. She advised the king and queen to have patience, and to mend their ways. The king returned disconsolate. The queen tried to comfort him.

" ' We will wait till she is older. She may then be able to suggest something herself. She will know at least how she feels, and explain things to us.'

" ' But what if she should marry ! ' exclaimed the king, in sudden consternation at the idea.

" ' Well, what of that ? ' rejoined the queen.

" ' Just think ! If she were to have any children ! In the course of a hundred years the air might be as full of floating children as of gossamers in autumn.'

" ' That is no business of ours,' replied the queen. ' Besides, by that time, they will have learned to take care of themselves.'

" A sigh was the king's only answer.

" He would have consulted the court physicians; but he was afraid they would try experiments upon her.

" Chapter VI. — She laughs too much.

" Meantime, notwithstanding awkward occurrences, and griefs that she brought her parents to, the little princess laughed and grew, — not fat, but plump and tall. She reached the age of seventeen, without having fallen into any worse scrape than a chimney; by rescuing her from which, a little bird-nesting urchin got fame and a black face. Nor, thoughtless as she was, had she committed anything worse than laughter at everybody and everything that came in her way. When she heard that General Clanrunfort was cut to pieces with all his forces, she laughed; when she heard that the enemy was on his way to besiege her papa's capital, she laughed hugely; but when she heard that the city would most likely be abandoned to the mercy of the enemy's soldiery, — why, then, she laughed immoderately. These were merely reports invented for the sake of experiment. But she never could be brought to see the serious side of anything. When her mother cried, she said: —

"'What queer faces mamma makes! And she squeezes water out of her cheeks! Funny mamma!'

"And when her papa stormed at her, she laughed, and danced round and round him, clapping her hands, and crying: —

"'Do it again, papa. Do it again! It's such fun. Dear, funny papa!'

"And if he tried to catch her, she glided from him in an instant; not in the least afraid of him, but thinking it part of the game not to be caught. With one push of her foot, she would be floating in the air above his head; or she would go dancing backwards and forwards and sideways, like a great butterfly. It happened several times, when her father and mother were holding a consultation about her in private, that they were interrupted by vainly repressed outbursts of laughter over their heads; and, looking up with indignation, saw her floating at full length in the air above them, whence she regarded them with the most comical appreciation of the position.

"One day an awkward accident happened. The princess had come out upon the lawn with one of her attendants, who held her by the hand. Spying her father at the other side of the lawn, she snatched her hand from the maid's, and sped across to him. Now, when she wanted to run alone, her custom was to catch up a stone in each hand, so that she might come down again after a bound. Whatever she wore as part of her attire had no effect in this way; even gold, when it thus became as it were a part of herself, lost all its weight for the time. But whatever she only held in her hands retained its downward tendency. On this occasion she could see nothing to catch up, but a huge toad, that was walking across the lawn as if he had a hundred years to do it in. Not knowing what disgust meant, for this was one of her peculiarities, she snatched up the toad, and bounded away. She had almost reached her father, and he was holding out his arms to receive her, and take from her lips the kiss which hovered on them like a butterfly on a rosebud, when a puff of wind blew her aside into the arms of a young page, who had just been receiving a message from his majesty. Now it was no great peculiarity in the princess that, once she was set a-going, it always cost her time and trouble to check herself. On this occasion there was no time. She *must* kiss, — and she kissed the page. She did not mind it much; for she had no shyness in her composition; and she knew, besides, that she could not help it. So she only laughed, like a musical-box. . The poor page fared the worst. For the princess, trying to correct the unfortunate tendency of the kiss, put out her hands to keep her off the page; so that, along with the kiss, he received, on the other cheek, a slap with a huge black toad, which she poked right into his eye. He tried to laugh, too; but it resulted in a very odd contortion of countenance, which showed that there was no danger of his pluming himself on the kiss. Indeed it is not safe to be kissed by princesses. As for the king, his dignity was greatly hurt, and he did not speak to the page for a whole month.

"I may here remark that it was very amusing to see her run, if her mode of progression could properly be called running. For first she would make a bound; then, having alighted, she would run a few steps, and make another bound. Sometimes she would fancy she had reached the ground before she actually had, and her feet would go backwards and forwards, running upon nothing at all, like those of a chicken on its back. Then she would laugh like the very spirit of fun; only in her laugh there was something missing. What it was, I find myself unable to describe. I think it was a certain tone, depending upon the possibility of sorrow, — *morbidezza,* perhaps. She never smiled."

"I am not sure about your physics, Mr. Smith," said the doctor. "If she had no gravity, no amount of muscular propulsion could have given her any momentum. And again, if she had no gravity, she must inevitably have ascended beyond the regions of the atmosphere."

"Bottle your philosophy, Harry, with the rest of your physics," said the clergyman, laughing. "Don't you see that she must have had some weight, only it wasn't worth mentioning, being no greater than the ordinary weight of the atmosphere? Besides, you know very well that a law of nature could not be destroyed. Therefore it was only witchcraft, you know; and the laws of that remain to be discovered, — at least so far as my knowledge goes. Mr. Smith you have gone in for a fairy-tale; and, if I were you, I would claim the immunities of Fairyland."

"So I do." I responded fiercely, and went on.

"Chapter VII. — Try metaphysics.

"After a long avoidance of the painful subject, the king and queen resolved to hold a counsel of three upon it; and so they sent for the princess. In she came, sliding and flitting and gliding from one piece of furniture to another, and put herself at last in an arm-chair, in a sitting posture. Whether she could be said *to sit*, seeing she received no support from the seat of the chair, I do not pretend to determine.

" 'My dear child,' said the king, ' you must be aware that you are not exactly like other people.'

" 'O you dear funny papa! I have got a nose and two eyes and all the rest. So have you. So has mamma.'

" 'Now be serious, my dear, for once,' said the queen.

" 'No, thank you, mamma; I had rather not.'

" 'Would you not like to be able to walk like other people?' said the king.

" 'No indeed, I should think not. You only crawl. You are such slow coaches! '

" 'How do you feel, my child?' he resumed, after a pause of discomfiture.

" ' Quite well, thank you.'

" ' I mean, what do you feel like?'

" ' Like nothing at all, that I know of.'

" ' You must feel like something.'

" ' I feel like a princess, with such a funny papa, and such a dear pet of a queen-mamma! '

" ' Now, really! ' began the queen; but the princess interrupted her.

" ' Oh! yes,' she added, ' I remember. I have a curious feeling sometimes, as if I were the only person that had any sense in the whole world.'

" She had been trying to behave herself with dignity; but now she burst into a violent fit of laughter, threw herself backwards over the chair, and went rolling about the floor in an ecstasy of enjoyment. The king picked her up easier than one does a down quilt, and replaced her in her former relation to the chair. The exact preposition expressing this relation I do not happen to know.

" ' Is there nothing you wish for? ' resumed the king, who had learned by this time that it was quite useless to be angry with her.

" ' O you dear papa! — yes,' answered she.

" ' What is it, my darling? '

" ' I have been longing for it, — oh, such a time! Ever since last night.'

" ' Tell me what it is.'

" ' Will you promise to let me have it? '

" The king was on the point of saying *yes ;* but the wiser queen checked him with a single motion of her head.

" ' Tell me what it is first? ' said he.

" ' No, no. Promise first.'

" ' I dare not. What is it? '

" ' Mind I hold you to your promise. It is — to be tied to the end of a string, — a very long string indeed, and be flown like a kite. Oh, such fun! I would rain rose-water, and hail sugar-plums, and snow whipt-cream, and, and, and — '

" A fit of laughing choked her; and she would have been off again, over the floor, had not the king started up and caught her just in time. Seeing that nothing but talk could be got out of her, he rang the bell, and sent her away with two of her ladies-in-waiting.

"'Now, queen,' he said, turning to her majesty, 'what *is* to be done?'

"'There is but one thing left,' answered she. 'Let us consult the college of metaphysicians.'

"'Bravo!' cried the king; 'we will.'

"Now at the head of this college were two very wise Chinese philosophers, by name, Hum-Drum, and Kopy-Keck. For them the king went, and straightway they came. In a long speech, he communicated to them what they knew very well already, — as who did not? — namely, the peculiar condition of his daughter in relation to the globe on which she dwelt; and requested them to consult together as to what might be the cause and probable cure of her *infirmity*. The king laid stress upon the word, but failed to discover his own pun. The queen laughed; but Hum-Drum and Kopy-Keck heard with humility and retired in silence. Their consultation consisted chiefly in propounding and supporting, for the thousandth time, each his favorite theories. For the condition of the princess afforded delightful scope for the discussion of every question arising from the division of thought, — in fact of all the Metaphysics of the Chinese Empire. But it is only justice to say that they did not altogether neglect the discussion of the practical question, *what was to be done.*

"Hum-Drum was a Materialist, and Kopy-Keck was a Spiritualist. The former was slow and sententious; the latter was quick and flighty; the latter had generally the first word; the former the last.

"'I assert my former assertion,' began Kopy-Keck, with a plunge. 'There is not a fault in the princess, body or soul; only they are wrong put together. Listen to me now, Hum-Drum, and I will tell you in brief what I think. Don't speak. Don't answer me. I *won't* hear you till I have done. At that decisive moment, when souls seek their appointed habitations, two eager souls met, struck, rebounded, lost their way, and arrived each at the wrong place. The soul of the princess was one of those, and she went far astray. She does not belong by rights to this world at all, but to some other planet, probably Mercury. Her proclivity to her true sphere destroys

all the natural influence which this orb would otherwise pos‑
sess over her corporeal frame. She cares for nothing here.
There is no relation between her and this world.

"' She must therefore be taught, by the sternest compulsion,
to take an interest in the earth as the earth. She must study
every department of its history, — its animal history; its vege‑
table history; its mineral history; its social history; its moral
history; its political history; its scientific history; its literary
history; its musical history; its artistical history; above all,
its metaphysical history. She must begin with the Chinese
Dynasty, and end with Japan. But, first of all, she must study
Geology, and especially the history of the extinct races of
animals, — their natures, their habits, their loves, their hates,
their revenges. She must — '

"' Hold, h‑o‑o‑old ! ' roared Hum-Drum. ' It is certainly
my turn now. My rooted and insubvertible conviction is that
the causes of the anomalies evident in the princess' condition
are strictly and solely physical. But that is only tantamount
to acknowledging that they exist. Hear my opinion. From
some cause or other, of no importance to our inquiry, the mo‑
tion of her heart has been reversed. That remarkable combi‑
nation of the suction and the force pump works the wrong
way, — I mean in the case of the unfortunate princess: it
draws in where it should force out, and forces out where it
should draw in. The offices of the auricles and the ventricles
are subverted. The blood is sent forth by the veins, and re‑
turns by the arteries. Consequently it is running the wrong
way through all her corporeal organism, — lungs and all. Is it
then at all mysterious, seeing that such is the case, that on the
other particular of gravitation as well, she should differ from
normal humanity? My proposal for the cure is this : —

"' Phlebotomize until she is reduced to the last point of
safety. Let it be effected, if necessary, in a warm bath. When
she is reduced to a state of perfect asphyxy, apply a ligature
to the left ankle, drawing it as tight as the bone will bear.
Apply, at the same moment, another of equal tension around
the right wrist. By means of plates constructed for the pur‑
pose, place the other foot and hand under the receivers of two
air-pumps. Exhaust the receivers. Exhibit a pint of French
brandy, and await the results.'

" ' Which would presently arrive in the form of grim Death,' said Kopy-Keck.

" ' If it should, she would yet die in doing our duty,' retorted Hum-Drum.

" But their majesties had too much tenderness for their volatile offspring to subject her to either of the schemes of the equally unscrupulous philosophers. Indeed, the most complete knowledge of the laws of nature would have been unserviceable in her case; for it was impossible to classify her. She was a fifth imponderable body, sharing all the other properties of the ponderable.

" Chapter VIII.— Try a drop of water.

" Perhaps the best thing for the princess would have been falling in love. But how a princess who had no gravity at all could fall into anything, is a difficulty, — perhaps *the* difficulty. As for her own feelings on the subject, she did not even know that there was such a beehive of honey and stings to be fallen into. And now I come to mention another curious fact about her.

" The palace was built on the shore of the loveliest lake in the world, and the princess loved this lake more than father or mother. The root of this preference, no doubt, — although the princess did not recognize it as such, — was, that the moment she got into it, she recovered the natural right of which she had been so wickedly deprived, — namely, gravity. Whether this was owing to the fact that water had been employed as the means of conveying the injury, I do not know. But it is certain that she could swim and dive like the duck that her old nurse said she was. The way that this alleviation of her misfortune was discovered, was as follows: One summer evening, during the carnival of the country, she had been taken upon the lake by the king and queen, in the royal barge. They were accompanied by many of the courtiers in a fleet of little boats. In the middle of the lake she wanted to get into the lord chancellor's barge, for his daughter, who was a great favorite with her, was in it with her father. The old king rarely condescended to make light of his misfortune, but on this occasion he happened to be in a particularly good-humor, and, as the barges approached each other, he caught up the princess to throw her into the chancellor's barge. He lost his balance, however, and, dropping into the bottom of the barge, lost his hold of his daughter, not, however, before imparting to her the downward tendency of his own person, though in a somewhat different direction, for, as the king fell into the boat, she fell into the water. With a burst of delighted laughter, she disappeared in the lake. A cry of horror ascended from the boats. They had never seen the princess go down before. Half the men were under water in a moment, but they had all, one after another, come up to the surface again for breath, when, — tinkle, tinkle, babble and gush, came the princess' laugh over the water from far away. There she was, swimming like a swan. Nor would she come out for king or queen, chancellor or daughter. But though she was obstinate, she seemed more sedate than usual. Perhaps that was because a great pleasure spoils laughing. After this the passion of her life was to get into the water, and she was always the better behaved and the more beautiful, the more she had of it. Summer and winter it was all the same, only she could not stay quite so long in the water when they had to break the ice to let her in. Any day, from morning till evening, she might be descried, — a streak of white in the blue water, — lying as still as the shadow of a cloud, or shooting along like a dolphin, disappearing, and coming up again far off, just where one did not expect her. She would have been in the lake of a night too, if she could have had her way, for the balcony of her window overhung a deep pool in it, and through a shallow reedy passage she could have swum out into the wide wet water, and no one would have been any the wiser. Indeed, when she happened to wake in the moonlight, she could hardly resist the temptation. But there was the sad difficulty of getting into it. She had as great a dread of the air as some children have of the water. For the slightest gust of wind would blow her away, and a gust might arise in the stillest moment. And if she gave herself a push towards the water and just failed of reaching it, her situation would be dreadfully awkward, irrespective of the wind, for at best there she would have to remain, suspended in her night-gown till she was seen and angled for by somebody from the window.

"'Oh! if I had my gravity,' thought she, contemplating the water, 'I would flash off this balcony like a long white sea-bird, headlong into the darling wetness. Heigh-ho!'

"This was the only consideration that made her wish to be like other people.

"Another reason for being fond of the water was that in it alone she enjoyed any freedom. For she could not walk out without a cortége, consisting in part of a troop of light horse, for fear of the liberties which the wind might take with her. And the king grew more apprehensive with increasing years, till at last he would not allow her to walk abroad without some twenty silken cords fastened to as many parts of her dress, and held by twenty noblemen. Of course horseback was out of the question. But she bade good-by to all this ceremony when she got into the water. So remarkable were its effects upon her, especially in restoring her for the time to the ordinary human gravity, that, strange to say, Hum-Drum and Kopy-Keck agreed in recommending the king to bury her alive for three years, in the hope that, as the water did her so much good, the earth would do her yet more. But the king had some vulgar prejudices against the experiment, and would not give his consent. Foiled in this, they yet agreed in another recommendation, which, seeing that the one imported his opinions from China and the other from Thibet, was very remarkable indeed. They said, that if water of external origin and application could be so efficacious, water from a deeper source might work a perfect cure; in short, that, if the poor, afflicted princess could by any means be made to cry, she might recover her lost gravity.

"But how was this to be brought about? Therein lay all the difficulty. The philosophers were not wise enough for this. To make the princess cry was as impossible as to make her weigh. They sent for a professional beggar, commanded him to prepare his most touching oracle of woe, helped him, out of the court charade-box, to whatever he wanted for dressing up, and promised great rewards in the event of his success. But it was all in vain. She listened to the mendicant artist's story, and gazed at his marvellous make-up, till she could contain herself no longer, and went into the most undignified contortions for relief, shrieking, positively screeching with laughter.

"When she had a little recovered herself, she ordered her attendants to drive him away, and not give him a single copper; whereupon his look of mortified discomfiture wrought her punishment and his revenge, for it sent her into violent hysterics, from which she was with difficulty recovered.

"But so anxious was the king that the suggestion should have a fair trial, that he put himself in a rage one day, and, rushing up to her room, gave her an awful whipping. But not a tear would flow. She looked grave, and her laughing sounded uncommonly like screaming, — that was all. The good old tyrant, though he put on his best gold spectacles to look, could not discover the smallest cloud in the serene blue, of her eyes.

"CHAPTER IX. — PUT ME IN AGAIN.

"It must have been about this time that the son of a king, who lived a thousand miles from Lagobel, set out to look for the daughter of a queen. He travelled far and wide, but as sure as he found a princess he found some fault with her. Of course he could not marry a mere woman, however beautiful; and there was no princess to be found worthy of him. Whether the prince was so near perfection that he had a right to demand perfection itself, I cannot pretend to say. All I know is, that he was a fine, handsome, brave, generous, well-bred and well-behaved youth, as all princes are.

In his wanderings he had come across some reports about our princess; but, as everybody said she was bewitched, he never dreamed that she could bewitch him. For what indeed could a prince do with a princess that had lost her gravity? Who could tell what she might not lose next? She might lose her visibility, or her tangibility; or, in short, the power of making impressions upon the radical sensorium; so that he should never be able to tell whether she was dead or alive. Of course he made no further inquiries about her.

"One day he lost sight of his retinue in a great forest. These forests are very useful in delivering princes from their courtiers, like a sieve that keeps back the bran. Then the princes get away to follow their fortunes. In this they have the advantage of the princesses, who are forced to marry before they have had a bit of fun. I wish our princesses got lost in a forest sometimes.

"One lovely evening, after wandering about for many days, he found that he was approaching the outskirts of this forest; for the trees had got so thin that he could see the sunset through them; and he soon came upon a kind of heath. Next he came upon signs of human neighborhood; but by this time it was getting late, and there was nobody in the fields to direct him.

"After travelling for another hour, his horse, quite worn out with long labor and lack of food, fell, and was unable to rise again. So he continued his journey on foot. At length he entered another wood, — not a wild forest, but a civilized wood, through which a footpath led him to the side of a lake. Along this path the prince pursued his way through the gathering darkness. Suddenly he paused, and listened. Strange sounds came across the water. It was, in fact, the princess laughing. Now, there was something odd in her laugh, as I have already hinted; for the hatching of a real hearty laugh requires the incubation of gravity; and, perhaps, this was how the prince mistook the laughter for screaming. Looking over the lake, he saw something white in the water; and, in an instant, he had torn off his tunic, kicked off his sandals, and plunged in. He soon reached the white object, and found that it was a woman. There was not light enough to show that she was a princess, but quite enough to show that she was a lady, for it does not want much light to see that.

"Now, I cannot tell how it came about, — whether she pretended to be drowning, or whether he frightened her, or caught her so as to embarrass her; but certainly he brought her to shore in a fashion ignominious to a swimmer, and more nearly drowned than she had ever expected to be; for the water had got into her throat as often as she had tried to speak.

"At the place to which he bore her, the bank was only a foot or two above the water; so he gave her a strong lift out of the water, to lay her on the bank. But, her gravitation ceasing the moment she left the water, away she went, up into the air, scolding and screaming : —

" ' You naughty, *naughty*, NAUGHTY, NAUGHTY man! '

" No one had ever succeeded in putting her into a passion before. When the prince saw her ascend, he thought he must have been bewitched, and have mistaken a great swan for a lady. But the princess caught hold of the topmost cone upon a lofty fir. This came off; but she caught at another; and, in fact, stopped herself by gathering cones, dropping them as the stalks gave way. The prince, meantime, stood in the water, forgetting to get out. But the princess disappearing, he scrambled on shore, and went in the direction of the tree. He found her climbing down one of the branches, towards the stem. But in the darkness of the wood, the prince continued in some bewilderment as to what the phenomenon could be; until, reaching the ground, and seeing him standing there, she caught hold of him, and said : —

" ' I ll tell papa.'

" ' Oh, no, you won't! ' rejoined the prince.

" ' Yes, I will,' she persisted. ' What business had you to pull me down out of the water, and throw me to the bottom of the air? I never did you any harm.'

" ' I am sure I did not mean to hurt you.'

" ' I don't believe you have any brains; and that is a worse loss than your wretched gravity. I pity you.'

" The prince now saw that he had come upon the bewitched princess, and had already offended her. Before he could think what to say next, the princess, giving a stamp with her foot that would have sent her aloft again, but for the hold she had of his arm, said angrily : —

" ' Put me up directly.'

" ' Put you up where, you beauty? ' asked the prince.

" He had fallen in love with her, almost, already; for her anger made her more charming than any one else had ever beheld her; and, as far as he could see, which certainly was not far, she had not a single fault about her, except, of course, that she had no gravity. A prince, however, must be incapable of judging of a princess by weight. The loveliness of a foot, for instance, is hardly to be estimated by the depth of the impression it can make in mud!

" 'Put you up where, you beauty?' said the prince.

" 'In the water, you stupid!' answered the princess.

" 'Come, then,' said the prince.

" The condition of her dress, increasing her usual difficulty in walking, compelled her to cling to him; and he could hardly persuade himself that he was not in a delightful dream, notwithstanding the torrent of musical abuse with which she overwhelmed him. The prince being in no hurry, they reached the lake at quite another part, where the bank was twenty-five feet high at least. When they stood at the edge, the prince, turning towards the princess, said : —

" 'How am I to put you in?'

" 'That is your business,' she answered, quite snappishly. 'You took me out, — put me in again.'

" 'Very well,' said the prince ; and, catching her up in his arms, he sprang with her from the rock. The princess had just time to give one delightful shriek of laughter before the water closed over them. When they came to the surface, the princess, for a moment or two, could not even laugh, for she had gone down with such a rush, that it was with difficulty that she recovered her breath. The moment they reached the surface : —

" 'How do you like falling in?' said the prince.

" After a few efforts, the princess panted out : —

" 'Is that what you call *falling in?*'

" 'Yes,' answered the prince, 'I should think it a very tolerable specimen.'

" 'It seemed to me like going up,' rejoined she.

" 'My feeling was certainly one of elevation, too,' the prince conceded.

" The princess did not appear to understand him, for she retorted his first question : —

" 'How do *you* like falling in?'

" 'Beyond everything,' answered he; 'for I have fallen in with the only perfect creature I ever saw.'

" 'No more of that; I am tired of it,' said the princess.

" Perhaps she shared her father's aversion to punning.

" 'Don't you like falling in, then?' said the prince.

" 'It is the most delightful fun I ever had in my life,' answered she. 'I never fell before. I wish I could learn.

To think I am the only person in my father's kingdom that can't fall ! '

" Here the poor princess looked almost sad.

" ' I shall be most happy to fall in with you any time you like,' said the prince, devotedly.

" 'Thank you. I don't know. Perhaps it would not be proper. But I don't care. At all events, as we have fallen in, let us have a swim together.'

" ' With all my heart,' said the prince.

" And away they went, swimming, and diving, and floating, until at last they heard cries along the shore, and saw lights glancing in all directions. It was now quite late, and there was no moon.

" ' I must go home,' said the princess. ' I am very sorry, for this is delightful.'

" ' So am I,' responded the prince. ' But I am glad I haven't a home to go to, — at least, I don't exactly know where it is.'

" ' I wish I hadn't one either," rejoined the princess ; ' it is so stupid ! I have a great mind,' she continued, ' to play them all a trick. Why couldn't they leave me alone ? They won't trust me in the lake for a single night ! You see where that green light is burning ? That is the window of my room. Now if you would just swim there with me very quietly, and when we are all but under the balcony, give me such a push — up you call it — as you did a little while ago, I should be able to catch hold of the balcony, and get in at the window ; and then they may look for me till to-morrow morning ! '

" ' With more obedience than pleasure,' said the prince. gallantly ; and away they swam, very gently.

" ' Will you be in the lake to-morrow night ? ' the prince ventured to ask.

" ' To be sure I will. I don't think so. Perhaps,' — was the princess' somewhat strange answer.

" But the prince was intelligent enough not to press her further ; and merely whispered, as he gave her the parting lift : ' Don't tell.' The only answer the princess returned was a roguish look. She was already a yard above his head. The look seemed to say : ' Never fear. It is too good fun to spoil that way.'

"So perfectly like other people had she been in the water, that even yet the prince could scarcely believe his eyes when he saw her ascend slowly, grasp the balcony, and disappear through the window. He turned, almost expecting to see her still by his side. But he was alone in the water. So he swam away quietly, and watched the lights roving about the shore for hours after the princess was safe in her chamber. As soon as they disappeared, he landed in search of his tunic and sword, and, after some trouble, found them again. Then he made the best of his way round the lake to the other side. There the wood was wilder, and the shore steeper, — rising more immediately towards the mountains which surrounded the lake on all sides, and kept sending it messages of silvery streams from morning to night, and all night long. He soon found a spot whence he could see the green light in the princess' room, and where, even in the broad daylight, he would be in no danger of being discovered from the opposite shore. It was a sort of cave in the rock, where he provided himself a bed of withered leaves, and lay down too tired for hunger to keep him awake. All night long he dreamed that he was swimming with the princess."

"All that is very improper, — to my mind," said Mrs. Cathcart. And she glanced towards the place where Percy had deposited himself, as if she were afraid of her boy's morals.

But if she was anxious on that score, her fears must have been dispersed the same moment by an indubitable snore from the youth, who was in his favorite position, — lying at full length on a couch.

"You must remember all this is in Fairyland, aunt," said Adela, with a smile. "Nobody does what papa and mamma would not like here. We must not judge the people in fairy-tales by precisely the same conventionalities we have. They must be good after their own fashion."

"Conventionalities! Humph!" said Mrs. Cathcart.

"Besides, I don't think the princess was quite accountable," said I.

"You should have made her so, then," rejoined my critic.

"Oh! wait a little, madam," I replied.

"I think," said the clergyman, "that Miss Cathcart's defence is very tolerably sufficient; and in my character of Master of the Ceremonies, I order Mr. Smith to proceed."

I made haste to do so, before Mrs. Cathcart should open a new battery.

"Chapter X. — Look at the moon.

"Early the next morning, the prince set out to look for something to eat, which he soon found at a forester's hut, where for many following days he was supplied with all that a brave prince could consider necessary. And, having plenty to keep him alive for the present, he would not think of wants not yet in existence. Whenever Care intruded, this prince always bowed him out in the most princely manner.

"When he returned from his breakfast to his watch-cave, he saw the princess already floating about in the lake, attended by the king and queen, — whom he knew by their crowns, — and a great company in lovely little boats, with canopies of all the colors of the rainbow, and flags and streamers of a great many more. It was a very bright day, and soon the prince, burned up with the heat, began to long for the water and the cool princess. But he had to endure till the twilight; for the boats had provisions on board, and it was not till the sun went down, that the gay party began to vanish. Boat after boat drew away to the shore, following that of the king and queen, till only one, apparently the princess' own boat, remained. But she did not want to go home even yet, and the prince thought he saw her order the boat to the shore without her. At all events, it rowed away; and now, of all the radiant company, only one white speck remained. Then the prince began to sing.

"And this was what he sang : —

> " ' Lady fair,
> Swan-white,
> Lift thine eyes,
> Banish night
> By the might
> Of thine eyes.

Snowy arms,
Oars of snow,
Oar her hither,
Plashing low.
Soft and slow,
Oar her hither.

Stream behind her
O'er the lake,
Radiant whiteness!
In her wake
Following, following for her sake,
Radiant whiteness!

Cling about her,
Waters blue;
Part not from her,
But renew
Cold and true
Kisses round her.
Lap me round,
Waters sad
That have left her;
Make me glad,
For ye had
Kissed her ere ye left her.

"Before he had finished his song, the princess was just under the place where he sat, and looking up to find him. Her ears had led her truly.

"'Would you like a fall, princess?' said the prince, looking down.

"'Ah! there you are. Yes, if you please, prince,' said the princess, looking up.

"'How do you know I am a prince, princess?' said the prince.

"'Because you are a very nice young man, prince,' said the princess.

"'Come up then, princess.'

"'Fetch me, prince.'

"The prince took off his scarf, then his sword-belt, then his tunic, and tied them all together, and let them down. But the line was far too short. He unwound his turban, and added it to the rest, when it was all but long enough, and his purse completed it. The princess just managed to lay hold of the knot of money, and was beside him in a moment. This rock was much higher than the other, and the splash and the dive were tremendous. The princess was in ecstasies of delight, and their swim was delicious.

"Night after night they met, and swam about in the dark, clear lake, where such was the prince's delight, that (whether the princess' way of looking at things infected him, or he was actually getting light-headed) he often fancied that he was swimming in the sky instead of the lake. But when he talked about being in heaven, the princess laughed at him dreadfully.

"When the moon came, she brought them fresh pleasure. Everything looked strange and new in her light, with an old, withered, yet unfading newness. When the moon was nearly full, one of their great delights was, to dive deep in the water, and then, turning round, look up through it at the great blot of light close above them, shimmering and trembling and wavering, spreading and contracting, seeming to melt away, and again grow solid. Then they would shoot up through it; and lo! there was the moon, far off, clear and steady and cold, and very lovely, at the bottom of a deeper and bluer lake than theirs, as the princess said.

"The prince soon found out that while in the water the princess was very like other people. And, besides this, she was not so forward in her questions, or pert in her replies at sea as on shore. Neither did she laugh so much; and when she did laugh it was more gently. She seemed altogether more modest and maidenly in the water than out of it. But when the prince, who had really fallen in love when he fell in the lake, began to talk to her about love, she always turned her head towards him and laughed. After a while she began to look puzzled, as if she were trying to understand what he meant, but could not, — revealing a notion that he meant something. But as soon as ever she left the lake, she was so altered, that the prince said to himself: 'If I marry her, I see no help for it, we must turn merman and mermaid, and go out to sea at once.'

"CHAPTER XI. — HISS!

"The princess' pleasure in the lake had grown to a passion, and she could scarcely bear to be out of it for an hour. Imagine, then, her consternation, when, diving with the prince one night, a sudden suspicion seized her, that the lake was not so deep as it used to be. The prince could not imagine what had happened. She shot to the surface, and, without a word, swam at full speed towards the higher side of the lake. He followed, begging to know if she was ill, or what was the matter. She never turned her head, or took the smallest notice of his question. Arrived at the shore she coasted the rocks with minute inspection. But she was not able to come to a conclusion, for the moon was very small, and so she could not see well. She turned therefore and swam home, without saying a word to explain her conduct to the prince, of whose presence she seemed no longer conscious. He withdrew to his cave, in great perplexity and distress.

"Next day she made many observations, which, alas! strengthened her fears. She saw that the banks were too dry, and that the grass on the shore and the trailing plants on the rocks were withering away. She caused marks to be made along the borders, and examined them day after day, in all directions of the wind, till at last the horrible idea became a certain fact, — that the surface of the lake was slowly sinking.

"The poor princess nearly went out of the little mind she had. It was awful to her, to see the lake which she loved more than any living thing, lie dying before her eyes. It sank away, slowly vanishing. The tops of rocks that had never been seen before began to appear far down in the clear water. Before long, they were dry in the sun It was fearful to think of the mud that would lie baking and festering, full of lovely creatures dying, and ugly creatures coming to life, like the unmaking of a world. And how hot the sun would be without any lake! She could not bear to swim in it, and began to pine away. Her life seemed bound up with it, and ever as the lake sank, she pined. People said she would not live an hour after the lake was gone. But she never cried.

"Proclamation was made to all the kingdom, that whosoever

should discover the cause of the lake's decrease would be rewarded after a princely fashion. Hum-Drum and Kopy-Keck applied themselves to their physics and metaphysics, but in vain. No one came forward to suggest a cause.

"Now the fact was, that the old princess was at the root of the mischief. When she heard that her niece found more pleasure in the water than any one else had out of it, she went into a rage, and cursed herself for her want of foresight.

"'But,' said she, 'I will soon set all right. The king and the people shall die of thirst; their brains shall boil and frizzle in their skulls, before I shall lose my revenge.'

"And she laughed a ferocious laugh, that made the hairs on the back of her black cat stand erect with terror.

"Then she went to an old chest in the room, and, opening it, took out what looked like a piece of dried sea-weed. This she threw into a tub of water. Then she threw some powder into the water, and stirred it with her bare arm, muttering over it words of hideous sound, and yet more hideous import. Then she set the tub aside, and took from the chest a huge bunch of a hundred rusty keys, that clattered in her shaking hands. Then she sat down and proceeded to oil them all. Before she had finished, out from the tub, the water of which had kept on a slow motion ever since she had ceased stirring it, came the head and half the body of a huge gray snake. But the witch did not look round. It grew out of the tub, waving itself backwards and forwards with a slow, horizontal motion, till it reached the princess, when it laid its head upon her shoulder, and gave a low hiss in her ear. She started — but with joy; and, seeing the head resting on her shoulder, drew it towards her and kissed it. Then she drew it all out of the tub, and wound it round her body. It was one of those dreadful creatures which few have ever beheld, — the White Snakes of Darkness.

"Then she took the keys and went down into her cellar; and, as she unlocked the door, she said to herself: —

"'This *is* worth living for!'

"Locking the door behind her, she descended a few steps into the cellar, and, crossing it, unlocked another door into a dark, narrow passage. This also she locked behind her, and descended a few more steps. If any one had followed the witch-princess, he would have heard her unlock exactly one hundred doors, and descend a few steps after unlocking each. When she had unlocked the last, she entered a vast cave, the roof of which was supported by huge natural pillars of rock. Now this roof was the underside of the bottom of the lake.

"She then untwined the snake from her body, and held it by the tail high above her. The hideous creature stretched up its head towards the roof of the cavern, which it was just able to reach. It then began to move its head backwards and forwards, with a slow, oscillating motion, as if looking for something. At the same moment, the witch began to walk round and round the cavern, coming nearer to the centre every circuit; while the head of the snake described the same path over the roof that she did over the floor, for she held it up still. And still it kept slowly oscillating. Round and round the cavern they went thus, ever lessening the circuit, till, at last, the snake made a sudden dart, and clung fast to the roof with its mouth. 'That's right, my beauty!' cried the princess; 'drain it dry.'

"She let it go, left it hanging, and sat down on a great stone, with her black cat, who had followed her all around the cave, by her side. Then she began to knit, and mutter awful words. The snake hung like a huge leech, sucking at the stone; the cat stood with his back arched, and his tail like a piece of cable, looking up at the snake; and the old woman sat and knitted and muttered. Seven days and seven nights they sat thus; when suddenly the serpent dropped from the roof, as if exhausted, and shrivelled up like a piece of dried sea-weed on the floor. The witch started to her feet, picked it up, put it in her pocket, and looked up at the roof. One drop of water was trembling on the spot where the snake had been sucking. As soon as she saw that, she turned and fled, followed by her cat. She shut the door in a terrible hurry, locked it, and, having muttered some frightful words, sped to the next, which also she locked and muttered over; and so with all the hundred doors, till she arrived in her own cellar. There she sat down on the floor ready to faint, but listening with malicious delight to the rushing of the water, which she could hear distinctly through all the hundred doors.

"But this was not enough. Now that she had tasted

revenge, she lost her patience. Without further measures, the lake would be too long in disappearing. So the next night, with the last shred of the dying old moon rising, she took some of the water in which she had revived the snake, put it in a bottle, and set out, accompanied by her cat. Ere she returned, she had made the entire circuit of the lake, muttering fearful words as she crossed every stream, and casting into it some of the water out of her bottle. When she had finished the circuit, she muttered yet again, and flung a handful of the water towards the moon. Every spring in the country ceased to throb and bubble, dying away like the pulse of a dying man. The next day there was no sound of falling water to be heard along the borders of the lake. The very courses were dry; and the mountains showed no silvery streaks down their dark sides. And not alone had the fountains of mother Earth ceased to flow; for all the babies throughout the country were crying dreadfully, — only without tears.

" Chapter XII. — Where is the Prince?

" Never since the night when the princess left him so abruptly, had the prince had a single interview with her. He had sent her once or twice in the lake; but as far as he could discover, she had not been in it any more at night. He had sat and sung, and looked in vain for his Nereid; while she, like a true Nereid, was wasting away with her lake, sinking as it sank, withering as it dried. When at length he discovered the change that was taking place in the level of the water, he was in great alarm and perplexity. He could not tell whether the lake was dying because the lady had forsaken it; or whether the lady would not come because the lake had begun to sink. But he resolved to know so much at least.

" He disguised himself, and, going to the palace, requested to see the lord chamberlain. His appearance at once gained his request; and the lord chamberlain, being a man of some insight, perceived that there was more in the prince's solicitation than met the ear. He felt likewise that no one could tell whence a solution of the present difficulties might arise. So he granted the prince's prayer to be made shoeblack to the princess. It was rather knowing in the prince to request such an easy post; for the princess could not possibly soil as many shoes as other princesses.

"He soon learned all that could be told about the princess. He went nearly distracted; but, after roaming about the lake for days, and diving in every depth that remained, all that he could do was to put an extra polish on the dainty pair of boots that was never called for.

"For the princess kept her room, with the curtains drawn to shut out the dying lake. But she could not shut it out of her mind for a moment. It haunted her imagination so that she felt as if her lake were her soul, drying up within her, first to become mud, and then madness and death. She brooded over the change, with all its dreadful accompaniments, till she was nearly out of her mind. As for the prince, she had forgotten him. However much she had enjoyed his company in the water, she did not care for him without it. But she seemed to have forgotten her father and mother too.

"The lake went on sinking. Small slimy spots began to appear, which glittered steadily amidst the changeful shine of the water. These grew to broad patches of mud, which widened and spread, with rocks here and there, and floundering fishes and crawling eels swarming about. The people went everywhere catching these, and looking for anything that might have been dropped into the water.

"At length the lake was all but gone; only a few of the deepest pools remaining unexhausted.

"It happened one day that a party of youngsters found themselves on the brink of one of these pools, in the very centre of the lake. It was a rocky basin of considerable depth. Looking in, they saw at the bottom something that shone yellow in the sun. A little boy jumped in and dived for it. It was a plate of gold, covered with writing. They carried it to the king.

"On one side of it stood these words: —

"'Death alone from death can save
Love is death, and so is brave.
Love can fill the deepest grave.
Love loves on beneath the wave.'

"Now this was enigmatical enough to the king and courtiers. But the reverse of the plate explained it a little. Its
contents amounted to this : —

"'If the lake should disappear, they must find the hole
through which the water ran. But it would be useless to try
to stop it by any ordinary means. There was but one effect-
ual mode. The body of a living man could alone stanch the
flow. The man must give himself of his own will; and the
lake must take his life as it filled. Otherwise the offering
would be of no avail. If the nation could not provide one
hero, it was time it should perish.'

"CHAPTER XIII. — HERE I AM.

"This was a very disheartening revelation to the king.
Not that he was unwilling to sacrifice a subject, but that he
was hopeless of finding a man willing to sacrifice himself. No
time could be lost, however; for the princess was lying motionless on her bed, and taking no nourishment but lake-water,
which was now none of the best. Therefore the king caused
the contents of the wonderful plate of gold to be published
throughout the country.

"No one, however, came forward.

"The prince, having gone several days' journey into the
forest, to consult a hermit whom he had met there on his way
to Lagobel, knew nothing of the oracle till his return.

"When he had acquainted himself with all the particulars,
he sat down and thought.

"'She would die, if I didn't do it; and life would be nothing to me without her; so I shall lose nothing by doing it.
And life will be as pleasant to her as ever, for she will soon
forget me, and there will be so much more beauty and happiness in the world. To be sure I shall not see it.' — Here the
poor prince gave a sigh. — 'How lovely the lake will be in
the moonlight, with that glorious creature sporting in it like a
wild goddess! It is rather hard to be drowned by inches,
though. Let me see, — that will be seventy inches of me to
drown.' — Here he tried to laugh, but could not. — 'The

longer the better, however,' he resumed; 'for can I not bargain that the princess shall be beside me all the time? So I shall see her once more, — kiss her perhaps, who knows? — and die looking in her eyes. It will be no death. At least I shall not feel it. And to see the lake filling for the beauty again! — All right! I am ready.'

"He kissed the princess' boot, laid it down, and hurried to the king's apartment. But feeling, as he went, that anything sentimental would be disagreeable, he resolved to carry off the whole affair with burlesque. So he knocked at the door of the king's counting-house, where it was all but a capital crime to disturb him. When the king heard the knock, he started up, and opened the door in a rage. Seeing only the shoe-black, he drew his sword. This, I am sorry to say, was his usual mode of asserting his regality, when he thought his dignity was in danger. But the prince was not in the least alarmed.

"'Please your majesty, I'm your butler,' said he.

"'My butler! you lying rascal! What do you mean?'

"'I mean, I will cork your big bottle.'

"'Is the fellow mad?' bawled the king, raising the point of his sword.

"'I will put a stopper, — plug, — what you call it, in your leaky lake, grand monarch,' said the prince.

"The king was in such a rage, that before he could speak he had time to cool, and to reflect that it would be great waste to kill the only man who was willing to be useful in the present emergency, seeing that in the end the insolent fellow would be as dead as if he had died by his majesty's own hand.

"'Oh!' said he at last, putting up his sword with difficulty, — it was so long; 'I am obliged to you, you young fool! Take a glass of wine?'

"'No, thank you,' replied the prince.

"'Very well,' said the king. 'Would you like to run and see your parents before you make your experiment?'

"'No, thank you,' said the prince.

"'Then we will go and look for the hole at once,' said his majesty, and proceeded to call some attendants.

"'Stop, please your majesty; I have a condition to make,' interposed the prince.

"'What!' exclaimed the king; 'a condition! and with me! How dare you?'

"'As you please,' said the prince, coolly. 'I wish your majesty good-morning.'

"'You wretch! I will have you put in a sack, and stuck in the hole.'

"'Very well, your majesty,' replied the prince, becoming a little more respectful, lest the wrath of the king should deprive him of the pleasure of dying for the princess. 'But what good will that do your majesty? Please to remember that the oracle says the victim must offer himself.'

"'Well, you *have* offered yourself,' retorted the king.

"'Yes, upon one condition.'

"'Condition again!' roared the king, once more drawing his sword. 'Begone! Somebody else will be glad enough to take the honor off your shoulders.'

"'Your majesty knows it will not be easy to get one to take my place.'

"'Well, what is your condition?' growled the king, feeling that the prince was right.

"'Only this,' replied the prince: 'that, as I must on no account die before I am fairly drowned, and the waiting will be rather wearisome, the princess, your daughter, shall go with me, feed me with her own hands, and look at me now and then, to comfort me; for you must confess it *is* rather hard. As soon as the water is up to my eyes, she may go and be happy, and forget her poor shoeblack.'

"Here the prince's voice faltered, and he very nearly grew sentimental, in spite of his resolutions.

"'Why didn't you tell me before what your condition was? Such a fuss about nothing!' exclaimed the king.

"'Do you grant it?' persisted the prince.

"'I do,' replied the king.

"'Very well. I am ready.'

"'Go and have some dinner, then, while I set my people to find the place.'

"The king ordered out his guards, and gave directions to the officers to find the hole in the lake at once. So the bed of the lake was marked out in divisions, and thoroughly examined; and in an hour or so the hole was discovered. It was in the middle of a stone, near the centre of the lake, in the very pool where the golden plate had been found. It was a three-cornered hole, of no great size. There was water all round the stone, but none was flowing through the hole.

"CHAPTER XIV. — THIS IS VERY KIND OF YOU.

"The prince went to dress for the occasion, for he was resolved to die like a prince.

"When the princess heard that a man had offered to die for her, she was so transported that she jumped off the bed, feeble as she was, and danced about the room for joy. She did not care who the man was; that was nothing to her. The hole wanted stopping; and if only a man would do, why, take one. In an hour or two more, everything was ready. Her maid dressed her in haste, and they carried her to the side of the lake. When she saw it, she shrieked, and covered her face with her hands. They bore her across to the stone, where they had already placed a little boat for her. The water was not deep enough to float it, but they hoped it would be, before long. They laid her on cushions, placed in the boat wines and fruits and other nice things, and stretched a canopy over all.

"In a few minutes, the prince appeared. The princess recognized him at once; but did not think it worth while to acknowledge him.

"'Here I am,' said the prince. 'Put me in.'

"'They told me it was a shoeblack,' said the princess.

"'So I am,' said the prince. 'I blacked your little boots three times a day, because they were all I could get of you. Put me in.'

"The courtiers did not resent his bluntness, except by saying to each other that he was taking it out in impudence.

"But how was he to be put in? The golden plate contained no instructions on this point. The prince looked at the hole, and saw but one way. He put both his legs into it, sitting on the stone, and, stooping forward, covered the two corners that remained open, with his two hands. In this

uncomfortable position he resolved to abide his fate, and, turning to the people, said : —

"'Now you can go.'

"The king had already gone home to dinner.

"'Now you can go,' repeated the princess after him, like a
parrot.

"The people obeyed her, and went.

"Presently a little wave flowed over the stone, and wetted
one of the prince's knees.   But he did not mind it much.   He
began to sing, and the song he sang was this : —

"'As a world that has no well,
Darkly bright in forest-dell ;
As a world without the gleam
Of the downward-going stream ;
As a world without the glance
Of the ocean's fair expanse ;
As a world where never rain
Glittered on the sunny plain, —
Such, my heart. thy world would be,
If no love did flow in thee.

"'As a world without the sound
Of the rivulets under ground ;
Or the bubbling of the spring
Out of darkness wandering ;
Or the mighty rush and flowing
Of the river's downward going ;
Or the music-showers that drop
On the outspread beech's top ;
Or the ocean's mighty voice,
When his lifted waves rejoice, —
Such, my soul, thy world would be,
If no love did sing in thee.

"'Lady, keep thy world's delight ;
Keep the waters in thy sight.
Love hath made me strong to go,
For thy sake, to realms below,
Where the water's shine and hum
Through the darkness never come :
Let, I pray, one thought of me
Spring, a little well, in thee ;
Lest thy loveless soul be found
Like a cry and thirsty ground.'

"'Sing again, prince.   It makes it less tedious,' said the
princess.

" But the prince was too much overcome to sing any more. And a long pause followed.

" ' This is very kind of you, prince,' said the princess at last, quite coolly, as she lay in the boat with her eyes shut.

" ' I am sorry I can't return the compliment,' thought the prince ; ' but you are worth dying for, after all.'

" Again a wavelet, and another, and another, flowed over the stone, and wetted both the prince's knees thoroughly ; but he did not speak or move. Two — three — four hours passed in this way, the princess apparently fast asleep, and the prince very patient. But he was much disappointed in his position. for he had none of the consolation he had hoped for.

" At last he could bear it no longer.

" ' Princess ! ' said he.

" But at the moment, up started the princess, crying : —

" ' I'm afloat ! I'm afloat ! '

" And the little boat bumped against the stone.

" ' Princess ! ' repeated the prince, encouraged by seeing her wide awake, and looking eagerly at the water.

" ' Well ? ' said she, without once looking round.

" ' Your papa promised that you should look at me ; and you haven't looked at me once.'

" ' Did he ? Then I suppose I must. But I am so sleepy ! '

" ' Sleep, then, darling, and don't mind me,' said the poor prince.

" ' Really, you are very good,' replied the princess. ' I think I will go to sleep again.'

" ' Just give me a glass of wine and a biscuit, first,' said the prince very humbly.

" ' With all my heart,' said the princess, and gaped as she said it.

She got the wine and the biscuit, however, and coming nearer with them : —

" ' Why, prince,' she said, ' you don't look well ! Are you sure you don't mind it ? '

" ' Not a bit,' answered he, feeling very faint indeed. ' Only, I shall die before it is of any use to you, unless I have something to eat.'

" ' There, then ! ' said she, holding out the wine to him.

" 'Ah! you must feed me. I dare not move my hands. The water would run away directly.'

" ' Good gracious! ' said the princess, and she began at once to feed him with bits of biscuit, and sips of wine.

" As she fed him, he contrived to kiss the tips of her fingers now and then. She did not seem to mind it, one way or the other. But the prince felt better.

" ' Now, for your own sake, princess,' said he, 'I cannot let you go to sleep. You must sit and look at me, else I shall not be able to keep up.'

" ' Well, I will do anything I can to oblige you,' answered she. with condescension, and, sitting down, she did look at him, and kept looking at him, with wonderful steadiness, considering all things.

" 'The sun went down, and the moon came up, and gush after gush the waters were flowing over the rock. They were up to the prince's waist now.

" ' Why can't we go and have a swim? ' said the princess. ' There seems to be water enough just about here.'

" ' I shall never swim more,' said the prince.

" ' Oh! I forgot,' said the princess, and was silent.

" So the water grew and grew, and rose up and up on the prince. And the princess sat and looked at him. She fed him now and then. The night wore on. The waters rose and rose. The moon rose likewise, higher and higher, and shone full on the face of the dying prince. The water was up to his neck.

" ' Will you kiss me, princess? ' said he feebly, at last, for the fun was all out of him now.

" ' Yes, I will,' answered the princess, and kissed him with a long, sweet, cold kiss.

" ' Now,' said he, with a sigh of content, ' I die happy.'

" He did not speak again. The princess gave him some wine for the last time: he was past eating. Then she sat down again, and looked at him. The water rose and rose. It touched his chin. It touched his lower lip. It touched between his lips. He shut them hard to keep it out. The princess began to feel strange. It touched his upper lip. He breathed through his nostrils. The princess looked wild. It covered his nostrils. Her eyes looked scared, and shone strange in the moonlight. His head fell back; the water closed over it; and the bubbles of his last breath bubbled up through the water. The princess gave a shriek, and sprang into the lake.

"She laid hold first of one leg, then of the other, and pulled and tugged, but she could not move either. She stopped to take breath, and that made her think that he could not get any breath. She was frantic. She got hold of him, and held his head above the water, which was possible, now his hands were no longer on the hole. But it was of no use, for he was past breathing.

"Love and water brought back all her strength. She got under the water, and pulled and pulled with her whole might, till, at last, she got one leg out. The other easily followed. How she got him into the boat she never could tell; but when she did, she fainted away. Coming to herself, she seized the oars, kept herself steady as best she could, and rowed and rowed, though she had never rowed before. Round rocks, and over shallows, and through mud she rowed, till she got to the landing stairs of the palace. By this time her people were on the shore, for they had heard her shriek. She made them carry the prince to her own room, and lay him in her bed, and light a fire, and send for the doctors.

" ' But the lake, your Highness,' said the chamberlain, who, roused by the noise, came in, in his night-cap.

" ' Go and drown yourself in it,' said she.

" This was the last rudeness of which the princess was ever guilty, and one must allow that she had good cause to feel provoked with the lord chamberlain.

"Had it been the king himself, he would have fared no better. But both he and the queen were fast asleep. And the chamberlain went back to his bed. So the princess and her old nurse were left with the prince. Somehow, the doctors never came. But the old nurse was a wise woman, and knew what to do.

"They tried everything for a long time without success. The princess was nearly distracted between hope and fear, but she tried on and on, one thing after another, and everything over and over again.

"At last, when they had all but given it up, just as the sun rose, the prince opened his eyes.

"Chapter XV. — Look at the Rain!

"The princess búrst into a passion of tears, and *fell* on the floor. There she lay for an hour, and her tears never ceased. All the pent-up crying of her life was spent now. And a rain came on, such as had never been seen in that country. The sun shone all the time, and the great drops, which fell straight to the earth, shone likewise. The palace was in the heart of a rainbow. It was a rain of rubies, and sapphires, and emeralds, and topazes. The torrents poured from the mountains like molten gold, and if it had not been for its subterraneous outlet, the lake would have overflowed and inundated the country. It was full from shore to shore.

"But the princess did not heed the lake. She lay on the floor and wept. And this rain within doors was far more wonderful than the rain out of doors. For when it abated a little, and she proceeded to rise, she found, to her astonishment, that she could not. At length, after many efforts, she succeeded in getting upon her feet. But she tumbled down again directly. Hearing her fall, her old nurse uttered a yell of delight, and ran to her, screaming : —

"'My darling child! She's found her gravity!'

"'Oh! that's it, is it?' said the princess, rubbing her shoulder and her knee alternately. 'I consider it very unpleasant. I feel as if I should be crushed to pieces.'

"'Hurrah!' cried the prince, from the bed. 'If you're all right, princess, so am I. How's the lake?'

"'Brimful,' answered the nurse.

"'Then we're all jolly.'

"'That we are, indeed!' answered the princess, sobbing.

"And there was rejoicing all over the country that rainy day. Even the babies forgot their past troubles, and danced and crowed amazingly. And the king told stories, and the queen listened to them. And he divided the money in his box, and she the honey in her pot, to all the children. And there was such jubilation as was never heard of before.

"Of course the prince and princess were betrothed at once. But the princess had to learn to walk, before they could be married with any propriety. And this was not so easy, at her time of life, for she could walk no more than a baby. She was always falling down and hurting herself.

" ' Is this the gravity you used to make so much of?' said she, one day to the prince. 'For my part, I was a great deal more comfortable without it.'

" ' No, no; that's not it. This is it,' replied the prince, as he took her up, and carried her about like a baby, kissing her all the time. 'This is gravity.'

" ' That's better,' said she. 'I don't mind that so much.'

" And she smiled the sweetest, loveliest smile in the prince's face. And she gave him one little kiss, in return for all his, and he thought them overpaid, for he was beside himself with delight. I fear she complained of her gravity more than once after this, notwithstanding.

"It was a long time before she got reconciled to walking. But the pain of learning it was quite counterbalanced by two things, either of which would have been sufficient consolation. The first was, that the prince himself was her teacher; and the second, that she could tumble into the lake as often as she pleased. Still, she preferred to have the prince jump in with her, and the splash they made before was nothing to the splash they made now.

" The lake never sank again. In process of time it wore the roof of the cavern quite through, and was twice as deep as before.

" The only revenge the princess took upon her aunt was to tread pretty hard on her gouty toe the next time she saw her. But she was sorry for it the very next day, when she heard that the water had undermined her house, and that it had fallen in the night, burying her in its ruins; whence no one ever ventured to dig up her body. There she lies to this day.

" So the prince and princess lived and were happy; and had crowns of gold, clothes of cloth, and shoes of leather, and children of boys and girls, not one of whom was ever known, on the most critical occasion, to lose the smallest atom of his or her due proportion of gravity."

" Bravo ! "
" Capital ! "
" Very good indeed ! "

"Quite a success!" — cried my complimentary friends.

"I don't think the princess could have rowed, though, — without gravity, you know," said the school-master.

"But she did," said Adela. "I won't have my uncle found fault with. It is a very funny, and a very pretty story."

"What is the moral of it?" drawled Mrs. Cathcart, with the first syllable of *moral* very long and very gentle.

"That you need not be afraid of ill-natured aunts, though they are witches," said Adela.

"No, my dear; that's not it," I said. "It is, that you need not mind forgetting your poor relations. No harm will come of it in the end."

"I think the moral is," said the doctor, "that no girl is worth anything till she has cried a little."

Adela gave him a quick glance, and then cast her eyes down. Whether he had looked at her I don't know. But I should think not. Neither the clergyman nor his wife had made any remark. I turned to them.

"I am afraid you do not approve of my poor story," I said.

"On the contrary," replied Mr. Armstrong, "I think there is a great deal of meaning in it, to those who can see through its fairy-gates. What do you think of it, my dear?"

"I was so pleased with the earnest parts of it, that the fun jarred upon me a little, I confess," said Mrs. Armstrong. "But I dare say that was silly."

"I think it was, my dear. But you can afford to be silly sometimes, in a good cause."

"You might have given us the wedding," said Mrs. Bloomfield.

"I am an old bachelor, you see. I fear I don't give weddings their due," I answered. "I don't care for them, — in stories, I mean."

"When will you dine with us again?" asked the colonel.

"When you please," answered the curate.

"To-morrow, then?"

"Rather too soon that, is it not? Who is to read the next story?"

"Why, you, of course," answered his brother.

"I am at your service," rejoined Mr. Armstrong. "But to-morrow!"

"Don't you think, Ralph," said his wife, "you could read better if you followed your usual custom of dining early?"

"I am sure I should, Lizzie. Don't you think, Colonel Cathcart, it would be better to come in the evening, just after your dinner? I like to dine early, and I am a great tea-drinker. If we might have a huge teakettle on the fire, and teapot to correspond on the table, and I, as I read my story, and the rest of the company, as they listen, might help ourselves, I think it would be very jolly, and very homely."

To this the colonel readily agreed. I heard the ladies whispering a little, and the words, "Very considerate indeed!" from Mrs. Bloomfield, reached my ears. Indeed, I had thought that the colonel's hospitality was making him forget his servants. And I could not help laughing to think what Beeves' face would have been like, if he had heard us all invited to dinner again, the next day.

Whether Adela suspected us now, I do not know. She said nothing to show it.

Just before the doctor left, with his brother and sister, he went up to her, and said, in a by-the-by sort of way : —

"I am sorry to hear that you have not been quite well of late, Miss Cathcart. You have been catching cold, I am afraid. Let me feel your pulse."

She gave him her wrist directly, saying : —

"I feel much better to-night, thank you."

He stood — listening to the pulse, you would have said, — his whole attitude was so entirely that of one listening, with his eyes doing nothing at all. He stood thus for a while, without consulting his watch, looking as if the pulse had brought him into immediate communication with the troubled heart itself, and he could feel every flutter and effort which it made. Then he took out his watch and counted.

Now that his eyes were quite safe, I saw Adela's eyes steal up to his face, and rest there for half a minute with a reposeful expression. I felt that there was something healing in the very presence and touch of the man, — so full was he of health and humanity ; and I thought Adela felt that he was a good man, and one to be trusted in.

He gave her back her hand, as it were, so gently did he let it go, and said : —

"I will send you something, as soon as I get home, to take at once. I presume you will go to bed soon?"

"I will, if you think it best."

And so Mr. Henry Armstrong was, without more ado, tacitly installed as physician to Miss Adela Cathcart; and she seemed quite content with the new arrangement.

CHAPTER VI.

THE BELL.

BEFORE the next meeting took place, namely, after breakfast on the following morning, Percy having gone to visit the dogs, Mrs. Cathcart addressed me:—

"I had something to say to my brother, Mr. Smith, but—"

"And you wish to be alone with him? With all my heart," I said.

"Not at all, Mr. Smith," she answered, with one of her smiles, which were quite incomprehensible to me, until I hit upon the theory that she kept a stock of them for general use, as stingy old ladies keep up their half-worn ribbons to make presents of to servant-maids: "I only wanted to know, before I made a remark to the colonel, whether Dr. Armstrong—"

"Mr. Armstrong lays no claim to the rank of a physician."

"So much the better for my argument. But is he a friend of yours, Mr. Smith?"

"Yes,—of nearly a week's standing."

"Oh, then, I am in no danger of hurting your feelings."

"I don't know that," thought I, but I did not say it.

"Well, Colonel Cathcart,—excuse the liberty I am taking,—but surely you do not mean to dismiss Dr. Wade, and give a young man like that the charge of your daughter's health at such a crisis."

"Dr. Wade is dismissed already, Jane. He did her no more good than any old woman might have done."

"But such a young man!"

"Not so very young," I ventured to say. "He is thirty at least."

But the colonel was angry with her interference; for, an impetuous man always, he had become irritable of late.

"Jane," he said, "is a man less likely to be delicate because he is young? Or does a man always become more refined as he grows older? For my part,"— and here his opposition to his unpleasant sister-in-law possibly made him say more than he would otherwise have conceded, — "I have never seen a young man whose manners and behavior I liked better."

"Much good that will do her! It will only hasten the mischief. You men are so slow to take a hint, brother; and it is really too hard to be forced to explain one's self always. Don't you see that, whether he cures her or not, he will make her fall in love with him? And you won't relish that, I fancy."

"You won't relish it, at all events. But mayn't he fall in love with her as well?" thought I; which thought, a certain expression in the colonel's face kept me from uttering. I saw at once that his sister's words had set a discord in the good man's music. He made no reply; and Mrs. Cathcart saw that her arrow had gone to the feather. I saw what she tried to conceal, — the flash of success on her face. But she presently extinguished it, and rose and left the room. I thought with myself that such an arrangement would be the very best thing for Adela; and that, if the blessedness of woman lies in any way in the possession of true manhood, she, let her position in society be what it might compared with his, and let her have all the earls in the kingdom for uncles, would be a fortunate woman indeed, to marry such a man as Harry Armstrong; — for so much was I attracted to the man, that I already called him Harry, when I and myself talked about him. But I was concerned to see my old friend so much disturbed. I hoped, however, that his good, generous heart would right its own jarring chords before long, and that he would not spoil a chance of Adela's recovery, however slight, by any hasty measures founded on nothing better than paternal jealousy. I thought, indeed, he had gone too far to make that possible for some time; but I did not know how far his internal discomfort might act upon his behavior as host, and so interfere with the homeliness of our story-club, upon which I depended not a little for a portion of the desired result.

The motive of Mrs. Cathcart's opposition was evident. She was a partisan of Percy; for Adela was a very tolerable fortune, as people say.

These thoughts went through my mind, as thoughts do, in no time at all; and when the lady had closed the door behind her with protracted gentleness, I was ready to show my game; in which I really considered my friend and myself partners.

"Those women," I said (women forgive me!), with a laugh, which I trust the colonel did not discover to be a forced one, — "those women are always thinking about falling in love and that sort of foolery. I wonder she isn't jealous of me now! Well, I do love Adela better than any man will, for some weeks to come. I've been a sweetheart of hers ever since she was in long clothes." Here I tried to laugh again, and, to judge from the colonel, I verily believe I succeeded. The cloud lightened on his face, as I made light of its cause, till at last he laughed too. If I thought it all nonsense, why should he think it earnest? So I turned the conversation to the club, about which I was more concerned than about the love-making at present, seeing the latter had positively no existence as yet.

"Adela seemed quite to enjoy the reading last night," I said.

"I thought she looked very grave," he answered.

The good man had been watching her face all the time, I saw, and evidently paying no heed to the story. I doubted if he was the better judge for this, — observing only *ab extra*, and without being in sympathy with her feelings as moved by the tale.

"Now that is just what I should have wished to see," I answered. "We don't want her merry all at once. What we want is, that she should take an interest in something. A grave face is a sign of interest. It is all the world better than a listless face."

"But what good can stories do in sickness?"

"That depends on the origin of the sickness. My convic-

tion is, that, near or far off, in ourselves, or in our ancestors,
— say Adam and Eve, for comprehension's sake, — all our
ailments have a moral cause. I think that if we were all
good, disease would, in the course of generations, disappear
utterly from the face of the earth."

"That's just like one of your notions, old friend! Rather
peculiar. Mystical, is it not?"

"But ·I meant to go on to say that, in Adela's case, I
believe, from conversation I have had with her, that the operation of mind on body is far more immediate than that I have
hinted at."

"You cannot mean to imply," said my friend, in some
alarm, "that Adela has anything upon her conscience?"

"Certainly not. But there may be moral diseases that do
not in the least imply personal wrong or fault. They may
themselves be transmitted, for instance. Or even if such
sprung wholly from present physical causes, any help given to
the mind would react on those causes. Still more would the
physical ill be influenced through the mental, if the mind be
the source of both.

"Now, from whatever cause, Adela is in a kind of moral atrophy, for she cannot digest the food provided for her, so as to get
any good of it. Suppose a patient, in a corresponding physical condition, should show a relish for anything proposed to
him, would you not take it for a sign that that was just the
thing to do him good? And we may accept the interest Adela
shows in any kind of mental pabulum provided for her, as an
analogous sign. It corresponds to relish, and is a ground for
expecting some benefit to follow, — in a word, some nourishment of the spiritual life. Relish may be called the digestion
of the palate; interest, the digestion of the inner ears; both
significant of further digestion to follow. The food thus relished may not be the best food; and yet it may be the best for
the patient, because she feels no repugnance to it, and can
digest and assimilate, as well as swallow it. For my part, I
believe in no cramming, bodily or mental. I think nothing
learned without interest can be of the slightest after benefit;
and although the effort may comprise a moral good it involves
considerable intellectual injury. All I have said applies with

still greater force to religious teaching, though that is not defi-
nitely the question now."

"Well, Smith, I can't talk philosophy like you; but what
you say sounds to me like sense. At all events, if Adela
enjoys it, that is enough for me. Will the young doctor tell
stories too?"

"I don't know. I fancy he *could*. But to-night we have
his brother."

"I shall make them welcome, anyhow."

This was all I wanted of him; and now I was impatient for
the evening, and the clergyman's tale. The more I saw of
him the better I liked him, and felt the more interest in him.
I went to church that same day, and heard him read prayers,
and liked him better still; so that I was quite hungry for the
story he was going to read to us.

The evening came, and with it the company. Arrange-
ments, similar to those of the evening before, having been
made, with some little improvements, the colonel now occupying the middle place in the half-circle, and the doctor seated,
whether by chance or design, at the corner farthest from the
invalid's couch, the clergyman said, as he rolled and unrolled
the manuscript in his hand: —

"To explain how I came to a story, the scene of which is
in Scotland, I may be allowed to inform the company that I
spent a good part of my boyhood in a town in Aberdeenshire,
with my grandfather, who was a thorough Scotchman. He had
removed thither from the south, where the name is indigenous,
being indeed a descendant of that Christy, whom his father,
Johnny Armstrang, hanging with the rope about his neck, ready
to be hanged, — or murdered, as the ballad calls it, — apostro-
phizes in these words: —

> "'And God be with thee, Christy, my son,
>   Where thou sits on thy nurse's knee,
> But an' thou live this hundred year,
>   Thy father's better thou'lt never be.'

"But I beg your pardon, ladies and gentlemen all, for this
has positively nothing to do with the story. Only please to
remember that in those days it was quite respectable to be
hanged."

We all agreed to this with a profusion of corroboration, except the colonel, who, I thought, winced a little. But presently our attention was occupied with the story, thus announced : —

"*The Bell. A Sketch in Pen and Ink.*

He read in a great, deep, musical voice, with a wealth of pathos in it, — always suppressed, yet almost too much for me in the more touching portions of the story.

"One interruption more," he said, before he began. "I fear you will find it a sad story."

And he looked at Adela.

I believe that he had chosen the story on the homœopathic principle.

"I like sad stories," she answered, and he went on at once.

"THE BELL.

"A Sketch in Pen and Ink.

"Elsie Scott had let her work fall on her knees, and her hands on her work, and was looking out of the wide, low window of her room, which was on one of the ground floors of the village street. Through a gap in the household shrubbery of fuchsias and myrtles filling the window-sill, one passing on the foot-pavement might get a momentary glimpse of her pale face, lighted up with two blue eyes, over which some inward trouble had spread a faint, gauze-like haziness. But almost before her thoughts had had time to wander back to this trouble, a shout of children's voices, at the other end of the street, reached her ear. She listened a moment. A shadow of displeasure and pain crossed her countenance, and, rising hastily, she betook herself to an inner apartment, and closed the door behind her.

"Meantime the sounds drew nearer, and by and by, an old man, whose strange appearance and dress showed that he had little capacity either for good or evil, passed the window. His clothes were comfortable enough in quality and condition, for they were the annual gift of a benevolent lady in the neighborhood, but, being made to accommodate his taste, both known and traditional, they were somewhat peculiar in cut and adornment. Both coat and trousers were of a dark gray cloth, but

the former, which, in its shape, partook of the military, had a
straight collar of yellow, and narrow cuffs of the same, while
upon both sleeves, about the place where a corporal wears his
stripes was expressed, in the same yellow cloth, a somewhat
singular device.   It was as close an imitation of a bell, with
its tongue hanging out of its mouth, as the tailor's skill could
produce from a single piece of cloth.   The origin of the military cut of his coat was well known.   His preference for it
arose in the time of the wars of the first Napoleon, when the
threatened invasion of the country caused the organization of
many volunteer regiments.   The martial show and exercises
captivated the poor man's fancy, and from that time forward
nothing pleased his vanity, and consequently conciliated his
good will more, than to style him by his favorite title, — the
Colonel.   But the badge on his arm had a deeper origin, which
will be partially manifest in the course of the story, — if story
it can be called.   It was, indeed, the baptism of the fool, the
outward and visible sign of his relation to the infinite and
unseen.   His countenance, however, although the features
were not of any peculiarly low or animal type, showed no
corresponding sign of the consciousness of such a relation,
being as vacant as human countenance could well be.

"The cause of Elsie's annoyance was that the fool was
annoyed, for he was followed by a troop of boys who turned
his rank into scorn, and assailed him with epithets hateful to
him.   Although the most harmless of creatures when let
alone, he was dangerous when roused; and now he stooped
repeatedly to pick up stones and hurl them at his tormentors,
who took care, while abusing him, to keep at a considerable
distance, lest he should get hold of them.   Amidst the sounds
of derision that followed him, might be heard the words
frequently repeated : '*Come hame! come hame!*'   But in a
few minutes the noise ceased, either from the interference of
some friendly inhabitant, or that the boys grew weary, and
departed in search of other amusement.   By and by, Elsie
might be seen again at her work in the window; but the cloud
over her eyes was deeper, and her whole face more sad.

" Indeed, so much did the persecution of the poor man affect
her, that an onlooker would have been compelled to seek the
cause in some yet deeper sympathy than that commonly felt

for the oppressed, even by women. And such a sympathy existed, strange as it may seem, between the beautiful girl (for many called her a *bonnie lassie*) and this 'tatter of humanity.' Nothing would have been farther from the thoughts of those that knew them, than the supposition of any correspondence or connection between them, yet this sympathy sprung in part from a real similarity in their history and present condition.

"All the facts that were known about *Feel Jock's* origin were these : that, seventy years ago, a man who had gone with his horse and cart some miles from the village, to fetch home a load of peat from a desolate *moss*, had heard, while toiling along as rough a road on as lonely a hill-side as any in Scotland, the cry of a child ; and, searching about, had found the infant, hardly wrapt in rags, and untended, as if the earth herself had just given him birth, — that desert moor, wide and dismal, broken and watery, the only bosom for him to lie upon, and the cold, clear night-heaven his only covering. The man had brought him home, and the parish had taken parish-care of him. He had grown up, and proved what he now was, — almost an idiot. Many of the townspeople were kind to him, and employed him in fetching water for them from the river and wells in the neighborhood, paying him for his trouble in victuals, or whiskey, of which he was very fond. He seldom spoke ; and the sentences he could utter were few ; yet the tone, and even the words of his limited vocabulary, were sufficient to express gratitude and some measure of love toward those who were kind to him, and hatred of those who teased and insulted him. He lived a life without aim, and apparently to no purpose ; in this resembling most of his more gifted fellow-men, who, with all the tools and materials needful for the building of a noble mansion, are yet content with a clay hut.

"Elsie, on the contrary, had been born in a comfortable farm-house, amidst homeliness and abundance. But at a very early age she had lost both father and mother ; not so early, however, but that she had faint memories of warm soft times on her mother's bosom, and of refuge in her mother's arms from the attacks of geese and the pursuit of pigs. Therefore, in after-times, when she looked forward to heaven, it was as much a reverting to the old heavenly times of childhood and

mother's love, as an anticipation of something yet to be revealed.   Indeed. without some such memory, how should we
ever picture to ourselves a perfect rest?   But sometimes it
would seem as if the more a heart was made capable of loving,
the less it had to love; and poor Elsie, in passing from a
mother's to a brother's guardianship, felt a change of spiritual
temperature, too keen.   He was not a bad man, or incapable
of benevolence when touched by the sight of want in anything
of which he would himself have felt the privation; but he was
so coarsely made, that only the purest animal necessities affected him; and a hard word, or unfeeling speech, could never
have reached the quick of his nature through the hide that
enclosed it.   Elsie, on the contrary, was excessively and painfully sensitive, as if her nature constantly portended an invisible multitude of half-spiritual, half-nervous antennæ, which
shrunk and trembled in every current of air at all below their
own temperature.   The effect of this upon her behavior was
such that she was called odd; and the poor girl felt that she
was not like other people, yet could not help it.   Her brother,
too, laughed at her without the slightest idea of the pain he
occasioned, or the remotest feeling of curiosity as to what the
inward and consistent causes of the outward abnormal condition might be.   Tenderness was the divine comforting she
needed; and it was altogether absent from her brother's character and behavior.

" Her neighbors looked on her with some interest, but they
rather shunned than courted her acquaintance; especially after
the return of certain nervous attacks, to which she had been
subject in childhood, and which were again brought on by the
events I must relate.   It is curious how certain diseases repel,
by a kind of awe, the sympathies of the neighbors; as if, by
the fact of being subject to them, the patient were removed
into another realm of existence, from which, like the dead with
the living, she can hold communion with those around her only
partially, and with a mixture of dread pervading the intercourse.   Thus some of the deepest, purest wells of spiritual
life are, like those in old castles, choked up by the decay of
the outer walls.   But what tended more than anything, perhaps, to keep up the painful unrest of her soul (for the beauty
of her character was evident in the fact that the irritation sel-

dom reached her *mind*), was a circumstance at which, in its present connection, some of my readers will smile, and others feel a shudder corresponding in kind to that of Elsie.

" Her brother was very fond of a rather small, but ferocious-looking, bull-dog, which followed close at his heels, wherever he went, with hanging head and slouching gait, never leaping or racing about like other dogs. When in the house, he always lay under his master's chair. He seemed to dislike Elsie, and she felt an unspeakable repugnance to him. Though she never mentioned her aversion, her brother easily saw it by the way which she avoided the animal ; and, attributing it entirely to fear, — which indeed had a great share in the matter, — he would cruelly aggravate it, by telling her stories of the fierce hardihood and relentless persistency of this kind of animal. He dared not yet further increase her terror by offering to set the creature upon her, because it was doubtful whether he might be able to restrain him ; but the mental suffering which he occasioned by this heartless conduct, and for which he had no sympathy, was as severe as many bodily sufferings to which he would have been sorry to subject her. Whenever the poor girl happened inadvertently to pass near the dog, which was seldom, a low growl made her aware of his proximity, and drove her to a quick retreat. He was, in fact, the animal impersona-tion of the animal opposition which she had continually to endure. Like chooses like ; and the bull-dog *in* her brother made choice of the bull-dog *out of* him for his companion. So her day was one of shrinking fear and multiform discom-fort.

" But a nature capable of so much distress must of necessity be *capable* of a corresponding amount of pleasure, and in her case this was manifest in the fact that sleep and the quiet of her own room restored her wonderfully. If she was only let alone, a calm mood, filled with images of pleasure, soon took possession of her mind.

" Her acquaintance with the fool had commenced some ten years previous to the time I write of, when she was quite a little girl, and had come from the country with her brother, who, having taken a small farm close to the town, preferred residing in the town to occupying the farm-house, which was not comfortable. She looked at first with some terror on his

uncouth appearance, and with much wonderment on his strange
dress. This wonder was heightened by a conversation she
overheard one day in the street, between the fool and a little
pale-faced boy, who, approaching him respectfully, said, 'Weel,
cornel!'—'Weel, laddie'' was the reply. 'Fat dis the wow say,
cornel?'—'Come hame! come hame!' answered the *colonel*,
with both accent and quantity heaped on the word *hame*. She
heard no more, and knew not what the little she had heard
meant. What the *wow* could be she had no idea, only, as the
years passed on, the strange word became in her mind inde-
scribably associated with the strange shape in yellow cloth on
his sleeves. Had she been a native of the town, she could not
have failed to know its import, so familiar was every one with
it, although the word did not belong to the local vocabulary;
but, as it was, years passed away before she discovered its
meaning. And when, again and again, the fool, attempting
to convey his gratitude for some kindness she had shown him,
mumbled over the words, '*The wow o' Rivven, the wow o'
Rivven,*' the wonder would return as to what could be the
idea associated with them in his mind; but she made no advance
towards their explanation.

"That, however, which most attracted her to the old man
was his persecution by the children. They were to him what
the bull-dog was to her,—the constant source of irritation
and annoyance. They could hardly hurt him, nor did he
appear to dread other injury from them than insult, to which,
fool though he was, he was keenly alive. Human gad-flies
that they were, they sometimes stung him beyond endurance,
and he would curse them in the impotence of his anger. Once
or twice Elsie had been so far carried beyond her constitutional
timidity, by sympathy for the distress of her friend, that she
had gone out and talked to the boys,—even scolded them, so
that they slunk away ashamed, and began to stand as much in
dread of her as of the clutches of their prey. So she, gentle
and timid to excess, acquired among them the reputation of a
termagant. Popular opinion among children, as among men,
is often just, but as often very unjust; for the same manifestations may proceed from opposite principles, and, therefore, as
indices to character, may mislead as often as enlighten.

"Next door to the house in which Elsie resided, dwelt a

tradesman and his wife, who kept an indefinite sort of shop, in which various kinds of goods were exposed to sale. Their youngest son was about the same age as Elsie, and while they were rather more than children, and less than young people, he spent many of his evenings with her, somewhat to the loss of position in his classes at the parish school. They were, indeed, much attached to each other, and, peculiarly constituted as Elsie was, one may imagine what kind of heavenly messenger a companion stronger than herself must have been to her. In fact, if she could have framed the undefinable need of her childlike nature into an articulate prayer, it would have been, 'Give me some one to love me stronger than I.' Any love was helpful, yes, in its degree, saving to her poor troubled soul; but the hope, as they grew older together, that the powerful yet tender-hearted youth really loved her, and would one day make her his wife, was like the opening of heavenly eyes of life and love in the hitherto blank and death-like face of her existence. But nothing had been said of love, although they met and parted like lovers.

"Doubtless if the circles of their thought and feeling had continued as now to intersect each other, there would have been no interruption to their affection; but the time at length arrived when the old couple, seeing the rest of their family comfortably settled in life, resolved to make a gentleman of the youngest, and so sent him from school to college. The facilities existing in Scotland for providing a professional training enabled them to educate him as a surgeon. He parted from Elsie with some regret, but, far less dependent on her than she was on him, and full of the prospects of the future, he felt none of that sinking at the heart which seemed to lay her whole nature open to a fresh inroad of all the terrors and sorrows of her peculiar existence. No correspondence took place between them. New pursuits and relations, and the development of his tastes and judgments, entirely altered the position of poor Elsie in his memory. Having been, during their intercourse, far less of a man than she of a woman, he had no definite idea of the place he had occupied in her regard, and in his mind she receded into the background of the past, without his having any idea that she would suffer thereby, or that he was unjust towards her, while, in her thoughts, his image stood in the highest and clearest relief. It was the centre-point from which and towards which all lines radiated and converged, and, although she could not but be doubtful about the future, yet there was much hope mingled with her doubts.

"But when, at the close of two years, he visited his native village, and she saw before her, instead of the homely youth who had left her that winter evening, one who, to her inexperienced eyes, appeared a finished gentleman, her heart sank within her, as if she had found Nature herself false in her ripening processes, destroying the beautiful promise of a former year by changing instead of developing her creations. He spoke kindly to her, but not cordially. To her ear the voice seemed to come from a great distance out of the past; and while she looked upon him, that optical change passed over her vision, which all have experienced after gazing abstractedly on any object for a time: his form grew very small, and receded to an immeasurable distance; till, her imagination mingling with the twilight haze of her senses, she seemed to see him standing far off on a hill, with the bright horizon of sunset for a background to his clearly defined figure.

"She knew no more till she found herself in bed in the dark; and the first message that reached her from the outer world was the infernal growl of the bull-dog from the room below. Next day she saw her lover walking with two ladies, who would have thought it some degree of condescension to speak to her; and he passed the house without once looking towards it.

"One who is sufficiently possessed by the demon of nervousness to be glad of the magnetic influences of a friend's company in a public promenade, or of a horse beneath him in passing through a church-yard, will have some faint idea of how utterly exposed and defenceless poor Elsie now felt on the crowded thoroughfare of life. And the insensibility which had overtaken her was not the ordinary swoon with which Nature relieves the overstrained nerves, but the return of the epileptic fits of her early childhood; and if the condition of the poor girl had been pitiable before, it was tenfold more so now. Yet she did not complain, but bore all in silence, though it was evident that her health was giving way. But now help came to her from a strange quarter; though many might not be willing to accord the name of help to that which rather hastened than retarded the progress of her decline.

" She had gone to spend a few of the summer days with a relative in the country, some miles from her home, if home it could be called. One evening, towards sunset, she went out for a solitary walk. Passing from the little garden gate, she went along a bare country road for some distance, and then, turning aside by a footpath through a thicket of low trees, she came out in a lonely little church-yard on the hill-side. Hardly knowing whether or not she had intended to go there, she seated herself on a mound covered with long grass, — one of many. Before her stood the ruins of an old church which was taking centuries to crumble. Little remained but the gable-wall, immensely thick, and covered with ancient ivy. The rays of the setting sun fell on a mound at its foot, not green like the rest, but of a rich, red-brown in the rosy sunset, and evidently but newly heaped up. Her eyes, too, rested upon it. Slowly the sun sank below the near horizon.

" As the last brilliant point disappeared, the ivy darkened, and a wind arose and shook all its leaves, making them look cold and troubled; and to Elsie's ear came a low, faint sound, as from a far-off bell. But close beside her — and she started and shivered at the sound — rose a deep, monotonous, almost sepulchral voice: ' *Come hame! come hame! The wow! the wow!* '

" At once she understood the whole. She sat in the church-yard of the ancient parish church of Ruthven; and when she lifted up her eyes, there she saw, in the half-ruined belfry, the old bell, all but hidden with ivy, which the passing wind had roused to utter one sleepy tone; and there, beside her, stood the fool with the bell on his arm; and to him and to her the *wow o' Rivven* said, ' *Come hame! come hame!* ' Ah, what did she want in the whole universe of God but a home? And though the ground beneath was hard, and the sky overhead far and boundless, and the hill-side lonely and companionless, yet somewhere within the visible, and beyond these the outer surfaces of creation, there might be a home for her; as round the wintry house the snows lie heaped up cold and white and dreary all the long *forenight*, while within, beyond the closed shutters, and giving no glimmer through the thick stone walls, the fires are blazing joyously, and the voices and laughter of young unfrozen children are heard, and nothing belongs to winter but the gray hairs on the heads of the parents, within whose warm hearts childlike voices are heard, and childlike thoughts move to and fro. The kernel of winter itself is spring, or a sleeping summer.

"It was no wonder that the fool, cast out of the earth on a far more desolate spot than this, should seek to return within her bosom at this place of open doors, and should call it *home*. For surely the surface of the earth had no home for him. The mound at the foot of the gable contained the body of one who had shown him kindness. He had followed the funeral that afternoon from the town, and had remained behind with the bell. Indeed, it was his custom, though Elsie had not known it, to follow every funeral going to this, his favorite church-yard of Ruthven; and, possibly in imitation of its booming, for it was still tolled at the funerals, he had given the old bell the name of *the wow*, and had translated its monotonous clangor into the articulate sounds, *come hame, come hame*. What precise meaning he attached to the words, it is impossible to say; but it was evident that the place possessed a strange attraction for him, drawing him towards it by the cords of some spiritual magnetism. It is possible that in the mind of the idiot there may have been some feeling about this church-yard and bell, which, in the mind of another, would have become a grand poetic thought, — a feeling as if the ghostly old bell hung at the church-door of the invisible world, and ever and anon rung out joyous notes (though they sounded sad in the ears of the living), calling to the children of the unseen to *come home, come home*. She sat for some time in silence, — for the bell did not ring again, and the fool spoke no more, — till the dews began to fall, when she rose and went home, followed by her companion, who passed the night in the barn.

"From that hour Elsie was furnished with a visual image of the rest she sought, — an image which, mingling with deeper and holier thoughts, became, like the bow set in the cloud, the earthly pledge and sign of the fulfilment of heavenly hopes. Often when the wintry fog of cold discomfort and homelessness filled her soul, all at once the picture of the little church-yard

— with the old gable and belfry, and the slanting sunlight steeping down to the very roots the long grass on the graves —arose in the darkened chamber (*camera obscura*) of her soul; and again she heard the faint Æolian sound of the bell, and the voice of the prophet-fool who interpreted the oracle; and the inward weariness was soothed by the promise of a long sleep. Who can tell how many have been counted fools simply because they were prophets; or how much of the madness in the world may be the utterance of thoughts true and just, but belonging to a region differing from ours in its nature and scenery ?

" But to Elsie, looking out of her window, came the mocking tones of the idle boys who had chosen as the vehicle of their scorn the very words which showed the relation of the fool to the eternal, and revealed in him an element higher far than any yet developed in them. They turned his glory into shame, like the enemies of David when they mocked the would-be king. And the best in a man is often that which is most condemned by those who have not attained to his goodness. The words, however, even as repeated by the boys, had not solely awakened indignation at the persecution of the old man ; they had likewise comforted her with the thought of the refuge that awaited both him and her.

" But the same evening a worse trial befell her. Again she sat near the window, oppressed by the consciousness that her brother had come in. He had gone upstairs, and his dog had remained at the door, exchanging surly compliments with some of his own kind, when the fool came strolling past, and, I do not know from what cause, the dog flew at him. Elsie heard his cry and looked up. Her fear of the brute vanished in a moment before her sympathy for her friend. She darted from the house and rushed towards the dog to drag him off the defenceless idiot, calling him by his name in a tone of anger and dislike. He left the fool, and, springing at Elsie, seized her by the arm above the elbow with such a gripe that, in the midst of her agony, she fancied she heard the bone crack. But she uttered no cry, for the most apprehensive are sometimes the most courageous. Just then, however, her former lover was coming along the street, and, catching a glimpse of what had happened, was on the spot in an instant, took the dog by the

throat with a gripe not inferior to his own, and having thus
compelled him to give up his hold, dashed him on the ground
with a force that almost stunned him, and then with a super-
added kick sent him away limping and howling; whereupon
the fool, attacking him furiously with a stick, would certainly
have finished him, had not his master descried his plight and
come to his rescue.

"Meantime the young surgeon had carried Elsie into the
house; for, as soon as she was rescued from the dog, she had
fallen down in one of her fits, which were becoming more and
more frequent of themselves, and little needed such a shock as
this to increase their violence. He was dressing her arm when
she began to recover; and when she opened her eyes, in a state
of half-consciousness, the first object she beheld was his face
bending over her. Recalling nothing of what had occurred, it
seemed to her, in the dreamy condition in which the fit had left
her, the same face, unchanged, which had once shone in upon
her tardy spring-time, and promised to ripen it into summer.
She forgot that it had departed and left her in the wintry cold.
And so she uttered wild words of love and trust; and the youth,
while stung with remorse at his own neglect, was astonished
to perceive the poetic forms of beauty in which the soul of the
uneducated maiden burst into flower. But as her senses recovered themselves, the face gradually changed to her, as if
the slow alteration of two years had been phantasmagorically
compressed into a few moments; and the glow departed from
the maiden's thoughts and words, and her soul found itself at
the narrow window of the present, from which she could behold but a dreary country. From the street came the iambic
cry of the fool, 'Come hame! come hame!'

"Tycho Brahe, I think, is said to have kept a fool, who
frequently sat at his feet in his study, and to whose mutter-
ings he used to listen in the pauses of his own thought. The
shining soul of the astronomer drew forth the rainbow of harmony
from the misty spray of words ascending over from the dark
gulf into which the thoughts of the idiot were ever falling. He
beheld curious concurrences of words therein, and could read
strange meanings from them, — sometimes even received wondrous hints for the direction of celestial inquiry, from what to
any other, and it may be to the fool himself, was but a cease-

less and aimless babble. Such power lieth in words. It is not then to be wondered at, that the sounds I have mentioned should fall on the ears of Elsie, at such a moment, as a message from God himself. This, then, — all this dreariness, — was but a passing show like the rest, and there lay somewhere for her a reality, — a home. The tears burst up from her oppressed heart. She received the message and prepared to go home. From that time her strength gradually sank, but her spirits as steadily rose.

"The strength of the fool, too, began to fail, for he was old. He bore all the signs of age, even to the gray hairs, which betokened no wisdom. But one cannot say what wisdom might be in him, or how far he had not fought his own battle, and been victorious. Whether any notion of a continuance of life and thought dwelt in his brain, it is impossible to tell; but he seemed to have the idea that this was not his home; and those who saw him gradually approaching his end might well anticipate for him a higher life in the world to come. He had passed through this world without ever awakening to such a consciousness of being as is common to mankind. He had spent his years like a weary dream through a long night, — a strange, dismal, unkindly dream, — and now the morning was at hand. Often in his dream had he listened with sleepy senses to the ringing of the bell, but that bell would awake him at last. He was like a seed buried too deep in the soil, to which the light has never penetrated, and which, therefore, has never forced its way upwards to the open air, never experienced the resurrection of the dead. But seeds will grow ages after they have fallen into the earth; and, indeed, with many kinds, and within some limits, the older the seed before it germinates, the more plentiful is the fruit. And may it not be believed of many human beings, that, the great Husbandman having sown them like seeds sown in the soil of human affairs, there they lie buried a life long; and, only after the upturning of the soil by death, reach a position in which the awakening of their aspiration and the consequent growth become possible. Surely he has made nothing in vain.

"A violent cold and cough brought him at last near to his end, and, hearing that he was ill, Elsie ventured one bright spring day to go to see him. When she entered the misera-

ble room where he lay, he held out his hand to her with something like a smile, and muttered feebly and painfully, 'I'm
gaein' to the wow, nae to come back again.' Elsie could not
restrain her tears; while the old man, looking fixedly at her,
though with meaningless eyes, muttered, for the last time,
' *Come hame! come hame!* ' and sank into a lethargy, from
which nothing could rouse him, till, next morning, he was
waked by friendly death from the long sleep of this world's
night. They bore him to his favorite church-yard, and buried
him within the site of the old church, below his loved bell,
which had ever been to him as the cuckoo-note of a coming
spring. Thus he at length obeyed its summons, and went
home.

"Elsie lingered till the first summer days lay warm on the
land. Several kind hearts in the village, hearing of her illness,
visited her and ministered to her. Wondering at her sweetness and patience, they regretted they had not known her
before. How much consolation might not their kindness have
imparted, and how much might not their sympathy have
strengthened her on her painful road! But they could not
long have delayed her going home. Nor, mentally constituted
as she was, would this have been at all to be desired. Indeed,
it was chiefly the expectation of departure that quieted and
soothed her tremulous nature. It is true, that a deep spring
of hope and faith kept singing on in her heart; but this alone,
without the anticipation of speedy release, could only have
kept her mind at peace. It could not have reached, at least
for a long time, the border land between body and mind, in
which her disease lay.

"One still night of summer, the nurse who watched by her
bedside heard her murmur through her sleep, 'I hear it: *come
hame! come hame!* I'm comin', I'm comin', — I'm gaein'
hame to the wow, nae to come back.' She awoke at the sound
of her own words, and begged the nurse to convey to her
brother her last request, that she might be buried by the side
of the fool, within the old church of Ruthven. Then she
turned her face to the wall, and in the morning was found
quiet and cold. She must have died within a few minutes
after her last words. She was buried according to her request,
and thus she, too, went home.

" Side by side rest the aged fool and the young maiden, for the bell called them, and they obeyed ; and surely they found the fire burning bright, and heard friendly voices, and felt sweet lips on theirs, in the home to which they went. Surely both intellect and love were waiting them there.

" Still the old bell hangs in the old gable ; and whenever another is borne to the old church-yard, it keeps calling to those who are left behind, with the same sad, but friendly and unchanging voice : ' *Come hame ! come hame ! come hame !* ' "

For a full minute, there was silence in the little company. I myself dared not look up ; but the movement of indistinct and cloudy white over my undirected eyes let me know that two or three, amongst them Adela, were lifting their handkerchiefs to their faces. At length a voice broke the silence.

" How much of your affecting tale is true, Mr. Armstrong ? "

The voice belonged to Mrs. Cathcart.

" I object to the question," said I. " I don't want to know. Suppose, Mrs. Cathcart, I were to put this story-club, members, stories, and all, into a book, how would any one like to have her real existence questioned ? It would at least imply that I had made a very bad portrait of that one."

The lady cast rather a frightened look at me, which I confess I was not sorry to see. But the curate interposed.

" What frightful sophistry, Mr. Smith ! " Then turning to Mrs. Cathcart, he continued : —

" I have not the slightest objection to answer your question, Mrs. Cathcart, and if our friend Mr. Smith does not want to hear the answer I will wait till he stops his ears."

He glanced to me, his black eyes twinkling with fun. I saw that it was all he could do to keep from winking, but he did.

" Oh, no," I answered, " I will share what is going."

" Well, then, the fool is a real character, in every point. But I learned, after I had written the sketch, that I had made one mistake. He was in reality about seventeen when he was found on the hill. The bell is a real character too. Elsie is a creature of my own. So, of course, are the brother and the dog."

"I don't know whether to be glad or sorry that there was no Elsie," said his wife. "But did you know the fool yourself?"

"Perfectly well, and had a great respect for him. When a little boy, I was quite proud of the way he behaved to me. He occasionally visited the general persecution of the boys upon any boy he chanced to meet on the road, but, as often as I met him, he walked quietly past me, muttering, '*Auntie's folk!*' or returning my greeting of *A fine day, colonel!*' with a grunted '*Ay!*'"

"What did he mean by 'Auntie's folk'?" asked Mrs. Armstrong.

"My grandmother was kind to him, and he always called her *Auntie*. I cannot tell how the fancy originated, but certainly he knew all her descendants somehow, — a degree of intelligence not to have been expected of him, — and invariably murmured 'Auntie's folk,' as often as he passed any of them on the road, as if to remind himself that these were friends, or relations. Possibly he had lived with an aunt before he was exposed on the moor."

"Is *wow* a word at all?" I asked.

"If you look into Jamieson's Dictionary," said Armstrong, "as I have done for the express purpose, you will find that the word is used differently in different quarters of the country, — chiefly, however, as a verb. It means *to bark, to howl;* likewise *to wave or beckon;* also *to woo,* or *make love* to. Any of these might be given as an explanation of his word. But I do not think it had anything to do with these meanings, nor was the word used, in that district, in either of the last two senses, in my time at least. It was used, however, in the meaning of *alas*, — a form of *woe* in fact, as *wow's me!* But I believe it was, in the fool's use, an attempt to reproduce the sound which the bell made. If you repeat the word several times, resting on the final *w*, and pausing between each repetition, — *wow! wow! wow!* — you will find that the sound is not at all unlike the tolling of a funeral bell, and therefore the word is most probably an onomatopoetic invention of the fool's own."

Adela offered no remark upon the story, and I knew from her countenance that she was too much affected to be inclined to speak. Her eyes had that fixed, forward look, which, combined with haziness, indicates deep emotion, while the curves of her mouth were nearly straightened out by the compression of her lips. I had thought, while the reader went on, that she could hardly fail to find in the story of Elsie some correspondence to her own condition and necessities; I now believed that she had found that correspondence. More talk was not desirable; and I was glad when, after a few attempts at ordinary conversation, Mr. and Mrs. Bloomfield rose to take their leave, which was accepted by the whole company as a signal for departure.

"But stay," I interposed; "who is to read or tell next?"

"Why, I will be revenged on Harry," said the clergyman.

"That you can't," said the doctor; "for I have nothing to give you."

"You don't mean to say you are going to jib?"

"No. I don't say I won't read. In fact I have a story in my head, and a bit of it on paper; but I positively can't read next time."

"Will you oblige us with a story, colonel?" said I.

"My dear fellow, you know I never put pen to paper in my life, except when I could not help it. I may tell you a story before it is all over, but write one I cannot."

"A tale that is told is the best tale of all," I said. "Shall we book you for next time?"

"No, no! not next time; positively not. My story must come of itself, else I cannot tell it at all."

"Well, there's nobody left but you, Mr. Bloomfield. So you can't get rid of it."

"I don't think I ever wrote what was worth calling a story; but I don't mind reading you something of the sort which I have at home, on one condition."

"What is that?"

"That nobody ask any questions about it."

"Oh! certainly."

"But my only reason is, that somehow I feel it would all come to pieces if you did. It is nothing as a story; but there are feelings expressed in it, which were very strong in me when I wrote it, and which I do not feel willing to talk about, although I have no objection to having them thought about."

"Well, that is settled. When shall we meet again?"

"To-morrow or the day after," said the colonel; "which you please."

"Oh! the day after, if I may have a word in it," said the doctor. "I shall be very busy to-morrow; and we mustn't crowd remedies either, you know."

The close of the sentence was addressed to me only. The rest of the company had taken leave, and were already at the door, when he made the last remark. He now came up to his patient, felt her pulse, and put the question : —

"How have you slept the last two nights?"

"Better, thank you."

"And do you feel refreshed when you wake?"

"More so than for some time."

"I won't give you anything to-night. Good-night."

"Good-night. Thank you."

This was all that passed between them. Jealousy, with the six eyes of Colonel, Mrs., and Percy Cathcart, was intent upon the pair during the brief conversation. And I thought Adela perceived the fact.

CHAPTER VII.

THE SCHOOL-MASTER'S STORY.

I WAS walking up the street the next day, when, finding I was passing the grammar-school, and knowing there was nothing going on there now, I thought I should not be intruding if I dropped in upon the school-master and his wife, and had a little chat with them. I already counted them friends; for I felt that, however different our training and lives might have been, we all meant the same thing now, and that is the true bond of fellowship. I found Mr. Bloomfield reading to his wife, — a novel, too. Evidently he intended to make the most of this individual holiday, by making it as unlike a work-day as possible.

"I see you are enjoying yourself," I said. "It's a shame to break in upon you."

"We are delighted to see you. Your interruption will only postpone a good thing to a better," said the kind-hearted school-master, laying down his book. "Will you take a pipe?"

"With pleasure, — but not here, surely?"

"Oh! we smoke everywhere in holiday time."

"You enjoy your holiday, I can see."

"I should think so. I don't believe one of the boys delights in a holiday quite as heartily as I do. You must not imagine I do not enjoy my work, though."

"Not in the least. Earnest work breeds earnest play. But you must find the labor wearisome at times."

"I confess I have felt it such. I have said to myself sometimes: "Am I to go on forever teaching boys Latin grammar, till I wish there had never been a Latin nation to leave such an incubus upon the bosom of after ages?" Then I would remind myself, that, under cover of grammar and geography, and all the other *farce*-meat (as the word *ought* to be written and pronounced), I put something better into my pupils; something that I loved myself, and cared to give to them. But I often ask myself to what it all goes. I learn to love my boys. I kill in them all the bad I can. I nourish in them all the good I can. I send them across the borders of manhood, — and they leave me, and most likely I hear nothing more of them. And I say to myself: 'My life is like a wind. It blows and will cease.' But something says in reply : 'Wouldst thou not be one of God's winds, content to blow, and scatter the rain and dew, and shake the plants into fresh life, and then pass away and know nothing of what thou hast done?' And I answer: 'Yes, Lord.'"

"You are not a wind; you are a poet, Mr. Bloomfield," I said, with emotion.

"One of the speechless ones, then," he returned, with a smile that showed plainly enough that the speechless longed for utterance. It was such a smile as would, upon the face of a child, wile anything out of you. Surely God, who needs no wiles to make him give what one is ready to receive, will let him sing some day, to his heart's content! And me, too, O Lord, I pray.

"What a pleasure it must be to you now, to have such a

man as Mr. Armstrong for your curate! He will be a brother to you," I said, as soon as I could speak.

"Mr. Smith, I cannot tell you what he is to me already. He is doing what I would fain have done, — what was denied to me."

"How do you mean?"

"I studied for the church. But I aimed too high. My heart burned within me, but my powers were small. I wanted to relight the ancient lamp, but my rush-light would not kindle it. My friends saw no light; they only smelt burning. I was heterodox. I hesitated, I feared, I yielded, I withdrew. To this day, I do not know whether I did right or wrong. But I am honored yet in being allowed to teach, and, if at the last I have the faintest 'Well done' from the Master, I shall be satisfied."

Mrs. Bloomfield was gently weeping; partly from regret, as I judged, that her husband was not in the position she would have given him, partly from delight in his manly goodness. A watery film stood in the school-master's eyes, and his wise, gentle face was irradiated with the light of a far-off morning, whose dawn was visible to his hope.

"The world is the better for you at least, Mr. Bloomfield," I said. "I wish some more of us were as sure as you of helping on the daily Creation, which is quite as certain a fact as that of old; and is even more important to us than that recorded in the book of Genesis. It is not great battles alone that build up the world's history, nor great poems alone that make the generations grow. There is a still, small rain from heaven that has more to do with the blessedness of nature and of human nature than the mightiest earthquake or the loveliest rainbow."

"I do comfort myself," he answered, "at this Christmas-time, and for the whole year, with the thought that, after all, the world was saved by a child. But that brings me to think of a little trouble I am in, Mr. Smith. The only paper I have, at all fit for reading to-morrow night, is much too short to occupy the evening. What is to be done?"

"Oh! we can talk about it."

"That is just what I could not bear. It is rather an odd

composition, I fear; but, whether it be worth anything or not, I cannot help having a great affection for it."

" Then it is true, I presume ? "

" There again! That is just one of the questions I don't want to answer. I quite sympathized with you last night in not wishing to know how much of Mr. Armstrong's story was true. Even if wholly fictitious, a good story is always true. But there are things which one would have no right to invent, which would be worth nothing if they were invented, from the very circumstance of their origin in the brain, and not in the world. The very beauty of them demands that they should be fact; or, if not, that they should not be told, — sent out poor unclothed spirits into the world before a body of fact has been prepared for them. But I have always found it impossible to define the kind of stories I mean. The nearest I can come to it is this : If the force of the lesson depends on the story being a fact, it must not be told except it is a fact. Then, again, there are true things that one would be shy of telling, if he thought they would be attributed to himself. Now this story of mine is made up of fiction and fact both. And I fear that if I were called upon to take it to pieces, it would lose the force of any little truth it possesses, besides exposing me to what I would gladly avoid. Indeed, I fear I ought not to read it at all."

" You are amongst friends, you know, Mr. Bloomfield."

" Entirely ? " he asked, with a half-comic expression.

" Well," I answered, laughing, "any exception that may exist is hardly worth considering, and, indeed, ought to be thankfully accepted, as tending to wholesomeness. Neither vinegar nor mustard would be desirable as food, you know; yet —"

" I understand you. I am ashamed of having made such a fuss about nothing. I will do my best, I assure you."

I fear that the fastidiousness of the good man will not be excuse enough for the introduction of such a long preamble to a story for which only a few will in the least care. But the said preamble happening to touch on some interesting subjects, I thought it well to record it. As to the story itself, there are some remarks of Balzac in the introduction to one of his, that would well apply to the school-master's. They are to the effect that some stories, which have nothing in them as stories, yet fill one with an interest both gentle and profound, if they are read in the mood that is exactly fitted for their just reception.

Mr. Bloomfield conducted me to the door.

"I hope you will not think me a grumbler," he said; "I should not like your disapprobation, Mr. Smith."

"You do me great honor," I said, honestly. "Believe me, there is no danger of that. I understand and sympathize with you entirely."

"My love of approbation is large," he said, tapping the bump referred to with his forefinger. "Excuse it and me too."

"There is no need, my dear friend," I said, "if I may call you such."

His answer was a warm squeeze of the hand, with which we parted.

As I returned home, I met Henry Armstrong, mounted on a bay mare of a far different sort from what a sportsman would consider a doctor justified in using for his purposes. In fact, she was a thorough hunter; no beauty certainly, with her ewe-neck, drooping tail, and white face and stocking; but she had an eye at once gentle and wild as that of a savage angel, if my reader will condescend to dream for a moment of such an anomaly; while her hind quarters were power itself, and her foreleg was flung right out from the shoulder with a gesture not of work but of delight; the step itself being entirely one of work, — long in proportion to its height. The lines of her fore and hind quarters converged so much that there was hardly more than room for the saddle between them. I had never seen such action. Altogether, although not much of a hunting man, the motion of the creature gave me such a sense of power and joy that I longed to be scouring the fields with her under me. It was a sunshiny day, with a keen, cold air, and a thin sprinkling of snow; and Harry looked so radiant with health, that one could easily believe he had health to convey, if not to bestow. He stopped and inquired after his patient.

"Could you not get her to go out with you, Mr. Smith?" he said.

"Would that be safe, Mr. Henry?"

"Perfectly safe, if she is willing to go; not otherwise. Get her to go willingly for ten minutes, and see if she is not the better for it. What I want is to make the blood go quicker and more plentifully through her brain. She has not fever enough. She does not live fast enough."

"I will try," I said. "Have you been far to-day?"

"Just come out. You might tell that by the mare. You should see her three hours after this."

And he patted her neck as if he loved her, — as I am sure he did, — and trotted gently away.

When I came up to the gate, Beeves was standing at it.

"A nice gentleman that, sir!" said he.

"He is, Beeves. I quite agree with you."

"And rides a good mare, sir; and rides as well as any man in the county. I never see him leave home in a hurry. Always goes gently out, and comes gently in. What has gone between, you may see by her skin when she comes home."

"Does he hunt, Beeves?"

"I believe not, sir; except the fox crosses him in one of his rounds. Then, if he is heading anywhere in his direction, they say doctor and mare go at it like mad. He's got two more in his stable, better horses to look at; but that's the one to go."

"I wonder how he affords such animals."

"They say he has a way of buying them lame, and a wonderful knack of setting them up again. They all go, anyhow."

"Will you say to your mistress that I should like very much if she would come to me here?"

Beeves stared, but said "Yes, sir," and went in. I was now standing in front of the house, doubtful of the reception Adela would give my message, but judging that curiosity would aid my desire. I was right. Beeves came back with the message that his mistress would join me in a few minutes. In a quarter of an hour she came, wrapt in furs. She was very pale, but her eye was brighter than usual, and it did not shrink from the cold glitter of the snow. She put her arm in mine, and we walked for ten minutes along the dry gravel walks, chatting cheerfully, about anything and nothing.

"Now you must go in," I said.

"Not yet, surely, uncle. By-the-by, do you think it was right of me to come out?"

"Mr. Henry Armstrong said you might."

She did not reply, but I thought a light rose-color tinged her cheek.

"But he said you must not be out more than ten minutes."

"Well, I suppose I must do as I am told."

And she turned at once, and went up the stair to the door almost as lightly as any other girl of her age.

There was some progress, plainly enough. But was that a rose-tinge I had seen on her cheek, or not?

The next evening after tea we arranged ourselves much as on the last occasion; and Mr. Bloomfield, taking a neat manuscript from his pocket, and evidently restraining himself from apology and explanation, although as evidently nervous about the whole proceeding, and jealous of his own presumption, began to read as follows: —

His voice trembled as he read, and his wife's face was a shade or two paler than usual.

"BIRTH, DREAMING, AND DEATH.

"In a little room, scantily furnished, lighted, not from the window, for it was dark without, and the shutters were closed, but from the peaked flame of a small, clear-burning lamp, sat a young man, with his back to the lamp and his face to the fire. No book or paper on the table indicated labor just forsaken; nor could one tell from his eyes, in which the light had all retreated inwards, whether his consciousness was absorbed in thought, or reverie only. The window-curtains, which scarcely concealed the shutters, were of coarse texture, but of brilliant scarlet, — for he loved bright colors; and the faint reflection they threw on his pale, thin face made it look more delicate than it would have seemed in pure daylight. Two or three book-shelves, suspended by cords from a nail in the wall, contained a collection of books, poverty-stricken as to numbers, with but few to fill up the chronological gap between the Greek New Testament and stray volumes of the poets of the present century. But his love for the souls of his individual books was the stronger that there was no possibility of its degenerating into avarice for the bodies or outsides whose aggregate constitutes the piece of house-furniture called a library.

"Some years before, the young man (my story is so short, and calls in so few personages, that I need not give him a name) had aspired, under the influence of religious and sympathetic feeling, to be a clergyman; but Providence, either in the form of poverty, or of theological difficulty, had prevented his prosecuting his studies to that end. And now he was only a village school-master, nor likely to advance further. I have said *only* a village school-master; but is it not better to be a teacher *of* babes than a preacher *to* men, at any time; not to speak of those troublous times of transition, wherein a difference of degree must so often assume the appearance of a difference of kind? That man is more happy — I will not say more blessed — who, loving boys and girls, is loved and revered by them, than he who, ministering unto men and women, is compelled to pour his words into the filter of religious suspicion, whence the water is allowed to pass away unheeded, and only the residuum is retained for the analysis of ignorant party-spirit.

"He had married a simple village girl, in whose eyes he was nobler than the noblest, — to whom he was the mirror, in which the real forms of all things around were reflected. Who dares pity my poor village school-master? I fling his pity away. Had he not found in her love the verdict of God, that he was worth loving? Did he not in her possess the eternal and the unchangeable? Were not her eyes openings through which he looked into the great depths that could not be measured or represented? She was his public, his society, his critic. He found in her the heaven of his rest. God gave unto him immortality, and he was glad. For his ambition, it had died of its own mortality. He read the words of Jesus, and the words of great prophets whom he has sent; and learned that the wind-tossed anemone is a word of God as real and true as the unbending oak beneath which it grows; that reality is an absolute existence precluding degrees. If his mind was, as his room, scantily furnished, it was yet lofty; if his light was small, it was brilliant. God lived, and he lived. Perhaps the highest moral height which a man can reach, and at the same time the most difficult of attainment, is the willingness to be *nothing* relatively, so that he attain that positive excellence which the original conditions of his being render not merely possible, but imperative. It is nothing to a man to be greater or less than another; to be esteemed or otherwise by the public or private world in which he moves. Does he, or does he not, behold and love and live the unchangeable, the essential, the divine? This he can only do according as God has made him. He can behold and understand God in the least degree, as well as in the greatest, only by the godlike within him; and he that loves thus the good and great has no room, no thought, no necessity, for comparison and difference. The truth satisfies him. He lives in his absoluteness. God makes the glowworm, as well as the star; the light in both is divine. If mine be an earth-star to gladden the wayside, I must cultivate humbly and rejoicingly its green earth-glow, and not seek to blanch it to the whiteness of the stars that lie in the fields of blue. For to deny God in my own being is to cease to behold him in any. God and man can meet only by the man's becoming that which God meant him to be. Then he enters into the house of life, which is greater than the house of fame. It is better to be a child in a green field than a knight of many orders in a state ceremonial.

"All night long he had sat there, and morning was drawing nigh. He has not heard the busy wind all night, heaping up snow against the house, which will make him start at the ghostly face of the world when at length he opens the shutters, and it stares upon him so white. For up in a little room above, white-curtained, like the great earth without, there has been a storm, too, half the night, — moanings and prayers — and some forbidden tears; but now, at length, it is over; and through the portals of two mouths instead of one flows and ebbs the tide of the great air-sea which feeds the life of man. With the sorrow of the mother, the new life is purchased for the child; our very being is redeemed from nothingness with the pains of a death of which we know nothing.

"An hour has gone by since the watcher below has been delivered from the fear and doubt that held him. He has seen the mother and the child, — the first she has given to life and him, — and has returned to his lonely room, quiet and glad.

"But not long did he sit thus before thoughts of doubt awoke in his mind. He remembered his scanty income, and the somewhat feeble health of his wife. One or two small debts he had contracted seemed absolutely to press on his bosom; and the new-born child — 'oh! how doubly welcome,' he thought, 'if I were but half as rich again as I am!' — brought with it, as its own love, so its own care. The dogs of need, that so often hunt us up to heaven, seemed hard upon his heels; and he prayed to God with fervor; and as he prayed he fell asleep in his chair, and as he slept he dreamed. The fire and the lamp burned on as before, but threw no rays into his soul; yet now, for the first time, he seemed to become aware of the storm without; for his dream was as follows: —

"He lay in his bed, and listened to the howling of the wintry wind. He trembled at the thought of the pitiless cold, and turned to sleep again, when he thought he heard a feeble knocking at the door. He rose in haste, and went down with a light. As he opened the door, the wind, entering with a gust of frosty particles, blew out his candle; but he found it unnecessary, for the gray dawn had come. Looking out, he saw nothing at first; but a second look, turned downwards, showed him a little half-frozen child, who looked quietly, but beseechingly, in his face. His hair was filled with drifted snow, and his little hands and cheeks were blue with cold. The heart of the school-master swelled to bursting with the spring-flood of love and pity that rose up within it. He lifted the child to his bosom, and carried him into the house, where, in the dream's incongruity, he found a fire blazing in the room in which he now slept. The child said never a word. He set him by the fire, and made haste to get hot water, and put him in a warm bath. He never doubted that this was a stray orphan who had wandered to him for protection, and he felt that he could not part with him again, even though the train of his previous troubles and doubts once more passed through the mind of the dreamer, and there seemed no answer to his perplexities for the lack of that cheap thing, gold, — yea, silver. But when he had undressed and bathed the little orphan, and having dried him on his knees, set him down to reach something warm to wrap him in, the boy suddenly looked up in his face, as if revived, and said with a heavenly smile, 'I am the child Jesus.' — 'The child Jesus!' said the dreamer, astonished. 'Thou art like any other child.' 'No, do not say so,' returned the boy, 'but say, *Any othei child is like me.'* And the child and the dream slowly faded away, and he awoke with these words sounding in his heart: 'Whosoever shall receive one of such children in my name, receiveth me; and whosoever shall receive me, receiveth not me, but him that sent me.' It was the voice of God saying to him : 'Thou wouldst receive the child whom I sent thee out of the cold, stormy night; receive the new child out of the cold waste into the warm human house, as the door by which it can enter God's house, its home. If better could be done for it, or for thee, would I have sent it hither? Through thy love, my little one must learn my love and be blessed. And thou shalt not keep it without thy reward. For thy necessities, — in thy little house, is there not yet room? in thy barrel, is there not yet meal? and thy purse is not empty quite. Thou canst not eat more than a mouthful at once. I have made thee so. Is it any trouble to me to take care of thee? Only I prefer to feed thee from my own hand, and not from thy store.' And the school-master sprang up in joy, ran upstairs, kissed his wife, and clasped the baby in his arms in the name of the child Jesus. And in that embrace, he knew that he received God to his heart. Soon, with a tender, beaming face, he was wading through the snow to the school-house, where he spent a happy day amidst the rosy faces and bright eyes of his boys and girls. These, likewise, he loved the more dearly and joyfully for that dream, and those words in his heart; so that, amidst their true child-faces (all going well with them, as not unfrequently happened in his school-room), he felt as if all the elements of Paradise were gathered around him, and knew that he was God's child, doing God's work.

"But while that dream was passing through the soul of the husband, another visited the wife, as she lay in the faintness and trembling joy of the new motherhood. For although she that has been mother before is not the less a new mother to the new child, her former relation not covering with its wings the fresh bird in the nest of her bosom, yet there must be a peculiar delight in the thoughts and feelings that come with the first-born. As she lay half in a sleep, half in a faint, with the vapors of a gentle delirium floating through her brain, without losing the sense of existence she lost the consciousness of its form, and thought she lay, not a young mother in her bed, but a nosegay of wild flowers in a basket, crushed, flattened and half withered. With her in the basket lay other bunches of flowers, whose odors, some rare as well as rich, revealed to her the sad contrast in which she was placed. Beside her lay a cluster of delicately curved, faintly tinged, tea-scented roses, while she was only blue hyacinth bells, pale primroses, amethyst anemones, closed blood-colored daisies, purple violets, and one sweet-scented, pure white orchis. The basket lay on the counter of a well-known little shop in the village, waiting for purchasers. By and by her own husband entered the shop, and approached the basket to choose a nosegay. 'Ah!' thought she, ' will he choose me? How dreadful if he should not, and I should be left lying here, while he takes another! But how should he choose me? They are all so beautiful, and even my scent is nearly gone. And he cannot know that it is I lying here. Alas! alas!' But as she thought thus, she felt his hand clasp her, heard the ransom-money fall, and felt that she was pressed to his face and lips, as he passed from the shop. He *had* chosen her; he *had* known her. She opened her eyes; her husband's kiss had awakened her. She did not speak, but looked up thankfully in his eyes, as if he had, in fact, like one of the old knights, delivered her from the transformation of some evil magic, by the counter-enchantment of a kiss, and restored her from a half-withered nosegay to be a woman, a wife, a mother. The dream comforted her much, for she had often feared that she, the simple, so-called uneducated girl, could not be enough for the great school-master. But soon her thoughts flowed into another channel; the tears rose in her dark eyes, shining clear from beneath a stream that was not of sorrow, and it was only weakness that kept her from uttering audible words like these: ' Father in heaven, shall I trust my husband's love, and doubt thine? Wilt thou meet less richly the fearing hope of thy child's heart, than he in my dream met the longing of his wife's? He was perfected in my eyes by the love he bore me; shall I find thee less complete? Here I lie on thy world, faint, and crushed, and withered; and my soul often seems as if it had lost all the odors that should float up in the sweet-smelling savor of thankfulness and love to thee. But thou hast only to take me, only to choose me, only to clasp me to thy bosom, and I shall be a beautiful singing angel, singing to God, and comforting my husband while I sing. Father take me, possess me, fill me!'

"So she lay patiently waiting for the summer-time of restored strength that drew slowly nigh. With her husband and her child near her, in her soul, and God everywhere, there was for her no death, and no hurt. When she said to herself, 'How rich I am!' it was with the riches that pass not away, — the riches of the Son of man; for in her treasures the human and the divine were blended, were one.

"But there was a hard trial in store for them. They had learned to receive what the Father sent; they had now to learn that what he gave he gave eternally, after his own being, — his own glory. For ere the mother awoke from her first sleep, the baby, — like a frolicsome child-angel, that but tapped at his mother's window and fled, — the baby died; died while the mother slept away the pangs of its birth; died while the father was teaching other babes out of the joy of his new fatherhood.

"When the mother woke, she lay still in her joy, — the joy of a doubled life; and knew not that death had been there, and had left behind only the little human coffin.

"'Nurse, bring me the baby,' she said at last. 'I want to see it.'

"But the nurse pretended not to hear.

"'I want to nurse it. Bring it.'

"She had not yet learned to say *him*; for it was her first baby.

"But the nurse went out of the room, and remained some minutes away. When she returned, the mother spoke more absolutely, and the nurse was compelled to reply — at last.

"'Nurse, do bring me the baby; I am quite able to nurse it now.'

"'Not yet, if you please, ma'am. Really you must rest a while first. Do try to go to sleep.'

"The nurse spoke steadily, and looked her, too, straight in the face; and there was a constraint in her voice, a determination to be calm, that at once roused the suspicion of the mother; for though her first-born was dead, and she had given birth to what was now, as far as the eye could reach, the waxen image of a son, a child had come from God, and had departed to him again ; and she *was* his mother.

"And the fear fell upon her heart that it might be as it was ; and, looking at her attendant with a face blanched yet more with fear than with suffering, she said : —

"'Nurse, is the baby — ?'

"She could not say *dead ;* for to utter the word would be at once to make it possible that the only fruit of her labor had been pain and sorrow.

"But the nurse saw that further concealment was impossible ; and, without another word, went and fetched the husband, who, with face pale as the mother's, brought the baby, dressed in its white clothes, and laid it by its mother's side, where it lay too still.

"'O ma'am, do not take on so,' said the nurse, as she saw the face of the mother grow like the face of the child, as if she were about to rush after him into the dark.

"But she was not 'taking on' at all. She only felt that pain at her heart, which is the farewell kiss of a long-cherished joy. Though cast out of paradise into a world that looked very dull and weary, yet, used to suffering, and always claiming from God the consolation it needed, and satisfied with that, she was able, presently, to look up in her husband's face, and try to reassure him of her well-being by a dreary smile.

"'Leave the baby,' she said ; and they left it where it was. Long and earnestly she gazed on the perfect tiny features of the little alabaster countenance, and tried to feel that this was the child she had been so long waiting for. As she looked, she fancied she heard it breathe, and she thought, 'What if it should be only asleep!' but, alas! the eyes would not open, and when she drew it close to her, she shivered to feel it so cold. At length, as her eyes wandered over and over the little face, a look of her husband dawned unexpectedly upon it ; and, as if the wife's heart awoke the mother's, she cried out, 'Baby! baby!' and burst into tears, during which weeping she fell asleep.

"When she awoke, she found the babe had been removed while she slept. But the unsatisfied heart of the mother longed to look again on the form of the child ; and again, though with remonstrance from the nurse, it was laid beside her. All day and all night long, it remained by her side, like a little frozen thing that had wandered from its home, and now lay dead by the door.

"Next morning the nurse protested that she must part with it, for it made her fret; but she knew it quieted her, and she would rather keep her little lifeless babe. At length the nurse appealed to the father; and the mother feared he would think it necessary to remove it; but to her joy and gratitude he said, 'No, no; let her keep it as long as she likes.' And she loved her husband the more for that; for he understood her.

"Then she had the cradle brought near the bed, all ready as it was for a live child that had open eyes, and therefore needed sleep, — needed the lids of the brain to close, when it was filled full of the strange colors and forms of the new world. But this one needed no cradle, for it slept on. It needed, instead of the little curtains to darken it to sleep, a great sunlight to waken it up from the darkness, and the ever-satisfied rest. Yet she laid it in the cradle, which she had set near her, where she could see it, with the little hand and arm laid out on the white coverlet. If she could only keep it so! Could not something be done, if not to awake it, yet to turn it to stone, and let it remain so forever? No; the body must go back to its mother, the earth, and the *form* which is immortal, being the thought of God, must go back to its Father, — the Maker. And as it lay in the white cradle, a white coffin was being made for it. And the mother thought: 'I wonder which trees are growing coffins for my husband and me.'

"But ere the child, that had the prayer of Job in his grief, and had died from its mother's womb, was carried away to be buried, the mother prayed over it this prayer: 'O God, if thou wilt not let me be a mother, I have one refuge: I will go back and be a child; I will be thy child more than ever. My mother-heart will find relief in childhood towards its Father. For is it not the same nature that makes the true mother and the true child? Is it not the same thought blossoming upward and blossoming downward? So there is God the Father and God the Son. Thou wilt keep my little son for me. He has gone home to be nursed for me. And when I grow well,

I will be more simple, and truthful, and joyful in thy sight.
And now thou art taking away my child, my plaything, from
me. But I think how pleased I should be, if I had a daughter,
and she loved me so well that she only smiled when I took her
plaything from her. Oh! I will not disappoint thee, — thou
shalt have thy joy. Here I am, do with me what thou wilt;
I will only smile.'

"And how fared the heart of the father? At first, in the
bitterness of his grief, he called the loss of his child a punishment for his doubt and unbelief; and the feeling of punishment made the stroke more keen, and the heart less willing to
endure it. But better thoughts woke within him ere long.

"The old woman who swept out his school-room came in
the evening to inquire after the mistress, and to offer her con-
dolences on the loss of the baby. She came likewise to tell
the news, that a certain old man of little respectability had
departed at last, unregretted by a single soul in the village
but herself, who had been his nurse through the last tedious
illness.

"The school-master thought with himself: —

"'Can that soiled and withered leaf of a man, and my little snow-flake of a baby, have gone the same road? Will they
meet by the way? Can they talk about the same thing, —
anything? They must part on the borders of the shining
land, and they could hardly speak by the way.'

"'He will live four-and-twenty hours, nurse,' the doctor
had said.

"'No, doctor; he will die to-night,' the nurse had replied,
during which whispered dialogue, the patient had lain breathing quietly, for the last of suffering was nearly over.

"He was at the close of an ill-spent life, not so much selfish-
ly towards others as indulgently towards himself. He had
failed of true joy by trying often and perseveringly to create
a false one; and now, about to knock at the gate of the other
world, he bore with him no burden of the good things of this;
and one might be tempted to say of him, that it were better
he had not been born. The great majestic mystery lay before
him; but when would he see its majesty?

"He was dying thus, because he had tried to live as Nature said he should not live; and he had taken his own wages

— for the law of the Maker is the necessity of his creature. His own children had forsaken him, for they were not perfect as their Father in heaven, who maketh his sun to shine on the evil and on the good. Instead of doubling their care as his need doubled, they had thought of the disgrace he brought on them, and not of the duty they owed him; and now, left to die alone for them, he was waited on by this hired nurse, who, familiar with death-beds, knew better than the doctor, — knew that he could live only a few hours.

"Stooping to his ear she had told him, as gently as she could, — for she thought she ought not to conceal it, — that he must die that night. He had lain silent for a few moments; then had called her, and, with broken and failing voice, had said, ' Nurse, you are the only friend I have; give me one kiss before I die.' And the woman-heart had answered the prayer.

" ' And,' said the old woman, 'he put his arms round my neck, and gave me a long kiss, — such a long kiss! — and then he turned his face away, and never spoke again.'

" So, with the last unction of a woman's kiss, with this baptism for the dead, he had departed.

" ' Poor old man ! he had not quite destroyed his heart yet,' thought the school-master. ' Surely it was the child-nature that woke in him at the last, when the only thing left for his soul to desire, the only thing he could think of as a preparation for the dread something, was a kiss. Strange conjunction, yet simple and natural ! Eternity — a kiss. Kiss me; for I am going to the Unknown ! — Poor old man !' the school-master went on in his thoughts, ' I hope my baby has met him, and put his tiny hand in the poor old shaking hand, and so led him across the borders into the shining land, and up to where Jesus sits and said to the Lord : "Lord, forgive this old man, for he knew not what he did." And I trust the Lord has forgiven him.'

" And then the bereaved father fell on his knees, and cried out : —

" ' Lord, thou hast not punished me. Thou wouldst not punish for a passing thought of troubled unbelief, with which I strove. Lord, take my child and his mother and me, and do what thou wilt with us. I know thou givest not, to take again."

"And ere the school-master could call his protestantism to his aid, he had ended his prayer with the cry : —

"'And, O God! have mercy upon the poor old man, and lay not his sins to his charge.'

"For, though a woman's kiss may comfort a man to eternity, it is not all he needs. And the thought of his lost child had made the soul of the father compassionate."

He ceased, and we sat silent.

CHAPTER VIII.

SONG.

I confess I was a little dismayed to find what a solemn. turn the club-stories had taken. But this dismay lasted for a moment only; for I saw that Adela was deeply interested, again wearing the look that indicates abstracted thought and feeling. I said to myself : —

"This is very different mental fare from what you have been used to, Adela."

But she seemed able to mark, learn, and inwardly digest it, for she had the appearance of one who is stilled by the strange newness of her thoughts. I was sure that she was now experiencing a consciousness of existence quite different from anything she had known before. But it had a curious outcome.

For, when the silence began to grow painful, no one daring to ask a question, and Mrs. Cathcart had resumed her knitting, Adela suddenly rose, and, going to the piano, struck a few chords, and began to sing. The song was one of Heine's strange ghost-dreams, so unreal in everything but feeling, and therefore, as dreams, so true. Why did she choose such a song after what we had been listening to ? I accounted for it by the supposition that, being but poorly provided as far as variety in music went, this was the only thing suggested to her by the tone of the paper, and, therefore, the nearest she could come to it. It served, however, to make a change and a transition; which was, as I thought, very desirable, lest any of the company should be scared from attending the club; and I resolved that I would divert the current, next time, if I could.

This was what Adela sang; and the singing of it was evidently a relief to her : —

> I dreamt of the daughter of a king,
>   With a cheek white, wet, and chill;
> Under the limes we sat murmuring,
>   And holding each other so still!
>
> "Oh! not thy father's sceptre of gold,
>   Nor yet his shining throne,
> Nor his diamond crown that glitters cold, —
>   'Tis thyself I want, my own!"
>
> "Oh! that is too good," she answered me,
>   "I lie in the grave all day;
> And only at night I come to thee,
>   For I cannot keep away."

It was something that she had volunteered a song, whatever it was. But it is a misfortune that, in writing a book, one cannot give the music of a song. Perhaps, by the time that music has its fair part in education, this may be done. But, meantime, we mention the fact of a song, and then give the words, as if that were the song. The music is the song, and the words are no more than the saddle on which the music sits, the singer being the horse, who could do without a saddle well enough. — May Adela forgive the comparison! — At the same time, a true word-song has music of its own, and is quite independent, for its music, both of that which it may beget, and of that with which it may be associated.

As she rose, she glanced towards the doctor, and said : —

"Now it is your turn, Mr. Armstrong."

Harry did not wait for a second invitation; for to sing was to him evidently a pleasure too great to be put in jeopardy. He rose at once, and, sitting down at the instrument, sang — I cannot say *as follows*, you see; I can only say *the following words* : —

> Autumn clouds are flying, flying,
>   O'er the waste of blue;
> Summer flowers are dying, dying,
>   Late so lovely new.

Laboring wains are slowly rolling
  Home with winter grain;
Holy bells are slowly tolling
  Over buried men.

Goldener lights set noon a-sleeping
  Like an afternoon;
Colder airs come stealing, creeping
  After sun and moon;
And the leaves, all tired of blowing,
  Cloudlike o'er the sun,
Change to sunset-colors, knowing
  That their day is done.

Autumn's sun is sinking, sinking
  Into Winter's night;
And our hearts are thinking, thinking
  Of the cold and blight.
Our life's sun is slowly going
  Down the hill of might;
Will our clouds shine golden-glowing
  On the slope of night?

But the vanished corn is lying
  In rich golden glooms.
In the church-yard, all the sighing
  Is above the tombs.
Spring will come, slow-lingering,
  Opening buds of faith.
Man goes forth to meet his spring,
  Through the door of death.

So we love, with no less loving,
  Hair that turns to gray;
Or a step less lightly moving.
  In life's autumn day.
And if thought, still-brooding, lingers
  O'er each bygone thing,
'Tis because old Autumn's fingers
  Paint in hues of Spring.

The whole tone of this song was practical and true, and so was fitted to correct the unhealthiness of imagination which might have been suspected in the choice of the preceding. "Words and music," I said to myself, "must here have come from the same hand; for they are one utterance. There is no setting of words to music here; but the words have brought their own music with them; and the music has brought its own words."

As Harry rose from the piano-forte, he said to me gayly: —

"Now, Mr. Smith, it is your turn. I know when you sing, it will be something worth listening to."

"Indeed, I hope so," I answered. "But the song-hour has not yet come to me. How good you all ought to be who can sing! I feel as if my heart would break with delight, if I could sing; and yet there is not a sparrow on the house-top that cannot sing a better song than I."

"Your hour will come," said the clergyman, solemnly. "Then you will sing, and all we shall listen. There is no inborn longing that shall not be fulfilled. I think that is as certain as the forgiveness of sins. Meantime, while your singing-robes are making, I will take your place with my song, if Miss Cathcart will allow me."

"Do, please," said Adela, very heartily; "we shall all be delighted."

The clergyman sang, and sang even better than his brother. And these were the words of his song : —

THE MOTHER MARY TO THE INFANT JESUS.

'Tis time to sleep, my little boy;
  Why gaze thy bright eyes so?
At night, earth's children, for new joy,
  Home to thy Father go.
But thou art wakeful. Sleep, my child;
  The moon and stars are gone;
The wind and snow they grow more wild,
  And thou art smiling on.

My child, thou hast immortal eyes,
  That see by their own light;
They see the innocent blood, — it lies
  Red-glowing through the night.
Through wind and storm unto thine ear
  Cry after cry doth run;
And yet thou seemest not to hear,
  And only smilest on.

When first thou camest to the earth,
  All sounds of strife were still:
A silence lay around thy birth,
  And thou didst sleep thy fill.
Why sleep'st thou, — nay, why weep'st thou not?
  Thy earth is woe-begone;
Babies and mothers wail their lot,
  And still thou smilest on.

I read thine eyes like holy book;
  No strife is pictured there;
Upon thy face I see the look
  Of one who answers prayer.
Ah, yes ! — Thine eyes, beyond this wild,
  Behold God's will well done;
Men's songs thine ears are hearing, child;
  And so thou smilest on.

The prodigals arise and go,
  And God goes forth to meet!
Thou seest them gather, weeping low,
  About the Father's feet.
And for their brothers men must bear,
  Till all are homeward gone.
O Eyes, ye see my answered prayer!
  Smile, Son of God, smile on!

As soon as the vibrations of this song, I do not mean on the
chords of the instrument, but in the echo-caves of our bosoms,
had ceased, I turned to the doctor and said : —

"Are you ready with your story yet, Mr. Henry ?"

"Oh, dear, no !" he answered, — "not for days. I am
not an idle man like you, Mr. Smith. I belong to the laboring class."

I knew that he could not have it ready.

"Well," I said, "if our friends have no objection, I will
give you another myself next time."

"Oh ! thank you, uncle," said Adela. "Another fairy-
tale, please."

"I can't promise you another fairy-tale just yet, but I can
promise you something equally absurd, if that will do."

"Oh, yes! Anything you like, uncle. *I*, for one, am
sure to like what you like."

"Thank you, my dear. Now I will go; for I see the
doctor waiting to have a word with you."

The company took their leave, and the doctor was not two
minutes behind them; for, as I went up to my room, after asking the curate when I might call upon him, I saw him come
out of the drawing-room and go downstairs.

"Monday evening, then," I had heard the colonel say, as
he followed his guests to the hall.

CHAPTER IX.

THE CURATE AND HIS WIFE.

As I approached the door of the little house in which the curate had so lately taken up his abode, he saw me from the window, and, before I had had time to knock, he had opened the door.

"Come in," he said. "I saw you coming. Come to my den, and we will have a pipe together."

"I have brought some of my favorite cigars," I said, "and I want you to try them."

"With all my heart."

The room to which he led me was small, but disfigured with no offensive tidiness. Not a spot of wall was to be seen for books, and yet there were not many books after all. We sat for some minutes enjoying the fragrance of the western incense, without other communion than that of the clouds we were blowing, and what I gathered from the walls. For I am old enough, as I have already confessed, to be getting long-sighted, and I made use of the gift in reading the names of the curate's books, as I had read those of his brother's. They were mostly books of the sixteenth and seventeenth centuries, with a large admixture from the nineteenth, and more than the usual proportion of the German classics; though, strange to say, not a single volume of German Theology could I discover. The curate was the first to break the silence.

"I find this a very painful cigar," he said, with a half laugh.

"I am sorry you don't like it. Try another."

"The cigar is magnificent."

"Isn't it thoroughfare, then?"

"Oh, yes! the cigar's all right. I haven't smoked such a cigar for more than ten years; and that's the reason."

"I wish I had known you seven years, Mr. Armstrong."

"You have known me a hundred and seven."

"Then I have a right to —"

"Poke my fire as much as you please."

And as Mr. Armstrong said so, he poked his own chest, to signify the symbolism of his words.

"Then I should like to know something of your early history, — something to account for the fact that a man like you, at your time of life, is only a curate."

"I can do all that, and account for the pain your cigar gives me. in one and the same story."

I sat full of expectation.

"You won't find me long-winded, I hope."

"No fear of that. Begin directly. I adjure you by our friendship of a hundred years."

"My father was a clergyman before me; one of those simple-hearted men who think that to be good and kind is the first step towards doing God's work; but who are too modest, too ignorant, and sometimes too indolent, to aspire to any second step, or even to inquire what the second step may be. The poor in his parish loved him and preyed upon him. He gave and gave, even after he had no more that he had a right to give.

"He was not by any means a rich man, although he had a little property besides his benefice; but he managed to send me to Oxford. Inheriting, as I suspect, a little tendency to extravagance, having at least no love of money except for what it would bring, and seeing how easily money might be raised there for need true or false, I gradually learned to think less and less of the burdens grievous to be borne, which a subjection to Mammon will accumulate on the shoulders of the unsuspecting ass. I think the old men of the sea, in 'Sindbad the Sailor,' must personify debt. At least *I* have found reason to think so. At the same time I wish I had done nothing worse than run into debt. Yet by far the greater part of it was incurred for the sake of having works of art about me. Of course pictures were out of the question; but good engravings and casts were within the reach of a borrower. At least it was not for the sake of whip-handles and trowsers, that I fell into the clutches of Moses Melchizedek, — for that was the devil to whom I betrayed my soul for money. Emulation, however, mingled with the love of art; and I must confess, too, that cigars cost me money as well as pictures: and, as I have already hinted, there was worse behind. But some things we can only speak to God about.

"I shall never forget the oily face of the villain — may God save him, and then he'll be no villain! — as he first hinted that he would lend me any money I might want, upon certain insignificant conditions, such as signing for a hundred and fifty, where I should receive only a hundred. The sunrise of the future glowed so golden, that it seemed to me the easiest thing in the world to pay my debts *there*. Here, there was what I wanted, cigars and all. There, there must be gold, else whence the hue? I could pay all my debts in the future with the utmost ease. *How* was no matter. I borrowed and borrowed. I flattered myself, besides, that in the things I bought I held money's worth; which, in the main, would have been true, if I had been a dealer in such things; but a mere owner can seldom get the worth of what he possesses, especially when he cannot choose but sell, and has no choice of his market. So when, horrified at last with the filth of the refuge into which I had run to escape the bare walls of heaven, I sold off everything but a few of my pet books," — here he glanced lovingly round his humble study, where shone no glories of print or cast, — "which I ought to have sold as well, I found myself still a thousand pounds in debt.

"Now, although I had never had a thousand pounds from Melchizedek, I had known perfectly well what I was about. I had been deluded, but not cheated; and in my deep I saw yet a lower depth, into which I *would* not fall, — for then I felt I should be lost indeed, — that of in any way repudiating my debts. But what was to be done I had no idea.

"I had studied for the church, and I now took holy orders. I had a few pounds a year from my mother's property, which all went in part-payment of the interest of my debt. I dared not trouble my father with any communication on the subject of my embarrassment, for I knew that he could not help me, and that the impossibility of doing so would make him more unhappy than the wrong I had done in involving myself. I seized the first offer of a curacy that presented itself. Its emoluments were just one hundred pounds a year, of which I had *not* to return twenty pounds, as some curates have had to do. Out of this I had to pay one half, in interest for the thousand pounds. On the other half, and the trifle my mother allowed me, I contrived to live.

"But the debt continued undiminished. It lay upon me as a mountain might crush a little Titan. There was no cracking frost, no cutting stream, to wear away, by slowest trituration, that mountain of folly and wickedness. But what I suffered most from was the fact that I must seem to the poor of my parish unsympathetic and unkind. For, although I still managed to give away a little, it seemed to me such a small, shabby sum, every time that I drew my hand from my pocket, in which perhaps I had left still less, that it was with a positive feeling of shame that I offered it. There was no high generosity in this. It was mostly selfish, — the effect of the transmission of my father's blind benevolence, working as an impulse in me. But it made me wretched. Add to this a feeling of hypocrisy, in the knowledge that I, the dispenser of sacred things to the people, was myself the slave of a money-lending Jew, and you will easily see how my life could not be to me the reality which it must be, for any true and healthy action, to every man. In a word, I felt that I was a humbug. As to my preaching, that could not have had much reality in it of any kind, for I had no experience yet of the relation of Christian Faith to Christian Action. In fact, I regarded them as separable, — not merely as distinguishable, in the necessity which our human nature, itself an analysis of the divine, has for analyzing itself. I respected everything connected with my profession, which I regarded as in itself eminently respectable; but, then, it was only the profession I respected, and I was only *doing church* at best. I have since altered my opinion about the profession, as such; and while I love my work with all my heart, I do not care to think about its worldly relations at all. The honor is to be a servant of men, whom God thought worth making, worth allowing to sin, and worth helping out of it at such a cost. But as far as regards the *profession*, is it a manly kind of work, to put on a white gown once a week, and read out of a book; and then put on a black gown, and read out of a paper you bought or wrote, — all about certain old time-honored legends which have some influence in keeping the common people on their good behavior, by promising them happiness after they are dead, if

they are respectable, and everlasting torture if they are
blackguards? Is it manly?"

"You are scarcely fair to the profession even as such, Mr.
Armstrong," I said.

"That's what I *feel* about it," he answered. "Look here,"
he went on, holding out a brawny right arm, with muscles like
a prize-fighter's; "they may laugh at what, by a happy hit,
they have called muscular Christianity, — I for one don't object
to being laughed at, — but I ask you, is that work fit for a
man to whom God has given an arm like that? I declare to
you, Smith, I would rather work in the docks, and leave the
churching to the softs and dandies; for then I should be able
to respect myself as giving work for my bread, instead of drawing so many pounds a year for talking *goody* to old wives and
sentimental young ladies; — for over men who are worth anything, such a man has no influence. God forbid that I should be
disrespectful to old women, or even sentimental young ladies!
They are worth *serving* with a man's whole heart, but not
worth pampering. I am speaking of the profession as pro-
fessed by a mere clergyman, — one in whom the professional
predominates."

"But you can't use those splendid muscles of yours in the
church."

"But I can give up the use of them for something better
and nobler. They indicate work; but if I can do real spiritual instead of corporeal work, I rise in the scale. I sacrifice
my thews on the altar of my faith. But by the mere clergyman,
there is no work done to correspond, — I do not say to *his*
capacity for work, but to the capacity for work indicated by such
a frame as mine, — work of some sort, if not of the high poetic
order, then of the lower porter-sort. But if there be a living
God, who is doing all he can to save men, to make them pure
and noble and high, humble and loving and true, to make them
live the life he cares to live himself; if he has revealed and is
revealing this to men, and needs for his purpose the work of
their fellow-men, who have already seen and known this purpose, — surely there is no nobler office than that of a parson;
for to him is committed the grand work of letting men see the
thoughts of God, and the work of God, — in a word, of telling
the story of Jesus, so that men shall see how true it is for *now*,

how beautiful it is for *ever;* and recognize it as in fact *the* story of God. Then a clergyman has simply to be more of a man than other men; whereas if he be but a clergyman he is less of a man than any other man who does honestly the work he has to do, whether he be farm-laborer, shoemaker, or shop-keeper. For such a work, a man may well pine in a dungeon, or starve in a curacy; yea, for such a work, a man will endure the burden of having to dispense the wealth of a bishop-ric after a divine fashion."

"But your story?" I said at last, unwilling as I was to interrupt his eloquence.

"Yes. This brings me back to it. Here was I starving for no high principle, only for the commonplace one of paying my debts; and paying my debts out of the church's money too, for which, scanty as it was, I gave wretched labor, — reading prayers as neatly as I could, and preaching sermons half evangelical, half scholastic, of the most unreal and uninteresting sort, feeling all the time hypocritical, as I have already said, and without the farthest prospect of deliverance.

"Then I fell in love."

"Worse and worse!"

"So it seemed, but so it wasn't, — like a great many things. At all events, she's downstairs now, busy at a baby's frock, I believe; God bless her! Lizzie is the daughter of a lieutenant in the army, who died before I knew her. She was living with her mother and elder sister, on a very scanty income, in the village where I had the good fortune to be the unhappy curate. I believe I was too unhappy to make myself agreeable to the few young ladies of my congregation, which is generally considered one of the first duties of a curate, in order, no doubt, to secure their co-operation in his charitable schemes; and certainly I do not think I received any great attention from them, — certainly not from Lizzie. I thought she pitied and rather despised me. I don't know whether she did, but I still suspect it. I am thankful to say I have no ground for thinking she does now. But we have been through a kind of a moderate-burning fiery furnace together, and that brings out the sense, and burns out the nonsense, in both men and women. Not that Lizzie had much nonsense to be burned out of her, as you will soon see.

"I had often been fool enough to wonder that, while she was most attentive and devout during the reading of the service, her face assumed, during the sermon, a far-off look of abstraction, that indicated no reception of what I said, further than as an influence of soporific quality. I felt that there was reproof in this. In fact, it roused my conscience yet more, and made me doubt whether there was anything genuine in me at all. Sometimes I felt as if I really could not go on, but must shut up my poor manuscript, which was 'an ill-favored thing, sir, but mine own,' and come down from the pulpit, and beg Miss Lizzie Payton's pardon for presuming to read it in her presence. At length that something, or rather want of something, in her quiet, unregarding eyes, aroused a certain opposition, ambition, indignation, in me. I strove to write better, and to do better generally. Every good sentence I launched at her, — I don't quite know whether I aimed at her heart or her head; I fear the latter; but I know that I looked after my arrow with a hurried glance, to see whether it had reached the mark. Seldom, however, did I find that my bow had the strength to arouse Miss Lizzie from the somniculose condition which, in my bitterness, I attributed to her. Since then I have frequently tried to bring home to her the charge, and wring from her the confession that, occasionally, just occasionally, she was really overpowered by — the weather. But she has never admitted more than one such lapse, which, happening in a hard frost, and the church being no warmer than condescension, she wickedly remarked must have been owing, not to the weight of the atmosphere, but the weight of something else. At length, in my anxiety for self-justification, I persuaded myself that her behavior was a sign of spiritual insensibility; that she needed conversion; that she looked with contempt from the far-off table-lands of the Broad church, or the dizzy pinnacles of snow-clad Puseyism, upon the humble efforts of one who followed in the footsteps of the first fishers of men, — for such I tried, in my self-protection, to consider myself.

"One day, I happened to meet her in a retired lane near the village. She was carrying a jug in her hand.

"'How do you do, Miss Lizzie? A labor of love?' I said, ass that I was!

"'Yes,' she answered; 'I've been over to Farmer Dale's, to fetch some cream for mamma's tea.'

"She knew well enough I had meant a ministration to the poor.

"'Oh! I beg your pardon,' I rejoined; 'I thought you had been round your district.'

"This was wicked; for I knew quite well that she had no district.

"'No,' she answered, 'I leave that to my sister. Mamma is my district. And, do you know, her headaches are as painful as any washerwoman's.'

"This shut me up rather; but I plucked up courage presently

"'You don't seem to like going to church, Miss Lizzie?'

"Her face flushed.

"'Who dares to say so? I am very regular in my attendance.'

"'Not a doubt of it. But you don't enjoy being there?'

"'I do.'

"'Confess, now. You don't like my sermons.'

"'Do you like them yourself, Mr. Armstrong?'

"Here was a floorer! Did I like them myself? I really couldn't honestly say I did. I was not greatly interested in them, further than as they were my own, and my best attempts to say something about something I knew nothing about. I was silent. She stood looking at me out of clear gray eyes.

"'Now you have begun this conversation, Mr. Armstrong, I will go on with it,' she said, at length. 'It was not of my seeking. I do not think you believe what you say in the pulpit.'

"Not believe what I said! Did I believe what I said? Or did I only believe that it was to be believed? The tables were turned with a vengeance. Here was the lay lamb, attacked and about to be worried by the wolf clerical, turning and driving the said wolf to bay. I stood and felt like a convicted criminal before the gray eyes of my judge. And somehow or other I did not hate those clear pools of light. They were very beautiful. But not one word could I find to say for myself. I stood and looked at her, and I fear I began to twitch at my neckcloth, with a vague instinct that I had better go and hang myself. I stared and stared, — and no doubt got as red as a turkey-cock, — till it began to be very embarrassing indeed. What refuge could there be from one who spoke the truth so plainly? And how do you think I got out of it?" asked Mr. Armstrong of me, John Smith, who, as he told the story, felt almost in as great confusion and misery as the narrator must have been in at the time, although now he looked amazingly jolly, and breathed away at his cigar with the slow exhalations of an epicure.

"Mortal cannot tell," I answered.

"One mortal can," rejoined he, with a laugh. "I fell on my knees, and made speechless love to her."

Here came a pause. The countenance of the Broad-churchman changed as if a lovely summer cloud had passed over it. The jolly air vanished, and he looked very solemn for a little while.

"There was no coxcombry in it, Smith. I may say that for myself. It was the simplest and truest thing I ever did in my life. How was I to help it? There stood the visible truth before me, looking out of the woman's gray eyes. What was I to do? I thank God I have never seen the truth plain before me, let it look ever so ghostly, without rushing at it. All my advances have been by a sudden act, — to me like an inspiration: — an act done in terror, almost, lest I should stop and think about it, and fail to do it. And here was no ghost, but a woman-angel, whose *Thou art the man* was spoken out of profundities of sweetness and truth. Could I turn my back upon her? Could I parley with her? — with the Truth? No. I fell on my knees, weeping like a child; for all my misery, all my sense of bondage and untruth, broke from me in those tears.

"My hat had fallen off as I knelt. My head was bowed on my hands. I felt as if she could save me. I dared not look up. She tells me since that she was bewildered and frightened; but I discovered nothing of that. At length I felt a light pressure, a touch of healing, fall on my bended head. It was her hand. Still I hid my face, for I was ashamed before her.

"'Come,' she said, in a low voice, which I dare say she compelled to be firm; 'come with me into the Westland Woods. There we can talk. Some one may come this way.'

"She has told me since that a kind of revelation came to

her at the moment; a sight not of the future but of the fact, and that this lifted her high above every feeling of mere propriety, substituting for it a conviction of right. She felt that God had given this man to her; and she no more hesitated to ask me to go with her into the woods than she would hesitate to go with me now if I asked her. And indeed, if she had not done so, I don't know what would have come of it, — how the story would have ended. I believe I should be kneeling there now, a whitened skeleton, to the terror and warning of all false churchmen who should pass through the lonely lane.

"I rose at once, like an obedient child, and turned in the direction of the Westland Woods, feeling that she was by my side, but not yet daring to look at her. Now there are few men to whom I would tell the trifle that followed. It was a trifle as to the outside of it; but it is amazing what *virtue*, in the old meaning of the word, may lie in a trifle. The recognition of virtue is at the root of all magical spells, and amulets, and talismans. Mind, I felt from the first that you and I would understand each other."

"You rejoice my heart," I said.

"Well, the first thing I had to do, as you may suppose, to make me fit to look at her, was to wipe my eyes. I put my hand in my pocket; then the other hand in the other pocket; then my first hand in the breast-pocket; and the slow-dawning, awful truth became apparent, that here was a great brute of a curate, who had been crying like a baby, and had no handkerchief. A moment of keen despair followed, —chased away by a vision of hope, in the shape of a little white cloud between me and the green grass. This cloud floated over a lady's hand, and was in fact a delicate handkerchief. I took it, and brought it to my eyes, which gratefully acknowledged the comfort. And the scent of the lavender, — not lavender water, but the lavender itself, that puts you in mind of country churches, and old Bibles, and dusky, low-ceiled parlors on Sunday afternoons, — the scent of the lavender was so pure and sweet, and lovely! It gave me courage.

" 'May I keep it?' I asked.

" 'Yes. Keep it,' she answered.

" 'Will you take my arm now?'

"For answer, she took my arm, and we entered the woods.

It was a summer afternoon. The sun had outflanked the thick clouds of leaves that rendered the woods impregnable from overhead, and was now shining in, a little sideways, with that slumberous light belonging to summer afternoons, in which everything, mind and all, seems half asleep and all dreaming.

" 'Let me carry the jug,' I said.

" 'No,' she answered, with a light laugh; 'you would be sure to spill the cream, and spoil both your coat and mamma's tea.'

" 'Then put it down in this hollow till we come back.'

" 'It would be full of flies and beetles in a moment. Besides, we won't come back this way, shall we? I can carry it quite well. Gentlemen don't like carrying things.'

" I feared lest the tone the conversation had assumed might lead me away from the resolution I had formed while kneeling in the lane. So, as usual with me, I rushed blindly on the performance.

" 'Miss Lizzie, I am a hypocritical and unhappy wretch.'

" She looked up at me with a face full of compassionate sympathy. I could have lost myself in that gaze. But I would not be turned from my purpose, of which she had no design, though her look had almost the power; and the flood-gates of speech once opened, out it came, the whole confession I have made to you, in what form or manner I found, the very first time I looked back upon the relation, that I had quite forgotten.

" All the time, the sun was sending ever so·many sloping ladders of light down through the trees, for there was a little mist rising that afternoon; and I felt as if they were the same kind of ladder that Jacob saw, inviting a man to climb up to the light and peace of God. I felt as if upon them invisible angels were going down all through the summer wood, and that the angels must love our woods as we love their skies. And amidst the trees and the ladders of ether, we walked, and I talked, and Lizzie listened to all I had to say, without uttering a syllable till I had finished.

" At length, having disclosed my whole bondage and grief, I ended with the question: —

" 'Now what is to be done?'

"She looked up in my face with those eyes of truth, and said : —

"'That money must be paid, Mr. Armstrong.'

"'But how?' I responded, in despair.

"She did not seem to heed my question, but she really answered it.

"'And, if I were you, I would do no more duty till it was paid.'

"Here was decision with a vengeance. It was more than I had bargained for. I was dumb. A moment's reflection, however, showed me that she was perfectly right; that what I had called *decision with a vengeance* was merely the utterance of a child's perception of the true way to walk in.

"Still I was silent; for long vistas of duty, and loss, and painful action and effort opened before me. At length I said :—

"' You are quite right, Miss Lizzie.'

"' I wish I could pay it for you,' she rejoined, looking up in my face with an expression of still tenderness, while the tears clouded her eyes just as clouds of a deeper gray come over the gray depths of some summer skies.

"' But you can help me to pay it.'

"' How?'

"' Love me,' I said, and no more. I could not.

"The only answer she made was to look up at me once more, then stop, and, turning towards me, draw herself gently against my side, as she held my arm. It was enough, — was it not?

"*Love me*, I said, and she did love me; and she's downstairs, as I told you; and I think she is not unhappy."

"But you're not going to stop there," I said.

"No, I'm not. That very evening I told the vicar that I must go. He pressed for my reasons; but I managed to avoid giving a direct answer. I begged him to set me at liberty as soon as possible, meaning, when he should have provided himself with a substitute. But he took offence at last, and told me I might go when I pleased; for he was quite able to perform the duties himself. Atfer this, I felt it would be unpleasant for him as well as for me, if I remained, and so I took him at his word. And right glad I was not to have to preach any more to Lizzie. It was time for me to act instead of talk.

"But what was I to do? The moment the idea of ceasing to *do church* was entertained by me, the true notion of what I was to do instead presented itself. It was this. I would apply to my cousin, the accountant. He was an older man, considerably, than myself, and had already made a fortune in his profession. We had been on very good terms indeed, considering that he was a dissenter, and all but hated the church; while, I fear, I quite despised dissenters. I had often dined with him, and he had found out that I had a great turn for figures, as he called it. Having always been fond of mathematics, I had been able to assist him in arriving at a true conclusion on what had been to him a knotty point connected with life insurance; and consequently he had a high opinion of my capacity in his department.

"I wrote to him, telling him I had resolved to go into business for a time. I did not choose to enlighten him further; and I fear I fared the better with him from his fancying that I must have begun to entertain doubts concerning church-establishments. I had the cunning not to ask him to employ me; for I thought it very likely he would request my services, which would put me in a better position with him. And it fell out as I had anticipated. He replied at once, offering me one hundred and fifty pounds to begin, with the prospect of an annual advance of twenty pounds, if, upon further trial, we both found the arrangement to our minds. I knew him to be an honorable man, and accepted the proposal at once. And I cannot tell how light-hearted I felt as I folded up my canonicals, and put them in a box to be left, for the mean time, in the charge of my landlady.

"I was troubled with no hesitation as to the propriety of the proceeding. Of course I felt that, if it had been mere money-making, a clergyman ought to have had nothing to do with it; but I felt now, on the other hand, that if any man was bound to pay his debts a clergyman was; in fact, that he could not do his duty till he had paid his debts; and that the wrong was not in turning to business now, but in having undertaken the office with a weight of filthy lucre on my back and my conscience which my pocket could never relieve them of. Any scruple about the matter I felt would be only superstition; that, in fact, it was a course of action worthy of a man. and therefore of a clergyman. I thought well enough of the church, too, to believe that every man of any manliness in it would say that I had done right. And, to tell the truth, so long as Lizzie was satisfied with me I did not care for archdeacon or bishop. I meant just to drop out of the ranks of the clergy without sign, and keep my very existence as secret as possible, until the moment I had achieved my end, when I would go to my bishop, and tell him all, requesting to be reinstated in my sacred office. There was only one puzzle in the affair, and that was how to act towards Mrs. Payton in regard to her daughter's engagement to me. The old lady was not gifted with much common sense, I knew; and I feared both that she would be shocked at the idea, and that she would not keep my secret. Of course, I consulted Lizzie about it. She had been thinking about it already, and had concluded that the best way would be for her to tell her mother the fact of our engagement, and for me to write to her from London that I did not intend taking a second charge for some time yet; and so leave Lizzie to act for the rest as occasion might demand. All this was very easily managed, and in the course of another week, chiefly devoted to the Westland Woods, I found myself at a desk in Cannon Street.

" And now began a real experience of life. I had resolved to regard the money I earned as the ransom-money of the church, paid by her for the redemption of an erring servant from the power of Mammon. I would therefore spend upon myself not one penny more than could be helped. With this view, and perhaps with a lurking notion of penance in some corner of my stupid brain, I betook myself to a lodging-house in Hatton Garden, where I paid just three shillings a week for a bedroom, if that could be called a room which was rather a box, divided from a dozen others by partitions of seven or eight feet in height. I had, besides, the use of a common room, with light and fire, and the use of a kitchen for cooking my own victuals, if I required any, presided over by an old man, who was rather dirtier than necessity could justify, or the amount of assistance he rendered could excuse. But I managed to avoid this region of the establishment, by both breakfasting and dining in eating-houses, of which I soon found out the best and cheapest. It is amazing upon how little a man with a good constitution, a good conscience, and an object, can live in London. I lived and throve. My bedroom, though as small as it could possibly have been, was clean, with all its appointments; and, for a penny a week additional, I had the use of a few newspapers. The only luxuries I indulged in, besides one pipe of bird's-eye a day, were writing verses, and teaching myself German. This last led to some little extravagance, for I soon came to buy German books at the bookstalls; but I thought the church would get the advantage of it by and by, and so I justified myself in it. I translated a great many German songs. Now and then you will hear my brother sing one of them. He was the only one of my family who knew where I lived. The others addressed their letters to my cousin's place of business. My father was dreadfully cut up at my desertion of the church, as he considered it. But I told my brother the whole story, and he went home, as he declared, prouder of his big brother than if he had been made a bishop of. I believe he soon comforted the dear old man, by helping him to see the matter in its true light, and not one word of reproach did I ever receive from his lips or his pen. He did his best likewise to keep the whole affair a secret.

"But a thousand pounds, with interest, was a dreadful sum. However, I paid the interest and more than fifty pounds of the principal the first year. One good thing was, I had plenty of clothes, and so could go a long time without becoming too shabby for business. I repaired them myself. I brushed my own boots. Occasionally I washed my own collars.

"But it was rather dreadful to think of the years that must pass before I could be clear, before I could marry Lizzie, before I could open my mouth again to utter truths which I now began to *see*, and which grew dearer to me than existence itself. As to Lizzie, I comforted myself by thinking that it did not matter much whether we were married or not, — we loved each other, and that was all that made marriage itself a good thing, and we had the good thing as it was. We corresponded regularly, and I need not say that this took a great many hours from German and other luxuries, and made the things I did not like much easier to bear.

"I am not stoic enough to be able to say that the baseness and meanness of things about me gave me no discomfort. In

my father's house, I had been used to a little simple luxury,
for he liked to be comfortable himself, and could not be so,
unless he saw every one comfortable about him as well At
college, likewise, I had not thwarted the tendency to self-in-
dulgence, as my condition now but too plainly testified. It
will be clear enough to you, Mr. Smith, that there must have
been things connected with such a mode of life exceedingly
distasteful to one who had the habits of a gentleman; but it
was not the circumstances, so much as the companions of my
location, that bred me discomfort. The people who shared the
same roof with me, I felt bound to acknowledge as so sharing,
although at first it was difficult to know how to behave to them,
and their conduct sometimes caused me excessive annoyance.
They were of all births and breedings, but almost all of them,
like myself, under a cloud. It was not much that I had to
associate with them, but even while glancing at a paper before
going up to my room, for I allowed myself no time for that at
the office, I could not help occasionally hearing language which
disgusted me to the backbone, and made me say to myself, as
I went slowly up the stairs, 'My sins have found me out, and
I am in hell for them.' Then, as I sat on the side of my bed
in my stall, the vision of the past would come before me in all
its beauty, — the Westland Woods, the open country, the comfortable abode, and, above all, the homely, gracious old church,
with its atmosphere of ripe sacredness and age-long belief; for
now I looked upon that reading-desk, and that pulpit, with new
eyes and new thoughts. as I will presently try to show you.
I had not really lost them, in the sense in which I regarded
them now, as types of a region of possibly noble work; but
even with their old aspect, they would have seemed more
honorable than this constant labor in figures from morning to
night, till I thought sometimes that the depth of punishment
would be to have to reckon to all eternity. But, as I have
said, I had my consolations, — Lizzie's letters, my books, a
walk to Hampstead Heath on a holiday, an occasional peep into Goethe or Schiller on a bright day in St. Lawrence Pountney
church-yard, to which I managed to get admittance, and — will
you believe it ? — going to a city church on Sundays. More of
this anon. So that, if I was in hell for my sins, it was, at
least, not one of Swedenborg's hells. Never before did I

understand what yet I had always considered one of the most exquisite sonnets I knew : —

> "Mourner, that dost deserve thy mournfulness,
>   Call thyself punished, call the earth thy hell;
>   Say, 'God is angry, and I earned it well,
> I would not have him smile and not redress.'
> Say this, and straightway all thy grief grows less.
>   'God rules at least, I find, as prophets tell,
>   And proves it in this prison.' Straight thy cell
> Smiles with an unsuspected loveliness.
>   A prison, — and yet from door and window-bar
>   I catch a thousand breaths of his sweet air;
>   Even to me, his days and nights are fair;
> He shows me many a flower, and many a star;
>   And though I mourn, and he is very far,
>   He does not kill the hope that reaches there.' "

"Where did you get that wonderful sonnet?" I cried, hardly interrupting him, for when he came to the end of it he paused with a solemn pause.

"It is one of the stars of the higher heavens, which I spied through my prison bars."

"Will you give me a copy of it?"

"With all my heart. It has never been in print."

"Then your star reminds me of that quaint simile of Henry Vaughan : —

> "'If a star were confined into a tomb,
>   Her captive flames must needs burn there;
> But when the hand that locked her up gives room,
>   She'll shine through all the sphere.'"

"Ah, yes; I know the poem. That is about the worst verse in it, though."

"Quite true."

"What a number of verses you know!"

"They stick to me somehow."

"Is the sonnet your own?"

"My dear fellow, how could I speak in praise of it as I do, if it were my own? I would say 'I wish it were!' only that would be worse selfishness than coveting a man's purse. No. It is not mine."

"Well, will you go on with your story, — if you will yet oblige me?"

" I will. But you will think it strange that I should be so communicative to one whose friendship I have so lately gained."

" I believe there is a fate in such things," I answered.

" Well, I yield to it, — if I do not weary you? "

" Go on. There is positively not the least danger of that."

" Well, it was not to hell I was really sent, but to school, — and that not a fashionable boarding, or expensive public school, but a day-school like a Scotch parish school, — to learn the conditions and ways and thoughts of my brothers and sisters.

" I soon got over the disgust I felt at the coarseness of the men I met. Indeed, I found amongst business gentlemen what affected me with the same kind of feeling, — only perhaps more profoundly, — a coarseness not of the social so much as of the spiritual nature; in a word, genuine selfishness; whereas this quality was rather less remarkable in those who had less to be selfish about. I do not say, therefore, that they had less of it. I soon saw that their profanity had chiefly a negative significance; but it was long before I could get sufficiently accustomed to their vileness, their beastliness, — I beg the beasts' pardon! — to keep from leaving the room when a vein of that sort was opened. But I succeeded in schooling myself to bear it. 'For,' thought I, 'there must be some bond — some ascertainable and recognizable bond — between these men and me; I mean some bond that might show itself as such to them and me.' I found out, before long, that there was a tolerably broad and visible one, — nothing less than our human nature, recognized as such. For by degrees I came to give myself to know them. I sat and talked to them, smoked with them, gave them tobacco, lent them small moneys, made them an occasional trifling present of some article of dress, of which I had more than I wanted; in short, gained their confidence. It was strange, but without any reproof from me, nothing more direct than simple silence, they soon ceased to utter a word that could offend me; and, before long, I had heard many of their histories. And what stories they were! Set any one to talk about himself, instead of about other people, and you will have a seam of the precious mental metal opened up to you at once: only ore, most likely, that needs much smelting and

refining; or, it may be, not gold at all, but a metal which
your mental alchemy may turn into gold.   The one thing I
learned was, that they and I were one; that our hearts were
the same.   How often I exclaimed inwardly, as some new
trait came to light, in the words, though without the general-
izing scorn, of Shakespeare's Timon, — 'More man!'
Sometimes I was seized with a kind of horror, beholding my
own visage in the mirror which some poor wretch's story held up
to me, — distorted perhaps by the flaws in the glass, but still
mine.   I saw myself in other circumstances and under other
influences, and felt sometimes, for a moment, as if I had been
guilty of the very deeds, more often of the very neglects,
that had brought my companion to misery.   I felt, in the
most solemn moods of reflection, that I might have done all
that, and become all that.   I saw but myself, over and over
again, with wondrous variations, none sufficient to destroy the
identity.   And I said to myself that, if I was so like them in
all that was undesirable, it must be possible for them to become
like me in all, whatever it was, that rendered me in any way
superior to them.

  "But wherein did this superiority consist?   I saw that,
whatever it was, I had little praise in it.   I said, 'What
have I done to be better than I found myself?   If Lizzie had
not taken me in hand, I should not have done even this.
What an effort it would need for one of these really to begin
to rouse and raise himself!   And what have I done to rouse
and raise myself, to whom it would surely be easier?   And
how can I hope to help them to rise till I have risen myself?
It is not enough to be above them; only by the strength of
my own rising can I help to raise them, for we are bound together by one cord.   Then how shall I rise?   Whose uprising
shall lift me?   On what cords shall I lay hold to be heaved
out of the pit?'   And then I thought of the story of the
Lord of men, who arose by his own might, not alone from the
body-tomb, but from all the death and despair of humanity,
and lifted with him our race, placing their tomb beneath their
feet, and them in the sunny hope that belongs to them, and
for which they were created, — the air of their own freedom.
'But,' I said to myself, 'this is ideal, and belongs to the race.
Before it comes true for the race, it must be done in the indi-

vidual. If it be true for the race, it can only be through its
being attainable by the individual. There must be something
in the story belonging to the individual. I will look at the
individual Christ, and see how he arose.'

" And then I saw that the Lord himself was clasped in the
love of the Father; that it was in the power of mighty communion that the daily obedience was done; that besides the
outward story of his devotion to men, there was the inward
story, — actually revealed to us men, marvellous as that is, —
the inward story of his devotion to his Father; of his speech
to him; of his upward look; of his delight in giving up to
him. And the answer to his prayers comes out in his deeds.
As Novalis says: ' In solitude the heavenly heart unfolded
itself to a flower-chalice of almighty love, turned towards the
high face of the Father.' I saw that it was in virtue of this,
that, again to use the words of Novalis, ' the mystery was un-
sealed. Heavenly spirits heaved the aged stone from the gloomy
grave; angels sat by the slumberer, bodied forth, in delicate
forms, from his dreams. Waking in new God-glories, he
clomb the height of the new-born world; buried with his own
hand the old corpse in the forsaken cavern, and laid thereon,
with almighty arm, the stone which no might raises again. Yet
weep thy beloved, tears of joy, and of boundless thanks at thy
grave; still ever, with fearful gladness, behold thee arisen,
and themselves with thee.' If then he is the captain of our
salvation, the head of the body of the human church, I must
rise by partaking in my degree of his food, by doing in my
degree his work. I fell on my knees and I prayed to the
Father. I rose, and, bethinking me of the words of the Son, I
went and tried to do them. I need say no more to you. A
new life awoke in me from that hour, feeble and dim, but yet
life; and often as it has stopped growing, that has always been
my own fault. Where it will end, thank God! I cannot tell.
But existence is an awful grandeur and delight.

" Then I understood the state of my fellow-men, with all
their ignorance, and hate, and revenge; some misled by passion, some blinded by dulness, some turned monomaniacs from
a fierce sense of injustice done them; and I said, ' There is
no way of helping them but by being good to them, and making
them trust me. But in every one of them there lies a secret

chamber, to which God has access from behind by a hidden door; while they know nothing of this chamber; and the other door, towards their own consciousness, is hidden by darkness and wrong, and ruin of all kinds. Sometimes they become dimly aware that there must be such a door. Some of us search for it, find it, turn back aghast; while God is standing behind the door waiting to be found, and ready to hold forth the arms of eternal tenderness to him who will open and look. Some of us have torn the door open, and, lo! there is the Father, at the heart of us, at the heart of all things.' I saw that he was leading these men through dark ways of disappointment and misery, the cure of their own wrong-doing, to find this door and find him. But could nothing be done to help them, — to lead them? They, too, must learn of Christ. Could they not be led to him? If he leads to the Father, could not man lead to him? True, he says that it is the leading of the Father that brings to him; for the Father is all in all; he fills and rounds the cycle. But he leads by the hand of man. Then I said, 'Is not this *the* work of the church?'

"And with this new test, I went to one church after another. And the prayers were beautiful. And my soul was comforted by them. And the troubles of the week sank back into the far distance, and God ruled in London city. But how could such as I thought of, love these prayers, or understand them? For them the voice of living man was needed. And surely the Spirit that dwelt in the church never intended to make less of the voice of a living man pleading with his fellow-men in his own voice, than the voice of many people pleading with God in the words which those who had gone to him had left behind them. If the Spirit be in the church, does it only pray? Yet almost as often as a man stood up to preach, I knew again why Lizzie had paid no heed to me. All he said had nothing to do with me or my wants. And if not with these, how could they have any influence on the all but outcasts of the social order? I justified Lizzie to the very full now; and I took refuge from the inanity of the sermon in thinking about her faithfulness. And that faithfulness was far beyond anything I knew yet.

"And now there awoke in me an earnest longing after the

office I had forsaken. Thoughts began to burn in me, and words to come unbidden, till sometimes I had almost to restrain myself from rising from the pew where I was seated, ascending the pulpit stairs, and requesting the man who had nothing to say, to walk down, and allow me, who had something to say, to take his place. Was this conceit? Considering what I was listening to, it could not have been *great* conceit at least. But I did restrain myself, for I thought an encounter with the police would be unseemly, and my motives scarcely of weight in the court to which they would lead me."

Here Mr. Armstrong relieved himself and me with a good laugh. I say relieved me, for his speech had held me in a state of tension such as to be almost painful.

"But I looked to the future in hope," he went on, "if ever I might be counted worthy, to resume the labor I had righteously abandoned; having had the rightness confirmed by the light I had received in carrying out the deed."

His voice here sank as to a natural pause, and I thought he was going to end his story.

"Tell me something more," I said.

"Oh!" returned he, "as far as story is concerned, the best of it is to come yet. About six months after I was fairly settled in London, I was riding in an omnibus, a rare enough accommodation with me, in the dusk of an afternoon. I was going out to Fulham to dine with my cousin, as I was sometimes forced to do. He was a good-hearted man, but — in short, I did not find him interesting. I would have preferred talking to a man who had barely escaped the gallows or the hulks. My cousin never did anything plainly wicked, and consequently never repented of anything. He thought no harm of being petty and unfair. He would not have taken a farthing that was not his own, but if he could get the better of you in an argument, he did not care by what means. He would put a wrong meaning on your words, that he might triumph over you, knowing all the time it was not what you meant. He would say, 'Words are words. I have nothing to do with your meanings. You may say you mean anything you like.' I wish it had been his dissent that made him such. But I won't say more about him, for I believe it is my chief fault, as to my profession, that I find commonplace people dreadfully uninteresting; and I am afraid I don't always give them quite fair play. I had to dine with him, and so I got into an omnibus going along the Strand. And I had not been long in it, before I began thinking about Lizzie. That was not very surprising.

"Next to me, nearer the top of the omnibus, sat a young woman, with a large brown-paper parcel on her lap. She dropped it, and I picked it up for her; but seeing that it incommoded her considerably I offered to hold it for her. She gave a kind of start when I addressed her, but allowed me to take the parcel. I could not see her face, because she was close to my side. But a strange feeling came over me, as if I was sitting next to Lizzie. I indulged in the fancy, not from any belief in it, only for the pleasure of it. But it grew to a great desire to see the young woman's face, and find whether or not she was at all like Lizzie. I could not, however, succeed in getting a peep within her bonnet; and so strong did the desire become, that, when the omnibus stopped at the circus, and she rose to get out, I got out first, without restoring the parcel, and stood to hand her out, and then give it back. Not yet could I see her face; but she accepted my hand, and, with a thrill of amazement, I felt a pressure of mine, which surely could be nobody's but Lizzie's. And it was Lizzie, sure enough! I kept the parcel; she put her arm in mine, and we crossed the street together, without a word spoken.

"'Lizzie!' I said, when we got into a quieter part.

"'Ralph!' she said, and pressed closer to my side.

"'How did you come here?'

"'Ah! I couldn't escape you.'

"'How did you come here?' I repeated.

"'You did not think,' she answered, with a low, musical laugh, 'that I was going to send you away to work, and take no share in it myself!'

"And then out came the whole truth. As soon as I had left, she set about finding a situation, for she was very clever with her needle and scissors. Her mother could easily do without her, as her elder sister was at home; and her absence would relieve their scanty means. She had been more fortunate than she could have hoped, and had found a good situation with a dressmaker in Bond street. Her salary was not

large, but it was likely to increase, and she had nothing
to pay for food or lodging; while, like myself, she was well
provided with clothes, and had, besides, facilities for procuring
more. And to make a long story as short as now may be,
there she remained in her situation as long as I remained in
mine; and every quarter she brought me all she could spare
of her salary for the Jew to gorge upon."

" And you took it?" I said, rather inadvertently.

"Took it! Yes. I took it, — thankfully, as I would the
blessing of Heaven. To have refused it would have argued me
unworthy of *her*. We understood each other too well for anything else. She shortened my purgatory by a whole year, —
my Lizzie! It is over now; but none of it will be over to all
eternity. She made a man of me."

A pause followed, as was natural, and neither spoke for some
moments. The ends of our cigars had been thrown away long
ago, but I did not think of offering another. At length I said,
for the sake of saying something : —

" And you met pretty often, I dare say ? "

" Every Sunday, at church."

" Of all places, the place where you ought to have met."

" It was. We met in a quiet old city church, where there
was nothing to attract us but the loneliness, the service, and
the bones of Milton."

" And when you had achieved your end — "

" It was but a means to an end. I went at once to a certain
bishop, told him the whole story, — not in quite such a lengthy
shape as I have told it to you, — and begged him to reinstate me
in my office."

" And what did he say ? "

" Nothing. The good man did not venture upon many
words. He held out his hand to me, shook mine warmly, and
here I am, you see, curate of St. Thomas', Purleybridge, and
husband of Lizzie Payton. Am I not a fortunate fellow ? "

" You are," I said, with emphasis, rising to take my leave.
" But it is too bad of me to occupy so much of your time on
a Saturday."

" Don't be uneasy about that. I shall preach all the better for it."

As I passed the parlor door, it was open, and Lizzie *was*

busy with a baby's frock. I think I should have known it
for one, even if I had not been put on the scent. She nodded
kindly to me as I passed out. I knew she was not one of the
demonstrative sort, else I should have been troubled that she
did not speak to me. I thought afterwards that she suspected,
from the sustained sound of her husband's voice, that he had
been telling his own story; and that therefore she preferred
letting me go away without speaking to me that morning.

"What a story for our club!" thought I. "Surely that
would do Adela good now."

But of course I saw at once that it would not do. I could
not for a moment wish that the curate should tell it. Yet I
did wish Adela could know it. So I have written it now;
and there it is, as nearly as he told it as I could manage to
record it.

The next day was Sunday. And here is a part of the curate's sermon : —

"My friends, I will give you a likeness, or a parable, which
I think will help you to understand what is the matter with
you all. For you all have something the matter with you;
and most of you know this to be the case, though you may
not know what is the matter. And those of you that feel
nothing amiss are far the worst off. Indeed you are ; for how
are things to be set right if you do not even know that there
is anything to be set right? There is the greatest danger of
everything growing much worse, before you find out that anything is wrong.

"But now for my parable.

"It is a cold winter forenoon, with the snow upon everything out of doors. The mother has gone out for the day, and
the children are amusing themselves in the nursery, — pretending to make such things as men make. But there is one among
them who joins in their amusement only by fits and starts.
He is pale and restless, yet inactive. His mother is away.
True, he is not well. But he is not very unwell ; and if she
were at home he would take his share in everything that was
going on, with as much enjoyment as any of them. But as it
is, his fretfulness and pettishness make no allowance for the
wilfulness of his brothers and sisters ; and so the confusions
they make in the room carry confusion into his heart and

brain, till at length a brighter noon entices the others out into the snow.

"Glad to be left alone, he seats himself by the fire and tries to read. But the book he was so delighted with yesterday is dull to-day. He looks up at the clock and sighs, and wishes his mother would come home. Again he betakes himself to his book, and the story transports his imagination to the great icebergs on the polar sea. But the sunlight has left them, and they no longer gleam and glitter and sparkle, as if spangled with all the jewels of the hot tropics, but shine cold and threatening as they tower over the ice-bound ship. He lays down the tale, and takes up a poem. But it, too, is frozen. The rhythm will not flow. And the sad feeling arises in his heart, that it is not so very beautiful, after all, as he had used to think it.

"'Is there anything beautiful?' says the poor boy at length, and wanders to the window. But the sun is under a cloud; cold, white, and cheerless, like death, lies the wide world out of doors; and the prints of his mother's feet in the snow all point towards the village and away from home. His head aches, and he cannot eat his dinner. He creeps upstairs to his mother's room. There the fire burns bright, and through the window falls a ray of sunlight. But the fire and the very sunlight are wintry and sad. 'Oh, when will mother be home?' He lays himself in a corner amongst soft pillows, and rests his head; but it is no nest for him, for the covering wings are not there. The bright-colored curtains look dull and gray; and the clock on the chimney-piece will not hasten its pace one second, but is very monotonous and unfeeling. Poor child! Is there any joy in the world? Oh, yes; but it always clings to the mother, and follows her about like a radiance, and she has taken it with her. Oh, when will she be home? The clock strikes as if it meant something, and then straightway goes on again with the old wearisome tic-tac.

"He can hardly bear it. The fire burns up within; daylight goes down without; the near world fades into darkness; the far-off worlds brighten and come forth, and look from the cold sky into the warm room; and the boy stares at them from the couch, and watches the motion of one of them, like the flight of a great golden beetle, against the divisions of the window-frame. Of this, too. he grows weary. Everything around him has lost its interest. Even the fire, which is like the soul of the room, within whose depths he has so often watched for strange forms and images of beauty and terror, has ceased to attract his tired eyes. He turns his back to it, and sees only its flickerings on the walls. To any one else, looking in from the cold, frosty night, the room would appear the very picture of afternoon comfort and warmth; and he, if he were descried thus nestling in its softest, warmest nook, would be counted a blessed child, without care, without fear, made for enjoyment, and knowing only fruition. But the mother is gone; and as that flame-lighted room would appear to the passing eye, without the fire, and with but a single candle to thaw the surrounding darkness and cold, so is that child's heart without the presence of the mother.

"Worn out at length with loneliness and mental want, he closes his eyes, and, after the slow lapse of a few more empty moments, reopens them on the dusky ceiling and the gray twilight window; no, — on two eyes near above him, and beaming upon him, the stars of a higher and holier heaven than that which still looks in through the unshaded windows. They are the eyes of the mother, looking closely and anxiously on her sick boy. 'Mother! mother!' His arms cling around her neck, and pull down her face to his.

"His head aches still, but the heart-ache is gone. When candles are brought, and the chill night is shut out of doors and windows, and the children are all gathered around the tea-table, laughing and happy, no one is happier, though he does not laugh, than the sick child, who lies on the couch and looks at his mother. Everything around is full of interest and use, glorified by the radiation of her presence. Nothing can go wrong. The splendor returns to the tale and the poem. Sickness cannot make him wretched. Now, when he closes his eyes, his spirit dares to go forth wandering under the shining stars and above the sparkling snow; and nothing is any more dull and unbeautiful. When night draws on, and he is laid in his bed, her voice sings him, and her hand soothes him, to sleep; nor do her influences vanish when he forgets everything in sleep; for he wakes in the morning well and happy, made whole by his faith in his mother. A power has gone forth from her love to heal and restore him.

"Brothers, sisters! do I not know your hearts from my own? — sick hearts, which nothing can restore to health and joy but the presence of Him who is Father and Mother both in one. Sunshine is not gladness, because you see Him not. The stars are far away, because He is not near; and the flowers, the smiles of old Earth, do not make you smile, because, although, thank God! you cannot get rid of the child's need, you have forgotten what it is the need of. The winter is dreary and dull, because, although you have the homeliest of homes, the warmest of shelters, the safest of nests to creep into and rest, — though the most cheerful of fires is blazing for you, and a table is spread, waiting to refresh your frozen and weary hearts, — you have forgot the way thither, and will not be troubled to ask the way; you shiver with the cold and hunger, rather than arise and say, 'I will go to my Father;' you will die in the storm rather than fight the storm; you will lie down in the snow rather than tread it under foot. The heart within you cries out for something, and you let it cry. It is crying for its God, — for its father and mother and home. And all the world will look dull and gray, — and if it does not look so now, the day will come when it must look so, — till your heart is satisfied and quieted with the known presence of Him in whom we live and move and have our being."

<hr />

CHAPTER X.

THE SHADOWS.

IT was again my turn to read. I opened my manuscript, and had just opened my mouth as well, when I was arrested for a moment. For, happening to glance to the other side of the room, I saw that Percy had thrown himself at full length on a couch, opposite to that on which Adela was seated, and was watching her face with all his eyes. But his look did not express love

so much as jealousy.   Indeed, I had seen small sign of his being attached to her.   If she had encouraged him, which certainly she did not, I dare say his love might have come out;
but I presume that he had been comfortably content until now,
when perhaps some remark of his mother had made him fear a
rival.   Mischief of some sort was evidently brewing.   A
human cloud, surcharging itself with electric fire, lay swelling
on the horizon of our little assembly; but I did not anticipate
much danger from any storm that could break from such a
quarter.   I believed that as far as my good friend, the colonel,
was concerned, Adela might at least refuse whom she pleased.
Whether she might find herself at equal liberty to choose
whom she pleased was a question that I was unprepared to
answer.   And I could not think about it now.   I had to read.
So I gave out the title, and went on : —

"THE SHADOWS.

" Old Ralph Rinkleham made his living by comic sketches,
and all but lost it again by tragic poems.   So he was just the
man to be chosen king of the fairies, for in Fairy-land the
sovereignty is elective."

" But, uncle," interrupted Adela, " you said it was not to
be a fairy-tale."
" Well, I don't think you will call it one, when you have
heard it," I answered.   " But I am not particular as to
names.   The fairies have not much to do with it anyhow."
" I beg your pardon, uncle," rejoined my niece; and I
went on.

" They did not mean to insist on his residence; for they
needed his presence only on special occasions.   But they must
get hold of him somehow, first of all, in order to make him
king.   Once he was crowned, they could get him as often as
they pleased; but, before this ceremony, there was a difficulty.
For it is only between life and death that the fairies have
power over grown-up mortals, and can carry them off to their
country.   So they had to watch for an opportunity.
" Nor had they to wait long.   For old Ralph was taken

dreadfully ill; and while hovering between life and death they carried him off, and crowned him king of Fairy-land. But after he was crowned, it was no wonder, considering the state of his health, that he should not be able to sit quite upright on the throne of Fairy-land; or that, in consequence, all the gnomes and goblins, and ugly, cruel things that live in the holes and corners of the kingdom, should take advantage of his condition, and run quite wild, playing him, king as he was, all sorts of tricks; crowding about his throne, climbing up the steps, and actually scrambling and quarrelling like mice about his ears and eyes, so that he could see and think of nothing else. But I am not going to tell anything more about this part of his adventures just at present. By strong and sustained efforts, he succeeded, after much trouble and suffering, in reducing his rebellious subjects to order. They all vanished to their respective holes and corners; and King Ralph, coming to himself, found himself in his bed, half propped up with pillows.

"But the room was full of dark creatures, which gambolled about in the firelight in such a strange, huge, but noiseless fashion, that he thought at first that some of his rebellious goblins had not been subdued with the rest, and had followed him beyond the bounds of Fairy-land into his own private house in London. How else could these mad, grotesque hip-popotamus-calves make their ugly appearance in Ralph Rinkelmann's bedroom? But he soon found out, that, although they were like the underground goblins, they were very different as well, and would require quite different treatment. He felt convinced that they were his subjects too, but that he must have overlooked them somehow at his late coronation, — if indeed they had been present; for he could not recollect that he had seen anything just like them before. He resolved, therefore, to pay particular attention to their habits, ways, and characters; else he saw plainly that they would soon be too much for him; as indeed this intrusion into his chamber, where Mrs. Rinkelmann, who must be queen if he was king, sat taking some tea by the fireside, plainly indicated. But she, perceiving that he was looking about him with a more composed expression than his face had worn for many days, started up, and came quickly and quietly to his side, and her face was bright with gladness. Whereupon the fire burned up more cheerily and the figures became more composed and respectful in their behavior, retreating towards the wall like well-trained attendants. Then the king of Fairy-land had some tea and dry toast, and, leaning back on his pillows, nearly fell asleep; but not quite, for he still watched the intruders.

"Presently the queen left the room to give some of the young princes and princesses their tea; and the fire burned lower; and, behold, the figures grew as black and as mad in their gambols as ever! Their favorite games seemed to be *Hide and Seek; Touch and Go; Grin and Vanish;* and many other such; and all in the king's bedchamber too; so that it was quite alarming. It was almost as bad as if the house had been haunted by certain creatures, which shall be nameless in a fairy-story, because with them Fairy-land will not willingly have much to do.

"'But it is a mercy that they have their slippers on!' said the king to himself; for his head ached.

"As he lay back, with his eyes half-shut and half-open, too tired to pay longer attention to their games, but, on the whole, considerably more amused than offended with the liberties they took, for they seemed good-natured creatures, and more frolicsome than positively ill-mannered, he became suddenly aware that two of them had stepped forward from the walls, upon which, after the manner of great spiders, most of them preferred sprawling, and now stood in the middle of the floor, at the foot of his majesty's bed, becking, and bowing, and ducking in the most grotesquely obsequious manner; while every now and then they turned solemnly round upon one heel, evidently considering that motion the highest token of homage they could show.

"'What do you want?' said the king.

"'That it may please your majesty to be better acquainted with us,' answered they. 'We are your majesty's subjects.'

"'I know you are; I shall be most happy,' answered the king.

"'We are not what your majesty takes us for, though. We are not so foolish as your majesty thinks us.'

"'It is impossible to take you for anything that I know of,' rejoined the king, who wished to make them talk, and said whatever came uppermost; — 'for soldiers, sailors, or any-thing; you will not stand still long enough. I suppose you really belong to the fire-brigade; at least, you keep putting its light out.'

" 'Don't jest, please your majesty.' And as they said the words, for they both spoke at once throughout the interview, they performed a grave somerset towards the king.

" 'Not jest!' retorted he; 'and with you? Why, you do nothing but jest. What are you?'

" 'The Shadows, sire. And when we do jest, sire, we al-ways jest in earnest. But perhaps your majesty does not see us distinctly.'

" 'I see you perfectly well,' replied the king.

" 'Permit me, however,' rejoined one of the Shadows; and as he spoke, he approached the king, and, lifting a dark fore-finger, drew it lightly, but carefully, across the ridge of his forehead, from temple to temple. The king felt the soft glid-ing touch go, like water, into every hollow, and over the top of every height of that mountain-chain of thought. He had involuntarily closed his eyes during the operation, and when he unclosed them again, as soon as the finger was withdrawn, he found that they were opened in more senses than one. The room appeared to have extended itself on all sides, till he could not exactly see where the walls were; and all about it stood the Shadows motionless. They were tall and solemn; rather awful, indeed, in their appearance, notwithstanding many re-markable traits of grotesqueness, looking, in fact, just like the pictures of Puritans drawn by Cavaliers, with long arms, and very long, thin legs, from which hung large, loose feet, while in their countenances length of chin and nose predominated. The solemnity of their mien, however, overcame all the oddity of their form, so that they were very *eerie* indeed to look at, dressed as they all were in funereal black. But a single glance was all that the king was allowed to have; for the former operator waved his dusky palm across his vision, and once more the king saw only the fire-lighted walls, and dark shapes flick-ering about upon them. The two who had spoken for the rest seemed likewise to have vanished. But at last the king dis-covered them, standing one on each side of the fireplace. They kept close to the chimney-wall, and talked to each other across the length of the chimney-piece; thus avoiding the direct rays of the fire, which, though light is necessary to their appearing to human eyes, do not agree with them at all, — much less give birth to them, as the king was soon to learn. After a few minutes, they again approached the bed, and spoke thus:—

"'It is now getting dark, please your majesty. We mean —out of doors in the snow. Your majesty may see, from where he is lying, the cold light of its great winding-sheet, — a famous carpet for the Shadows to dance upon, your majesty. All our brothers and sisters will be at church now, before going to their night's work.'

"'Do they always go to church before they go to work?'

"'They always go to church first.'

"'Where is it?'

"'In Iceland. Would your majesty like to see it?'

"'How can I go and see it, when, as you know very well, I am ill in bed? Besides I should be sure to take cold in a frosty night like this, even if I put on the blankets, and took the feather-bed for a muff.'

"A sort of quivering passed over their faces, which seemed to be their mode of laughing. The whole shape of the face shook and fluctuated as if it had been some dark fluid, till, by slow degrees of gathering calm, it settled into its former rest. Then one of them drew aside the curtains of the bed, and, the window-curtains not having been yet drawn, the king beheld the white glimmering night outside, struggling with the heaps of darkness that tried to quench it; and the heavens full of stars, flashing and sparkling like live jewels. The other Shadow went towards the fire and vanished in it.

"Scores of Shadows immediately began an insane dance all about the room; disappearing, one after the other, through the uncovered window, and gliding darkly away over the face of the white snow; for the window looked at once on a field of snow. In a few moments, the room was quite cleared of them; but, instead of being relieved by their absence, the king felt immediately as if he were in a dead-house, and could hardly breathe for the sense of emptiness and desolation that fell upon him. But as he lay looking out on the snow, which stretched blank and wide before him, he spied in the distance a long dark line, which drew nearer and nearer, and showed itself at last to be all the Shadows, walking in a double row, and carrying in the midst of them something like a bier. They vanished under the window, but soon reappeared, having somehow climbed up the wall of the house; for they entered in perfect order by the window, as if melting through the transparency of the glass.

"They still carried the bier or litter. It was covered with richest furs, and skins of gorgeous·wild beasts, whose eyes were replaced by sapphires and emeralds, that glittered and gleamed in the fire and snow light. The outermost skin sparkled with frost, but the inside ones were soft and warm and dry as the down under a swan's wing. The Shadows approached the bed, and set the litter upon it. Then a number of them brought a huge fur-robe, and, wrapping it round the king, laid him on the litter in the midst of the furs. Nothing could be more gentle and respectful than the way in which they moved him; and he never thought of refusing to go. Then they put something on his head, and, lifting the litter, carried him once round the room, to fall into order. As he passed the mirror, he saw that he was covered with royal ermine, and that his head wore a wonderful crown, — of gold set with none but red stones: rubies and carbuncles and garnets, and others whose names he could not tell, glowed gloriously around his head, like the salamandrine essence of all the Christmas fires over the world. A sceptre lay beside him, — a rod of ebony, surmounted by a cone-shaped diamond, which, cut in a hundred facets, flashed all the hues of the rainbow, and threw colored gleams on every side, that looked like shadows more ethereal than those that bore him. Then the Shadows rose gently to the window, passed through it, and, sinking slowly upon the field of outstretched snow, commenced an orderly gliding rather than march along the frozen surface. They took it by turns to bear the king, as they sped, with the swiftness of thought, in a straight line towards the north. The pole-star rose above their heads with visible rapidity; for indeed they moved quite as fast as sad thoughts, though not with all the speed of happy desires. England and Scotland slid past the litter of the king of the Shadows. Over rivers and lakes they skimmed and glided. They climbed the high mountains, and crossed the valleys with an unfelt bound; till they came to John-o'-Groat's house and the northern sea. The sea was not frozen; for all the stars shone as clear out of the deeps below as they shone out of the deeps above; and as the bearers slid along the blue-gray surface, with never a furrow in their track, so clear was the water beneath, that the king saw neither surface, bottom, nor substance to it, and seemed to be gliding only through the blue sphere of heaven, with the stars above him, and the stars below him, and between the stars and him nothing but an emptiness, where, for the first time in his life, his soul felt that it had room enough.

"At length they reached the rocky shores of Iceland, where they landed, still pursuing their journey. All this time the king felt no cold; for the red stones in his crown kept him warm, and the emerald and sapphire eyes of the wild beasts kept the frosts from settling upon his litter.

"Oftentimes upon their way, they had to pass through forests, caverns, and rock-shadowed paths, where it was so dark that at first the king feared he would lose his Shadows altogether. But as soon as they entered such places, the diamond in his sceptre began to shine and glow and flash, sending out streams of light of all the colors that painter's soul could dream of; in which light the Shadows grew livelier and stronger than ever, speeding through the dark ways with an all but blinding swiftness. In the light of the diamond, too, some of their forms became more simple and human, while others seemed only to break out into a yet more untamable absurdity. Once, as they passed through a cave, the king actually saw some of their eyes, — strange shadow-eyes; he had never seen any of their eyes before. But at the same moment when he saw their eyes, he knew their faces too, for they turned them full upon him for an instant; and the other Shadows, catching sight of these, shrank and shivered, and nearly vanished. Lovely faces they were; but the king was very thoughtful after he saw them, and continued rather troubled all the rest of the journey. He could not account for those faces being there, and the faces of Shadows too, with living eyes."

"What does that mean?" asked Adela.

And I am rather ashamed to say that I could only answer, "I am not sure," and make haste to go on again.

" At last they climbed up the bed of a little stream, and then passing through a narrow rocky defile, came out suddenly upon the side of a mountain, overlooking a blue frozen lake in the very heart of mighty hills. Overhead the *aurora borealis* was shivering and flashing like a battle of ten thousand spears. Underneath, its beams passed faintly over the blue ice and the sides of the snow-clad mountains, whose tops shut up like huge icicles all about, with here and there a star sparkling on the very tip of one. But as the northern lights in the sky above, so wavered and quivered, and shot hither and thither, the Shadows on the surface of the lake below; now gathering groups, and now shivering asunder; now covering the whole surface of the lake, and anon condensed into one dark knot in the centre. Every here and there on the white mountains, might be seen two or three shooting away towards the tops, and vanishing beyond them. Their number was gradually, though hardly visibly, diminishing.

" ' Please your majesty,' said the Shadows, ' this is our church, — the Church of the Shadows.'

" And so saying the king's body-guard set down the litter upon a rock, and mingled with the multitudes below. They soon returned, however, and bore the king down into the middle of the lake. All the Shadows came crowding round him, respectfully but fearlessly; and sure never such a grotesque assembly revealed itself before to mortal eyes. The king had seen all kinds of gnomes, goblins, and kobolds, at his coronation; but they were quite rectilinear figures, compared with the insane lawlessness of form in which the Shadows rejoiced; and the wildest gambols of the former were orderly dances of ceremony, beside the apparently aimless and wilful contortions of figure, and metamorphoses of shape, in which the latter indulged. They retained, however, all the time, to the surprise of the king, an identity, each of his own type, inexplicably perceptible through every change. Indeed, this preservation of the primary idea of each form was quite as wonderful as the bewildering and ridiculous alterations to which the form itself was every moment subjected.

" ' What are you ? ' said the king, leaning on his elbow, and looking around him.

" ' The Shadows, your majesty,' answered several voices at once.

" ' What Shadows ? '

" ' The human Shadows. The Shadows of men, and women, and their children.'

" ' Are you not the shadows of chairs, and tables, and poker, and tongs, just as well ? '

" At this question a strange jarring commotion went through the assembly with a shock. Several of the figures shot up as high as the aurora, but instantly settled down again to human size, as if overmastering their feelings, out of respect to him who had roused them. One who had bounded to the highest visible icy peak, and as suddenly returned, now elbowed his way through the rest, and made himself spokesman for them during the remaining part of the dialogue.

" ' Excuse our agitation, your majesty,' said he. 'I see your majesty has not yet thought proper to make himself acquainted with our nature and habits.'

" ' I wish to do so now,' replied the king.

" ' We are the Shadows,' repeated the Shadow, solemnly.

" ' Well ? ' said the king.

" ' We do not often appear to men.'

" ' Ha ! ' said the king.

" ' We do not belong to the sunshine at all. We go through it unseen, and only by a passing chill do men recognize an unknown presence.'

" ' Ha ! ' said the king, again.

" ' It is only in the twilight of the fire, or when one man or woman is alone with a single candle, or when any number of people are all feeling of the same thing at once, making them one, that we show ourselves, and the truth of things.

" ' Can that be true that loves the night ? ' said the king.

" ' The darkness is the nurse of light,' answered the Shadow.

" ' Can that be true which mocks at forms ? ' said the king.

" ' Truth rides abroad in shapeless storms,' answered the Shadow.

" ' Ha ! ha ! ' thought Ralph Rinkelmann, ' it rhymes. The Shadow caps my questions with his answers. —Very strange ! ' And he grew thoughtful again.

" The Shadow was the first to resume.

" ' Please your majesty, may we present our petition ? '

" ' By all means,' replied the king. ' I am not well enough to receive it in proper state.'

" ' Never mind, your majesty. We do not care for much ceremony; and indeed none of us are quite well as present. The subject of our petition weighs upon us.'

" ' Go on,' said the king.

" ' Sire,' began the Shadow, ' our very existence is in danger. The various sorts of artificial light, both in houses and in men, women, and children, threaten to end our being. The use and the disposition of gas-lights, especially high in the centres, blind the eyes by which alone we can be perceived. We are all but banished from towns. We are driven into villages and lonely houses, chiefly old farm-houses, out of which even our friends the fairies are fast disappearing. We therefore petition our king, by the power of his art, to restore us to our rights in the house itself, and in the hearts of its dwellers.'

" ' But,' said the king, ' you frighten the children.'

" ' Very seldom, your majesty ; and then only for their good. We seldom seek to frighten anybody. We only want to make people silent and thoughtful; to awe them a little, your majesty.'

" ' You are much more likely to make them laugh,' said the king.

" ' Are we ? ' said the Shadow.

" And, approaching the king one step, he stood quite still for a moment. The diamond of the king's sceptre shot out a vivid flame of violet light, and the king stared at the Shadow in silence, and his lips quivered."

" Now what *does* that mean ? " said Adela, again.

" How can I tell ? " I answered, and went on : —

" ' It is only,' resumed the Shadow, ' when our thoughts are not fixed upon any particular object, that our bodies are subject to all the vagaries of elemental influences. Generally, amongst worldly men and frivolous women, we only attach ourselves to some article of furniture or of dress ; and they never doubt that we are mere foolish and vague results of the dashing of

the waves of the light against the solid forms of which their
houses are full. We do not care to tell them the truth, for
they would never see it.   But let the worldly man — or the
frivolous woman — and then — '

"At each of the pauses indicated, the mass of Shadows
throbbed and heaved with emotion, but soon settled again into
comparative stillness.   Once more the Shadow addressed himself to speak. But suddenly they all looked up, and the king,
following their gaze, saw that the aurora had begun to pale.

" ' The moon is rising,' said the Shadow.   'As soon as she
looks over the mountains into the valley, we must be gone, for
we have plenty to do by the moon; we are powerful in her
light.   But if your majesty will come here to-morrow night,
your majesty may learn a great deal more about us, and judge
for himself whether it be fit to accord our petition; for then
will be our grand annual assembly, in which we report to our
chiefs the deeds we have attempted, and the good or bad success we have had.'

" ' If you send for me,' replied the king, ' I will come.'

" Ere the Shadow could reply, the tip of the moon's cres-
cent horn peeped up from behind an icy pinnacle, and one slender ray fell on the lake.   It shone upon no Shadows.   Ere
the eye of the king could again seek the earth after beholding the first brightness of the moon's resurrection, they had
vanished; and the surface of the lake glittered cold and blue
in the pale moonlight.

" There the king lay, alone in the midst of the frozen lake,
with the moon staring at him.   But at length he heard from
somewhere a voice that he knew.

" ' Will you take another cup of tea, dear? ' said Mrs. Rinkelmann ; and Ralph, coming slowly to himself, found that he
was lying in his own bed.

" ' Yes, I will," he answered; ' and rather a large piece of
toast, if you please ; for I have been a long journey since I
saw you last.'

" ' He has not come to himself quite,' said Mrs. Rinkelmann, between her and herself.

" ' You would be rather surprised,' continued Ralph, ' if I
told you where I had been, and all about it.'

" ' I dare say I should,' responded his wife.

" ' Then I will tell you,' rejoined Ralph.

" But, at that moment, a great Shadow bounced out of the fire with a single huge leap, and covered the whole room. Then it settled in one corner, and Ralph saw it shaking its fist at him from the end of a preposterous arm. So he took the hint, and held his peace. And it was as well for him. For I happen to know something about the Shadows too; and I know that if he had told his wife all about it just then, they would not have sent for him the following evening.

" But as the king, after taking his tea and toast, lay and looked about him, the dancing shadows in his room seemed to him odder and more inexplicable than ever. The whole chamber was full of mystery. So it generally was, but now it was more mysterious than ever. After all that he had seen in the Shadow-church, his own room and its shadows were yet more wonderful and unintelligible than those.

" This made it the more likely that he had seen a true vision; for, instead of making common things look commonplace, as a false vision would have done, it made common things disclose the wonderful that was in them.

" ' The same applies to all true art,' thought Ralph Rinkelmann.

" The next afternoon, as the twilight was growing dusky, the king lay wondering whether or not the Shadows would fetch him again. He wanted very much to go, for he had enjoyed the journey exceedingly, and he longed, besides, to hear some of the Shadows tell their stories. But the darkness grew deeper and deeper, and the Shadows did not come. The cause was, that Mrs. Rinkelmann sat by the fire in the gloaming; and they could not carry off the king while she was there. Some of them tried to frighten her away, by playing the oddest pranks on the walls, and floor, and ceiling; but altogether without effect; the queen only smiled, for she had a good conscience. Suddenly, however, a dreadful scream was heard from the nursery, and Mrs. Rinkelmann rushed upstairs to see what was the matter. No sooner had she gone, than the two warders of the chimney-corners stepped out into the middle of the room, and said, in a low voice: —

" ' Is your majesty ready?'

" ' Have you no hearts ? ' said the king; ' or are they as black as your faces? Did you not hear the child scream ? I must know what is the matter with her before I go.'

" ' Your majesty may keep his mind easy on that point,' replied the warders. ' We had tried everything we could think of, to get rid of her majesty the queen, but without effect. So a young madcap Shadow, half against the will of the older ones of us, slipped upstairs into the nursery; and has, no doubt, succeeded in appalling the baby, for he is very lithe and long-legged. — Now, your majesty.'

" ' I will have no such tricks played in my nursery,' said the king, rather angrily. ' You might put the child beside itself.'

" ' Then there would be twins, your majesty. And we rather like twins.'

" ' None of your miserable jesting! You might put the child out of her wits.'

" ' Impossible, sire; for she has not got into them yet.'

" ' Go away,' said the king.

" ' Forgive us, your majesty. Really, it will do the child good; for that Shadow will, all her life, be to her a symbol of what is ugly and bad. When she feels in danger of hating or envying any one, that Shadow will come back to her mind, and make her shudder.'

" ' Very well,' said the king. ' I like that. Let us go.'

" The Shadows went through the same ceremonies and preparations as before, during which the young Shadow before-mentioned contrived to make such grimaces as kept the baby in terror, and the queen in the nursery, till all was ready. Then with a bound that doubled him up against the ceiling, and a kick of his legs six feet out behind him, he vanished through the nursery door, and reached the king's bedchamber just in time to take his place with the last who were melting through the window in the rear of the litter, and settling down upon the snow beneath. Away they went, a gliding blackness over the white carpet, as before. And it was Christmas Eve.

" When they came in sight of the mountain-lake, the king saw that it was crowded over its whole surface with a changeful intermingling of Shadows. They were all talking and listening alternately, in pairs, trios, and groups of every size.

Here and there, large companies were absorbed in attention to one elevated above the rest, not in a pulpit, or on a platform, but on the stilts of his own legs, elongated for the nonce. The aurora, right overhead, lighted up the lake and the sides of the mountains, by sending down from the zenith, nearly to the surface of the lake, great folded vapors, luminous with all the colors of a faint rainbow.

"Many, however, as the words were that passed on all sides, not a whisper of a sound reached the ears of the king; their shadow speech could not enter his corporeal organs. One of his guides, however, seeing that the king wanted to hear and could not, went through a strange manipulation of his head and ears : after which he could hear perfectly, though still only the voice to which, for the time, he directed his attention. This, however, was a great advantage, and one which the king longed to carry back with him to the world of men.

"The king now discovered that this was not merely the church of the Shadows, but their news-exchange at the same time. For, as the Shadows have no writing or printing, the only way in which they can make each other acquainted with their doings and thinkings is to meet and talk at the word-mart and parliament of shades. And as, in the world, people read their favorite authors, and listen to their favorite speakers, so here the Shadows seek their favorite Shadows, listen to their adventures, and hear generally what they have to say.

"Feeling quite strong, the king rose and walked about amongst them, wrapped in his ermine robe, with his red crown on his head, and his diamond sceptre in his hand. Every group of Shadows to which he drew near ceased talking as soon as they saw him approach; but at a nod they went on again directly, conversing and relating and commenting as if no one was there of other kind or of higher rank than themselves. So the king heard a good many stories, at some of which he laughed, and at some of which he cried. But if the stories that the Shadows told were printed, they would make a book that no publisher could produce fast enough to satisfy the buyers. I will record some of the things that the king heard, for he told them to me soon after. In fact, I was for some time his private secretary, and that is how I come to know all about his adventures.

" ' I made him confess before a week was over,' said a gloomy old Shadow.

" ' But what was the good of that?' said a pert young one; ' that could not undo what was done.'

" ' Yes, it might.'

" ' What! bring the dead to life ?'

" ' No; but comfort the murderer. I could not bear to see the pitiable misery he was in. He was far happier with the rope round his neck than he was with the purse in his pocket. I saved him from killing himself too.'

" ' How did you make him confess ?'

" ' Only by wallowing on the wall a little.'

" ' How could that make him tell ?'

" ' *He* knows.'

" He was silent; and the king turned to another.

" ' I made a fashionable mother repent.'

" ' How ?' broke from several voices, in whose sound was mingled a touch of incredulity.

" ' Only by making a little coffin on the wall,' was the reply.

" ' Did the fashionable mother then confess ?'

" ' She had nothing more to confess than everybody knew.'

" ' What did everybody know then ?'

" ' That she might have been kissing a living child, when she followed a dead one to the grave. The next will fare better."

" ' I put a stop to a wedding," said another.

" ' Horrid shade!' remarked a poetic imp.

" ' How?' said others; ' tell us how.'

" ' Only by throwing a darkness, as if from the branch of a sconce, over the forehead of a fair girl. They are not married yet, and I do not think they will be. But I loved the youth who loved her. How he started! It was a revelation to him.'

" ' But did it not deceive him ?'

" ' Quite the contrary.'

" ' But it was only a shadow from the outside, not a shadow coming through from the soul of the girl.'

" ' Yes. You may say so. But it was all that was wanted to let the meaning of her forehead come out, — yes, of her whole face, which had now and then, in the pauses of his passion, perplexed the youth. All of it — curled nostrils, pouting lips, projecting chin — instantly fell into harmony with that darkness between her eyebrows. The youth understood it in a moment, and went home miserable. And they're not married *yet*.'

" 'I caught a toper alone, over his magnum of port,' said a very dark Shadow; 'and didn't I give it him! I made *delirium tremens* first; and then I settled into a funeral, passing slowly along the whole of the dining-room wall. I gave him plenty of plumes and mourning coaches. And then I gave him a funeral service; but I could not manage to make the surplice white, which was all the better for such a sinner. The wretch stared till his face passed from purple to gray, and actually left his fifth glass only, unfinished, and, took refuge with his wife and children in the drawing-room, much to their surprise. I believe he actually drank a cup of tea; and, although I have often looked in again, I have never seen him drinking, alone at least.'

" ' But does he drink less? Have you done him any good?'

" ' I hope so; but I am sorry to say I can't feel sure about it.'

" 'Humph! Humph! Humph!' grunted various Shadow throats.

" ' I had much fun once!' cried another. 'I made such game of a young clergyman!'

" ' You have no right to make game of any one.'

" ' Oh, yes, I have, — when it is for his good. He used to study his sermons, — where do you think?'

" ' In his study, of course.'

" ' Yes and no. Guess again.'

" ' Out amongst the faces in the streets.'

" ' Guess again.'

" ' In still green places in the country?'

" ' Guess again.'

" ' In old books?'

" ' Guess again.'

" ' No, no. Tell us.'

" ' In the looking-glass. Ha! ha! ha!'

" ' He was fair game; fair Shadow-game.'

" ' I thought so. And I made such fun of him one night on the wall! He had sense enough to see that it was himself, and very like an ape. So he got ashamed, turned the mirror with its face to the wall, and thought a little more about his people, and a little less about himself. I was very glad; for, please your majesty,' — and here the speaker turned towards the king, — ' we don't like the creatures that live in the mirrors. You call them ghosts, don't you ? '

" Before the king could reply, another had commenced. But the mention of the clergyman made the king wish to hear one of the Shadow-sermons. So he turned him towards a long Shadow, who was preaching to a very quiet and listening crowd. He was just concluding his sermon : —

" ' Therefore, dear Shadows, it is the more needful that we love one another as much as we can, because that is not much. We have no excuse for not loving, as mortals have, for we do not die like them. I suppose it is the thought of that death that makes them hate so much. Then again, we go to sleep all day, most of us, and not in the night, as men do. And you know that we forget everything that happened the night before ; therefore, we ought to love well, for the love is short. Ah ! dear Shadow, whom I love now with all my shadowy soul, I shall not love thee to-morrow eve ; I shall not know thee ; I shall pass thee in the crowd and never dream that the Shadow whom I now love is near me then. Happy Shades ! for we only remember our tales until we have told them here, and then they vanish in the Shadow church-yard, where we bury only our dead selves. Ah ! brethren, who would be a man and remember ? Who would be a man and weep ? We ought indeed to love one another, for we alone inherit obliv-ion ; we alone are renewed with eternal birth ; we alone have no gathered weight of years. I will tell you the awful fate of one Shadow who rebelled against his nature, and sought to remember the past. He said, " I *will* remember this eve." He fought with the genial influences of kindly sleep when the sun rose on the awful dead day of light ; and, although he could not keep quite awake, he dreamed of the foregone eve, and he never forgot his dream. Then he tried again the next night, and the next, and the next ; and he tempted another Shadow to try it with him. At last their awful fate overtook them ; and, instead of being Shadows any longer, they began to have shadows stick-ing to them ; and they thickened and thickened till they van-ished out of our world ; and they are now condemned to walk the earth, a man and a woman, with death behind them, and memories within them. Ah! brother Shades! let us love one another, for we shall soon forget. We are not men, but Shadows.'

"The king turned away, and pitied the poor Shadows far more than they pitied men.

"'Oh! how we played with a musician one night,' exclaimed one of another group, to which the king had directed a passing thought. He stopped to listen. 'Up and down we went, like the hammers and dampers on his piano. But he took his revenge on us. For after he had watched us for half an hour .n the twilight, he rose and went to his instrument, and played a Shadow-dance that fixed us all in sound forever. Each could tell the very notes meant for him; and as long as he played we could not stop, but went on dancing and dancing after the music, just as the magician — I mean the musician — pleased. And he punished us well; for he nearly danced us all off our legs and out of shape, into tired heaps of collapsed and palpitating darkness. We won't go near him for some time again, if we can only remember it. He had been very miserable all day, he was so poor; and we could not think of any way of comforting him except making him laugh. We did not succeed, with our best efforts; but it turned out better than we had expected, after all; for his Shadow-dance got him into notice, and he is quite popular now, and making money fast. If he does not take care, we shall have other work to do with him by and by, poor fellow!'

"'I and some others did the same for a poor playwright once. He had a Christmas piece to write, and, not being an original genius, he could think of nothing that had not been done already twenty times. I saw the trouble he was in, and collecting a few stray Shadows, we acted in dumb show, of course, the funniest bit of nonsense we could think of; and it was quite successful. The poor fellow watched every motion, roaring with laughter at us, and delight at the ideas we put into his head. He turned it all into words and scenes and actions; and the piece came off "with a success unprecedented in the annals of the stage;"—at least so said the reporter of the "Punny Palpitator."'

"Now don't you try, uncle, there's a dear, to make any fun; for you know you can't. It's always a failure," said Adela, looking as mischievous as she could. "You can only make people cry; you can't make them laugh. So don't try it. It hurts my feelings dreadfully when you fail; and gives me a pain in the back of my neck besides."

I heard her with delight, but went on, saying : —

"I must read what I have written, you monkey ! "

"'But how long we have to look for a chance of doing anything worth doing ! " said a long, thin, especially lugubrious Shadow. 'I have only done one deed worth telling, ever since we met last. But I am proud of that.'

"'What was it? What was it?' rose from twenty voices.

"'I crept into a dining-room, one twilight, soon after last Christmas day. I had been drawn thither by the glow of a bright fire through red window-curtains. At first I thought there was no one there, and was on the point of leaving the room, and going out again into the snowy street, when I suddenly caught the sparkle of eyes, and saw that they belonged to a little boy who lay very still on a sofa. I crept into a dark corner by the sideboard, and watched him. He seemed very sad, and did nothing but stare into the fire. At last he sighed out, ' I wish mamma would come home.' — 'Poor boy ! ' thought I; 'there is no help for that but mamma.' Yet I would try to while away the time for him. So out of my corner I stretched a long Shadow arm, reaching all across the ceiling, and pretended to make a grab at him. He was rather frightened at first; but he was a brave boy, and soon saw that it was all a joke. So when I did it again, he made a clutch at me; and then we had such fun ! For though he often sighed and wished mamma would come home, he always began again with me; and on we went with the wildest game. At last his mother's knock came to the door, and, starting up in delight, he rushed into the hall to meet her, and forgot all about poor black me. But I did not mind that in the least; for when I glided out after him into the hall, I was well repaid for my trouble, by hearing his mother say to him, ' Why, Charlie, my dear, you look ever so much better since I left you ! ' At that moment I slipped through the closing

door, and, as I ran across the snow, I heard the mother say,
'What Shadow can that be, passing so quickly?' And Charlie answered with a merry laugh, 'O mamma, I suppose it
must be the funny Shadow that has been playing such games
with me, all the time you were out.' As soon as the door was
shut, I crept along the wall, and looked in at the dining-room
window. And I heard his mamma say, as she led him into
the room, "What an imagination the boy has!" Ha! ha! ha!
Then she looked at him very earnestly for a minute, and the
tears came in her eyes; and, as she stooped down over him, I
heard the sounds of a mingling kiss and sob.'"

"Ah, I thought so!" cried Adela, who espied, peeping,
that I had this last tale on a separate slip of paper, — "I
thought so. That is yours, Mr. Armstrong, and not uncle's
at all. He stole it out of your sermon."

"You are excessively troublesome to-night, Adela," I rejoined. "But I confess the theft."

"He had quite a right to take what I had done with, Miss
Cathcart," said the curate; and once more I resumed.

"'I always look for nurseries full of children,' said
another; 'and this winter I have been very fortunate. I am
sure we belong especially to children. One evening, looking
about in a great city, I saw through the window into a large
nursery, where the odious gas had not yet been lighted.
Round the fire sat a company of the most delightful children I
had ever seen. They were waiting patiently for their tea. It
was too good an opportunity to be lost. I hurried away, and,
gathering together twenty of the best Shadows I could find,
returned in a few moments to the nursery. There we began
on the walls one of our best dances. To be sure it was mostly
extemporized; but I managed to keep it in harmony by singing this song, which I made as we went on. Of course the
children could not hear it; they only saw the motions that
answered to it. But with them they seemed to be very much
delighted indeed, as I shall presently show you. This was
the song: —

> "'Swing, swang, swingle, swuff,
> Flicker, flacker, fling, fluff!

Thus we go,
To and fro,
Here and there,
Everywhere,
Born and bred;
Never dead,
 Only gone.

On! Come on!
Looming, glooming,
Spreading, fuming,
Shattering, scattering,
Parting, darting,
Settling, starting,
All our life
Is a strife,
And a wearying for rest
On the darkness' friendly breast.

Joining, splitting,
Rising, sitting,
Laughing, shaking,
Sides all aching,
Grumbling, grim and gruff,
Swingle, swangle, swuff!

Now a knot of darkness;
Now dissolvéd gloom;
Now a pall of blackness
Hiding all the room.
Flicker, flucker, fluff!
Black and black enough!

Dancing now like demons;
Lying like the dead;
Gladly would we stop it,
And go down to bed!
But our work we still must do,
Shadow men, as well as you.

Rooting, rising, shooting,
Heaving, sinking, creeping;
Hid in corners crooning;
Splitting, poking, leaping,
Gathering, towering, swooning,
 When we're lurking,
 Yet we're working,
For our labor we must do,
Shadow men, as well as you.
 Flicker, flacker, fling, fluff!
 Swing, swang, swingle, swuff!'

" ' How thick the Shadows are ! ' said one of the children, —
a thoughtful little girl

" ' I wonder where they come from?' said a dreamy little boy.

" ' I think they grow out of the wall,' answered the little girl; ' for I have been watching them come; first one and then another, and then a whole lot of them. I am sure they grow out of the walls.'

" ' Perhaps they have papas and mammas,' said an older boy, with a smile.

" ' Yes, yes; the doctor brings them in his pocket,' said another consequential little maiden.

" ' No; I'll tell you,' said the older boy. ' They're ghosts.'

" ' But ghosts are white.'

" ' Oh, these have got black coming down the chimney.

" ' No,' said a curious-looking, white-faced boy of fourteen, who had been reading by the firelight, and had stopped to hear the little ones talk; 'they're body-ghosts; they're not soul-ghosts.'

" A silence followed, broken by the first, the dreamy-eyed boy, who said : —

" ' I hope they didn't make me;' at which they all burst out laughing, just as the nurse brought in their tea. When she proceeded to light the gas, we vanished.

" ' I stopped a murder,' cried another.

" ' How? How? How?'

" ' I will tell you. I had been lurking about a sick-room for some time, where a miser lay, apparently dying. I did not like the place at all, but I felt as if I was wanted there. There were plenty of lurking-places about, for it was full of all sorts of old furniture, — especially cabinets, chests, and presses. I believe he had in that room every bit of the property he had spent a long life in gathering. And I knew he had lots of gold in those places; for one night, when his nurse was away, he crept out of bed, mumbling and shaking, and managed to open one of his chests, though he nearly fell down with the effort. I was peeping over his shoulder, and such a gleam of gold fell upon me that it nearly killed me. But, hearing his nurse coming, he slammed the lid down, and I recovered. I tried very hard, but I could not do him any good. For, although I made all sorts of shapes on the walls and ceiling, representing evil deeds that he had done, of which there were plenty to choose from, I could make no shapes on his brain or conscience. He had no eyes for anything but gold. And it so happened that his nurse had neither eyes nor heart for anything else either.

" 'One day as she was seated beside his bed, but where he could not see her, stirring some gruel in a basin, to cool it for him, I saw her take a little phial from her bosom, and I knew by the expression of her face both what it was and what she was going to do with it. Fortunately the cork was a little hard to get out, and this gave me one moment to think.

" 'The room was so crowded with all sorts of things, that although there were no curtains on the four-post bed to hide from the miser the sight of his precious treasures, there was yet but one spot on the ceiling suitable for casting myself upon in the shape I wished to assume. And this spot was hard to reach. But I discovered that upon this very spot there was a square gleam of firelight thrown from a strange old dusty mirror that stood away in some corner, so I got in front of the fire, spied where the mirror was, threw myself upon it, and bounded from its face upon the square pool of dim light on the ceiling, assuming, as I passed, the shape of an old stooping hag, pouring something from a phial into a basin. I made the handle of the spoon with my own nose, ha! ha!'

" 'And the Shadow-hand caressed the Shadow-tip of the Shadow-nose, before the Shadow-tongue resumed.

" 'The old miser saw me. He would not taste the gruel that night, although his nurse coaxed and scolded till they were both weary. She pretended to taste it, and to think it very good; and at last retired into a corner, and made as if she were eating it herself; but I saw that she took good care to pour it all out.'

" 'But she must either succeed, or starve him, at last.'

" 'I will tell you.'

" 'But,' interposed another, 'he was not worth saving.'

" 'He might repent,' said another more benevolent Shadow.

" 'No chance of that,' returned the former. 'Misers never do. The love of money has less in it to cure itself than any other wickedness into which wretched men can fall. What a mercy it is to be born a Shadow! Wickedness does not stick to us. What do we care for gold! — Rubbish!'

"'Amen! Amen! Amen!.' came from a hundred Shadow-voices.

"'You should have let her murder him, and so have had done with him.'

"'And, besides, how was he to escape at last? He could never get´rid of her, — could he?'

"'I was going to tell you,' resumed the narrator, 'only you had so many Shadow-remarks to make, that you would not let me.'

"'Go on; go on.'

"'There was a little grandchild who used to come and see him sometimes, — the only creature the miser cared for. Her mother was his daughter; but the old man would never see her, because she had married against his will. Her husband was now dead, but he had not forgiven her yet. After the shadow he had seen, however, he said to himself, as he lay awake that night, — I saw the words on his face, — "How shall I get rid of that old devil? If I don't eat I shall die. I wish little Mary would come to-morrow. Ah! her mother would never serve me so, if I lived a hundred years more." He lay awake, thinking such things over and over again all night long, and I stood watching him from a dark corner; till the dayspring came and shook me out. When I came back next night, the room was tidy and clean. His own daughter, a sad-faced, still beautiful woman, sat by his bedside; and little Mary was curled up on the floor, by the fire, imitating us, by making queer shadows on the ceiling with her twisted hands. But she could not think how ever they got there. And no wonder, for I helped her to some very unaccountable ones.'

"'I have a story about a grand-daughter, too,' said another, the moment that speaker ceased.

"'Tell it. Tell it.'

"'Last Christmas day,' he began, 'I and a troop of us set out in the twilight, to find some house where we could all have something to do; for we had made up our minds to act together. We tried several, but found objections to them all. At last we espied a large lonely country-house, and, hastening

to it, we found great preparations making for the Christmas
dinner. We rushed into it, scampered all over it, and made
up our mind in a moment that it would do. We amused ourselves in the nursery first, where there were several children
being dressed for dinner. We generally do go to the nursery
first, your majesty. This time we were especially charmed
with a little girl about five years old, who clapped her hands
and danced about with delight at the antics we performed; and
we said we would do something for her if we had a chance.
The company began to arrive; and at every arrival we rushed
to the hall, and cut wonderful capers of welcome. Between
times, we scudded away to see how the dressing went on.
One girl about eighteen was delightful. She dressed herself
as if she did not care much about it, but could not help doing
it prettily. When she took her last look of the phantom in
the glass, she half·smiled to it. But we do not like those
creatures that come into the mirrors at all, your majesty. We
don't understand them. They are dreadful to us. She looked
rather sad and pale, but very sweet and hopeful. We wanted
to know all about her, and soon found out that she was a distant relation and a great favorite of the gentleman of the
house, an old man, with an expression of benevolence mingled
with obstinacy and a deep shade of the tyrannical. We could
not admire him much; but we would not make up our minds
all at once : Shadows never do.

"The dinner-bell rang, and down we hurried. The children all looked happy, and we were merry. There was one
cross fellow among the servants waiting, and didn't we plague
him! and didn't we get fun out of him! When he was bringing up dishes, we lay in wait for him at every corner, and
sprung upon him from the floor, and from over the banisters,
and down from the cornices. He started and stumbled and
blundered about, so that his fellow-servants thought he was
tipsy. Once he dropped a plate, and had to pick up the
pieces, and hurry away with them. Didn't we pursue him as
he went! It was lucky for him his master did not see him;
but we took care not to let him get into any· real scrape,
though his eyes were quite dazed with the dodging of the
unaccountable Shadows. Sometimes he thought the walls
were coming down upon him; sometimes that the floor was

gaping to swallow him; sometimes that he would be knocked in pieces by the hurrying to and fro, or be smothered in the black crowd.

" 'When the blazing plum-pudding was carried in, we made a perfect Shadow-carnival about it, dancing and mumming in the blue flames, like mad demons. And how the children screamed .with delight!

" 'The old gentleman, who was very fond of children, was laughing his heartiest laugh, when a loud knock came to the hall-door. The fair maiden started, turned paler, and then red as the Christmas fire. I saw it, and flung my hands across her face. She was very glad, and I know she said in her heart, " You kind Shadow! " which paid me well. Then I followed the rest into the hall, and found there a jolly, handsome, brown-faced sailor, evidently a son of the house. The old man received him with tears in his eyes, and the children with shouts of joy. The maiden escaped in the confusion, just in time to save herself from fainting. We crowded about the lamp to hide her retreat, and nearly put it out. The butler could not get it to burn up before she had glided into her place again, delighted to find the room so dark. The sailor only had seen her go, and now he sat down beside her, and, without a word got hold of her hand in the gloom. But now we all scattered to the walls and the corners; and the lamp blazed up again, and he let her hand go.

" 'During the rest of the dinner the old man watched them both, and saw that there was something between them, and was very angry; for he was an important man in his own estimation, — and they had never consulted him. The fact was, they had never known their own minds till the sailor had gone upon his last voyage; and had learned each other's only this moment. We found out all this by watching them, and then talking together about it afterwards. The old gentleman saw, too, that his favorite, who was under such obligation to him for loving her so much, loved his son better than him; and this made him so jealous, that he soon overshadowed the whole table with his morose looks and short answers. That kind of shadowing is very different from ours; and the Christmas dessert grew so gloomy that we Shadows could not bear it, and were delighted when the ladies rose to go to the drawing-room. The gentlemen would not stay behind the ladies, even for the sake of the well-known wine. So the moody host, notwithstanding his hospitality, was left alone at the table, in the great silent room. We followed the company upstairs to the drawing-room, and thence to the nursery for snap-dragon. While they were busy with this most shadowy of games, nearly all the Shadows crept downstairs again to the dining-room, where the old man still sat, gnawing the bone of his own selfishness. They crowded into the room, and by using every kind of expansion, — blowing themselves out like soap-bubbles, — they succeeded in heaping up the whole room with shade upon shade. They clustered thickest about the fire and the lamp, till at last they almost drowned them in hills of darkness.

" ' Before they had accomplished so much, the children tired with fun and frolic, were put to bed. But the little girl of five years old, with whom we had been so pleased when first we arrived, could not go to sleep. She had a little room of her own ; and I had watched her to bed, and now kept her awake by gambolling in the rays of the night-light. When her eyes were once fixed upon me, I took the shape of her grandfather, representing him on the wall, as he sat in his chair, with his head bent down, and his arms hanging listlessly by his sides. And the child remembered that that was just as she had seen him last ; for she had happened to peep in at the dining-room door, after all the rest had gone upstairs. " What if he should be sitting there still," thought she, " all alone in the dark ! " She scrambled out of bed and crept down.

" ' Meantime the others had made the room below so dark that only the face and white hair of the old man could be dimly discerned in the shadowy crowd. For he had filled his own mind with shadows, which we Shadows wanted to draw out of him. Those shadows are very different from us, your majesty knows. He was thinking of all the disappointments he had had in life, and of all the ingratitude he had met with. He thought far more of the good he had done than the good others had got. " After all I have done for them," said he, with a sigh of bitterness, " not one of them cares a straw for me. My own children will be glad when I am gone ! " At that instant he lifted up his eyes and saw, standing close by the door, a tiny

figure in a long night-gown. The door behind her was shut.
It was my little friend, who had crept in noiselessly. A pang
of icy fear shot to the old man's heart; but it melted away
as fast, for we made a lane through us for a single ray from
the fire to fall on the face of the little sprite; and he thought
it was a child of his own that had died when just the age of
her little niece, who now stood looking for her grandfather
among the Shadows. He thought she had come out of her
grave in the old darkness, to ask why her father was sitting
alone on Christmas day. And he felt he had no answer to
give his little ghost, but one would be ashamed for her to hear.
But the little girl saw him now. She walked up to him with
a childish stateliness, — stumbling once or twice on what seemed
her long shroud. Pushing through the crowded Shadows, she
reached him, climbed upon his knee, laid her little long-haired
head on his shoulders, and said: "Ganpa! you goomy? Isn't
it your Kismass day, too, ganpa?"

"'A new fount of love seemed to burst from the clay of
the old man's heart. He clasped the child to his bosom, and
wept. Then, without a word, he rose with her in his arms,
carried her up to her room, and, laying her down in her bed,
covered her up, kissed her sweet little mouth unconscious of
reproof, and then went to the drawing-room.

"'As soon as he entered, he saw the culprits in a quiet
corner alone. He went up to them, took a hand of each, and,
joining them in both his, said, "God bless you!" Then he
turned to the rest of the company, and "Now," said he,
"let's have a Christmas carol." And well he might; for
though I have paid many visits to the house, I have never
seen him cross since; and I am sure that must cost him a good
deal of trouble.'

"'We have just come from a great palace, said another,
'where we knew there were many children, and where we
thought to hear glad voices, and see royally merry looks. But as
soon as we entered, we became aware that one mighty Shadow
shrouded the whole; and that Shadow deepened and deepened,
till it gathered in darkness about the reposing form of a wise
prince. When we saw him, we could move no more, but clung
heavily to the walls, and by our stillness added to the sorrow
of the hour. And when we saw the mother of her people weeping

with bowed head for the loss of him in whom she had trusted, we were seized with such a longing to be Shadows no longer, but winged angels, which are the white shadows cast in heaven from the Light of Light, so to gather around her, and hover over her with comforting, that we vanished from the walls and found ourselves floating high above the towers of the palace, where we met the angels on their way; and knew that our service was not needed.'

" By this time there was a glimmer of approaching moon-light, and the king began to see several of those stranger Shadows, with human faces and eyes, moving about amongst the crowd. He knew at once that they did not belong to his dominion. They looked at him, and came near him, and passed slowly, but they never made any obeisance, or gave sign of homage. And what their eyes said to him, the king only could tell. And he did not tell.

" ' What are those other Shadows that move through the crowd?' said he to one of his subjects near him.

" The Shadow started, looked round, shivered slightly, and laid his finger on his lips. Then leading the king a little aside, and looking carefully about him once more: —

" ' I do not know,' said he, in a low tone, ' what they are. I have heard of them often, but only once did I ever see any of them before. That was when some of us one night paid a visit to a man who sat much alone, and was said to think a great deal. We saw two of those sitting in the room with him, and he was as pale as they were. We could not cross the threshold, but shivered and shook, and felt ready to melt away. Is not your majesty afraid of them too?'

" But the king made no answer; and before he could speak again the moon had climbed above the mighty pillars of the Church of the Shadows, and looked in at the great window of the sky.

" The shapes had all vanished; and the king, again lifting up his eyes, saw but the wall of his own chamber, on which flickered the Shadow of a Little Child He looked down, and there, sitting on a stool by the fire, he saw one of his own little ones, waiting to say good-night to his father, and go to bed early, that he might rise as early, and be very good and happy all Christmas day.

" And Ralph Rinkelmann rejoiced that he was a man, and not a Shadow."

When I had finished my story, the not unusual silence followed. It was soon broken by Adela.

" But what were those other shadows, mysteries in the midst of mystery?" persisted she.

" My dear, as the child said shadows were the ghosts of the body, so I say these were the shadows of the mind. Will that do?"

" I must think. I don't know. I can't trust you. I *do* believe, uncle, you write whatever comes into your head; and then when any one asks you the meaning of this or that, you hunt round till you find a meaning just about the same size as the thing itself, and stick it on. Don't you, now?"

" Perhaps *yes*, and perhaps *no*, and perhaps both," I answered.

" You have the most confounded imagination I ever knew, Smith, my boy!" said the colonel. " You run right away, and leave me to come hobbling after as I best can."

" Oh, never mind; I always return to my wife and children," I answered; and, being an old bachelor, this passed for a good joke with the kind-hearted company. No more remarks were made upon my Shadow story, though I was glad to see the curate pondering over it. Before we parted, the usual question of who was to read the next had to be settled.

" I propose, for a change," said the curate, " that the club meet at my house the next time, and that the story be omitted for once. We'll have some music, and singing, and poetry, and all that sort of thing. What do you say, Lizzie?"

" With all my heart," answered Mrs. Armstrong.

" You forget," said the colonel, " that Adela is not well enough to go out yet."

Adela looked as if she thought that was a mistake, and glanced towards the doctor. I think Percy caught sight of the glance as it passed him.

" If I may be allowed to give a professional opinion," said Harry, " I think she could go without the smallest danger, if she were well wrapped up."

"You can have the carriage, of course, my love," said her father, "if you would like to go."

"I should very much like to go," said Adela.

And so it was settled to the evident contentment of all except the mother and son, who, I suppose, felt that Adela was slipping through their fingers, in this strengthening of adverse influences. I was sure myself that nothing could be better for her, in either view of the case. Harry did not stay behind to ask her any questions this evening, but left with the rest.

The next day, the bright, frosty weather still continuing, I took Adela out for a walk.

"You are much better, I think, my dear," I said.

"Very much," she answered. "I think Mr. Armstrong's prescription is doing me a great deal of good. It seems like magic. I sleep very well indeed now. And somehow life seems a much more possible thing than it looked a week or two ago. And the whole world appears more like the work of God."

"I am very glad, my dear. If all your new curate tries to teach us be true, the world need not look very dreary to any of us."

"But do you believe it all, uncle?"

"Yes, I do, my dear. I believe that the grand, noble way of thinking of God and his will must be the true way, though it never can be grand or noble enough; and that belief in beauty and truth, notwithstanding so many things that are neither beautiful nor true, is essential to a right understanding of the world. Whatever is not good and beautiful is doomed by the very death that is in it; and when we find such things in ourselves or in other people, we may take comfort that these must be destroyed one day, even if it be by that form of divine love which appears as a consuming fire."

"But that is very dreadful too, is it not, uncle?"

"Yes, my dear. But there is a refuge from it; and then the fear proves a friend."

"What refuge?"

"God himself. If you go close up to him, his spirit will become your spirit, and you will need no fire then. You will find that that which is fire to them that are afar off is a mighty graciousness to them that are nigh. They are both the same thing."

Adela made me no answer. Perhaps I tried to give her more than she was ready to receive. Perhaps she needed more leading, before she would be able to walk in that road. If so, then Providence was leading her; and I need not seek to hasten a divine process.

But at least she enjoyed her walk that bright winter day, and came home without being wearied, or the cold getting any victory over her.

As we passed some cottages on our way home, Adela said : —

"There is a poor woman lives in one of these cottages, who used to be a servant of ours. She is in bad health, and I dare say is not very well off in this frost, for her husband is only a laborer. I should like to go and see her."

"With all my heart, my dear," I answered.

"This is the house," said Adela; and she lifted the latch and went in gently, I following.

No one had heard our entrance, and when Adela knocked at the inner door there was no reply. Whereupon she opened the door, and then we saw the woman seated on one side of the fire, and the man on the other side with his pipe in his mouth ; while between them sat the curate with his hands in his pockets, and his pipe likewise in his mouth. But they were blowing but a small cloud between them, and were evidently very deep in an earnest conversation.

I overheard a part of what the cottager was saying, and could not help listening to the rest.

"And the man was telling them, sir, that God had picked out so many men, women, and children, to go right away to glory, and left the rest to be damned forever and ever in hell. And I up and spoke to him; and ' Sir,' says I, ' if I was tould as how I was to pick out so many out o' my childeren, and take 'em with me to a fine house, and leave the rest to be burnt up i' the old one, which o' them would I choose ? ' — ' How can I tell ? ' says he. ' No doubt,' says I; ' they aint your sons and darters. But I can. I wouldn't move a foot, sir; but I'd take my chance wi' the poor things. And, sir,' says I, ' we're all God's childeren ; and which o' us is he to choose, and which is he to leave out ? I don't believe he'd know a bit better how to choose one and leave another than I should, sir, — that is, his heart wouldn't let him lose e'er a one o' us, or he'd be miserable forever, as I should be, if I left one o' mine i' the fire.' ''

Here Adela had the good sense to close the door again, yet more softly than she had opened it; and we retired.

"That's the right sort of man," said I, "to get a hold of the poor. He understands them, being himself as poor in spirit as they are in pocket, — or, indeed, I might have said, as he is in pocket himself. But depend upon it he comes out both ways poorer than he went in."

"It should not be required of a curate to give money," said Adela.

"Do you grudge him the blessedness of giving, Adela?"

"Oh, no. I only think it is too hard on him."

"It is as necessary for a poor man to give away, as for a rich man. Many poor men are more devoted worshippers of Mammon than some rich men."

And then I took her home.

CHAPTER XI.

THE EVENING AT THE CURATE'S.

As I led Adela, well wrapped in furs, down the steps to put her into the carriage, I felt by the wind, and saw by the sky, that a snow-storm was at hand. This set my heart beating with delight, for after all I am only what my friends call me, — an old boy; and so I am still very fond of snow and wind. Of course this pleasure is often modified by the recollection that it is to most people no pleasure, and to some a source of great suffering. But then I recover myself by thinking that I did not send for the snow, and that my enjoyment of it will neither increase their pains nor lessen my sympathies. And so I enjoy it again with all my heart It is partly the sense of being lapt in a mysterious fluctuating depth of exquisite shapes of evanescent matter, falling like a cataract from an unknown airy gulf, where they grow into being and form out of the in-

visible — well-named by the prophet Job; for a prophet he
was in the truest sense, all-seated in his ashes and armed with
his potsherd — the womb of the snow; partly the sense of
motion and the goings of the wind through the ethereal mass;
partly the delight that always comes from contest with nature,
— a contest in which no vile passions are aroused, and no weak
enemy goes helpless to the ground. I presume that in a right
condition of our nervous nature, instead of our being as some
would tell us, less exposed to the influences of nature, we should
in fact be altogether open to them. Our nerves would be a
thoroughfare for nature in all and each of her moods and
feelings, stormy or peaceful, sunshiny or sad. The true refuge from the slavery to which this would expose us, the subjection of man to circumstance, is to be found, not in the dead-
ening of the nervous constitution, or in a struggle with the influences themselves, but in the strengthening of the moral and
refining of the spiritual nature; so that, as the storms rave
through the vault of heaven without breaking its strong arches
with their winds, or staining its ethereal blue with their rain-
clouds, the soul of man should keep clear and steady and great,
holding within it its own feelings and even passions, knowing
that, let them moan or rave as they will, they cannot touch the
nearest verge of the empyrean dome, in whose region they have
their birth and being.

For me, I felt myself now, just an expectant human snow-
storm; and as I sat on the box by the coachman I rejoiced to
greet the first flake, which alighted on the tip of my nose even before we had cleared our own grounds. Before we had got *up
street*, the wind had risen, and the snow thickened, till the
horses seemed inclined to turn their tails to the hill and the
storm together, for the storm came down the hill in their faces.
It was soon impossible to see one's hand before one's eyes; and
the carriage lamps served only to reveal a chaotic fury of snow-
flakes, crossing each other's path at all angles, in the eddies of
the wind amongst the houses. The coachman had to keep en-
couraging his horses to get them to face it at all. The
ground was very slippery; and so fast fell the snow that it
had actually begun to ball in the horses' feet before we reached
our destination. When we were all safe in Mrs. Armstrong's
drawing-room, we sat for a while listening to the wind roar-

ing in the chimney, before any of us spoke. And then I did not join in the conversation, but pleased myself with looking at the room ; for, next to human faces, I delight in human abodes, which will always, more or less, according to the amount of choice vouchsafed in the occupancy, be like the creatures who dwell in them. Even the soldier-crab must have some likeness to the snail of whose house he takes possession, else he could not live in it at all.

The first thing to be done by one who would read a room is, to clear it as soon as possible of the air of the marvellous, the air of the story-book which pervades every place at the first sight of it. But I am not now going to write a treatise upon this art, for which I have not time to invent a name ; but only to give as much of a description of this room as will enable my readers to feel quite at home with us in it during our evening there. It was a large, low room, with two beams across the ceiling at unequal distances. There was only a drugget on the floor, and the window-curtains were scanty. But there was a glorious fire on the hearth, and the tea-board was filled with splendid china, as old as the potteries. The chairs, I believe, had been brought from old Mr. Armstrong's lumber-room, and so they all looked as if they could tell stories themselves. At all events they were just the proper chairs to tell stories in, and I could not help regretting that we were not to have any to-night. The rest of the company had arrived before us. A warm corner in an old-fashioned sofa had been prepared for Adela, and as soon as she was settled in it our hostess proceeded to pour out the tea with a simplicity and grace which showed that she had been just as much a lady when carrying parcels for the dress-maker, and would have been a lady if she had been a house-maid. Such women are rare in every circle, the best of every kind being rare. It is very disappointing to the imaginative youth when, coming up to London and going into society, he finds so few of men and women he meets come within the charmed circle of his ideal refinement.

I said to myself: "I am sure she could write a story if she would. I must have a try for one from her."

When tea was over, she looked at her husband, and then went to the piano, and sang the following ballad : —

" ' Traveller, what lies over the hill?
    Traveller, tell to me;
I am only a child — from the window-sill
    Over I cannot see.'

" ' Child, there's a valley over there,
    Pretty and woody and shy:
And a little brook that says — " Take care,
    Or I'll drown you by and by." '

" ' And what comes next?' — ' A little town;
    And a towering hill again;
More hills and valleys, up and down,
    And a river now and then.

" ' And what comes next?' — 'A lonely moor,
    Without a beaten way;
And gray clouds sailing slow, before
    A wind that will not stay.'

" ' And then?'—' Dark rocks and yellow sand,
    And a moaning sea beside.'
' And then?' — ' More sea, more sea, more land,
    And rivers deep and wide.'

" ' And then?' — ' Oh! rock and mountain and vale,
    Rivers and fields and men:
Over and over — a weary tale —
    And round to your home again.'

" ' Is that the end?   It is weary at best.'
    ' No, child; it is not the end.
On summer eves, away in the west,
    You will see a stair ascend;

" ' Built of all colors of lovely stones, —
    A stair up into the sky;
Where no one is weary, and no one moans,
    Or wants to be laid by.'

" ' I will go.' — ' But the steps are very steep;
    If you would climb up there,
You must lie at its foot, as still as sleep,
    And be a step of the stair,

" ' For others to put their feet on you,
    To reach the stones high-piled;
Till Jesus comes and takes you too,
    And leads you up, my child!' "

" That is one of your parables, I am sure, Ralph," said the
doctor, who was sitting, quite at his ease, on a footstool, with

his back against the wall, by the side of the fire opposite to
Adela, casting every now and then a glance across the fiery
gulf, just as he had done in church when I first saw him. And
Percy was there to watch them, though, from some high words
I overheard, I had judged that it was with difficulty his mother
had prevailed on him to come. I could not help thinking myself that two pairs of eyes met and parted rather oftener than
any other two pairs in the room; but I could find nothing to
object.

"Now, Miss Cathcart, it is your turn to sing."

"Would you mind singing another of Heine's songs?" said
the doctor, as he offered his hand to lead her to the piano.

"No," she answered. "I will not sing one of that sort.
It was not liked last time. Perhaps what I do sing won't be
much better though.

> "The waters are rising and flowing
> Over the weedy stone, —
> Over and over it going:
> It is never gone.
>
> "So joy on joy may go sweeping
> Over the head of pain, —
> Over and over it leaping:
> It will rise again."

"Very lovely, but not much better than what I asked for.
In revenge, I will give you one of Heine's that my brother
translated. It always reminds me, with a great difference, of
one in 'In Memoriam,' beginning: *Dark house.*"

So spake Harry, and sang: —

> "The shapes of the days forgotten
> Out of their graves arise,
> And show me what once my life was,
> In the presence of thine eyes.
>
> "All day through the streets I wandered,
> As in dreams men go and come;
> The people in wonder looked at me,
> I was so mournful dumb.
>
> "It was better though, at night-fall,
> When through the empty town
> I and my shadow together
> Went silent up and down.

"With echoing footstep,
  Over the bridge I walk;
The moon breaks out of the waters,
  And looks as if she would talk.

"I stood still before thy dwelling,
  Like a tree that prays for rain;
I stood gazing up at thy window, —
  My heart was in such pain.

"And thou lookedst through thy curtains, —
  I saw thy shining hand;
And thou sawest me, in the moonlight,
  Still as a statue stand."

"Excuse me," said Mrs. Cathcart, with a smile, "but I don't think such sentimental songs good for anybody. They can't be *healthy*, — I believe that is the word they use nowadays."

"I don't say they are," returned the doctor; "but many a pain is relieved by finding its expression. I wish he had never written worse."

"That is not why I like them," said the curate. "They seem to me to hold the same place in literature that our dreams do in life. If so much of our life is actually spent in dreaming, there must be some place in our literature for what corresponds to dreaming. Even in this region, we cannot step beyond the boundaries of our nature. I delight in reading Lord Bacon now; but one of Jean Paul's dreams will often give me more delight than one of Bacon's best paragraphs. It depends upon the mood. Some dreams like these, in poetry or in sleep, arouse individual states of consciousness altogether different from any of our waking moods, and not to be recalled by any mere effort of the will. All our being, for the moment, has a new and strange coloring. We have another kind of life. I think myself, our life would be much poorer without our dreams; a thousand rainbow tints and combinations would be gone; music and poetry would lose many an indescribable exquisiteness and tenderness. You see I like to take our dreams seriously, as I would even our fun. For I believe that those new, mysterious feelings that come to us in sleep, if they be only from dreams of a richer grass and a softer wind than we have known awake, are indications of wells of feeling and delight which have not yet broken out of their hiding-places in our souls, and are only to be suspected from these rings of fairy green that spring up in the high places of our sleep."

"I say, Ralph," interrupted Harry, "just that strangest of Heine's ballads, that — "

"Oh, no, no! not that one. Mrs. Cathcart would not like it at all."

"Yes, please do," said Adela.

"Pray don't think of me, gentlemen," said the aunt.

"No, I won't," said the curate.

"Then I will," said the doctor, with a glance at Adela, which seemed to say, "If you want it, you shall have it, whether they like it or not."

He repeated, with just a touch of the recitative in his tone, the following verses : —

> "Night lay upon mine eyelids :
>   Upon my mouth lay lead ;
> With withered heart and sinews,
>   I lay among the dead.

> "How long I lay and slumbered,
>   I knew not in the gloom,
> I wakened up, and listened
>   To a knocking at my tomb.

> "'Wilt thou not rise, my Henry?
>   Immortal day draws on ;
> The dead are all arisen ;
>   The endless joy begun.'

> "'My love, I cannot raise me ;
>   Nor could I find the door ;
> My eyes with bitter weeping
>   Are blind for evermore.'

> "'But from thine eyes, dear Henry,
>   I'll kiss away the night ;
> Thou shalt behold the angels,
>   And heaven's own blessed light.

> "'My love, I cannot raise me ;
>   The blood is flowing still,
> Where thou, heart-deep, didst stab me,
>   With a dagger speech to kill.'

> "'Oh! I will lay my hand, Henry,
>   So soft upon thy heart ;
> And that will stop the bleeding,
>   Stop all the bitter smart.'

" ' My love, I cannot raise me;
   My head is bleeding too.
When thou wast stolen from me,
   I shot it through and through.'

" ' With my thick hair, my Henry,
   I will stop the fountain red;
Press back again the blood-stream,
   And heal thy wounded head.'

" She begged so soft, so dearly,
   I could no more say *no ;*
Writhing, I strove to raise me,
   And to the maiden go.

" Then the wounds again burst open;
   And afresh the torrents break
From head and heart — life's torrents
   And lo! I am awake."

"There now, that is enough ! " said the curate.

" That is not nice, — is it, Mrs. Cathcart? "

Mrs. Cathcart smiled, and said : —

" I should hardly have thought your time well-spent in translating it, Mr. Armstrong."

" It took me a few idle minutes only," said the curate. " But my foolish brother, who has a child's fancy for horrid things, took a fancy to that; and so he won't let my sins be forgotten. But I will take away the taste of it with another of Heine's, seeing we have fallen upon him. I should never have dreamed of introducing him here. It was Miss Cathcart's first song that opened the vein, I believe."

" I am the guilty person," said Adela; "and I fear I am not sorry for my sins, — the consequences have been too pleasant. Do go on, Mr. Armstrong."

He repeated : —

" PEACE.

" High in the heavens the sun was glowing;
   Around him the white clouds, like waves were flowing;
The sea was very still and gray.
Dreamily thinking as I lay,
Close by the gliding vessel's wheel,
A sleepless slumber did o'er me steal;
And I saw the Christ, the healer of woe,
In white and waving garments go;
Walking in giant form went he
Over the land and sea.

High in the heaven he towered his head,
And his hands in blessing forth he spread
Over the land and sea.
And for a heart, oh, wonder meet!
In his breast the sun did throb and beat;
In his breast, for a heart to the only One,
Shone the red, the flaming sun.
The flaming red sun-heart of the Lord
Forth its gracious life-beams poured;
Its fair and love-benignant light
Softly shone, with warming might,
Over the land and sea.

" Sounds of solemn bells that go
Through the still air to and fro,
Draw, like swans, in a rosy band,
The gliding ship to the grassy land,
Where a mighty city, towered and high,
Breaks and jags the line of the sky.

" Oh, wonder of peace, how still was the town!
The hollow tumult had all gone down
Of the bustling and babbling trades.
Men and women, and youths and maids,
White clothes wearing,
Palm branches bearing,
Walked through the clean and echoing streets,
And when one with another meets,
They look at each other with eyes that tell
That they understand each other well;
And, trembling with love and sweet restraint,
Each kisses the other upon the brow,
And looks above, like a hoping saint,
To the holy, healing sun-heart's glow;
Which atoning all, its red blood streams
Downward in still outwelling beams;
Till, threefold blessed, they call aloud,
The single hearts of a happy crowd,
    Praised be Jesus Christ!"

"You will like that better," concluded the curate, again
addressing Mrs. Cathcart.

"Fanciful," she answered. "I don't like fancies about
sacred things."

"I fear, however," replied he, "that most of our serious
thoughts about sacred things are a little better than fancies."

"Sing that other of his about the flowers, and I promise
you never to mention his name in this company again," said
Harry.

"Very well, I will, on that condition," answered Ralph.

"In the sunny summer morning,
   Into the garden I come;
The flowers are whispering and speaking,
   But I, I wander dumb.

"The flowers are whispering and speaking,
   And they gaze at my visage wan:
'You must not be cross with our sister,
   You melancholy man!'"

"Is that all?" said Adela.

"Yes, that's all," answered the singer.

"But we cannot let you off with that only," she said.

"What an awful night it is!" interrupted the colonel, rising and going to the window to peep out. "Between me and the lamp, the air looks solid with driving snow."

"Sing one of your winter songs, Ralph," said the curate's wife. "This is surely stormy enough for one of your Scotch winters that you are so proud of."

Thus adjured, Mr. Armstrong sang:—

"A morning clear, with frosty light
   From sunbeams late and low;
They shine upon the snow so white,
   And shine back from the snow.

"From icy spears a drop will run,—
   Not fall: at afternoon,
It shines a diamond for the sun,
   An opal for the moon.

"And when the bright, sad sun is low
   Behind the mountain-dome,
A twilight wind will come, and blow
   All round the children's home;

"And waft about the powdery snow,
   As night's dim footsteps pass;
But waiting, in its grave below,
   Green lies the summer-grass."

"Now it seems to me," said the colonel, "though I am no authority in such matters, that it is just in such weather as this that we don't need songs of that sort. They are not very exhilarating."

"There is truth in that," replied Mr. Armstrong. "I think

it is in winter chiefly that we want songs of summer, as the Jews sang, — if not the songs of Zion, yet of Zion, in a strange land. Indeed, most of our songs are of this sort."

" Then sing one of your own summer songs."

" No, my dear ; I would rather not. I don't altogether like them. Besides, if Harry could sing that *Tryst* of Schiller's, it would bring back the feeling of the summer better than any brooding over the remembrances of it could do."

" Did you translate that too ? " I asked.

" Yes. As I told you, at one time of my life translating was a constant recreation to me. I have had many half-successes, some of which you have heard. I think this one better."

" What is the name of it ? "

" It is ' Die Erwartung,' — *The Waiting*, literally, or *Expectation*. But the Scotch word *Tryst* (Rendezvous) is a better name for a poem, though English. It is often curious how a literal rendering, even when it gives quite the meaning, will not do, because of the different ranks of the two words in their respective languages."

" I have heard you say," said Harry, " that the principles of the translation of lyrics have yet to be explored."

" Yes. But what I have just said applies nearly as much to prose as to the verse. — Sing, Harry. You know it well enough."

" Part is in recitative."

" So it is. Go on."

" To enter into the poem, you must suppose a lover waiting in an arbor for his lady-love. First come two recited lines of expectation ; then two more, in quite a different measure, of disappointment ; and then a long-lined song of meditation ; until expectation is again aroused, to be again disappointed, and so through the poem.

"THE TRYST.

"That was the wicket a-shaking!
That was its clang as it fell!
No, 'twas but the night-wind waking,
And the poplars' answering swell.

" Put on thy beauty, foliage-vaulted roof,
  To greet her entrance, radiant all with grace;
Ye branches, weave a holy tent, star-proof;
  With lovely darkness, silent, her embrace;
Sweet, wandering airs, creep through the leafy woof,
  And toy and gambol round her rosy face,
When with its load of beauty, lightly borne,
Glides in the fairy foot, and brings my morn.

    " Hush! I hear timid, yet daring
      Steps that are almost a race!
        No, a bird — some terror scaring —
        Started from its roosting-place.

" Quench thy sunk torch, Hyperion! Night, appear!
  Dim, ghostly Night, lone loveliness entrancing!
Spread, purple blossoms, round us, in a sphere;
  Twine, lattice-boughs, the mystery enhancing;
Love's joy would die, if more than two were here, —
  She shuns the daybeam indiscreetly glancing.
Eve's star alone — no envious tell-tale she —
Gazes unblamed, from far across the sea.

    " Hark! distant voices, that lightly
      Ripple the silence deep!
        No; the swans that, circling nightly,
        Through the silver waters sweep.

" Around me wavers an harmonious flow;
  The fountain's fall swells in delicious rushes;
The flower beneath the west wind's kiss bends low;
  A trembling joy from each to all outgushes.
Grape-clusters beckon; peaches luring glow,
  Behind dark leaves hiding their crimson blushes;
The winds, cooled with the sighs of flowers asleep,
Light waves of odor o'er my forehead sweep.

    " Hear I not echoing footfalls,
      Hither along the pleached walk?
        No; the over-ripened fruit falls,
        Heavy-swollen, from off its stalk.

" Dull is the eye of day that flamed so bright;
  In gentle death, its colors all are dim;
Unfolding fearless in the fair half light,
  The flower-cups ope, that all day closed their brim
Calm lifts the moon her clear face on the night;
  Dissolved in masses faint, Earth's features swim;
Each grace withdraws the soft relaxing zone, —
Beauty unrobed shines full on me alone.

    " See I not, there, a white shimmer? —
      Something with pale silken shine?
        No; it is the column's glimmer,
        'Gainst the gloomy hedge of pine.

"O longing heart! no more thyself delight
With shadow-forms, — a sweet, deceiving pleasure;
Filling thy arms but as the vault of night
Infoldeth darkness without hope or measure.
Oh, lead the living beauty to my sight,
That living love her loveliness may treasure!
Let but her shadow fall across my eyes,
And straight my dreams exulting truths will rise!

And soft as, when, purple and golden,
The clouds of the evening descend,
So had she drawn nigh unbeholden,
And wakened with kisses her friend."

Never had song a stranger accompaniment than this song; for the air was full of fierce noises near and afar. Again the colonel went to the window. When he drew back the curtains, at Adela's request, and pulled up the blind, you might have fancied the dark wind full of snowy Banshees, fleeting and flickering by, and uttering strange, ghostly cries of warning. The friends crowded into the bay-window, and stared out into the night with a kind of happy awe. They pressed their brows against the panes, in the vain hope of seeing where there was no light. Every now and then the wind would rush up against the window in fierce attack, as if the creatures that rode by upon the blast had seen the row of white faces, and it angered them to be thus stared at, and they rode their airy steeds full tilt against the thin rampart of glass that protected the human weaklings from becoming the spoil of their terrors.

While every one was silent with the intensity of this outlook, and with the awe of such an uproar of wild things without souls, there came a loud knock at the door, which was close to the window where they stood. Even the old colonel, whose nerves were as hard as piano-wires, started back and cried "God bless me!" The doctor, too, started, and began mechanically to button his coat, but said nothing. Adela gave a little, suppressed scream, and, ashamed of the weakness, crept away to her sofa-corner.

The servant entered, saying that Dr. Armstrong's man wanted to see him. Harry went into the passage, which was just outside the drawing-room, and the company overheard the following conversation, every word : —

"Well, William?"

"There's a man come after you from Cropstone Farm, sir. IIis missus is took sudden."

"What? — It's not the old lady then? It's the young mistress?"

"Yes; she's in labor, sir; leastways she *was*, — he's been three hours on the road. I reckon it's all over by this time. You won't go, sir! It's morally unpossible."

"Won't go! It's morally impossible not. You knew I would go. That's the mare outside."

"No, sir. It's Tilter."

"Then you *did* think I wouldn't go! You knew well enough Tilter's no use for a job like this. The mare's my only chance."

"I beg your pardon, sir. I did *not* think you would go."

"Home with you, as hard as Tilter can drive — confound him! — And bring the mare instantly. She's had her supper?"

"I left her munching, sir."

"Don't let her drink. I'll give her a quart of ale at Job Timpson's."

"You won't go that way, surely, sir?"

"It's the nearest; and the snow can't be very deep yet."

"I've brought your boots and breeches, sir."

"All right."

The man hurried out, and Harry was heard to run upstairs to his brother's room. The friends stared at each other in some perturbation. Presently Harry re-entered, in the articles last mentioned, saying: —

"Ralph, have you an old shooting-coat you could lend me?"

"I should think so, Harry. I'll fetch you one."

Now at length the looks of the circle found some expression in the words of the colonel: —

"Mr. Armstrong, I am an old soldier, and I trust I know what duty is. The only question is, *Can* this be done?"

"Colonel, no man can tell what can or cannot be done till he tries. I think it can."

The colonel held out his hand — his sole reply.

The school-master and his wife ventured to expostulate. To them IIarry made fun of the danger. Adela had come from the corner to which she had retreated and joined the group. She laid her hand on Harry's arm, and he saw that she was pale as death.

"Don't go," she said.

As if to enforce her words, the street-door, which I suppose William had not shut properly, burst open with a bang against the wall, and the wind went shrieking through the house, as if in triumph at having forced an entrance.

"The woman is in labor," said Harry, in reply to Adela, forgetting, in the stern reality both for the poor woman and himself, that girls of Adela's age and social position are not accustomed to hear such facts so plainly expressed from a man's lips. Adela, however, simply accepted the fact, and replied : —

"But you will be too late anyhow."

"Perhaps just in time," he answered, as his brother entered with a coat over his arm.

"Ralph," he went on, with a laugh, "they are trying to persuade me not to go."

"It's a tempting of Providence," said Mrs. Bloomfield.

"Harry, my boy," said the curate, solemnly, "I would rather have you brought home dead to-morrow than see you sitting by that fire five minutes after your mare comes. But you'll put on a great-coat?"

"No, thank you. I shall do much better without one. How comical I shall look in Farmer Prisphig's Sunday clothes! I'm not going to be lost this storm, Mrs. Bloomfield; for I second-see myself at this moment, sitting by the farmer's kitchen fire, in certain habiliments a world too wide for my unshrunk shanks, but doing my best to be worthy of them by the attention I am paying to my supper."

Here he stooped to Lizzie and whispered in her ear : —

"Don't let them make a fuss about my going. There is really no particular danger. And I don't want my patient there frightened and thrown back, you know."

Mrs. Armstrong nodded a promise. In a moment more, Harry had changed his coat; for the storm had swept away ceremony at least. Lizzie ran and brought him a glass of wine; but he begged for a glass of milk instead, and was soon supplied; after which he buttoned up his coat, tightened the straps of his spurs, which had been brought slack on his boots, put on one of a thick pair of gloves which he found in his brother's coat, bade them all good-night, drew on the other glove, and stood prepared to go.

Did he or did he not see Adela's eyes gazing out of her pale face with an expression of admiring apprehension, as she stood bending forward, and looking up at the strong man about to fight the storm. and all ready to meet it? I don't know. I only put it to his conscience.

In a moment more, the knock came again, — the only sign, for no one could hear the mare's hoofs in the wind and snow. With one glance and one good-night he hurried out. The wind once more, for a brief moment, held an infernal carnival in the house. They crowded to the window, — saw a dim form heave up on horseback, and presently vanish. All space lay beyond; but, for them, he was swallowed up by the jaws of the darkness. They knew no more. A flash of pride in his brother shot from Ralph's eyes, as, with restrained excitement, for which he sought some outlet, he walked towards the piano. His wife looked at Ralph with the same light of pride, tempered by thankfulness; for she knew, if he had been sent for, he would have gone all the same as Harry; but then he was not such a horseman as his brother. The fact was, he had neither seat nor hands, though no end of pluck.

"He will have to turn back," said the colonel. "He can't reach Cropstone Farm to-night. It lies right across the moor. It is impossible."

"Impossible things are always being done," said the curate, "else the world would have been all moor by this time."

"The wind is dead against him," said the school-master.

"Better in front than in flank," said the colonel. "It won't blow him out of the saddle."

Adela had crept back to her corner, where she sat shading her eyes, and listening. I saw that her face was very pale. Lizzie joined her, and began talking to her.

I had not much fear for Harry, for I could not believe that his hour was come yet. I had great confidence in him and his mare. And I believed in the God that made Harry, and the mare, and the storm too, through which he had sent them to the aid of one who was doing her part to keep his world going.

But now Mr. Armstrong had found a vent for his excitement in another of his winter songs, which might be very well for his mood, though it was not altogether suited to that of some of the rest of us. He sang : —

> " Oh, wildly wild the winter-blast
> Is whirling round the snow ;
> The wintry storms are up at last,
> And care not how they go.
>
> " In wreaths and mists, the frozen white
> Is torn into the air ;
> It pictures, in the dreary light,
> An ocean in despair.
>
> " Come, darkness ! rouse the fancy more ;
> Storm ! wake the silent sea ;
> Till, roaring in the tempest-roar,
> It rave to ecstasy ;
>
> " And death-like figures, long and white,
> Sweep through the driving spray ;
> And, fading in the ghastly night,
> Cry faintly far away."

I saw Adela shudder. Presently she asked her papa whether it was not time to go home. Mrs. Armstrong proposed that she should stay all night ; but she evidently wished to go. It would be rather perilous work to drive down the hill with the wind behind, in such a night ; but a servant was sent to hasten the carriage notwithstanding. The colonel and Percy and I ran alongside of it, ready to render any assistance that might be necessary ; and, although we all said we had never been out in such an uproar of the elements, we reached home in safety.

As Adela bade us good-night in the hall, I certainly felt very uneasy as to the effects of the night's adventures upon her, — she looked so pale and wretched.

She did not come down to breakfast.

But she appeared at lunch, nothing the worse, and in very good spirits.

If I did not think that this had something to do with another fact I have come to the knowledge of since, I don't know that the particulars of the evening need have been related so minutely. The other fact was this; that in the gray dawn of the morning, by which time the snow had ceased, though the wind still blew, Adela saw from her window a weary rider and wearier horse pass the house, going up the street. The heads of both were sunk low. You might have thought the poor mare was looking for something she had lost last night in the snow; and perhaps it was not all fatigue with Harry Armstrong. Perhaps he was giving thanks that he had saved two lives instead of losing his own. He was not so absorbed, however, but that he looked up at the house as he passed, and I believe he saw the blind of her window drop back into its place.

But how did she come to be looking out just at the moment?

If a lady has not slept all night, and has looked out of window ninety-nine times before, it is not very wonderful that at the hundredth time she should see what she was looking for; that is, if the object desired has not been lost in the snow, or drowned in a moorland pit; neither of which had happened to Harry Armstrong. Nor is it unlikely that, after seeing what she has watched for, she will fall too fast asleep to be roused by the breakfast-bell.

CHAPTER XII.

PERCY AND HIS MOTHER.

At luncheon the colonel said : —

"Well, Adela, you will be glad to know that our hero of last night returned quite safe this morning."

"I am glad to know it, papa."

"He is one of the right sort, that young fellow. Duty is the first thing with him."

"Perhaps duty may not have been his only motive," said Mrs. Cathcart, coldly. "It was too good an opportunity to be lost."

Adela seemed to understand her, for she blushed; but not with embarrassment alone, for the fire that made her cheek glow red flashed in flames from her eyes.

"Some people, aunt," she said, trying to follow the cold tone in which Mrs. Cathcart had spoken, "have not the faculty for the perception of the noble and self-denying. Their own lives are so habitually elevated, that they see nothing remarkable in the devotion of others."

"Well, I do see nothing remarkable in it," returned the aunt, in a tone that indicated she hardly knew what to make of Adela's sarcasm. "Mr. Armstrong would have been liable to an action at law if he had refused to go. And then to come into the drawing-room in his boots and spurs, and change his coat before ladies. It was all just of a piece with the coarse speech he made to you when you were simple enough to ask him not to go. I can't think what you admire about the man, I am sure."

Adela rose and left the room.

"You are too hard on Mr. Armstrong," said the colonel.

"Perhaps I am, colonel; but I have my reasons. If you will be blind to your daughter's interests, that is only the more reason why I should keep my eyes open to them."

So saying, Mrs. Cathcart rose, and followed her niece out of the room, but no farther, I will venture to say. Fierce as the aunt was, there had been that in the niece's eyes, as she went, which I do not believe the vulgar courage of the aunt could have faced.

I concluded that Mrs. Cathcart had discovered Adela's restlessness the night before; had very possibly peeped into her room; and, as her windows looked in the same direction, might have seen Harry riding home from his selfish task in the cold gray morning; for scheming can destroy the rest of some women as perfectly as loving can destroy the rest of others. She might have made the observation, too, that Adela had lain as still as a bird unhatched, after that apparition of weariness had passed.

The colonel again sank into an uncomfortable mood. He had loved his dead brother very dearly, and had set his heart on marrying Adela to Percy. Besides, there was quite enough of worldliness left in the heart of the honorable old soldier to make him feel that a country practitioner, of very moderate means, was not to be justified in aspiring to the hand of his daughter. Moreover, he could hardly endure the thought of his daughter's marriage at all, for he had not a little of the old man's jealousy in him; and the notion of Percy being her husband was the only form in which the thought could present itself, that was in the least degree endurable to him. Yet he could not help admiring Harry; and, until his thoughts had been turned into their present channel by Mrs. Cathcart's remarks, he had felt that that lady was unjust to the doctor. But to think that his line, for he had no son, should merge into that of the Armstrongs, who were of somewhat dubious descent in his eyes, and Scotch, too, — though, by the way his own line was Scotch, a few hundred years back, — was sufficient to cause him very considerable uneasiness; *pain* would be the more correct word.

I have, for many pages, said very little about Percy; simply because there has been very little to say about him. He was always present at our readings, but did not appear to take any interest in them. He would generally lie on a couch, and stare either at Adela or the fire till he fell asleep. If he did not succeed in getting to sleep, he would show manifest signs of being bored. No doubt he considered the whole affair a piece of sentimental humbug. And during the day I saw very little of him. He had hunted once or twice, on one of his uncle's horses; they had scarcely seen the hounds this season. But that was a bore, no doubt. He went skating occasionally, and had once tried to get Adela to accompany him; but she would not. These amusements, with a few scattered hours of snipe-shooting, composed his Christmas enjoyments; the intervals being filled up with yawning, teasing the dogs, growling at his mother and the cold, and sleeping the "innocent sleep."

Whether he had any real regard for Adela I could not quite satisfy myself, — I mean *real* by the standard and on the scale of his own being; for, of course, as compared with the love of men like the Armstrongs, the attachment of a lad like Percy could hardly be considered *real* at all. But even that, as I say, I could not clearly find out. His jealousy seemed rather the jealousy of what was his, or ought to be his, than any more profound or tragical feeling. But he evidently disliked the doctor; and the curate, too, whether for his own sake or for the doctor's, is of little consequence.

In the course of this forenoon I came upon Master Percy in the kitchen-garden. He had set an old shutter against one of the walls for a target, and was peppering away at it with a revolver; apparently quite satisfied if he succeeded in hitting the same panel twice running at twelve paces. Guessing at the nonsense that was in his head, I sauntered up to him, and watched his practice for a while. He pulled the trigger with a jerk that threw the muzzle up half an inch every time he fired, else I don't believe he would have hit the board at all. But he held his breath beforehand, till he was red in the face, because he had heard that, in firing at a mark, pistol-shooters did not even breathe, to avoid the influence of the motion of the chest upon the aim.

"Ah!" I said, "pretty well. But you should see Mr. Henry Armstrong shoot."

Whereupon Mr. Percy Cathcart deliberately damned Mr. Henry Armstrong, expressly and by name. I pretended not to have heard him, and, continuing to regard the said condemned as still alive and comfortable, went on : —

. "Just ask him, the next time you find him at home, to let you see him drive a nail with three pistol-bullets."

He threw the pistol from him, exploded himself like a shell, in twenty different fragments of oaths, and left me the kitchen garden and the pistol, which latter I took a little practice with myself, for the sake of emptying two of the chambers still charged. Whether Henry Armstrong even knew how to fire a pistol, I did not know; but I dare say he was a first-rate shot, if I only had known it. I sent the pistol up to Mr. Percy's room by the hand of Mr. Beeves; but I never heard him practising any more.

The next night the curate was to read us another story. The time arrived, and with it all our company, except Harry. Indeed it was a marvel that he had been able to attend so often as he had attended. I presume the severe weather had by this time added to his sick-list.

Although I fear the chief end of our readings was not so fully attained as hitherto, or, in other words, that Adela did not enjoy the evenings so much as usual, I will yet record all with my usual faithfulness.

The curate and his wife were a little late, and when they arrived they found us waiting for them in music. As soon as they entered Adela rose from the piano.

"Do go on, Miss Cathcart," said the curate.

"I had just finished," she replied.

"Then if you will allow me, I will sing a song first, which I think will act as an antidote to those sentimental ones which we had at my house, and of which Mrs. Cathcart did not **ap** prove."

"Thank you," said everybody, Mrs. Cathcart included.

Whereupon the curate sang : —

> "I am content. In trumpet-tones,
>   My song, let people know.
> And many a mighty man, with throne
>   And sceptre, is not so.
> And if he is, I joyful cry,
> Why, then, he's just the same as I.
>
> "The Mogul's gold, the Sultan's show
>   His bliss, supreme too soon,
> Who, lord of all the world below,
>   Looked up unto the moon —
> I would not pick it up — all that
> Is only fit for laughing at.
>
> "My motto is, — *Content with this.*
>   Gold — place — I prize not such.
> That which I have, my measure is;
>   Wise men desire not much.
> Men wish and wish and have their will,
> And wish again, as hungry still.
>
> "And gold and honor are besides
>   A very brittle glass;
> And time, in his unresting tides,
>   Makes all things change and pass,
> Turns riches to a beggar's dole;
> Sets glory's race an infant's goal.
>
> "Be noble, — that is more than wealth;
>   Do right, — that's more than place;
> Then in the spirit there is health,
>   And gladness in the face;
> Then thou art with thyself at one
> And, no man hating, fearest none.

> "I am content. In trumpet tones,
>   My song, let people know.
> And many a mighty man, with throne
>   And sceptre, is not so;
> And if he is, I joyful cry,
> Why, then, he's just the same as I."

"Is that one of your own, Mr. Armstrong?" asked the colonel.

"It is, like most of those you have heard from me and my brother, only a translation.

"I am no judge of poetry, but it seems to me that if he was content he need not say so much about it."

"There is something in what you say. But there was no show-off in Claudius, I think. He was a most simple-hearted, amiable man, to all appearance. A man of business, too, — manager of a bank at Altona, in the beginning of the present century. But as I have not given a favorable impression of him, allow me to repeat a little bit of innocent humor of his, — a cradle song, — which I like fully better than the other."

"Most certainly; it is only fair," answered the colonel.

> "Sleep, baby boy, sleep sweet, secure;
>   Thou art thy father's miniature;
> That art thou, though thy father goes
> And swears that thou hast not his nose.

> "A moment gone, he looked at thee,
>   My little budding rose,
> And said, No doubt there's much of me.
>   But he has not my nose.

> "I think myself, it is too small,
>   But it is *his* nose after all;
> For if thy nose his nose be not,
>   Whence came the nose that thou hast got?

> "Sleep, baby, sleep; don't half-way doze:
>   To tease me, — that's his part.
> No matter if you've not his nose,
>   So be you've got his heart!"

CHAPTER XIII.

THE BROKEN SWORDS.

EVERY one liked this, except Mrs. Cathcart, who opined, with her usual smile, that it was rather silly.

"Well, I hope a father may be silly sometimes," said the curate, with a glance at his wife, which she did not acknowledge. "At least, I fear I should be silly enough, if I were a father."

No more remarks were made, and, as it was now quite time to begin the story, Mr. Armstrong took his place, and the rest took their places. He began at once.

"THE BROKEN SWORDS.

"The eyes of three, two sisters and a brother, gazed for the last time on a great pale-golden star, that followed the sun down the steep west. It went down to arise again; and the brother about to depart might return, but more than the usual doubt hung upon his future. For between the white dresses of the sisters shone his scarlet coat and golden sword-knot, which he had put on for the first time, more to gratify their pride than his own vanity. The brightening moon, as if prophetic of a future memory, had already begun to dim the scarlet and the gold, and to give them a pale, ghostly hue. In her thoughtful light the whole group seemed more like a meeting in the land of shadows than a parting in the substantial earth. But which should be called the land of realities? — the region where appearance, and space, and time drive between, and stop the flowing currents of the soul's speech? or that region where heart meets heart, and appearance has become the slave to utterance, and space and time are forgotten?

"Through the quiet air came the far-off rush of water, and the near cry of the land-rail. Now and then a chilly wind blew unheeded through the startled and jostling leaves that shady the ivy-seat. Else, there was calm everywhere, rendered yet deeper and more intense by the dusky sorrow that filled their hearts. For, far away, hundreds of miles beyond

the hearing of their ears, roared the great war-guns; next
week their brother must sail with his regiment to join the army; and to-morrow he must leave his home.

"The sisters looked on him tenderly, with vague fears about
his fate. Yet little they divined it. That the face they loved
might lie pale and bloody, in a heap of slain, was the worst
image of it that arose before them; but this, had they seen the
future, they would, in ignorance of the further future, have infinitely preferred to that which awaited him. And even while
they looked on him, a dim feeling of the unsuitableness of his
lot filled their minds. For, indeed, to all judgments it must
have seemed unsuitable that the home-boy, the loved of
his mother, the pet of his sisters, who was happy, woman-
like (as Coleridge says), if he possessed the signs of love,
having never yet sought for its proofs, — that he should
be sent amongst soldiers, to command and be commanded; to
kill, or perhaps to be himself crushed out of the fair earth in
the uproar that brings back for the moment the reign of Night
and Chaos. No wonder that to his sisters it seemed strange
and sad. Yet such was their own position in the battle of life,
in which their father had died with doubtful conquest, that
when their old military uncle sent the boy an ensign's commis-
sion, they did not dream of refusing the only path open, as
they thought, to an honorable profession, even though it
might lead to the trench-grave. They heard it as the voice of
destiny, wept, and yielded.

"If they had possessed a deeper insight into his character,
they would have discovered yet further reason to doubt the
fitness of the profession chosen for him; and if they had ever
seen him at school, it is possible the doubt of fitness might
have strengthened into a certainty of incongruity. His comparative inactivity amongst his school-fellows, though occasioned
by no dulness of intellect, might have suggested the necessity
of a quiet life, if inclination and liking had been the arbiters
in the choice. Nor was this inactivity the result of defective
animal spirits either, for sometimes his mirth and boyish frolic
were unbounded; but it seemed to proceed from an over-activity
of the inward life, absorbing, and in some measure checking,
the outward manifestation. He had so much to do in his own
hidden kingdom, that he had not time to take his place in the

polity and strife of the commonwealth around him. Hence, while other boys were acting, he was thinking. In this point of difference he felt keenly the superiority of many of his companions; for another boy would have the obstacle overcome, or the adversary subdued, while he was meditating on the propriety, or on the means, of effecting the desired end. He envied their promptitude, while they never saw reason to envy his wisdom; for his conscience, tender and not strong, frequently transformed slowness of determination into irresolution; while a delicacy of the sympathetic nerves tended to distract him from any predetermined course, by the diversity of their vibrations, responsive to influences from all quarters, and destructive to unity of purpose.

"Of such a one, the *à priori* judgment would be, that he ought to be left to meditate and grow for some time, before being called upon to produce the fruits of action. But add to these mental conditions a vivid imagination, and a high sense of honor, nourished in childhood by the reading of the old knightly romances, and then put the youth in a position in which action is imperative, and you have elements of strife sufficient to reduce that fair kingdom of his to utter anarchy and madness. Yet so little do we know ourselves, and so different are the symbols with which the imagination works its algebra, from the realities which those symbols represent, that as yet the youth felt no uneasiness, but contemplated his new calling with a glad enthusiasm and some vanity; for all his prospect lay in the glow of the scarlet and the gold. Nor did this excitement receive any check till the day before his departure, on which day I have introduced him to my readers, when, accidentally taking up a newspaper of a week old, his eye fell on these words: '*Already crying women are to be met in the streets.*' With this cloud afar on his horizon, which, though no bigger than a man's hand, yet cast a perceptible shadow over his mind, he departed next morning. The coach carried him beyond the consecrated circle of home-laws and impulses, out into the great tumult, above which rises ever and anon the cry of Cain, ' Am I my brother's keeper ? '

"Every tragedy of higher order, constructed in Christian times, will correspond more or less to the grand drama of the Bible; wherein the first act opens with a brilliant sunset vision

of Paradise, in which childish sense and need are served with
all the profusion of the indulgent nurse. But the glory fades
off into gray and black, and night settles down upon the heart
which, rightly uncontent with the childish, and not having yet
learned the childlike, seeks knowledge and manhood as a thing
denied by the Maker, and yet to be gained by the creature;
so sets forth alone to climb the heavens, and, instead of climbing, falls into the abyss. Then follows the long dismal night
of feverish efforts and delirious visions, or, it may be, helpless
despair; till at length a deeper stratum of the soul is heaved
to the surface; and amid the first dawn of morning, the youth
says within him, 'I have sinned against my *Maker* — I will
arise and go to my *Father*.' More or less, I say, will Christian tragedy correspond to this, — a fall and a rising again;
not a rising only, but a victory; not a victory merely, but a
triumph. Such, in its way and degree, is my story. I have
shown, in one passing scene, the home-paradise; now I have to
show a scene of a far differing nature.

" The young ensign was lying in his tent, weary, but wakeful. All day long the cannon had been bellowing against the
walls of the city, which now lay with wide, gaping breach,
ready for the morrow's storm, but covered yet with the friendly
darkness. His regiment was ordered to be ready with the
earliest dawn to march up to the breach. That day, for the
first time, there had been blown on his sword, — there the
sword lay, a spot on the chased hilt still. He had cut down
one of the enemy in a skirmish with a sallying party of the
besieged, and the look of the man, as he fell, haunted him. He
felt, for the time, that he dared not pray to the Father, for the
blood of a brother had rushed forth at the stroke of his arm,
and there was one fewer of living souls on the earth because
he lived thereon. And to-morrow he must lead a troop of men
up to that poor disabled town, and turn them loose upon it,
not knowing what might follow in the triumph of enraged and
victorious foes, who for weeks had been subjected, by the con-
stancy of the place, to the greatest privations. It was true the
general had issued his commands against all disorder and pil-
lage; but if the soldiers once yielded to temptation, what might
not be done before the officers could reclaim them! All the
wretched tales he had read of the sack of cities rushed back on

his memory. He shuddered as he lay. Then his conscience began to speak, and to ask what right he had to be there. Was the war a just one? He could not tell; for this was a bad time for settling nice questions. But there he was, right or wrong, fighting and shedding blood on God's earth, beneath God's heaven.

"Over and over he turned the question in his mind; again and again the spouting blood of his foe, and the death-look in his eye, rose before him; and the youth who at school could never fight with a companion, because he was not sure that he was in the right, was alone in the midst of undoubting men of war, amongst whom he was driven helplessly along, upon the waves of a terrible necessity. What wonder that in the midst of these perplexities his courage should fail him! What wonder that the consciousness of fainting should increase the faintness! or that the dread of fear and its consequences should hasten and invigorate its attacks! To crown all, when he dropped into a troubled slumber at length, he found himself hurried, as on a storm of fire, through the streets of the captured town, from all the windows of which looked forth familiar faces, old and young, but distorted from the memory of his boyhood by fear and wild despair. On one spot laid the body of his father, with his face to the earth; and he woke at the cry of horror and rage that burst from his own lips, as he saw the rough, bloody hand of a soldier twisted in the loose hair of his elder sister, and the younger fainting in the arms of a scoundrel belonging to his own regiment.

"He slept no more. As the gray morning broke, the troops appointed for the attack assembled without sound of trumpet or drum, and were silently formed in fitting order. The young ensign was in his place, weary and wretched after his miserable night. Before him he saw a great, broad-shouldered lieutenant, whose brawny hand seemed almost too large for his sword-hilt, and in any one of whose limbs played more animal life than in the whole body of the pale youth. The firm-set lips of this officer, and the fire of his eye, showed a concentrated resolution, which, by the contrast, increased the misery of the ensign, and seemed, as if the stronger absorbed the weaker, to draw out from him the last fibres of self-possession: the sight of unattainable determination, while it in-

creased the feeling of the arduousness of that which required
such determination, threw him into the great gulf which lay
between him and it.   In this disorder of his nervous and mental condition, with a doubting conscience and a shrinking heart,
is it any wonder that the terrors which lay before him at the
gap in those bristling walls, should draw near, and, making sudden inroad upon his soul, overwhelm the government of a will
worn out by the tortures of an unassured spirit?   What share
fear contributed to unman him, it was impossible for him, in
the dark, confused conflict of differing emotions, to determine;
but doubtless a natural shrinking from danger, there being no
excitement to deaden its influence, and no hope of victory to en-
courage to the struggle, seeing victory was dreadful to him as
defeat, had its part in the sad result.   Many men who have courage, are dependent on ignorance and a low state of the moral feeling for that courage; and a further progress towards the development of the higher nature would, for a time at least,
entirely overthrow it.   Nor could such loss of courage be
rightly designated by the name of cowardice.

"But, alas! the colonel happened to fix his eyes upon him
as he passed along the file; and this completed his confusion.
He betrayed such evident symptoms of perturbation, that that
officer ordered him under arrest; and the result was, that,
chiefly for the sake of example to the army, he was, upon trial
by court-martial, expelled from the service, and had his sword
broken over his head.   Alas for the delicate-minded youth!
Alas for the home-darling!

"Long after, he found at the bottom of his chest the pieces of
the broken sword, and remembered that, at the time, he had lifted them from the ground and carried them away.   But he could
not recall under what impulse he had done so.   Perhaps the
agony he suffered, passing the bounds of mortal endurance,
had opened for him a vista into the eternal, and had shown
him, if not the injustice of the sentence passed upon him, yet
his freedom from blame, or, endowing him with dim prophetic
vision, had given him the assurance that some day the stain would
be wiped from his soul, and leave him standing clear before the
tribunal of his own honor.   Some feeling like this, I say, may
have caused him, with a passing gleam of indignant protest. to
lift the fragments from the earth, and carry them away; even

as the friends of a so-called traitor may bear away his mutilated body from the wheel. But, if such was the case, the vision was soon overwhelmed and forgotten in the succeeding anguish. He could not see that, in mercy to his doubting spirit, the
question which had agitated his mind almost to madness, and
which no results of the impending conflict could have settled for
him, was thus quietly set aside for the time; nor that. painful as
was the dark, dreadful existence that he was now to pass in
self-torment and moaning, it would go by, and leave his spirit
clearer far, than if, in his apprehension, it had been stained with
further blood-guiltiness, instead of the loss of honor. Years
after, when he accidentally learned that on that very morning
the whole of his company, with parts of several more, had, or
ever they began to mount the breach, been blown to pieces by
the explosion of a mine, he cried aloud in bitterness, 'Would
God that my fear had not been discovered before I reached that
spot!' But surely it is better to pass into the next region
of life having reaped some assurance, some firmness of character, determination of effort, and consciousness of the worth of
life, in the present world; so approaching the future steadily
and faithfully, and if in much darkness and ignorance, yet not
in the oscillations of moral uncertainty.

"Close upon the catastrophe followed a torpor, which lasted
he did not know how long, and which wrapped in a thick fog
all the succeeding events. For some time he can hardly be
said to have had any conscious history. He awoke to life and
torture when half way across the sea towards his native country, where was no home any longer for him. To this point,
and no further, could his thoughts return in after years. But
the misery which he then endured is hardly to be understood,
save by those of like delicate temperament with himself. All
day long he sat silent in his cabin; nor could any effort of the
captain, or others on board, induce him to go on deck till night
came on, when, under the starlight, he ventured into the open
air. The sky soothed him then, he knew not how. For the
face of nature is the face of God, and must bear expressions
that can influence, though unconsciously to them, the most ignorant and hopeless of his children. Often did he watch the
clouds in hope of a storm, his spirit rising and falling as the
sky darkened or cleared; he longed, in the necessary selfish-

ness of such suffering, for a tumult of waters to swallow the vessel; and only the recollection of how many lives were involved in its safety besides his own, prevented him from praying to God for lightning and tempest, borne on which he might dash into the haven of the other world. One night, following a sultry calm day, he thought that Mercy had heard his unuttered prayer. The air and sea were intense darkness, till a light as intense for one moment annihilated it, and the succeeding darkness seemed shattered with the sharp reports of the thunder that cracked without reverberation. He who had shrunk from battle with his fellow-men rushed to the mainmast, threw himself on his knees, and stretched forth his arms in speechless energy of supplication; but the storm passed away overheard, and left him kneeling still by the uninjured mast. At length the vessel reached her port. He hurried on shore to bury himself in the most secret place he could find. *Out of sight* was his first, his only thought. Return to his mother he would not, he could not; and, indeed, his friends never learned his fate, until it had carried him far beyond their reach.

"For several weeks he lurked about like a malefactor, in low lodging-houses, in narrow streets of the seaport to which the vessel had borne him, heeding no one, and but little shocked at the strange society and conversation with which, though only in bodily presence, he had to mingle. These formed the subjects of reflection in after times; and he came to the conclusion that, though much evil and much misery exist, sufficient to move prayers and tears in those who love their kind, yet there is less of both than those looking down from a more elevated social position upon the weltering heap of humanity are ready to imagine, especially if they regard it likewise from the pedestal of self-congratulation on which a meagre type of religion has elevated them. But at length his little stock of money was nearly expended, and there was nothing that he could do, or learn to do, in this seaport. He felt impelled to seek manual labor, partly because he thought it more likely he could obtain that sort of employment, without a request for reference as to his character, which would lead to inquiry about his previous history; and partly, perhaps, from an instinctive feeling that hard bodily labor would tend to lessen his inward suffering.

"He left the town, therefore, at night-fall of a July day, carrying a little bundle of linen, and the remains of his money, somewhat augmented by the sale of various articles of clothing and convenience, which his change of life rendered superfluous and unsuitable. He directed his course northwards, travelling principally by night, — so painfully did he shrink from the gaze even of footfarers like himself; and sleeping during the day in some hidden nook of wood or thicket, or under the shadow of a great tree in a solitary field. So fine was the season, that for three successive weeks he was able to travel thus without inconvenience, lying down when the sun grew hot in the forenoon, and generally waking when the first faint stars were hesitating in the great darkening heavens that covered and shielded him. For above every cloud, above every storm, rise up, calm, clear, divine, the deep infinite skies; they embrace the tempest even as the sunshine; by their permission it exists within their boundless peace: therefore it cannot hurt, and must pass away, while there they stand as ever, domed up eternally, lasting, strong, and pure.

"Several times he attempted to get agricultural employment; but the whiteness of his hands and the tone of his voice not merely suggested unfitness for labor, but generated suspicion as to the character of one who had evidently dropped from a rank so much higher, and was seeking admittance within the natural masonic boundaries and secrets and privileges of another. Disheartened somewhat, but hopeful, he journeyed on. I say hopeful; for the blessed power of life in the universe, in fresh air and sunshine absorbed by active exercise in winds, yea, in rain, though it fell but seldom, had begun to work its natural healing, soothing effect, upon his perturbed spirit. And there was room for hope in his new endeavor. As his bodily strength increased, and his health, considerably impaired by inward suffering, improved, the trouble of his soul became more endurable; and in some measure to endure is to conquer and destroy. In proportion as the mind grows in the strength of patience, the disturber of its peace sickens and fades away. At length, one day, a widow lady in a village through which his road led him, gave him a day's work in her garden. He labored hard and well, notwithstanding his soon-blistered hands, received his wages thankfully, and found a resting-place for the night on the low part of a hay-stack from which the upper portion had been cut away. Here he ate his supper of bread and cheese, pleased to have found such comfortable quarters, and soon fell fast asleep.

"When he awoke, the whole heavens and earth seemed to give a full denial to sin and sorrow. The sun was just mounting over the horizon, looking up the clear cloud-mottled sky. From millions of water-drops hanging on the bending stalks of grass sparkled his rays in varied refraction, transformed here to a gorgeous burning ruby, there to an emerald green as the grass, and yonder to a flashing sunny topaz. The chanting priest-lark had gone up from the low earth as soon as the heavenly light had begun to enwrap and illumine the folds of its tabernacle ; and had entered the high heavens with his offering, whence, unseen, he now dropped on the earth the sprinkled sounds of his overflowing blessedness. The poor youth rose but to kneel, and cry, from a bursting heart, 'Hast thou not, O Father, some care for me? Canst thou not restore my lost honor? Can anything befall thy children for which thou hast no help? Surely, if the face of thy world lie not, joy and not grief is at the heart of the universe. Is there none for me?'

"The highest poetic feeling of which we are now conscious springs not from the beholding of perfected beauty, but from the mute sympathy which the creation with all its children manifests with us in the groaning and travailing which look for the sonship. Because of our need and aspiration, the snow-drop gives birth in our hearts to a loftier spiritual and poetic feeling than the rose most complete in form, color, and odor. The rose is of Paradise ; the snow-drop is of the striving, hoping, longing earth. Perhaps our highest poetry is the expression of our aspirations in the sympathetic forms of visible nature. Nor is this merely a longing for a restored paradise ; for even in the ordinary history of men, no man or woman that has fallen can be restored to the position formerly held. Such must rise to a yet higher place, whence they can behold their former standing far beneath their feet. They must be restored by the attainment of something better than they ever possessed before, or not at all. If the law be a weariness, we must escape it by taking refuge with the spirit, for not otherwise can we fulfil the law than by being above the law. To escape the overhanging rocks of Sinai, we must climb to its secret top.

> " ' Is thy strait horizon dreary?
> Is thy foolish fancy chill?
> Change the feet that have grown weary,
> For the wings that never will.'

"Thus, like one of the wandering knights searching the wide earth for the Sangreal, did he wander on, searching for his lost honor, or rather (for that he counted gone forever) seeking unconsciously for the peace of mind which had departed from him, and taken with it, not the joy merely, but almost the possibility, of existence.

"At last, when his little store was all but exhausted, he was employed by a market-gardener, in the neighborhood of a large country town, to work in his garden, and sometimes take his vegetables to market. With him he continued for a few weeks, and wished for no change; until, one day, driving his cart through the town, he saw approaching him an elderly gentleman, whom he knew at once, by his gait and carriage, to be a military man. Now he had never seen his uncle, the retired officer, but it struck him that this might be he; and under the tyranny of his passion for concealment, he fancied that if it it were he, he might recognize him by some family likeness, — not considering the improbability of his looking at him. This fancy, with the painful effect which the sight of an officer, even in plain clothes, had upon him, recalling the torture of that frightful day, so overcame him, that he found himself at the other end of an alley before he recollected that he had the horse and cart in charge. This increased his difficulty; for now he dared not return, lest his inquiries after the vehicle, if the horse had strayed from the direct line, should attract attention, and cause interrogations which he would be unable to answer. The fatal want of self-possession seemed again to ruin him. He forsook the town by the nearest way, struck across the country to another line of road, and, before he was missed, was miles away, still in a northerly direction.

"But although he thus shunned the face of man, especially of any one who reminded him of the past, the loss of his reputation in their eyes was not the cause of his inward grief. That would have been comparatively powerless to disturb him, had he not lost his own respect. He quailed before his own thoughts; he was dishonored in his own eyes. His perplexity had not yet sufficiently cleared away to allow him to see the extenuating circumstances of the case; not to say the fact, that the peculiar mental condition in which he was at the time removed the case quite out of the class of ordinary instances of cowardice. He condemned himself more severely than any of his judges would have dared; remembering that portion of his mental sensations which had savored of fear, and forgetting the causes which had produced it. He judged himself a man stained with the foulest blot that could cleave to a soldier's name, a blot which nothing but death, not even death, could efface. But, inwardly condemned and outwardly degraded, his dread of recognition was intense; and feeling that he was in more danger of being discovered where the population was sparser, he resolved to hide himself once more in the midst of poverty; and, with this view, found his way to one of the largest of the manufacturing towns.

"He reached it during the strike of a great part of the workmen; so that, though he found some difficulty in procuring employment, as might be expected from his ignorance of machine-labor, he yet was sooner successful than he would otherwise have been. Possessed of a natural aptitude for mechanical operations, he soon became a tolerable workman; and he found that his previous education assisted to the fitting execution of those operations even which were most purely mechanical.

"He found also, at first, that the unrelaxing attention requisite for the mastering of the many niceties of his work, of necessity drew his mind somewhat from its brooding over his misfortune, hitherto almost ceaseless. Every now and then, however, a pang would shoot suddenly to his heart, and turn his face pale, even before his consciousness had time to inquire what was the matter. So by degrees, as attention became less necessary, and the nervo-mechanical action of his system increased with use, his thoughts again returned to their old misery. He would wake at night in his poor room, with the feeling that a ghostly nightmare sat on his soul; that a want — a loss — miserable, fearful — was present; that something of his heart was gone from him; and through the darkness he would hear the snap of the breaking sword, and lie for a moment overwhelmed beneath the assurance of the incredible fact. Could it be true that *he* was a coward? that *his* honor was gone, and in its place a stain? that *he* was a thing for men — and worse, for women — to point the finger at, laughing bitter laughter? Never lover or husband could have mourned with the same desolation over the departure of the loved; the girl alone, weeping scorching tears over *her* degradation, could resemble him in his agony, as he lay on his bed, and wept and moaned.

"His sufferings had returned with the greater weight, that he was no longer upheld by the 'divine air' and the open heavens, whose sunlight now only reached him late in an afternoon, as he stood at his loom, through windows so coated with dust that they looked like frosted glass; showing, as it passed through the air to fall on the dirty floor, how the breath of life was thick with dust of iron and wood, and films of cotton; amidst which his senses were now too much dulled by custom to detect the exhalations from greasy wheels and overtasked human-kind. Nor could he find comfort in the society of his fellow-laborers. True, it was a kind of comfort to have those near him who could not know of his grief; but there was so little in common between them, that any interchange of thought was impossible. At least, so it seemed to him. Yet sometimes his longing for human companionship would drive him out of his dreary room at night, and send him wandering through the lower part of the town, where he would gaze wistfully on the miserable faces that passed him, as if looking for some one — some angel, even there — to speak good will to his hungry heart.

"Once he entered one of those gin-palaces, which, like the golden gates of hell, entice the miserable to a worse misery, and seated himself close to a half-tipsy, good-natured wretch, who made room for him on a bench by the wall. He was comforted even by this proximity to one who would not repel him. But soon the paintings of warlike action — of knights and horses, and mighty deeds done with battle-axe and broad-sword, which adorned the panels all round—drove him forth even from this heaven of the damned; yet not before the impious thought had arisen in his heart, that the brilliantly painted and sculptured roof, with the gilded vine-leaves and bunches of grapes trained up the windows, all lighted with the great shining chandeliers, was only a microcosmic repetition of the bright heavens and the glowing earth that overhung and surrounded the misery of man. But the memory of how kindly they had comforted and elevated him, at one period of his painful history, not only banished the wicked thought, but brought him more quiet, in the resurrection of a past blessing, than he had known for some time. The period, however, was now at hand, when a new grief, followed by a new and more elevated activity, was to do its part towards the closing up of the fountain of bitterness.

"Amongst his fellow-laborers, he had for a short time taken some interest in observing a young woman, who had lately joined them. There was nothing remarkable about her, except what at first sight seemed a remarkable plainness. A slight scar over one of her rather prominent eyebrows increased this impression of plainness. But the first day had not passed, before he began to see that there was something not altogether common in those deep eyes; and the plain look vanished before a closer observation, which also discovered, in the forehead and the lines of the mouth, traces of sorrow or other suffering. There was an expression, too, in the whole face of fixedness of purpose, without any hardness of determination. Her countenance altogether seemed the index to an interesting mental history. Signs of mental trouble were always an attraction to him; in this case so great, that he overcame his shyness, and spoke to her one evening as they left the works. He often walked home with her after that; as, indeed, was natural, seeing that she occupied an attic in the same poor lodging-house in which he lived himself. The street did not bear the best character; nor, indeed, would the occupations of all the inmates of the house have stood investigation; but so retiring and quiet was this girl, and so seldom did she go abroad after work-hours, that he had not discovered till then that she lived in the same street, not to say the same house, with himself.

"He soon learned her history, — a very common one as to outward events, but not surely insignificant because common. Her father and mother were both dead, and hence she had to find her livelihood alone, and amidst associations which were always disagreeable, and sometimes painful. Her quick womanly instinct must have discovered that he, too, had a history ; for though, his mental prostration favoring the operation of outward influences, he had greatly approximated in appearance to those amongst whom he labored, there were yet signs, besides the educated accent of his speech, which would have distinguished him to an observer ; but she put no questions to him, nor made any approach towards seeking a return of the confidence she reposed in him. It was a sensible alleviation to his sufferings to hear her kind voice, and look in her gentle face, as they walked home together ; and at length the expectation of this pleasure began to present itself, in the midst of the busy, dreary work-hours, as the shadow of a heaven to close up the dismal, uninteresting day.

"But one morning he missed her from her place, and a keener pain passed through him than he had felt of late ; for he knew that the Plague was abroad, feeding in the low, stagnant places of human abode ; and he had but too much reason to dread that she might be now struggling in its grasp. He seized the first opportunity of slipping out and hurrying home. He sprang upstairs to her room. He found the door locked, but heard a faint moaning within. To avoid disturbing her, while determined to gain an entrance, he went down for the key of his own door, with which he succeeded in unlocking hers, and so crossed her threshold for the first time. There she lay on her bed, tossing in pain, and beginning to be delirious. Careless of his own life, and feeling that he could not die better than in helping the only friend he had ; certain, likewise, of the difficulty of finding a nurse for one in this disease and of her station in life ; and sure, likewise, that there could be no question of propriety either in the circumstances with which they were surrounded, nor in this case of terrible fever almost as hopeless for her as dangerous to him, he instantly began the duties of a nurse, and returned no more to his employment. He had a little money in his possession, for he would not, in the way in which he lived, spend all his wages ;

so he proceeded to make her as comfortable as he could, with all the pent-up tenderness of a loving heart finding an outlet at length. When a boy at home, he had often taken the place of nurse, and he felt quite capable of performing its duties. Nor was his boyhood far behind yet, although the trials he had come through made it appear an age since he had lost his light heart. So he never left her bedside, except to procure what was necessary for her. She was too ill to oppose any of his measures, or to seek to prohibit his presence. Indeed, by the time he had returned with the first medicine, she was insensible; and she continued so through the whole of the following week, during which time he was constantly with her.

"That action produces feeling is as often true as its converse; and it is not surprising that, while he smoothed the pillow for her head, he should have made a nest in his heart for the helpless girl. Slowly and unconsciously he learned to love her. The chasm between his early associations and the circumstances in which he found her, vanished as he drew near to the simple, essential womanhood. His heart saw hers and loved it; and he knew that, the centre once gained, he could, as from the fountain of life, as from the innermost secret of the holy place, the hidden germ of power and possibility, transform the outer intellect and outermost manners as he pleased. With what a thrill of joy, a feeling for long time unknown to him, and till now never known in this form or with this intensity, the thought arose in his heart that here lay one who some day would love him; that he should have a place of refuge and rest; one to lie in his bosom and not despise him! 'For,' said he to himself, 'I will call forth her soul from where it sleeps, like an unawakened echo in an unknown cave; and like a child, of whom I once dreamed, that was mine, and to my delight turned in fear from all besides, and clung to me, this soul of hers will run with bewildered, half-sleeping eyes, and tottering steps, but with a cry of joy on its lips, to me as the life-giver. She will cling to me and worship me. Then will I tell her, for she must know all, that I am low and contemptible; that I am an outcast from the world, and that, if she receive me, she will be to me as God. And I will fall down at her feet and pray her for comfort, for life, for restoration to myself; and she will throw herself beside me, and weep and love me, I know. And we will go through life together, working hard, but for each other; and when we die, she shall lead me into Paradise, as the prize her angel-hand found cast on a desert shore, from the storm of winds and waves which I was too weak to resist — and raised, and tended, and saved.' Often did such thoughts as these pass through his mind while watching by her bed; alternated, checked, and sometimes destroyed, by the fears which attended her precarious condition, but returning with every apparent betterment or hopeful symptom.

" I will not stop to decide the nice question, how far the intention was right, of causing her to love him before she knew his story. If in the whole matter there was too much thought of self, my only apology is the sequel. One day, the ninth from the commencement of her illness, a letter arrived, addressed to her; which he, thinking he might prevent some inconvenience thereby, opened and read, in the confidence of that love which already made her and all belonging to her appear his own. It was from a soldier, — *her lover*. It was plain that they had been betrothed before he left for the continent a year ago; but this was the first letter which he had written to her. It breathed changeless love, and hope, and confidence in her. He was so fascinated that he read it through without pause.

" Laying it down, he sat pale, motionless, almost inanimate. From the hard-won, sunny heights, he was once more cast down into the shadow of death. The second storm of his life began, howling and raging, with yet more awful lulls between. 'Is she not *mine?*' he said, in agony. 'Do I not feel that she is mine? Who will watch over her as I? Who will kiss her soul to life as I? Shall she be torn away from me, when my soul seems to have dwelt with hers forever in an eternal house? But have I not a right to her? Have I not given my life for hers? Is he not a soldier, and are there not many chances that he may never return? And it may be, that although they were engaged in word, soul has never touched soul with them; their love has never reached that point where it passes from the mortal to the immortal, the indissoluble; and so, in a sense, she may yet be free. Will he do for her what I will do? Shall this precious heart of hers, in which I see the buds of so many beauties, be left to wither and die?'

"But here the voice within him cried out, 'Art thou the disposer of destinies? Wilt thou, in a universe where the visible God hath died for the Truth's sake, do evil that a good, which he might neglect or overlook, may be gained? Leave thou her to him, and do thou right.' And he said within himself, 'Now is the real trial for my life! Shall I conquer or no?' And his heart awoke and cried, 'I will. God forgive me for wronging the poor soldier! A brave man, brave at least, is better for her than I.'

"A great strength arose within him, and lifted him up to depart. 'Surely I may kiss her once,' he said. For the crisis was over, and she slept. He stooped towards her face, but before he had reached her lips he saw her eyelids tremble; and he who had longed for the opening of those eyes, as of the gates of heaven, that she might love him, stricken now with fear lest she should love him, fled from her, before the eyelids that hid such strife and such victory from the unconscious maiden had time to unclose. But it was agony, — quietly to pack up his bundle of linen in the room below, when he knew she was lying awake above with her dear, pale face, and living eyes! What remained of his money, except a few shillings, he put up in a scrap of paper, and went out with his bundle in his hand, first to seek a nurse for his friend, and then to go he knew not whither. He met the factory people with whom he had worked, going to dinner, and amongst them a girl who had herself but lately recovered from the fever, and was yet hardly able for work. She was the only friend the sick girl had seemed to have amongst the women at the factory, and she was easily persuaded to go and take charge of her. He put the money in her hand, begging her to use it for the invalid, and promising to send the equivalent of her wages for the time he thought she would have to wait on her. This he easily did by the sale of a ring, which, besides his mother's watch, was the only article of value he had retained. He begged her likewise not to mention his name in the matter; and was foolish enough to expect that she would entirely keep the promise she made him.

"Wandering along the street, purposeless now and bereft,

he spied a recruiting party at the door of a public house; and on coming nearer, found, by one of those strange coincidences which do occur in life, and which have possibly their root in a hidden and wondrous law, that it was a party, perhaps a remnant, of the very regiment in which he had himself served, and in which his misfortune had befallen him. Almost simultaneously with the shock which the sight of the well-known number on the soldiers' knapsacks gave him, arose in his mind the romantic, ideal thought, of enlisting in the ranks of this same regiment, and recovering, as private soldier and unknown, that honor which as officer he had lost. To this determination, the new necessity in which he now stood for action and change of life, doubtless contributed, though unconsciously. He offered himself to the sergeant; and, notwithstanding that his dress indicated a mode of life unsuitable as the antecedent to a soldier's, his appearance, and the necessity for recruits combined, led to his easy acceptance.

"The English armies were employed in expelling the enemy from an invaded and helpless country. Whatever might be the political motives which had induced the government to this measure, the young man was now able to feel that he could go and fight, individually and for his part, in the cause of liberty. He was free to possess his own motives for joining in the execution of the schemes of those who commanded his commanders.

"With a heavy heart, but with more of inward hope and strength than he had ever known before, he marched with his comrades to the seaport and embarked. It seemed to him that, because he had done right in his last trial, here was a new, glorious chance held out to his hand. True, it was a terrible change, to pass from a woman in whom he had hoped to find healing, into the society of rough men, to march with them, '*mit gleichem Tritt und Schritt*,' up to the bristling bayonets or the horrid vacancy of the cannon-mouth. But it was the only cure for the evil that consumed his life.

"He reached the army in safety, and gave himself, with religious assiduity, to the smallest duties of his new position. No one had a brighter polish on his arms, or whiter belts than he. In the necessary movements, he soon became precise to a degree that attracted the attention of his officers; while his character was remarkable for all the virtues belonging to a perfect soldier.

"One day, as he stood sentry, he saw the eyes of his colonel intently fixed on him. He felt his lip quiver, but he compressed and stilled it, and tried to look as unconscious as he could; which effort was assisted by the formal bearing required by his position. Now the colonel, such had been the losses of the regiment, had been promoted from a lieutenancy in the same, and had belonged to it at the time of the ensign's degradation. Indeed, had not the changes in the regiment been so great, he could hardly have escaped so long without discovery. But the poor fellow would have felt that his name was already free of reproach, if he had seen what followed on the close inspection which had awakened his apprehensions, and which, in fact, had convinced the colonel of his identity with the disgraced ensign. With a hasty and less soldierly step than usual, the colonel entered his tent, threw himself on his bed, and wept like a child. When he rose he was overheard to say these words, — and these only escaped his lips, — 'He is nobler than I.'.

"But this officer showed himself worthy of commanding such men as this private; for right nobly did he understand and meet his feelings. He uttered no word of the discovery he had made, till years afterwards; but it soon began to be remarked that whenever anything arduous, or in any manner distinguished, had to be done, this man was sure to be of the party appointed. In short, as often as he could, the colonel 'set him in the fore-front of the battle.' Passing through all with wonderful escape, he was soon as much noticed for his reckless bravery, as hitherto for his precision in the discharge of duties bringing only commendation and not honor. But his final lustration was at hand.

"A great part of the army was hastening, by forced marches, to raise the siege of a town which was already on the point of falling into the hands of the enemy. Forming one of a reconnoitring party, which preceded the main body at some considerable distance, he and his companions came suddenly upon one of the enemy's outposts, occupying a high, and on one side precipitous rock, a short way from the town, which it commanded. Retreat was impossible, for they were already discovered, and the bullets were falling amongst them like the first of a hail-storm The only possibility of escape remaining for them was a nearly hopeless improbability. It lay in forcing the post on this steep rock ; which if they could do before assistance came to the enemy, they might, perhaps, be able to hold out, by means of its defences, till the arrival of the army. Their position was at once understood by all ; and, by a sudden, simultaneous impulse, they found themselves half-way up the steep ascent, and in the struggle of a close conflict, without being aware of any order to that effect from their officers. But their courage was of no avail; the advantages of the place were too great; and in a few minutes the whole party was cut to pieces, or stretched helpless on the rock. Our youth had fallen amongst the foremost; for a musket-ball had grazed his skull, and laid him insensible.

" But consciousness slowly returned, and he succeeded at last in raising himself and looking around him. The place was deserted. A few of his friends, alive, but grievously wounded, lay near him. The rest were dead. It appeared that learning the proximity of the English forces from this rencontre with part of their advanced guard, and dreading lest the town, which was on the point of surrendering, should after all be snatched from their grasp, the commander of the enemy's forces had ordered an immediate and general assault; and had for this purpose recalled from their outposts the whole of his troops thus stationed, that he might make the attempt with the utmost strength he could accumulate.

" As the youth's power of vision returned, he perceived, from the height where he lay, that the town was already in the hands of the enemy. But looking down into the level space immediately below him, he started to his feet at once; for a girl, bare-headed, was fleeing towards the rock, pursued by several soldiers. ' Aha ! ' said he, divining her purpose, — the soldiers behind and the rock before her, — ' I will help you to die ! ' And he stooped and wrenched from the dead fingers of a sergeant the sword which they clenched by the bloody hilt. A new throb of life pulsed through him to his very finger-tips; and on the brink of the unseen world he stood, with the blood rushing through his veins in a wild dance of excitement. One who lay near him wounded, but recovered afterwards, said that he looked like one inspired. With a keen eye he watched the chase. The girl drew nigh; and rushed up the path near which he was standing. Close on her footsteps came the soldiers, the distance gradually lessening between them.

"Not many paces higher up was a narrower part of the ascent, where the path was confined by great stones, or pieces of rock. Here had been the chief defence in the preceding assault, and in it lay many bodies of his friends. Thither he went and took his stand.

"On the girl came, over the dead, with rigid hands and flying feet, the bloodless skin drawn tight on her features, and her eyes awfully large and wild. She did not see him, though she bounded past so near that her hair flew in his eyes. 'Never mind!' said he; 'we shall meet soon.' And he stepped into the narrow path just in time to face her pursuers, — between her and them. Like the red lightning the bloody sword fell, and a man beneath it. Cling! clang! went the echoes in the rocks — and another man was down; for, in his excitement, he was a destroying angel to the breathless pursuers. His stature rose, his chest dilated; and as the third foe fell dead, the girl was safe; for her body lay a broken, empty, but undesecrated temple, at the foot of the rock. That moment his sword flew in shivers from his grasp. The next instant he fell pierced to the heart; and his spirit rose triumphant, free, strong, and calm, above the stormy world, which at length lay vanquished beneath him."

"A capital story!" cried our host, the moment the curate had ceased reading. "But you should not have killed him. You should have made a general of him. By heaven! he deserved it."

Mr. Armstrong was evidently much pleased that the colonel so heartily sympathized with his tale. And every one else added some words of commendation. I could not help thinking with myself that he had only embodied the story of his own life in other more striking forms But I knew that, if I said so, he would laugh at me, and answer that all he had done was quite easy to do, — he had found no difficulty in it; whereas this man was a hero, and did the thing that he found very difficult indeed. Still I was sure that the story was at least the outgrowth of his own mind.

"May we ask," I said, "how much of the tale is fact?"

"I am sorry it is not all fact," he answered.

"Tell us how much, then," I said.

"Well, I will tell what made me write it. I heard an old lady at a dinner-table mention that she had once known a young officer who had his sword broken over his head, and was dismissed from the army for cowardice. I began trying first to understand his feelings: then to see how the thing could have happened; and then to discover what could be done for him. And hence the story. That was all, I am sorry to say."

"I thought as much," I rejoined.

"Will you excuse me if I venture to make a remark?" said Mrs. Bloomfield.

"With all my heart," answered the curate.

"It seemed to me that there was nothing Christian in the story. And I cannot help feeling that a clergyman might, therefore, have done better."

"I allow that in words there is nothing Christian," answered Mr. Armstrong; "I am quite ready to allow also that it might have been better if something of the kind you mean had been expressed in it. The whole thing, however, is only a sketch. But I cannot allow that, in spirit and scope, it is anything other than Christian, or indeed anything but Christian. It seems to me that the whole might be used as a Christian parable."

While the curate spoke, I had seen Adela's face flush; but the cause was not *visible* to me. As he uttered the last words, a hand was laid on his shoulder, and Harry's voice said:—

"At your parables again, Ralph?"

He had come in so gently that the only sign of his entrance had been the rose-light on Adela's cheeks. — Was he the sun? And was she a cloud of the east?

"Glad to see you safe amongst us again," said the colonel, backed by almost every one of the company.

"What's your quarrel with my parables, Harry?" said the curate.

"Quarrel? None at all. They are the delight of my heart.

I only wish you would give our friends one of your best, — 'The Castle,' for instance."

" Not yet a while, Harry. It is not my turn for some time, I hope. Perhaps Miss Cathcart will be tired of the whole affair, before it comes round to me again."

" Then I shall deserve to be starved of stories all the rest of my life," answered Adela, laughing.

" If you will allow me, then," said Harry, " I will give you a parable, called ' The Lost Church,' from the German poet, Uhland."

" Softly, Harry," said his brother; " you are ready enough with what is not yours to give; but where is your own story that you promised, and which indeed we should have a right to demand, whether you had promised it or not ? "

" I am working at it, Ralph, in my spare moments, which are not very many; and I want to choose the right sort of night to tell it in, too. This one wouldn't do at all. There's no moon."

" If it is a horrid story, it is a pity you did not read it last time, before you set out to cross the moor."

" Oh, that night would not have done at all. A night like that drives all fear out of one's head. But, indeed, it is not finished yet. — May I repeat the parable now, Miss Cathcart?"

" What do you mean by *a parable*, Mr. Henry ? " interrupted Mrs. Cathcart. " It sounds rather profane to me."

" I mean a picture in words, where more is meant than meets the ear."

" But why call it a parable ? "

" Because it is one."

" Why not speak in plain words then ? "

" Because a good parable is plainer than the plainest words. You remember what Tennyson says, — that

" ' truth embodied in a tale
Shall enter in at lowly doors' ? "

" Goethe," said the curate, " has a little parable about poems, which is equally true about parables : —

" ' Poems are painted window-panes.
If one looks from the square into the church,
Dusk and dimness are his gains, —
Sir Philistine is left in the lurch.

The sight, so seen, may well enrage him,
Nor any words henceforth assuage him.
  But come just inside what conceals;
Cross the holy threshold quite —
All at once, 'tis rainbow-bright;
Device and story flash to light;
  A gracious splendor truth reveals.
This, to God's children, is full measure;
It edifies and gives them pleasure.' "

"I can't follow that," said Adela.

"I will write it out for you," said Harry; "and then you will be able to follow it perfectly."

"Thank you very much. Now for your parable."

"It is called 'The Lost Church'; and I assure you it is full of meaning."

"I hope I shall be able to find it out."

"You will find the more the longer you think about it.

" ' Oft in the far wood, overhead,
    Tones of a bell are heard obscurely;
How old the sounds no sage has said,
    Or yet explained the story surely.
From the lost church, the legend saith,
    Out on the winds, the ringeth goeth;
Once full of pilgrims was the path, —
    Now, where to find it, no one knoweth.

" ' Deep in the wood I lately went,
    Where no foot-trodden path is lying;
From the time's woe and discontent,
    My heart went forth to God in sighing.
When in the forest's wild repose,
    I heard the ringing somewhat clearer;
The higher that my longing rose,
    Downward it rang the fuller, nearer.

" ' So on its thoughts my heart did brood,
    My sense was with the sound so busy,
That I have never understood
    How I clomb up the height so dizzy.
To me it seemed a hundred years
    Had passed away in dreaming, sighing, —
When lo! high o'er the clouds, appears
    An open space in sunlight lying.

" ' The heaven, dark-blue, above it bowed;
    The sun shone o'er it, large and glowing;
Beneath, a minster's structure proud
    Stood in the gold light, golden showing.

It seemed on those great clouds, sun-clear,
  Aloft to hover, as on pinions;
Its spire-point seemed to disappear,
  Melting away in high dominions.

" ' The bell's clear tones, entrancing, full, —
  The quivering tower, they, booming, swung it;
No human hand the rope did pull, —
  The holy storm-winds sweeping rung it,
The storm, the stream, came down, came near,
  And seized my heart with longing holy;
Into the church I went, with fear,
  With trembling step, and gladness lowly.

" ' The threshold crossed — I cannot show
  What in me moved: words cannot paint it.
Both dark and clear, the windows glow
  With noble forms of martyrs sainted.
I gazed and saw — transfigured glory!
  The pictures swell and break their barriers;
I saw the world and all its story
  Of holy women, holy warriors.

" ' Down at the altar I sank slowly;
  My heart was like the face of Stephen,
Aloft, upon the arches holy,
  Shone out in gold the glow of heaven.
I prayed; I looked again; and lo!
  The dome's high sweep had flown asunder;
The heavenly gates wide open go,
  And every veil unveils a wonder.

" ' What gloriousness I then beheld,
  Kneeling in prayer, silent and wondrous;
What sounds triumphant on me swelled,
  Like organs and like trumpets thunderous, —
My mortal words can never tell;
  But who for such is sighing sorest,
Let him give heed unto the bell
  That dimly soundeth in the forest.' "

" Splendid ! " cried the school-master, with enthusiasm.

" What is the lost church ? " asked Mrs. Cathcart.

" No one can tell, but him who finds it, like the poet," answered the curate.

" But I suppose *you* at least consider it the Church of England," returned the lady, with one of her sweetest attempts at a smile.

" God forbid ! " exclaimed the clergyman, with a kind of sacred horror.

"Not the Church of England!" cried Mrs. Cathcart, in a tone of horror likewise, dashed with amazement.

"No, madam, — the Church of God; the great cathedral-church of the universe; of which Church I trust the Church of England is a little Jesus-chapel."

"God bless you, Mr. Armstrong!" cried the school-master.

The colonel likewise showed some sign of emotion. Mrs. Cathcart looked set-down and indignant. Percy stared. Adela and Harry looked at each other.

"Whoever finds God in his own heart," said the clergyman, solemnly, "has found the lost Church, — the Church of God."

And he looked at Adela as he spoke. She cast down her eyes, and thanked him with her heart.

A silence followed.

"Harry, you must come up with your story next time — positively," said Mr. Armstrong, at length.

"I don't think I can. I cannot undertake to do so, at all events."

"Then what is to be done? — I have it. Lizzie, my dear, you have got that story you wrote once for a Christmas paper, have you not?"

"Yes, I have, Ralph; but that is far too slight a thing to be worth reading here."

"It will do at least to give Harry a chance for his. I mustn't praise it 'afore fowk,' you know."

"But it was never quite finished, — at least so people said."

"Well, you can finish it to-morrow well enough."

"I haven't time."

"You needn't be working at that — all day long and every day. There is no such hurry."

The blank indicates a certain cessation of intelligible sound occasioned by the close application of Lizzie's palm to Ralph's lips. She did not dare, however, to make any further opposition to his request.

"I think we have some claim on you, Mrs. Armstrong," said the host. "It will be my sister's turn next time, and after that Percy's."

Percy gave a great laugh; and his mother said, with a slight toss of her head: —

"I am not so fond of being criticised myself!"

"Has criticism been *your* occupation, Mrs. Cathcart," I said, "during our readings? If so, then indeed we have a claim on you greater than I had supposed."

She could not hide some degree of confusion and annoyance. But I had had my revenge, and I had no wish for her story; so I said nothing more.

We parted with the understanding that Mrs. Armstrong would read her story on the following Monday.

Again, before he took his leave, Mr. Harry had a little therapeutic *tête-à-tête* with Miss Adela, which lasted about two minutes, Mrs. Cathcart watching them every second of the time, with her eyes as round and wide as she could make them, for they were by nature very long, and by art very narrow, for she rarely opened them to any width at all. They were not pleasant eyes, those eyes of Mrs. Cathcart's. Percy's were like them, only better, for though they had a reddish tinge he did open them wider.

CHAPTER XIV.

MY UNCLE PETER.

"Why don't you write a story, Percy?" said his mother to him next morning at breakfast.

"Plenty of quill-driving at Somerset-House, mother. I prefer something else in the holidays."

"But I don't like to see you showing to disadvantage, Percy," said his uncle, kindly. "Why don't you try?"

"The doctor-fellow hasn't read one yet. And I don't think he will."

"Have patience. I think he will."

"I don't care. I don't want to hear it. It's all a confounded bore. They're nothing but goody humbug, or sentimental whining. His would be sure to smell of black draught. I'm not partial to drugs."

The mother frowned, and the uncle tried to smile kindly and excusingly. Percy rose and left the room.

"You see he's jealous of the doctor," remarked his mother, with an upward toss of the head.

The colonel did not reply, and I ventured no remark.

"There is a vein of essential vulgarity in both the brothers," said the lady.

"I don't think so," returned the colonel; and there the conversation ended.

Adela was practising at her piano the greater part of the day. The weather would not admit of a walk.

When we were all seated once more for our reading, and Mrs. Armstrong had her paper in her hand, after a little delay of apparent irresolution, she said all at once : —

"Ralph, I can't read. Will you read it for me ?"

"Do try to read it yourself, my dear," said her husband.

"I am sure I shall break down," she answered.

"If you were able to write it, surely you are able to read it," said the colonel. "I know what my difficulty would be."

"It is a very different thing to read one's own writing. I could read anything else well enough. Will you read it for me, Henry ?"

"With pleasure, if it must be any other than yourself. I know your handwriting nearly as well as my own. It's none of your usual lady-hands, — all point and no character. But what do you say, Ralph ?"

"Read it by all means, if she will have it so. The company has had enough of my reading. It will be a change of voice at least."

I saw that Adela looked pleasedly expectant.

"Pray don't look for much," said Mrs. Armstrong, in a pleading tone. "I assure you it is nothing, or at best a mere trifle. But I could not help myself, without feeling obstinate. And my husband lays so much on the cherished obstinacy of Lady Macbeth, holding that to be the key to her character, that he has terrified me from every indulgence of mine."

She laughed very sweetly ; and, her husband joining in the laugh, all further hindrance was swept away in the music of their laughter ; and Harry, taking the papers from his sister's hand, commenced at once. It was partly in print, and partly in manuscript.

"I will tell you the story of my Uncle Peter, who was born on Christmas day. He was very anxious to die on Christmas day as well; but I must confess that was rather ambitious in Uncle Peter. Shakespeare is said to have been born on St. George's day, and there is some ground for believing that he died on St. George's day. He thus fulfilled a cycle. But we cannot expect that of any but great men, and Uncle Peter was not a great man, though I think I shall be able to show that he was a good man. The only pieces of selfishness I ever discovered in him were, his self-gratulation at having been born on Christmas day, and the ambition with regard to his death, which I have just recorded; and that this selfishness was not of a kind to be very injurious to his fellow-men, I think I shall be able to show as well.

"The first remembrance that I have of him is his taking me one Christmas eve to the largest toy-shop in London, and telling me to choose any toy whatever that I pleased. He little knew the agony of choice into which this request of his — for it was put to me as a request, in the most polite, loving manner — threw his astonished nephew. If a general right of choice from the treasures of the whole world had been unanimously voted me, it could hardly have cast me into greater perplexity. I wandered about, staring like a distracted ghost at the 'wealth of Ormus and of Ind,' displayed about me. Uncle Peter followed me with perfect patience; nay, I believe, with a delight that equalled my perplexity, for, every now and then, when I looked round to him with a silent appeal for sympathy in the distressing dilemma into which he had thrown me, I found him rubbing his hands and spiritually chuckling over his victim. Nor would he volunteer the least assistance to save me from the dire consequences of too much liberty. How long I was in making up my mind I cannot tell; but as I look back upon this splendor of my childhood, I feel as if I must have wandered for weeks through interminable forest-alleys of toy-bearing trees. As often as I read the story of Aladdin, — and I read it now and then still, for I have children about, and their books about, — the subterranean orchard of jewels always brings back to my inward vision the

me that Christmas eve. As soon as, in despair of choosing
well, I had made a desperate plunge at decision, my Uncle
Peter, as if to forestall any supervention of repentance, began
buying like a maniac, giving me everything that took his
fancy or mine, till we and our toys nearly filled the cab which
he called to take us home.

" Uncle.Peter was a little, round man, not *very* fat, resembling both in limbs and features an overgrown baby. And I
believe the resemblance was not merely an external one; for,
though his intellect was quite up to par, he retained a degree of
simplicity of character and of tastes that was not childlike only,
but bordered, sometimes, upon the childish. To look at him,
you could not have fancied a face or a figure with less of the
romantic about them; yet I believe that the whole region of
his brain was held in fee-simple, whatever that may mean, by
a race of fairy architects, who built aerial castles therein,
regardless of expense. His imagination was the most distin-
guishing feature of his character. And, to hear him defend
any of his extravagances, it would·appear that he considered
himself especially privileged in that respect. ' Ah, my dear,'
he would say to my mother when she expostulated with him
on making some present far beyond the small means he at that
time possessed, ' ah, my dear, you see I was born on Christmas
-day.' Many a time he would come in from town, where he
was a clerk in a merchant's office, with the water running out
of his boots, and his umbrella carefully tucked under his arm;
and we would know very well that he had given the last cop-
pers he had, for his omnibus home, to some beggar or crossing-
sweeper, and had then been so delighted with the pleasure he had
given, that he forgot to make the best of it by putting up his
umbrella. Home he would trudge, in his worn suit of black,
with his steel watch-chain and bunch of ancestral seals swing-
ing and ringing from his fob, and the rain running into his
trowsers pockets, to the great endangerment of the health of
his cherished old silver watch, which never went wrong, because
it was put right every day by St. Paul's. He was quite poor
then, as I have said. I do not think he had more than a hundred pounds a year, and he must have been five and thirty. I
suppose his employers showed their care for the morals of their
clerks. by never allowing them any margin to misspend. But

Uncle Peter lived in constant hope and expectation of some unexampled good luck befalling him; 'for,' said he, 'I was born on Christmas day.'

"He was never married. When people used to jest with him about being an old bachelor, he used to smile, for anything would make him smile; but I was a very little boy indeed when I began to observe that the smile on such occasions was mingled with sadness, and that Uncle Peter's face looked very much as if he were going to cry. But he never said anything on the subject, and not even my mother knew whether he had had any love-story or not. I have often wondered whether his goodness might not come in part from his having lost some one very dear to him, and having his life on earth purified by the thoughts of her life in heaven. But I never found out. After his death, — for he did die, though not on Christmas day, — I found a lock of hair folded in paper with a date on it, — that was all, — in a secret drawer of his old desk. The date was far earlier than my first recollections of him. I reverentially burnt it with fire.

"He lived in lodgings by himself not far from our house; and, when not with us, was pretty sure to be found seated in his easy-chair, for he was fond of his simple comforts, beside a good fire, reading by the light of one candle. He had his tea always as soon as he came home, and some buttered toast or a hot muffin, of which he was sure to make me eat three-quarters if I chanced to drop in upon him at the right hour, which, I am rather ashamed to say, I not unfrequently did. He dared not order another, as I soon discovered. Yet I fear that did not abate my appetite for what there was. You see, I was never so good as Uncle Peter. When he had finished his tea, he turned his chair to the fire and read, — what do you think? Sensible Travels and Discoveries, or Political Economy, or Popular Geology? No: Fairy Tales, as many as he could lay hold of; and when they failed him, Romances or Novels. Almost anything in this way would do that was not bad. I believe he had read every word of Richardson's novels, and most of Fielding's and De Foe's. But once I saw him throw a volume in the fire, which he had been fidgeting over for a while. I was just finishing a sum I had brought across to him to help me with. I looked up and saw the volume in the fire.

The heat made it writhe open, and I saw the author's name, and that was *Sterne*. He had bought it at a book-stall as he came home. He sat awhile, and then got up and took down his Bible and began reading a chapter in the New Testament, as if for an antidote to the book he had destroyed."

"I put in that piece," said the curate.

"But Uncle Peter's luck came at last, — at least, he thought it did, when he received a lawyer's letter announcing the *demise* of a cousin of whom he had heard little for a great many years, although they had been warm friends while at school together. This cousin had been brought up to some trade in the wood line, — had been a cooper or a carpenter, and had somehow or other got landed in India, and, though not in the Company's service, had contrived in one way and another to amass what might be called a large fortune in any rank of life. I am afraid to mention the amount of it, lest it should throw discredit on my story. The whole of this fortune he left to Uncle Peter, for he had no nearer relation, and had always remembered him with affection.

"I happened to be seated beside my uncle when the lawyer's letter arrived. He was reading 'Peter Wilkins.' He laid down the book with reluctance, thinking the envelope contained some advertisement of slaty coal for his kitchen-fire, or cottony silk for his girls' dresses. Fancy my surprise when my little uncle jumped up on his chair, and thence on the table, upon which he commenced a sort of demoniac hornpipe. But that sober article of furniture declined giving its support to such proceedings for a single moment, and fell with an awful crash to the floor. My uncle was dancing amidst its ruins like Nero in blazing Rome, when he was reduced to an awful sense of impropriety by the entrance of his landlady. I was sitting in open-mouthed astonishment at my uncle's extravagance, when he suddenly dropped into his chair like a lark into its nest, leaving heaven silent. But silence did not reign long.

"'*Well!* Mr. Belper,' began his landlady, in a tone as difficult of description as it is easy of conception, for her fists had already planted themselves in her own opposing sides. But, to my astonishment, my uncle was not in the least awed, although I am sure, however much he tried to hide it, that I have often seen him tremble in his shoes at the distant roar of this tigress. But it is wonderful how much courage a pocketful of sovereigns will give. It is far better for rousing the pluck of a man than any number of bottles of wine in his head. What a brave thing a whole fortune must be then!

"'Take that rickety old thing away,' said my uncle.

"'Rickety, Mr. Belper! I'm astonished to hear a decent gentleman like you slander the very table as you've eaten' off, for the last —'

"'We won't be precise to a year, ma'am,' interrupted my uncle.

"'And if you will have little scapegraces of neveys into my house to break the furniture, why, them as breaks pays, Mr. Belper.'

"'Very well. Of course I will pay for it. I broke it myself, ma'am; and if you don't get out of my room I'll —'

"Uncle Peter jumped up once more, and made for the heap of ruins in the middle of the floor. The landlady vanished in a moment, and my uncle threw himself again into his chair, and absolutely roared with laughter.

"'Shan't we have rare fun, Charlie, my boy?' said he at last, and went off into another fit of laughter.

"'Why, uncle, what is the matter with you?' I managed to say, in utter bewilderment.

"'Nothing but luck, Charlie. It's gone to my head. I'm not used to it, Charlie, that's all. I'll come all right by and by. Bless you, my boy!'

"What do you think was the first thing my uncle did to relieve himself of the awful accession of power which had just befallen him? The following morning he gathered together every sixpence he had in the house, and went out of one grocer's shop into another, and out of one baker's shop into another, until he had changed the whole into three-penny pieces. Then he walked to town, as usual, to business. But one or two of his friends who were walking the same way, and followed behind him, could not think what Mr. Belper was about. Every crossing that he came to he made use of to cross to the other side. He crossed and recrossed the same street twenty times, they said. But at length they observed, that, with a legerdemain worthy of

a professor, he slipped something into every sweeper's hand as
he passed him. It was one of the threepenny pieces. When he
walked home in the evening, he had nothing to give, and besides
went through one of the wet experiences to which I have already
alluded. To add to his discomfort, he found, when he got home,
that his tobacco-jar was quite empty, so that he was forced to put
on his wet shoes again, — for he never, to the end of his days,
had more than one pair at a time, — in order to come across to
my mother to borrow sixpence. Before the legacy was paid to
him, he went through a good many of the tortures which result
from being ' a king and no king.' The inward consciousness
and the outward possibility did not in the least correspond. At
length, after much much manœuvring with the lawyers, who
seemed to sympathize with the departed cousin in this, that
they, too, would prefer keeping the money till death parted them
and it, he succeeded in getting a thousand pounds of it on
Christmas eve.

" ' NOW ! ' said Uncle Peter, in enormous capitals. That
night a thundering knock came to our door. We were all
sitting in our little dining-room, — father, mother, and seven
children of us, — talking about what we should do next day.
The door opened, and in came the most grotesque figure you
could imagine. It was seven feet high at least, without any
head, a mere walking tree-stump, as far as shape went, only
it looked soft. The little ones were terrified, but not the bigger ones of us; for from top to toe (if it had a toe) it was
covered with toys of every conceivable description, fastened on
to it somehow or other. It was a perfect treasure-cave of Ali
Baba turned inside out. We shrieked with delight. The
figure stood perfectly still, and we gathered round it in a group
to have a nearer view of the wonder. We then discovered that
there were tickets on all the articles, which we supposed at first
to record the price of each. But, upon still closer examination, we discovered that every one of the tickets had one or other
of our names upon it. This caused a fresh explosion of joy.
Nor was it the children only that were thus remembered. A
little box bore my mother's name. When she opened it, we
saw a real gold watch and chain, and seals and dangles of
every sort, of useful and useless kind; and my mother's initials
were on the watch. My father had a silver flute, and to the

music of it we had such a dance! the strange figure, now considerably lighter, joining in it without uttering a word. During the dance one of my sisters, a very sharp-eyed little puss, espied about half way up the monster two bright eyes looking out of a shadowy depth of something like the skirts of a great-coat. She peeped and peeped; and at length, with a perfect scream of exultation, cried out, 'It's Uncle Peter! It's Uncle Peter!' The music ceased; the dance was forgotten; we flew upon him like a pack of hungry wolves; we tore him to the ground; despoiled him of coats, and plaids, and elevating sticks; and discovered the kernel of the beneficent monster in the person of real Uncle Peter; which, after all, was the best present he could have brought us on Christmas eve, for we had been very dull for want of him, and had been wondering why he did not come.

"But Uncle Peter had laid great plans for his birthday, and for the carrying out of them he took me into his confidence, — I being now a lad of fifteen, and partaking sufficiently of my uncle's nature to enjoy at least the fun of his benevolence. He had been for some time perfecting his information about a few of the families in the neighborhood; for he was a bit of a gossip, and did not turn his landlady out of the room when she came in with a whisper of news, in the manner in which he had turned her out when she came to expostulate about the table. But she knew her lodger well enough never to dare to bring him any scandal. From her he had learned that a certain artist in the neighborhood was very poor. He made inquiry about him where he thought he could hear more, and finding that he was steady and hard-working (Uncle Peter never cared to inquire whether he had genius or not; it was enough to him that the poor fellow's pictures did not sell), resolved that he should have a more pleasant Christmas than he expected. One other chief outlet for his brotherly love, in the present instance, was a dissenting minister and his wife, who had a large family of little children. They lived in the same street with himself. Uncle Peter was an unwavering adherent to the Church of England, but he would have felt himself a dissenter at once if he had excommunicated any one by withdrawing his sympathies from him. He knew that this minister was a thoroughly good man, and he had even gone to hear him preach once or twice. He knew, too, that his congregation was not the more liberal to him that he was liberal to all men. So he resolved that he would act the part of one of the black angels that brought bread and meat to Elijah in the wilderness. Uncle Peter would never have pretended to rank higher than one of the foresaid ravens.

"A great part of the forenoon of Christmas day was spent by my uncle and me in preparations. The presents he had planned were many, but I will only mention two or three of them in particular. For the minister and his family he got a small bottle with a large mouth. This he filled as full of new sovereigns as it would hold; labelled it outside, '*Pickled Mushrooms;*' 'for doesn't it grow in the earth without any seed?' said he; and then wrapped it up like a grocer's parcel. For the artist, he took a large shell from his chimney-piece; folded a fifty-pound note in a bit of paper, which he tied up with a green ribbon; inserted the paper in the jaws of the shell, so that the ends of the ribbon should hang out; folded it up in paper and sealed it; wrote outside, '*Inquire within;*' enclosed the whole in a tin box and directed it, '*With Christmas-day's compliments;*' 'for wasn't I born on Christmas day?' concluded Uncle Peter for the twentieth time that forenoon. Then there were a dozen or two of the best port he could get, for a lady who had just had a baby, and whose husband and his income he knew from business relations. Nor were the children forgotten. Every house in his street and ours, in which he knew there were little ones, had a parcel of toys and sweet things prepared for it.

"As soon as the afternoon grew dusky, we set out with as many as we could carry. A slight disguise secured me from discovery, my duty being to leave the parcels at the different houses. In the case of the more valuable of them, my duty was to ask for the master or mistress, and see the packet in safe hands. In this I was successful in every instance. It must have been a great relief to my uncle when the number of parcels were sufficiently diminished to restore to him the use of his hands, for to him they were as necessary for rubbing as a tail is to a dog for wagging, — in both cases for electrical reasons, no doubt. He dropped several parcels in the vain attempt to hold them and perform the usual frictional move-

ment notwithstanding; so he was compelled instead to go
through a kind of solemn pace, which got more and more rapid
as the parcels decreased in number, till it became at last, in
its wild movements, something like a Highlander's sword-
dance. We had to go home several times for more, keeping the
best till the last. When Uncle Peter saw me give the 'pickled mushrooms' into the hands of the lady of the house, he
uttered a kind of laugh, strangled into a crow, which startled
the good lady, who was evidently rather alarmed already at
the weight of the small parcel, for she said, with a scared
look : —

"'It's not gunpowder, is it?'

"'No,' I said; 'I think it's shot.'

"'Shot!' said she, looking even more alarmed. 'Don't
you think you had better take it back again?'

"She held out the parcel to me, and made as if she would
shut the door.

"'Why, ma'am,' I answered, 'you would not have me
taken up for stealing it?'

"It was a foolish reply; but it answered the purpose if not
the question. She kept the parcel and shut the door. When
I looked round I saw my uncle going through a regular series
of convolutions, corresponding exactly to the bodily contortions he must have executed at school every time he received
a course of what they call *palmies* in Scotland; if, indeed,
Uncle Peter was ever even suspected of improper behavior at
school. It consisted first of a dance, then a double-up; then
another dance, then another double-up, and so on.

"'Some stupid hoax, I suppose!' said the artist, as I put
the parcels into his hands. He looked gloomy enough, poor
fellow!

"'Don't be too sure of that, if you please,' sir, said I, and
vanished.

"Everything was a good joke to uncle all that evening.

"'Charlie,' said he, 'I never had such a birthday in my
life before; but, please God, now I've begun, this will not
be the last of the sort. But, you young rascal, if you split,
why, I ll thrash the life out of you. No, I won't,' — here
my uncle assumed a dignified attitude, and concluded with

mock solemnity, — 'no, I won't. I will cut you off with a shilling.'

"This was a *crescendo* passage, ending in a howl, upon which he commenced once more an edition of the Highland fling, with impromptu variations.

"When all the parcels were delivered, we walked home together to my uncle's lodgings, where he gave me a glass of wine and a sovereign for my trouble. I believe I felt as rich as any of them.

"But now I must tell you the romance of my uncle's life. I do not mean the suspected hidden romance, for that no one knew, — except, indeed, a dead one knew all about it. It was a later romance, which, however, nearly cost him his life once.

"One Christmas eve we had been occupied, as usual, with the presents of the following Christmas day, and — will you believe it? — in the same lodgings too, for my uncle was a thorough Tory in his hatred of change. Indeed, although two years had passed, and he had had the whole of his property at his disposal since the legal term of one year, he still continued to draw his salary of £100, of Messrs. Buff and Codgers. One Christmas eve, I say, I was helping him to make up parcels, when, from a sudden impulse, I said to him : —

"'How good you are, uncle!'

"'Ha! ha! ha!' laughed he; 'that's the best joke of all. Good, my boy! Ha! ha! ha! Why, Charlie, you don't fancy I care one atom for all these people, do you? I do it all to please myself. Ha! ha! ha! It's the cheapest pleasure at the money, considering the quality, that I know. That *is* a joke. Good, indeed! Ha! ha! ha!'

"I am happy to say I was an old enough bird not to be caught with this metaphysical chaff. But my uncle's face grew suddenly very grave, even sad in its expression; and after a pause he resumed, but this time without any laughing : —

"'Good, Charlie! Why, I'm no use to anybody.'

"'You do me good, anyhow, uncle,' I answered. 'If I'm not a better man for having you for an uncle, why, I shall be a great deal the worst, that's all.'

"'Why, there it is!' rejoined my uncle; 'I don't know whether I do good or harm. But for you, Charlie, you're a good boy, and don't want any good done to you. It would break my heart, Charlie, if I thought you weren't a good boy.'

"He always called me a boy after I was a grown man. But then I believe he always felt like a boy himself, and quite forgot that we were uncle and nephew.

"I was silent, and he resumed : —

"'I wish I could be of real, unmistakable use to any one. But I fear I am not good enough to have that honor done me.'

"Next morning, — that was Christmas day, — he went out for a walk alone, apparently oppressed with the thought with which the serious part of our conversation on the preceding evening had closed. Of course nothing less than a three-penny piece would do for a crossing-sweeper on Christmas day ; but one tiny little girl touched his heart so that the usual coin was doubled. Still this did not relieve the heart of the giver sufficiently ; for the child looked up in his face in a way, whatever the way was, that made his heart ache. So he gave her a shilling. But he felt no better after that. I am following his own account of feelings and circumstances.

"'This won't do,' said Uncle Peter to himself. 'What is your name?' said Uncle Peter to the little girl.

"'Little Christmas,' she answered.

"'Little Christmas!' exclaimed Uncle Peter. 'I see why that wouldn't do now. What do you mean?'

"'Little Christmas, sir; please, sir.'

"'Who calls you that?'

"'Everybody, sir.'

"'Why do they call you that?'

"'It's my name, sir.'

"'What's your father's name?'

"'I ain't got none, sir.'

"'But you know what his name was?'

"'No, sir.'

"'How did you get your name then? It must be the same as your father's, you know.'

"'Then I suppose my father was Christmas day, sir, for I knows of none else. They always calls me Little Christmas.'

"'H'm! A little sister of mine, I see,' said Uncle Peter to himself.

"'Well, who's your mother?'

"'My aunt, sir. She knows I'm out, sir.'

"There was not the least impudence in the child's tone or manner in saying this. She looked up at him with her gypsy eyes in the most confident manner. She had not struck him in the least as beautiful; but the longer he looked at her, the more he was pleased with her.

"'Is your aunt kind to you?'

"'She gives me my wittles.'

"'Suppose you did not get any money all day, what would she say to you?'

"'Oh, she won't give me a hidin' to-day, sir, supposin' I gets no more. You've giv' me enough already, sir; thank you, sir. I'll change it into ha'pence.'

"'She does beat you sometimes, then?'

"'Oh, my!'

"Here she rubbed her arms and elbows as if she ached all over at the thought, and these were the only parts she could reach to rub for the whole.

"'I *will*,' said Uncle Peter to himself.

"'Do you think you were born on Christmas day, little one?'

"'I think I was once, sir.'

"'I shall teach the child to tell lies if I go on asking her questions in this way,' thought my uncle. 'Will you go home with me?' he said, coaxingly.

"'Yes, sir, if you will tell me where to put my broom, for I must not go home without it, else aunt would wallop me.'

"'I will buy you a new broom.'

"'But aunt would wallop me all the same if I did not bring home the old one for our Christmas fire.'

"'Never mind. I will take care of you. You may bring your broom if you like, though,' he added, seeing a cloud come over the little face.

"'Thank you, sir,' said the child; and, shouldering her broom, she trotted along behind him, as he led the way home.

"But this would not do, either. Before they had gone twelve paces, he had the child in one hand; and before they had gone a second twelve, he had the broom in the other. And so Uncle Peter walked home with his child and his broom. The latter he set down inside the door, and the former he led upstairs to his room. There he seated her on a chair by the fire, and, ringing the bell, asked the landlady to bring a basin of bread and milk. The woman cast a look of indignation and wrath at the poor little immortal. She might have been the impersonation of Christmas day in the catacombs, as she sat with her feet wide apart, and reaching half way down the legs of the chair, and her black eyes staring from the midst of knotted tangles of hair that never felt comb or brush, or were defended from the wind by bonnet or hood. I dare say uncle's poor apartment, with its cases of stuffed birds and its square piano that was used for a cupboard, seemed to her the most sumptuous of conceivable abodes. But she said nothing — only stared. When her bread and milk came, she ate it up without a word, and when she had finished it sat still for a moment, as if pondering what it became her to do next. Then she rose, dropped a courtesy, and said, 'Thank you, sir. Please, sir, where's my broom?'

" 'Oh, but I want you to stop with me, and be my little girl.'

" 'Please, sir, I would rather go to my crossing.'

"The face of Little Christmas lengthened visibly, and she was upon the point of crying. Uncle Peter saw that he had been too precipitate, and that he must woo the child before he could hope to win her; so he asked her for her address. But though she knew the way to her home perfectly, she could give only what seemed to him the most confused directions how to find it. No doubt to her they seemed as clear as day. Afraid of terrifying her by following her, the best way seemed to him to promise her a new frock on the morrow, if she would come and fetch it. Her face brightened so at the sound of a new frock, that my uncle had very little fear of the fault being hers if she did not come.

" 'Will you know the way back, my dear?'

" 'I always know my way anywheres,' answered she. So she was allowed to depart with her cherished broom.

"Uncle Peter took my mother into council upon the affair of the frock. She thought an old one of my sister's would do best. But my uncle had said a *new* frock, and a new one it must be. So next day my mother went with him to buy one, and was excessively amused with his entire ignorance of what was suitable for the child. However, the frock being purchased, he saw how absurd it would be to put a new frock over such garments as she must have below, and accordingly made my mother buy-everything to clothe her completely. With these treasures he hastened home, and found poor Little Christmas and her broom waiting for him outside the door, for the landlady would not let her in. This roused the wrath of my uncle to such a degree, that, although he had borne wrongs innumerable and aggravated for a long period of years without complaint, he walked in and gave her notice that he would leave in a week. I think she expected he would forget all about it before the day arrived; but, with his further designs for Little Christmas, he was not likely to forget it; and I fear I have seldom enjoyed anything so much as the consternation of the woman (whom I heartily hated) when she saw a truck arrive to remove my uncle's few personal possessions from her inhospitable roof. I believe she took her revenge by giving her cronies to understand that she had turned my uncle away at a week's warning for bringing home improper companions to her respectable house. But to return to Little Christmas. She fared all the better for the landlady's unkindness; for my mother took her home and washed her with her own soft hands from head to foot; and then put all the new clothes on her, and she looked charming. How my uncle would have managed I can't think. He was delighted at the improvement in her appearance. I saw him turn round and wipe his eyes with his handkerchief.

" ' Now, Little Christmas, will you come and live with me ? ' said he.

" She pulled the same face, though not quite so long as before, and said, ' I would rather go to my crossing, please, sir.'

" My uncle heaved a sigh and let her go.

" She shouldered her broom, as if it had been the rifle of a giant, and trotted away to her work.

" But next day, and the next, and the next, she was not to be seen at her wonted corner. When a whole week had passed and she did not make her appearance, my uncle was in despair.

" ' You see, Charlie,' said he, ' I am fated to be of no use to anybody, though I was born on Christmas day.'

"The very next day, however, being Sunday, my uncle found her as he went to church. She was sweeping a new crossing. She seemed to have found a lower deep still, for, alas! all her new clothes were gone, and she was more tattered and wretched-looking than before. As soon as she saw my uncle she burst into tears.

"'Look,' she said, pulling up her little frock, and showing her thigh with a terrible bruise upon it; '*she* did it.'

"A fresh burst of tears followed.

"'Where are your new clothes, Little Christmas?' asked my uncle.

"'She sold them for gin, and then beat me awful. Please, sir, I couldn't help it.'

"The child's tears were so bitter, that my uncle, without thinking, said: —

"'Never mind, dear; you shall have another frock.'

"Her tears ceased, and her face brightened for a moment; but the weeping returned almost instantaneously with increased violence, and she sobbed out: —

"'It's no use, sir; she'd only serve me the same, sir.'

"'Will you come home and live with me, then?'

"'Yes, please.'

"She flung her broom from her into the middle of the street. nearly throwing down a cab-horse, betwixt whose fore-legs it tried to pass; then, heedless of the oaths of the man, whom my uncle, had pacified with a shilling, put her hand in that of her friend and trotted home with him. From that day till the day of his death she never left him, — of her own accord, at least.

"My uncle had by this time, got into lodgings with a woman of the right sort, who received the little stray lamb with open arms and open heart. Once more she was washed and clothed from head to foot, and from skin to frock. My uncle never allowed her to go out without him, or some one who was capable of protecting her. He did not think it at all necessary to supply the woman, who might not be her aunt after all, with gin unlimited, for the privilege of rescuing Little Christmas from her cruelty. So he felt that she was in great danger of being carried off, for the sake either of her earnings or her ransom; and, in fact, some very suspicious-looking characters were several times observed prowling about in the neighborhood. Uncle

Peter, however, took what care he could to prevent any report of this reaching the ears of Little Christmas, lest she should live in terror ; and contented himself with watching her carefully. It was some time before my mother would consent to our playing with her freely and beyond her sight ; for it was strange to hear the ugly words which would now and then break from her dear little innocent lips. But she was very easily cured of this, although, of course, some time must pass before she could be quite depended upon. She was a sweet-tempered, loving child. But the love seemed for some time to have no way of showing itself, so little had she been used to ways of love and tenderness. When we kissed her she never returned the kiss, but only stared ; yet whatever we asked her to do she would do as if her whole heart was in it ; and I did not doubt it was. Now I know it was.

" After a few years, when Christmas began to be considered tolerably capable of taking care of herself, the vigilance of my uncle gradually relaxed a little. A month before her thirteenth birthday, as near as my uncle could guess, the girl disappeared. She had gone to the day-school as usual, and was expected home in the afternoon ; for my uncle would never part with her to go to a boarding-school, and yet wished her to have the benefit of mingling with her fellows, and not being always tied to the button-hole of an old bachelor. But she did not return at the usual hour. My uncle went to inquire about her. She had left the school with the rest. Night drew on. My uncle was in despair. He roamed the streets all night ; spoke about his child to every policeman he met ; went to the station-house of the district, and described her ; had bills printed, and offered a hundred pounds' reward for her restoration. All was unavailing. The miscreants must have seen the bills, but feared to repose confidence in the offer. Before the month was out, his clothes were hanging about him like a sack. He could hardly swallow a mouthful ; hardly even sit down to a meal. I believe he loved his Little Christmas every whit as much as if she had been his own daughter, — perhaps more, — for he could not help thinking of what she might have been if he had not rescued her ; and he felt that God had given her to him as certainly as if she had been his own child, only that she had come in another way. He would get out of bed in the middle of the night, unable to sleep, and go wandering up and down the streets, and into dreadful places, sometimes, to try to find her. But fasting and watching could not go on long without bringing friends with them. Uncle Peter was seized with a fever, which grew and grew till his life was despaired of. He was very delirious at times, and then the strangest fancies had possession of his brain. Sometimes he seemed to see the horrid woman she called her aunt, torturing the poor child; sometimes it was old Pagan Father Christmas, clothed in snow and ice, come to fetch his daughter; sometimes it was his old landlady shutting her out in the frost; or himself finding her afterwards, but frozen so hard to the ground that he could not move her to get her in-doors. The doctors seemed doubtful, and gave as their opinion — a decided shake of the head.

"Christmas day arrived. In the afternoon, to the wonder of all about him, although he had been wandering a moment before, he suddenly said: —

"'I was born on Christmas day, you know. This is the first Christmas day that didn't bring me good luck.'

"Turning to me, he added: —

"'Charlie, my boy, it's a good thing ANOTHER besides me was born on Christmas day, isn't it?'

"'Yes, dear uncle,' said I; and it was all I could say. He lay quite quiet for a few minutes, when there came a gentle knock to the street door.

"'That's Chrissy!' he cried, starting up in bed, and stretching out his arms with trembling eagerness. 'And me to say this Christmas day would bring me no good!'

"He fell back on his pillow, and burst into a flood of tears.

"I rushed down to the door, and reached it before the servant. I stared. There stood a girl about the size of Chrissy, with an old, battered bonnet on, and a ragged shawl. She was standing on the door-step, trembling. I felt she was trembling somehow, for I don't think I saw it. She had Chrissy's eyes too, I thought; but the light was dim now, for the evening was coming on.

"All this passed through my mind in a moment, during which she stood silent.

"'What is it?' I said, in a tremor of expectation.

"'Charlie, don't you know me?' she said, and burst into tears.

"We were in each other's arms in a moment, — for the first time. But Chrissy is my wife now. I led her upstairs in triumph, and into my uncle's room.

"'I knew it was my lamb!' he cried, stretching out his arms, and trying to lift himself up, only he was too weak.

"Chrissy flew to his arms. She was very dirty, and her clothes had such a smell of poverty! But there she lay in my uncle's bosom both of them sobbing, for a long time; and when at last she withdrew, she tumbled down on the floor, and there she lay motionless. I was in a dreadful fright, but my mother came in at the moment, while I was trying to put some brandy within her cold lips, and got her into a warm bath, and put her to bed.

"In the morning she was much better, though the doctor would not let her get up for a day or two. I think, however, that was partly for my uncle's sake.

"When at length she entered the room one morning, dressed in her own nice clothes, for there were plenty in the wardrobe in her room, my uncle stretched out his arms to her once more and said: —

"'Ah! Chrissy, I thought I was going to have my own way, and die on Christmas day; but it would have been one too soon, before I had found you, my darling.'

CHAPTER XV.

MY UNCLE PETER. — CONTINUED.

"It was resolved that, on that same evening, Chrissy should tell my uncle her story. We went out to walk together; and, though she was not afraid to go, the least thing startled her. A voice behind her would make her turn pale and look hurriedly round. Then she would smile again, even before the color had had time to come back to her cheeks, and say, 'What a goose I am! But it is no wonder.' I could see, too,

that she looked down at her nice clothes now and then with
satisfaction. She does not like me to say so, but she does
not deny it either, for Chrissy can't tell a story even about her
own feelings. My uncle had given us five pounds each to
spend, and that was jolly. We bought each other such a lot
of things, besides some for other people. And then we came
home and had dinner *tête-à-tête* in my uncle's dining-room; after
which we went up to my uncle's room, and sat over the fire in
the twilight till his afternoon-nap was over, and he was ready
for his tea. This was ready for him by the time he awoke.
Chrissy got up on the bed beside him; I got up at the foot of
the bed, facing her, and we had the tea-tray and plenty of *et
ceteras* between us.

" ' Oh! I *am* happy!' said Chrissy, and began to cry.

" ' So am I, my darling!' rejoined Uncle Peter, and followed her example.

" ' So am I,' said I; 'but I don't mean to cry about it.'
And then I did.

" We all had one cup of tea, and some bread and butter in
silence after this. But when Chrissy had poured out the second
cup for Uncle Peter, she began of her own accord to tell us
her story.

" ' It was very foggy when we came out of school that afternoon, as you may remember, dear uncle.'

" ' Indeed I do,' answered Uncle Peter, with a sigh.

" ' I was coming along the way home with Bessie, — you
know Bessie, uncle, — and we stopped to look in at a bookseller's window, where the gas was lighted. It was full of
Christmas things already. One of them I thought very pretty,
and I was standing staring at it, when all at once I saw that a
big drabby woman had poked herself in between Bessie and me.
She was staring in at the window too. She was so nasty that
I moved away a little from her, but I wanted to have one more
look at the picture. The woman came close to me. I moved
again. Again she pushed up to me. I looked in her face, for
I was rather cross by this time. A horrid feeling, I cannot
tell you what it was like, came over me as soon as I saw her.
I know how it was now, but I did not know then why I was
frightened. I think she saw I was frightened, for she instantly
walked against me, and shoved and hustled me round the cor-

ner, — it was a corner-shop, — and before I knew, I was in
another street. It was dark and narrow. Just at the moment
a man came from the opposite side and joined the woman. Then
they caught hold of my hands, and before my fright would let
me speak I was deep into the narrow lane, for they ran with me
as fast as they could. Then I began to scream, but they said
such horrid words that I was forced to hold my tongue; and in
a minute more they had me inside a dreadful house, where the
plaster was dropping away from the walls, and the skeleton-ribs
of the house were looking through. I was nearly dead with
terror and disgust. I don't think it was a bit less dreadful to
me from having dim recollections of having known such places
well enough at one time of my life. I think that only made me
the more frightened, because so the place seemed to have a claim
upon me. What if I ought to be there, after all, and these
dreadful creatures were my father and mother!

" ' I thought they were going to beat me at once, when the
woman, whom I suspected to be my aunt, began to take off my
frock. I was dreadful frightened, but I could not cry. However it was only my clothes that they wanted. But I cannot
tell you how frightful it was. They took almost everything I
had on, and it was only when I began to scream in despair — sit
still, Charlie, it's all over now — that they stopped, with a nod
to each other, as much as to say, "We can get the rest afterwards." Then they put a filthy frock on me; brought me
some dry bread to eat; locked the door, and left me. It was
nearly dark now. There was no fire. And all my warm clothes
were gone. — Do sit still, Charlie. — I was dreadfully cold.
There was a wretched-looking bed in one corner; but I think I
would have died of cold rather than get into it. And the air
in the place was frightful. How long I sat there in the dark,
I don't know.'

" ' What did you do all the time?' said I.

" ' There was only one thing to be done, Charlie. I think
that is a foolish question to ask.'

" ' Well, what *did* you do, Chrissy?'

" ' Said my prayers, Charlie.'

" ' And then?'

" ' Said them again.'

" ' And nothing else?'

" ' Yes; I tried to get out of the window, but that was of no use; for I could not open it. And it was one story high at least.'

" ' And what did you do next? '

" ' Said over all my hymns.'

" ' And then, — what *did* you do next? '

" ' Why do you ask me so many times? '

" ' Because I want to know.'

" ' Well, I will tell you. — I left my prayers alone; and I began at the beginning, and I told God the whole story, as if he had known nothing about it, from the very beginning when Uncle Peter found me on the crossing down to the minute when I was talking there to him in the dark.'

" ' Ah! my dear,' said my uncle, with faltering voice, ' you felt better after that, I dare say. And here was I in despair about you, and thought he did not care for any of us. I was very naughty, indeed.'

" ' And what next? ' I said.

" ' By and by I heard a noise of quarrelling in the street, which came nearer and nearer. The door was burst open by some one falling against it. Blundering steps came upstairs. The two who had robbed me, evidently tipsy, were trying to unlock the door. At length they succeeded, and tumbled into the room.

" ' Where is the unnatural wretch,' said the woman, ' who ran away and left her own mother in poverty and sickness? ' —

" ' O uncle, can it be that she is my mother? ' said Chrissy, interrupting herself.

" ' I don't think she is,' answered Uncle Peter. ' She only wanted to vex you, my lamb. But it doesn't matter whether she is or not.'

" ' Doesn't it, uncle? — I am ashamed of her.'

" ' But you are God's child. And he can't be ashamed of you. For he gave you the mother you had, whoever she was, and never asked you which you would have. So you need not mind. We ought always to like best to be just what God has made us.'

" ' I am sure of that, uncle. — Well, she began groping about to find me, for it was very dark. I sat quite still, except for trembling all over, till I felt her hands on me, when I jumped up, and she fell on the floor. She began swearing dreadfully, but did not try to get up. I crept away to another corner. I heard the man snoring, and the woman breathing loud. Then I felt my way to the door, but, to my horror, found the man lying across it on the floor, so that I could not open it. Then I believe I cried for the first time. I was nearly frozen to death, and there was all the long night to bear yet. How I got through it, I cannot tell. It did go away. Perhaps God destroyed some of it for me. But when the light began to come through the window, and show me all the filth of the place, the man and the woman lying on the floor, the woman with her head cut and covered with blood, I began to feel that the darkness had been my friend. I felt this yet more when I saw the state of my own dress, which I had forgotten in the dark. I felt as if I had done some shameful thing, and wanted to follow the darkness, and hide in the skirts of it. It was an old gown of some woollen stuff, but it was impossible to tell what, it was so dirty and worn. I was ashamed that even those drunken creatures should wake and see me in it. But the light would come, and it came and came, until at last it waked them up, and the first words were so dreadful! They quarrelled and swore at each other and at me, until I almost thought there couldn't be a God who would let that go on so, and never stop it. But I suppose he wants them to stop, and doesn't care to stop it himself, for he could easily do that of course, if he liked.'

" ' Just right, my darling ! ' said Uncle Peter, with emotion.

" Chrissy saw that my uncle was too much excited by her story, although he tried *not* to show it, and with a wisdom which I have since learned to appreciate, cut it short.

" ' They did not treat me cruelly, though, the worst was, that they gave me next to nothing to eat. Perhaps they wanted to make me thin and wretched-looking, and I believe they succeeded. — Charlie, you'll turn over the cream, if you don't sit still. — Three days passed this way. I have thought all over it, and I think they were a little puzzled how to get rid of me. They had no doubt watched me for a long time, and now they had got my clothes they were afraid. At last one night they took me out. My aunt, if aunt she is, was respectably dressed, — that is, comparatively, — and the man had

a great-coat on, which covered his dirty clothes. They helped
me into a cart which stood at the door, and drove off. I resolved
to watch the way we went. But we took so many turnings
through narrow streets before we came out in a main road, that
I soon found it was all one mass of confusion in my head; and
it was too dark to read any of the names of the streets, for the
man kept as much in the middle of the road as possible. We
drove some miles, I should think, before we stopped at the gate
of a small house with a big porch, which stood alone. My
aunt got out and went up to the house, and was admitted.
After a few minutes she returned, and, making me get out, she
led me up to the house, where an elderly lady stood, holding
the door half open. When we reached it my aunt gave me a
sort of shove in, saying to the lady, "There she is." Then she
said to me, "Come now, be a good girl, and don't tell lies," and,
turning hastily, ran down the steps, and got into the cart at
the gate, which drove off at once the way we had come. The
lady looked at me from head to foot, sternly but kindly too, I
thought, and so glad was I to find myself clear of those dreadful creatures, that I burst out crying. She instantly began
to read me a lecture on the privilege of being placed with
Christian people, who would instruct me how my soul might
be saved, and teach me to lead an honest and virtuous life. I
tried to say that I had led an honest life. But as often as I
opened my mouth to tell anything about myself or my uncle,
or, indeed, to say anything at all, I was stopped by her saying, "Now don't tell lies. Whatever you do, don't tell lies."
This shut me up quite. I could not speak when I knew she
would not believe me. But I did not cry; I only felt my face
get very hot and somehow my backbone grew longer, though
I felt my eyes fixed on the ground.

"'But,' she went on, 'you must change your dress. I
will show you the way to your room, and you will find a print
gown there, which I hope you will keep clean. And above
all things don't tell lies.'

"Here Chrissy burst out laughing, as if it was such fun to
be accused of lying; but presently her eyes filled, and she
made haste to go on.

"'You may be sure I made haste to put on the nice clean
frock, and, to my delight, found other clean things for me as

well. I declare I felt like a princess for a whole day after, notwithstanding the occupation. For I soon found that I had been made over to Mrs. Sprinx, as a servant of all work. I think she must have paid these people for the chance of reclaiming one whom they had represented as at least a great liar. Whether my wages were to be paid to them, or even what they were to be, I never heard. I made up my mind at once that the best thing would be to do the work without grumbling, and do it as well as I could, for that would be doing no harm to any one, but the contrary, while it would give me the better chance of making my escape. But though I was determined to get away the first opportunity, and was miserable when I thought how anxious you would all be about me, yet I confess it was such a relief to be clean and in respectable company, that I caught myself singing once or twice the very first day. But the old lady soon stopped that. She was about in the kitchen the greater part of the day till dinner-time, and taught me how to cook and save my soul both at once.'

" ' Indeed,' interrupted Uncle Peter, ' I have read receipts for the salvation of the soul that sounded very much as if they came out of a cookery book.' And the wrinkles of his laugh went up into his night-cap. Neither Chrissy nor I understood this at the time, but I have often thought of it since.

" Chrissy went on : —

" ' I had finished washing up my dinner things, and sat down for a few minutes, for I was tired. I was staring into the fire, and thinking and thinking how I should get away, and what I should do when I got out of the house, and feeling as if the man and the woman were always prowling about it, and watching me through the window, when suddenly I saw a little boy in a corner of the kitchen, staring at me with great brown eyes. He was a little boy, perhaps about six years old, with a pale face, and very earnest look. I did not speak to him, but waited to see what he would do. A few minutes passed, and I forgot him. But as I was wiping my eyes, which would get wet sometimes, notwithstanding my good fortune, he came up to me, and said in a timid whisper : —

" ' Are you a princess ?'

" ' What makes you think that ?' I said.

" ' You have got such white hands,' he answered.

" ' No, I am not a princess,' I said.

" ' Aren't you Cinderella?'

" ' No, my darling,' I replied; 'but something like her; for they have stolen me away from home and brought me here. I wish I could get away.'

" ' And here I confess I burst into a downright fit of crying.

" ' Don't cry,' said the little fellow, stroking my cheek. ' I will let you out some time. Shall you be able to find your way home all by yourself?'

" ' Yes, I think so,' I answered; but at the same time I felt very doubtful about it, because I always fancied those people watching me. But before either of us spoke again, in came Mrs. Sprinx.

" ' You naughty boy! What business have you to make the servant neglect her work?'

" · For I was still sitting by the fire, and my arm was round the dear little fellow, and his head was leaning on my shoulder.

" ' She's not a servant, auntie!' cried he, indignantly. ' She's a real princess, though of course she won't own to it.'

" ' What lies you have been telling the boy! You ought to be ashamed of yourself. Come along directly. Get the tea at once, Jane.'

" ' My little friend went with his aunt, and I rose and got the tea. But I felt much lighter-hearted since I had the sympathy of the little boy to comfort me. Only I was afraid they would make him hate me. But, although I saw very little of him the rest of the time, I knew they had not succeeded in doing so; for, as often as he could, he would come sliding up to me, saying, "How do you do, princess?" and then run away, afraid of being seen and scolded.

" ' I was getting very desperate about making my escape, for there was a high wall about the place, and the gate was always locked at night. When Christmas eve came, I was nearly crazy with thinking that to-morrow was uncle's birthday; and that I should not be with him. But that very night, after I had gone to my room, the door opened, and in came little Eddie in his night-gown, his eyes looking very bright and black over it.

" 'There, princess!' said he, 'there is the key of the gate Run.'

" 'I took him in my arms and kissed him, unable to speak. He struggled to get free, and ran to the door. There he turned and said : —

" 'You will come back and see me some day, — will you not?'

" 'That I will,' I answered.

" 'That you shall,' said Uncle Peter.

" 'I hid the key, and went to bed, where I lay trembling. As soon as I was sure they must be asleep, I rose and dressed. I had no bonnet or shawl but those I had come in; and, though they disgusted me, I thought it better to put them on. But I dared not unlock the street door, for fear of making a noise. So I crept out of the kitchen window, and then I got out at the gate all safe. No one was in sight. So I locked it again, and threw the key over. But what a time of fear and wandering about I had in the darkness, before I dared to ask any one the way! It was a bright, clear night; and I walked very quietly till I came upon a great wide common. The sky, and the stars, and the wideness frightened me, and made me gasp at first. I felt as if I should fall away from everything into nothing. And it was so lonely! But then I thought of God, and in a moment I knew that what I had thought loneliness was really the presence of God. And then I grew brave again, and walked on. When the morning dawned, I met a brick-layer going to his work, and found that I had been wandering away from London all the time; but I did not mind that. Now I turned my face towards it, though not the way I had come. But I soon got dreadfully tired and faint, and once I think I fainted quite. I went up to a house, and asked for a piece of bread, and they gave it to me, and I felt much better after eating it But I had to rest so often, and got so tired, and my feet got so sore, that — you know how late it was before I got home to my darling uncle.'

" 'And me too!' I expostulated.

" 'And you, too, Charlie,' she answered; and we all cried over again.

" 'This shan't happen any more!' said my uncle.

" After tea was over, he asked for writing-things, and wrote a note, which he sent off.

"The next morning, about eleven, as I was looking out of the window, I saw a carriage drive up and stop at our door.

"'What a pretty little brougham!' I cried. 'And such a jolly horse! Look here, Chrissy!'

"Presently Uncle Peter's bell rang, and Miss Chrissy was sent for. She came down again, radiant with pleasure.

"'What do you think, Charlie! That carriage is mine, — all my own. And I am to go to school in it always. Do come and have a ride in it.'

"You may be sure I was delighted to do so.

"'Where shall we go?' I said.

"'Let us ask uncle if we may go and see the little darling who set me free.'

"His consent was soon obtained, and away we went. It was a long drive, but we enjoyed it beyond everything. When we reached the house, we were shown into the drawing-room. There was Mrs. Sprinx and little Eddie. The lady stared; but the child knew Cinderella at once, and flew into her arms.

"'I knew you were a princess!' he cried. 'There, auntie!'

"But Mrs. Sprinx had put on an injured look, and her hands shook very much.

"'Really, Miss Belper, if that is your name, you have behaved in a most unaccountable way. Why did you not tell me, instead of stealing the key of the gate, and breaking the kitchen window? A most improper way for a young lady to behave, — to run out of the house at midnight!'

"'You forget, madam,' replied Chrissy, with more dignity than I had ever seen her assume, 'that as soon as ever I attempted to open my mouth, you told me not to tell lies. You believed the wicked people who brought me here rather than myself. However, as you will not be friendly, I think we had better go. Come, Charlie!'

"'Don't go, princess,' pleaded little Eddie.

"'But I must, for your auntie does not like me,' said Chrissy.

"'I am sure I always meant to do my duty by you. And I will do so still. Beware, my dear young woman, of the deceitfulness of riches. Your carriage won't save your soul!'

"Chrissy was on the point of saying something rude, as she confessed when we got out; but she did not. She made her bow, turned and walked away. I followed, and poor Eddie would have done so too, but was laid hold of by his aunt. I confess this was not quite proper behavior on Chrissy's part; but I never discovered that till she made me see it. She was very sorry afterwards, and my uncle feared the brougham had begun to hurt her already, as she told me. For she had narrated the whole story to him, and his look first let her see that she had been wrong. My uncle went with her afterwards to see Mrs. Sprinx, and thank her for having done her best; and to take Eddie such presents as my uncle only knew how to buy for children. When he went to school, I know he sent him a gold watch. From that time till now that she is my wife, Chrissy has had no more such adventures; and if Uncle Peter did not die on Christmas day, it did not matter much, for Christmas day makes all the days of the year as sacred as itself."

CHAPTER XVI.

THE GIANT'S HEART.

WHEN Harry had finished reading, the colonel gallantly declared that the story was the best they had had. Mrs. Armstrong received this as a joke, and begged him not to be so unsparing.

"Ah! Mrs. Armstrong," returned he, laughing, "you are not old enough yet to know the truth from a joke. Don't you agree with me about the story, Mrs. Cathcart?"

"I think it is very pretty and romantic. Such men as Uncle Peter are not very common in the world. The story is not too true to Nature."

This she said in a tone intended to indicate superior acquaintance with the world and its nature. I fear Mrs. Cathcart, and some others whom I could name, mean by *Nature* something very bad indeed, which yet an artist is bound to be loyal to.   The colonel, however, seemed to be of a different opinion.

"If there never was such a man as Uncle Peter," said he, "there ought to have been ; and it is all the more reason for putting him into a story that he is not to be found in the world."

"Bravo!" cried I.   "You have answered a great question in a few words."

"I don't know," rejoined our host.   "Have I ? It seems to me as plain as the catechism."

I thought he might have found a more apt simile, but I held my peace.

Next morning, I walked out in the snow.   Since the storm of that terrible night, it had fallen again quietly and plentifully; and now in the sunlight, the world — houses and trees, ponds and rivers — was like a creation, more than blocked out, but far from finished — in marble.

"And this," I said to myself, as I regarded the wondrous loveliness with which the snow had at once clothed and disfigured the bare branches of the trees, "this is what has come of the chaos of falling flakes!   To this repose of beauty has that storm settled and sunk !   Will it not be so with our mental storms as well ? "

But here the figure displeased me ; for those were not the true right shapes of the things ; and the truth does not stick to things, but shows itself out of them.

"This lovely show," I said, "is the result of a busy fancy. This white world is the creation of a poet such as Shelley, in whom the fancy was too much for the intellect.   Fancy settles upon anything ; half destroys its form, half beautifies it with something that is not its own.   But the true creative imagination, the form-seer, and the form-bestower, falls like the rain in the spring night, vanishing amid the roots of the trees ; not settling upon them in clouds of wintry white, but breaking forth from them in clouds of summer green."

And then my thoughts very naturally went from Nature to my niece ; and I asked myself whether within the last few days I had not seen upon her countenance the expression of a mental spring-time.   For the mind has its seasons four, with many changes, as well as the world, only that the cycles are generally longer; they can hardly be more mingled than as here in our climate.

Let me confess, now that the subject of the confession no longer exists, that there had been something about Adela that, pet-child of mine as she was, had troubled me. In all her behavior, so far as I had had any opportunity of judging, she had been as good as my desires at least. But there was a want in her face, a certain flatness of expression, which I did not like. I love the common with all my heart, but I hate the commonplace ; and, foolish old bachelor that I am, the commonplace in a woman troubles me, annoys me, makes me miserable. Well, it was something of the commonplace in Adela's expression that had troubled me. Her eyes were clear, with lovely long dark lashes, but somehow the light in them had been always the same ; and occasionally when I talked to her of the things I most wished to care about, there was such an immobile condition of the features, associated with such a ready assent in words, that I felt her notion of what I meant must be something very different indeed from what I did mean. Her face looked as if it were made of something too thick for the inward light to shine through, — wax, and not living muscle and skin. The fact was, the light within had not been kindled, else that face of hers would have been ready enough to let it shine out. Hitherto she had not seemed to me to belong at all to that company that praises God with sweet looks, as Thomas Hood describes Ruth as doing. What was wanting I had found it difficult to define. Her soul was asleep. She was dreaming a child's dreams, instead of seeing a woman's realities, — realities that awake the swift play of feature, as the wind of God arouses the expression of a still landscape. So there seemed after all a gulf between her and me. She did not see what I saw, feel what I felt, seek what I sought. Occasionally even, the delicate young girl, pure and bright as the snow that hung on the boughs around me, would shock the wizened old bachelor with her worldliness, — a worldliness that lay only in the use of current worldly phrases of selfish contentment, or selfish care. Ah! how little do young beauties understand of the pitiful emotions which they sometimes rouse in the breasts of men whom they suppose to be absorbed in admiration of them ! But for faith that these girls are God's work and only

half made yet, one would turn from them with sadness, almost
painful dislike, and take refuge with some noble-faced grandmother, or withered old maid, whose features tell of sorrow
and patience. And the beauty would think with herself that
such a middle-aged gentleman did not admire pretty girls, and
was severe and unkind and puritanical; whereas it was the
lack of beauty that made him turn away; the disappointment
of a face, — dull, that ought to be radiant; or the presence
of only that sort of beauty, which in middle age, except
the deeper nature should meantime come into play, would be
worse than commonplace, — would be mingled with the trail
of more or less guilty sensuality. Many a woman at forty is
repulsive, whom common men found at twenty irresistibly attractive; and many a woman at seventy is lovely to the eyes
of the man who would have been compelled to allow that she
was decidedly plain at seventeen.

"Maidens' bairns are aye weel guided," says the Scotch
proverb; and the same may be said of bachelors' wives. So
I will cease the strain, and return to Adela, the change in whom
first roused it.

Of late, I had seen a glimmer of something in her countenance which I had never seen before, — a something which,
the first time I perceived it, made me say to her, in my own
hearing only, "Ah, my dear, we shall understand each other
by and by!" And now and then the light in her eye would
be dimmed as by the foreshadowing of a tear, when there was
no immediate and visible cause to account for it; and — which
was very strange — I could not help fancying she began to be
a little shy of her old uncle. Could it be that she was afraid
of his insight reaching to her heart, and reading there more
than she was yet willing to confess to herself? But whatever the cause of the change might be, there was certainly a
responsiveness in her, a readiness to meet every utterance, and
take it home, by which the vanity of the old bachelor would
have been flattered to the full, had not his heart come first,
and forestalled the delight.

So absorbed was I in considering these things, that the time
passed like one of my thoughts; and before I knew I found
myself on the verge of the perilous moor over which Harry
had ridden in the teeth and heart of the storm. How smooth,

yet cruel, it looked in its thick covering of snow! There was heather beneath, within which lay millions of purple bells, ready to rush out at the call of summer, and ring peals of merry gladness, making the desolate place not only blossom, but rejoice, as the rose. And there were cold wells of brown water beneath that snow, of depth unknown, which nourished nothing but the green grass that hid the cold glare of their presence from the eyes of the else warefully affrighted traveller. And I thought of Adela when I thought of heather; and of some other women whom I had known, when I thought of the wells.

When I came home, I told Adela where I had been, and what a desolate place it was. And the flush that rose on her pale cheek was just like the light of the sunset which I had left shining over the whiteness of that snowy region. And I said to myself, "It *is* so. And I trust it may be well."

As I walked home, I had bethought myself of a story which I had brought down with me in the hope of a chance of reading it, but which Adela's illness had put out my mind; for it was only a child's story; and although I hoped older people might find something in it, it would have been absurd to read it without the presence of little children. So I said to Adela : —

"Don't you know any little children in Purleybridge, Adela?"

"Oh, yes; plenty."

"Couldn't you ask some of them one night, and I would tell them a story. I think at this season they should have a share in what is going, and I have got one I think they would like."

"I shall be delighted. I will speak to papa about it at once. But next time — "

"Yes, I know. Next time Harry Armstrong was going to read; but to tell you the truth, Adela, I doubt if he will be ready. I know he is dreadfully busy just now, and I believe he will be thankful to have a reprieve for a day or two, and his story, which I expect will be a good one, will be all the better for it."

"Then I will speak to papa about it the moment he comes in; and you will tell Mr. Henry. And mind, uncle. you take the change upon your own shoulders."

" Trust me, my dear," I said, as I left the room.

As I had anticipated, Harry was grateful.　Everything was arranged.

So, the next evening but one, we had a merry, pretty company of boys and girls, none older, or at least looking older, than twelve.　It did my heart good to see how Adela made herself at home with them, and talked to them as if she were one of themselves.　By the time tea was over, I had made friends with them all, which was a stroke in its way nearly equal to Chaucer's, who made friends with all the nine and twenty Canterbury pilgrims before the sun was down.　And the way I did was this.　I began with the one next me, asking her the question : —

" Do you like fairy stories ? "

" Yes, I do," answered she, heartily.

" Did you ever hear of the princess with the blue foot? "

" No.　Will you tell me, please ? "

Then I turned to the one on my other side, and asked her :—

" Did you ever hear of a giant that was all skin, — not skin and bone, you know, but all skin ? "

" No-o," she answered, and her round blue eyes got rounder and bluer.

The next was a boy.　I asked him : —

" Did you ever hear of Don Worm, of Wakemup ? "

" No.　Do please tell us about it."

And so I asked them, round the room.　And by that time all eyes were fixed upon me.　Then I said : —

" You see I cannot tell you all these stories to-night.　But would you all like one of some sort ? "

A chorus of *I should* filled the room.

" What shall it be about, then ? "

" A wicked fairy."

" No; that's stupid.　I'm tired of wicked fairies," said a scornful little girl.

" A good giant, then," said a priggish imp, with a face as round as the late plum pudding.

" I am afraid I could not tell you a story about a *good* giant ; for, unfortunately, all the good giants I ever heard of were very stupid ; so stupid that a story would not make itself about them ; so stupid, indeed, that they were always made game of by creatures not half so big or half so good, and I don't like such stories. Shall I tell you about the wicked giant that grew little children in his garden instead of radishes, and then carried them about in his waistcoat-pocket, and ate one as often as he remembered he had got some?"

"Yes, yes; please do."

"He used to catch little children and plant them in his garden, where you might see them in rows, with their heads only above ground, rolling their eyes about, and growing awfully fast. He liked greedy boys best, — boys that ate plum-pudding till they felt as if their belts were too tight."

Here the fat-faced boy stuck both his hands inside his belt.

"Because he was so fond of radishes," I went on, "he lived just on the borders of Giantland, where it touched on the country of common people. Now, everything in Giantland was so big, that the common people saw only a mass of awful mountains and clouds; and no living man had ever come from it, as far as anybody knew, to tell what he had seen in it.

"Somewhere near these borders, on the other side, by the edge of a great forest, lived a laborer, with his wife and a great many children. One day Tricksey-Wee, as they called her, teased her brother Buffy-Bob, till he could not bear it any longer, and gave her a box on the ear. Tricksey-Wee cried; and Buffy-Bob was so sorry and ashamed of himself that he cried too, and ran off into the wood. He was so long gone, that Tricksey-Wee began to be frightened, for she was very fond of her brother; and she was so sorry that she had first teased him, and then cried, that at last she ran into the wood to look for him, though there was more chance of losing herself than of finding him. And, indeed, so it seemed likely to turn out; for, running on without looking, she at length found herself in a valley she knew nothing about. And no wonder; for what she thought was a valley, with round, rocky sides, was no other than the space between two of the roots of a great tree that grew on the borders of Giantland. She climbed over the side of it, and right up to what she took for a black, round-topped mountain, far away; but she soon discovered that it was close to her, and was a hollow place so great that she could not tell what it was hollowed out of. Staring at it, she found that it was a door-way; and, going nearer and staring harder, she saw the door, far in, with a knocker of iron upon it, a great many yards above her head, and as large as the anchor of a big ship. Now, nobody had ever been unkind to Tricksey-Wee, and therefore she was not afraid of anybody. For Buffy-Bob's box on the ear she did not think worth considering. So, spying a little hole at the bottom of the door, which had been nibbled by some giant mouse, she crept through it, and found herself in an enormous hall, as big as if the late Mr. Martin, R.A., had been the architect. She could not have seen the other end of it at all, except for the great fire that was burning there, diminished to a spark in the distance. Towards this fire she ran as fast as she could, and was not far from it when something fell before her with a great clatter, over which she tumbled, and went rolling on the floor. She was not much hurt, however, and got up in a moment. Then she saw that she had fallen over something not unlike a great iron bucket. When she examined it more closely, she discovered that it was a thimble; and, looking up to see who had dropped it, behold a huge face, with spectacles as big as the round windows in a church, bending over her, and looking everywhere for the thimble. Tricksey-Wee immediately laid hold of it in both her arms, and lifted it about an inch nearer to the nose of the peering giantess. This movement made the old lady see where it was, and, her finger popping into it, it vanished from the eyes of Tricksey-Wee, buried in the folds of a white stocking, like a cloud in the sky, which Mrs. Giant was busy darning. For it was Saturday night, and her husband would wear nothing but white stockings on Sunday."

" But how could he be so particular about white stockings on Sunday, and eat little children ? " asked one of the group.

" Why, to be sure," I answered, " he did eat little children, but only *very* little ones ; and if ever it crossed his mind that it was wrong to do so, he always said to himself that he wore whiter stockings on Sunday than any other giant in all Giant-land.

" At that instant, Tricksey-Wee heard a sound like the wind in a tree full of leaves, and could not think what it could be ; till, looking up, she found that it was the giantess whispering to her; and when she tried very hard, she could hear what she said.well enough.

"'Run away, dear little girl,' she said, 'as fast as you can: for my husband will be home in a few minutes.'

"'But I've never been naughty to your husband,' said Tricksey Wee, looking up in the giantess' face.

"'That doesn't matter. You had better go. He is fond of little children, particularly little girls.'

"'Oh! Then he won't hurt me.'

"'I am not sure of that. He is so fond of them that he eats them up; and I am afraid he couldn't help hurting you a little. He's a very good man though.'

"'Oh! then—' began Tricksey Wee, feeling rather frightened; but before she could finish her sentence, she heard the sound of footsteps very far apart and very heavy. The next moment who should come running towards her, full speed, and as pale as death, but Buffy-Bob! She held out her arms, and he ran into them. But when she tried to kiss him, she only kissed the back of his head; for his white face and round eyes were turned to the door.

"'Run, children; run and hide,' said the giantess.

"'Come, Buffy,' said Tricksey; 'yonder's a great brake; we'll hide in it.'

"The brake was a big broom; and they had just got into the bristles of it, when they heard the door open with a sound of thunder; and in stalked the giant. You would have thought you saw the whole earth through the door when he opened it, so wide was it; and, when he closed it, it was like nightfall.

"'Where is that little boy?' he cried, with a voice like the bellowing of cannon. 'He looked a very nice boy, indeed. I am almost sure he crept through the mouse-hole at the bottom of the door. Where is he, my dear?'

"'I don't know,' answered the giantess.

"'But you know it is wicked to tell lies; don't you, dear?' retorted the giant.

"'Now, you ridiculous old Thunderthump!' said his wife, with a smile as broad as the sea in the sun; 'how can I mend your white stockings, and look after little boys? You have got plenty to last you over Sunday, I am sure. Just look what good little boys they are!'

"Tricksey-Wee and Buffy-Bob peered through the bristles, and discovered a row of little boys, about a dozen, with very fat faces, and goggle eyes, sitting before the fire, and looking stupidly into it. Thunderthump intended the most of these for seed, and was feeding them well before planting them. Now and then, however, he could not keep his teeth off them, and would eat one by-the-by, without salt."

"Now, you know that's all nonsense; for little children don't grow in gardens, I know. *You* may believe in the radish beds; *I* don't," said one pert little puss.

"I never said I did," replied I. "If the giant did, that's enough for my story. I told you the good giants are very stupid; so you may think what the bad ones are. Indeed, the giant never really tried the plan. No doubt he did plant the children; but he always pulled them up and ate them before they had a chance of increasing.

"He strode up to the wretched children. Now, what made them very wretched indeed was, that they knew if they could only keep from eating, and grow thin, the giant would dislike them, and turn them out to find their way home; but, notwithstanding this, so greedy were they, that they ate as much as ever they could hold. The giantess, who fed them, comforted herself with thinking that they were not real boys and girls, but only little pigs, pretending to be boys and girls.

"'Now tell me the truth,' cried the giant, bending his face down over them. They shook with terror, and every one hoped it was somebody else the giant liked best. 'Where is the little boy that ran into the hall just now? Whoever tells me a lie shall be instantly boiled.'

"'He's in the broom,' cried one dough-faced boy. 'He's in there, and a little girl with him.'

"'The naughty children,' cried the giant, 'to hide from *me!*' And he made a stride towards the broom.

"'Catch hold of the bristles, Bobby. Get right into a tuft, and hold on,' cried Tricksey-Wee, just in time.

"The giant caught up the broom, and, seeing nothing under it, set it down again with a bang that threw them both on the floor. He then made two strides to the boys, caught the dough-faced one by the neck, took the lid off a great pot that was boiling on the fire, popped him in as if he had been a trussed chicken, put the lid on again, and saying, 'There, boys! See what comes of lying!' asked no more questions; for, as he always kept his word, he was afraid he might have to do the same to them all; and he did not like boiled boys. He liked to eat them crisp, as radishes, whether forked or not, ought to be eaten. He then sat down, and asked his wife if his supper was ready. She looked into the pot, and throwing the boy out with the ladle, as if he had been a black-beetle that had tumbled in and had had the worst of it, answered that she thought it was. Whereupon he rose to help her; and, taking the pot from the fire, poured the whole contents, bubbling and splashing, into a dish like a vat. Then they sat down to supper. The children in the broom could not see what they had; but it seemed to agree with them; for the giant talked like thunder, and the giantess answered like the sea, and they grew chattier and chattier. At length the giant said : —

"'I don't feel quite comfortable about that heart of mine.' And as he spoke, instead of laying his hand on his bosom, he waved it away towards the corner where the children were peeping from the broom-bristles, like frightened little mice.

"'Well, you know, my darling Thunderthump,' answered his wife, 'I always thought it ought to be nearer home. But you know best of course.'

"'Ha! ha! You don't know where it is, wife. I moved it a month ago.'

"'What a man you are, Thunderthump! You trust any creature alive rather than your wife.'

"Here the giantess gave a sob, which sounded exactly like a wave going flop into the mouth of a cave up to the roof.

"'Where have you got it now?' she resumed, checking her emotion.

"'Well, Doodlem, I don't mind telling *you*,' said the giant, soothingly. 'The great she-eagle has got it for a nest-egg. She sits on it night and day, and thinks she will bring the greatest eagle out of it that ever sharpened his beak on the rocks of Mount Skycrack. I can warrant no one else will touch it while she has got it. But she is rather capricious, and I confess I am not easy about it; for the least scratch of one of her claws would do for me at once. And she *has* claws.' "

" What funny things you do make up ! " said a boy. " How could the giant's heart be in an eagle's nest, and the giant himself alive and well without it ? "

" Whatever you may think of it, Master Fred, I assure you I did not make it up. If it ever was made up, no one can tell who did it; for it was written in the chronicles of Giantland long before one of us was born. It was quite common," said I, in an injured tone, " for a giant to put his heart out to nurse, because he did not like the trouble and responsibility of doing it himself. It was, I confess, a dangerous sort of thing to do. But do you want any more of my story or not ? "

" Oh ! yes, please," cried Frederick, very heartily.

"Then don't you find any more fault with it, or I will stop."

Master Fred was straightway silent, and I went on.

" All this time Buffy-Bob and Tricksey-Wee were listening with long ears. *They* did not dispute about the giant's heart, and impossibility, and all that; for they were better educated than Master Fred, and knew all about it. ' Oh ! ' thought Tricksey-Wee, ' if I could but find the giant's cruel heart, wouldn't I give it a squeeze ! '

" The giant and giantess went on talking for a long time. The giantess kept advising the giant to hide his heart somewhere in the house; but he seemed afraid of the advantage it would give her over him.

" ' You could hide it at the bottom of the flour-barrel,' said she.

" ' That would make me feel chokey,' answered he.

" ' Well, in the coal-cellar, or in the dust-hole. That's the place! No one would think of looking for your heart in the dust-hole.'

" ' Worse and worse ! ' cried the giant.

" ' Well, the water-butt,' said she.

" ' No, no; it would grow spongy there,' said he.

" ' Well, what will you do with it ? '

" ' I will leave it a month longer where it is, and then I will give it to the Queen of the Kangaroos, and she will carry it in her pouch for me. It is best to change, you know, and then my enemies can't find it. But, dear Doodlem, it's a fretting care to have a heart of one's own to look after. The responsibility is too much for me. If it were not for a bite of a radish now and then, I never could bear it.'

" Here the giant looked lovingly towards the row of little boys by the fire, all of whom were nodding, or asleep on the floor.

" ' Why don't you trust it to me, dear Thunderthump ? ' said his wife. ' I would take the best possible care of it.'

" ' I don't doubt it, my love. But the responsibility would be too much for *you*. You would no longer be my darling, light-hearted, airy, laughing Doodlem. It would transform you into a heavy, oppressed woman, weary of life, — as I am.'

" The giant closed his eyes and pretended to go to sleep. His wife got his stockings, and went on with her darning. Soon, the giant's pretence became reality, and the giantess began to nod over her work.

" ' Now, Buffy,' whispered Tricksey-Wee. ' now's our time. I think it's moonlight, and we had better be off. There's a door with a hole for the cat just behind us.'

" ' All right! ' said Bob ; ' I'm ready.'

" So they got out of the broom-brake, and crept to the door. But, to their great disappointment, when they got through it, they found themselves in a sort of shed. It was full of tubs and things, and, though it was built of wood only, they could not find a crack.

" ' Let us try this hole,' said Tricksey ; for the giant and giantess were sleeping behind them, and they dared not go back.

" ' All right,' said Bob. He seldom said anything else than *All right*.

" Now this hole was in a mound that came in through the wall of the shed and went along the floor for some distance. They crawled into it, and found it very dark. But groping their way along, they soon came to a small crack, through which they saw grass, pale in the moonshine. As they crept on, they found the hole began to get wider and lead upwards.

" ' What is that noise of rushing ? ' said Buffy-Bob.

" ' I can't tell,' replied Tricksey; ' for, you see, I don't know what we are in.'

" The fact was, they were creeping along a channel in the heart of a giant tree ; and the noise they heard was the noise of the sap rushing along in its wooden pipes. When they laid their ears to the wall, they heard it gurgling along with a pleasant noise.

" ' It sounds kind and good,' said Tricksey. ' It is water running. Now it must be running from somewhere to somewhere. I think we had better go on, and we shall come somewhere.'

" It was now rather difficult to go on, for they had to climb as if they were climbing a hill; and now the passage was wide. Nearly worn out, they saw light overhead at last, and, creeping through a crack into the open air, found themselves on the fork of a huge tree. A great, broad, uneven space lay around them, out of which spread boughs in every direction, the smallest of them as big as the biggest tree in the country of common people. Overhead were leaves enough to supply all the trees they had ever seen. Not much moonlight could come through, but the leaves would glimmer white in the wind at times. The tree was full of giant birds. Every now and then, one would sweep through, with a great noise. But, except an occasional chirp, sounding like a shrill pipe in a great organ, they made no noise. All at once an owl began to hoot. He thought he was singing. As soon as he began, other birds replied, making rare game of him. To their astonishment, the children found they could understand every word they sang. And what they said was something like this : —-

" ' I will sing a song.
I am the owl.'—
' Sing a song, you sing-song,
Ugly fowl !
What will you sing about,
Now the light is out ? '

" ' Sing about the night;
I'm the owl.'—
' You could not see for the light,
Stupid fowl.'

> 'Oh! the moon! and the dew
> And the shadows! — tu-whoo!'

"The owl spread out his silent, soft, sly wings, and, lighting between Tricksey-Wee and Buffy-Bob, nearly smothered them, closing up one under each wing. It was like being buried in a down bed. But the owl did not like anything between his sides and his wings, so he opened his wings again, and the children made haste to get out. Tricksey-Wee immediately went in front of the bird, and looking up into his huge face, which was as round as the eyes of the giantess' spectacles, and much bigger, dropped a pretty courtesy, and said : —

"'Please, Mr. Owl, I want to whisper to you.'

"'Very well, small child,' answered the owl, looking important, and stooping his ear towards her. 'What is it?'

"'Please tell me where the eagle lives that sits on the giant's heart.'

"'O you naughty child! That's a secret. For shame!'

"And with a great hiss that terrified them, the owl flew into the tree. All birds are fond of secrets; but not many of them can keep them so well as the owl.

"So the children went on, because they did not know what else to do. They found the way very rough and difficult, the tree was so full of humps and hollows. Now and then they plashed into a pool of rain; now and then they came upon twigs growing out of the trunk where they had no business, and they were as large as full-grown poplars. Sometimes they came upon great cushions of soft moss, and on one of them they lay down and rested. But they had not laid long before they spied a large nightingale sitting on a branch, with its bright eyes looking up at the moon. In a moment more he began to sing, and the birds about him began to reply, but in a very different tone from that in which they had replied to the owl. Oh, the birds did call the nightingale such pretty names! The nightingale sang, and the birds replied like this : —

> "'I will sing a song.
> I'm the nightingale.' —
> 'Sing a song, long, long,
> Little Neverfail!
> What will you sing about,
> Light in or light out?'

" ' Sing about the light
  Gone away;
Down, away, and out of sight —
  Poor lost day!
Mourning for the day dead,
  O'er his dim bed.'

" The nightingale sang so sweetly that the children would
have fallen asleep but for fear of losing any of the song.
When the nightingale stopped they got up and wandered on.
They did not know where they were going, but they thought it
best to keep going on, because then they might come upon
something or other. They were very sorry they forgot to ask
the nightingale about the eagle's nest; but his music had put
everything else out of their heads. They resolved, however,
not to forget the next time they had a chance. They went on
and on, till they were both tired, and Tricksey-Wee said at
last, trying to laugh: —

" ' I declare my legs feel just like a Dutch doll's.'

" ' Then here's the place to go to bed in,' said Buffy-Bob.

" They stood at the edge of a last year's nest, and looked
down with delight into the round, mossy cave. Then they
crept gently in, and, lying down in each other's arms, found it
so deep, and warm, and comfortable, and soft, that they were
soon fast asleep.

" Now close beside them, in a hollow, was another nest, in
which lay a lark and his wife; and the children were awakened
very early in the morning, by a dispute between Mr. and Mrs.
Lark.

" ' Let me up,' said the lark.

" ' It is not time, said the lark's wife.

" ' It is,' said the lark, rather rudely. ' The darkness is quite
thin. I can almost see my own beak.'

" ' Nonsense! ' said the lark's wife. ' You know you came
home yesterday morning quite worn out, — you had to fly so
very high before you saw him. I am sure he would not mind
if you took it a little easier. Do be quiet and go to sleep
again.'

" ' That's not it at all,' said the lark. ' He doesn't want
me. I want him. Let me up, I say.'

" He began to sing; and Tricksey-Wee and Buffy-Bob, having now learned the way, answered him : —

" 'I will sing a song,
  I'm the Lark.' —
'Sing, sing, Throat-strong,
  Little Kill-the-dark.
What will you sing about,
  Now the night is out?

" ' I can only call;
  I can't think.
Let me up, that's all.
  Let me drink !
Thirsting all the long night
  For a drink of light.'

" By this time the lark was standing on the edge of his nest
and looking at the children.

" ' Poor little things ! You can't fly,' said the lark.

" ' No; but we can look up,' said Tricksey.

" ' Ah ! you don't know what it is to see the very first of
the sun.'

" ' But we know what it is to wait till he comes. He's no
worse for your seeing him first, is he ? '

" ' Oh ! no, certainly not,' answered the lark, with condescension ; and then, bursting into his *jubilate*, he sprung aloft,
clapping his wings like a clock running down.

" ' Tell us where —' began Buffy-Boy.

" But the lark was out of sight. His song was all that was
left of him. That was everywhere, and he was nowhere.

" ' Selfish bird ! ' said Buffy. ' It's all very well for larks
to go hunting the sun, but they have no business to despise
their neighbors, for all that.'

" ' Can I be of any use to you ? ' said a sweet bird-voice out
of the nest. This was the lark's wife, who stayed at home with
the young larks while her husband went to church.

" ' Oh ! thank you. If you please,' answered Tricksey-
Wee.

" And up popped a pretty brown head ; and then up came
a brown feathery body ; and last of all came the slender legs
on to the edge of the nest. There she turned, and, looking
down into the nest, from which came a whole litany of chirp-
ings for breakfast, said, ' Lie still, little ones.' Then she
turned to the children. ' My husband is King of the Larks,'
she said.

"Buffy-Bob took off his cap, and Tricksey-Wee courtesied very low.

"'Oh, it's not me,' said the bird, looking very shy. 'I am only his wife. It's my husband.' And she looked up after him into the sky, whence his song was still falling like a shower of musical hailstones. Perhaps she could see him.

"'He's a splendid bird,' said Buffy-Bob; 'only you know he *will* get up a little too early.'

"'Oh, no! he doesn't. It's only his way, you know. But tell me what I can do for you.'

"'Tell us, please, Lady Lark, where the she-eagle lives that sits on Giant Thunderthump's heart.'

"'Oh! that is a secret.'

"'Did you promise not to tell?'

"'No; but larks ought to be discreet. They see more than other birds.'

"'But you don't fly up high like your husband, do you?'

"'Not often. But it's no matter. I come to know things for all that.'

"'Do tell me, and I will sing you a song,' said Tricksey-Wee.

"'Can you sing too?'

"'Yes. And I will sing you a song I learned the other day about a lark and his wife.'

"'Please do,' said the lark's wife. 'Be quiet, children, and listen.'

"Tricksey-Wee was very glad she happened to know a song which would please the lark's wife, at least, whatever the lark himself might have thought of it, if he had heard it. So she sang:—

"'Good morrow, my lord!' in the sky alone,
Sang the lark, as the sun ascended his throne.
'Shine on me, my lord; I only am come,
Of all your servants, to welcome you home.
I have flown for an hour, right up, I swear,
To catch the first shine of your golden hair!'

"'Must I thank you, then,' said the king, 'Sir Lark,
For flying so high, and hating the dark?
You ask a full cup for half a thirst:
Half is love of me, and half love to be first.
There's many a bird that makes no haste,
But waits till I come. That's as much to my taste.'

" And the king hid his head in a turban of cloud;
  And the lark stopped singing, quite vexed and cowed.
  But he flew up higher, and thought, ' Anon,
  The wrath of the king will be over and gone;
  And his crown, shining out of the cloudy fold,
  Will change my brown feathers to a glory of gold.'

" So he flew, with the strength of a lark he flew.
  But, as he rose, the cloud rose too;
  And not a gleam of the golden hair
  Came through the depth of the misty air;
  Till, weary with flying, with sighing sore,
  The strong sun-seeker could do no more.

" His wings had had no chrism of gold;
  And his feathers felt withered and worn and old;
  And he sank, and quivered, and dropped like a stone.
  And there on his nest, where he left her, alone,
  Sat his little wife on her little eggs,
  Keeping them warm with wings and legs.

" Did I say alone?   Ah, no such thing!
  Full in her face was shining the king.
  ' Welcome, Sir Lark!   You look tired,' said he.
  ' *Up* is not always the best way to me.
  While you have been singing so high and away,
  I've been shining to your little wife all day.'

" He had set his crown all about the nest,
  And out of the midst shone her little brown breast;
  And so glorious was she in russet gold,
  That for wonder and awe Sir Lark grew cold.
  He popped his head under her wing, and lay
  As still as a stone, till the king was away.

" As soon as Tricksey-Wee had finished her song, the lark's wife began a low, sweet, modest little song of her own; and after she had piped away for two or three minutes, she said : —

" ' You dear children, what can I do for you?'

" ' Tell us where the she-eagle lives, please,' said Tricksey-Wee.

" ' Well, I don't think there can be much harm in telling such wise, good children,' said Lady Lark ; ' I am sure you don't want to do any mischief.'

" ' Oh, no; quite the contrary,' said Buffy-Bob.

" ' Then I'll tell you.   She lives on the very topmost peak of Mount Skycrack; and the only way to get up is, to climb on the spiders' webs that cover it from top to bottom.'

" ' That's rather serious,' said Tricksey-Wee.

" ' But you don't want to go up, you foolish little thing! You can't go. And what do you want to go up for? '

" ' That is a secret,' said Tricksey-Wee.

" ' Well, it's no business of mine,' rejoined Lady Lark, a little offended, and quite vexed that she had told them. So she flew away to find some breakfast for her little ones, who by this time were chirping very impatiently. The children looked at each other, joined hands, and walked off.

" In a minute more the sun was up, and they soon reached the outside of the tree. The bark was so knobby and rough, and full of twigs, that they managed to get down, though not without great difficulty. Then, far away to the north, they saw a huge peak, like the spire of a church, going right up into the sky. They thought this must be Mount Skycrack, and turned their faces towards it. As they went on, they saw a giant or two, now and then, striding about the fields or through the woods, but they kept out of their way. Nor were they in much danger; for it was only one or two of the border giants that were so very fond of children. At last they came to the foot of Mount Skycrack. It stood in a plain alone, and shot right up, I don't know how many thousand feet, into the air, a long, narrow, spearlike mountain. The whole face of it, from top to bottom, was covered with a net-work of spiders' webs, with threads of various sizes, from that of silk to that of whipcord. The webs shook, and quivered, and waved in the sun, glittering like silver. All about ran huge, greedy spiders, catching huge, silly flies, and devouring them.

" Here they sat down to consider what could be done. The spiders did not heed them, but ate away at the flies. At the foot of the mountain, and all round it, was a ring of water, not very broad, but very deep. Now, as they sat watching, one of the spiders, whose web was woven across this water, somehow or other lost his hold, and fell on his back. Tricksey-Wee and Buffy-Bob ran to his assistance, and, laying hold each of one of his legs, succeeded, with the help of the other legs, which struggled spiderfully, in getting him out upon dry land. As soon as he had shaken himself, and dried himself a little, the spider turned to the children, saying : —

" ' And now, what can I do for you? '

" 'Tell us, please,' said they, ' how we can get up the mountain to the she-eagle's nest.'

" ' Nothing is easier,' answered the spider. 'Just run up there, and tell them all I sent you, and nobody will mind you.'

" ' But we haven't got claws like you, Mr. Spider,' said Buffy.

" ' Ah! no more you have, poor unprovided creatures! Still I think we can manage it. Come home with me.'

" ' You won't eat us, will you?' said Buffy.

" ' My dear child,' answered the spider, in a tone of injured dignity, ' I eat nothing but what is mischievous or useless. You have helped me, and now I will help you.'

" The children rose at once, and, climbing as well as they could, reached the spider's nest in the centre of the web. They did not find it very difficult; for, whenever too great a gap came, the spider, spinning a strong cord, stretched it just where they would have chosen to put their feet next. He left them in his nest, after bringing them two enormous honey-bags, taken from bees that he had caught. Presently about six of the wisest of the spiders came back with him. It was rather horrible to look up and see them all round the mouth of the nest, looking down on them in contemplation, as if wondering whether they would be nice eating. At length one of them said : —

" ' Tell us truly what you want with the eagle, and we will try to help you.'

" Then Tricksey-Wee told them that there was a giant on the borders who treated little children no better than radishes, and that they had narrowly escaped being eaten by him; that they had found out that the great she-eagle of Mount Sky-crack was at present sitting on his heart; and that, if they could only get hold of the heart, they would soon teach the giant better behavior.

" ' But,' said their host, 'if you get at the heart of the giant, you will find it as large as one of your elephants. What can you do with it?'

" ' The least scratch will kill it,' answered Buffy-Bob.

" ' Ah! but you might do better than that,' said the spider. ' Now we have resolved to help you. Here is a little bag of spider-juice. The giants cannot bear spiders, and this juice is dreadful poison to them. We are all ready to go up with you, and drive the eagle away. Then you must put the heart into this other bag, and bring it down with you; for then the giant will be in your power.'

" ' But how can we do that?' said Buffy. ' The bag is not much bigger than a pudding-bag.'

" ' But it is as large as you will find convenient to carry.'

" ' Yes; but what are we to do with the heart?'

" ' Put it into the bag, to be sure. Only, first, you must squeeze a drop out of the other bag upon it. You will see what will happen.'

" ' Very well; we will,' said Tricksey-Wee. ' And now, if you please, how shall we go?'

" ' Oh, 'that's our business,' said the first spider. ' You come with me, and my grandfather will take your brother. Get up.'

" So Tricksey-Wee mounted on the narrow part of the spider's back, and held fast. And Buffy-Bob got on the grandfather's back. And up they scrambled, over one web after another, up and up. And every spider followed; so that, when Tricksey-Wee looked back, she saw a whole army of spiders scrambling after them.

" ' What can we want with so many?' she thought; but she said nothing.

" The moon was now up, and it was a splendid sight below and around them. All Giantland was spread out under them, with its great hills, lakes, trees, and animals. And all above them was the clear heaven, and Mount Skycrack rising into it, with its endless ladders of spider-webs, glittering like cords made of moonbeams. And up the moonbeams went, crawling, and scrambling, and racing, a huge army of huge spiders.

" At length they reached all but the very summit, where they stopped. Tricksey-Wee and Buffy-Bob could see above them a great globe of feathers, that finished off the mountain like an ornamental knob.

" ' How shall we drive her off?' said Buffy.

" ' We'll soon manage that,' said the grandfather spider. ' Come on, you, down there.'

" Up rushed the whole army, past the children, over the edge of the nest, on to the she-eagle, and buried themselves in her feathers. In a moment she became very restless, and went picking about with her beak. All at once she spread out her wings, with a sound like a whirlwind, and flew off to bathe in the sea; and then the spiders began to drop from her in all directions on their gossamer wings. The children had to hold fast to keep the wind of the eagle's flight from blowing them off. As soon as it was over, they looked into the nest, and there lay the giant's heart, an awful and ugly thing.

"'Make haste, child,' said Tricksey's spider. So Tricksey took her bag, and squeezed a drop out of it upon the heart. She thought she heard the giant give a far-off roar of pain, and she nearly fell from her seat with terror. The heart instantly began to shrink. It shrunk and shrivelled till it was nearly gone; and Buffy-Bob caught it up and put it into the bag. Then the two spiders turned and went down again as fast as they could. Before they got to the bottom, they heard the shrieks of the she-eagle over the loss of her egg; but the spiders told them not to be alarmed, for her eyes were too big to see them. By the time they reached the foot of the mountain, all the spiders had got home, and were busy again catching flies, as if nothing had happened. So the children, after renewed thanks to their friends, set off, carrying the giant's heart with them.

"'If you should find it at all troublesome, just give it a little more spider-juice directly,' said the grandfather, as they took their leave.

"Now, the giant had given an awful roar of pain, the moment they anointed his heart, and had fallen down in a fit, in which he lay so long that all the boys might have escaped if they had not been so fat. One did, — and got home in safety. For days the giant was unable to speak. The first words he uttered were : —

"'Oh, my heart! my heart!'

"'Your heart is safe enough, dear Thunderthump,' said his wife. 'Really a man of your size ought not to be so nervous and apprehensive. I am ashamed of you.'

"'You have no heart, Doodlem,' answered he. 'I assure you that at this moment mine is in the greatest danger. It has fallen into the hands of foes, though who they are I cannot tell.'

"Here he fainted again; for Tricksey-Wee, finding the heart

20

begin to swell a little, had given it the least touch of spider-juice.

" Again he recovered, and said : —

" ' Dear Doodlem, my heart is coming back to me. It is coming nearer and nearer.'

" After lying silent for a few hours, he exclaimed : —

" ' It is in the house, I know ! ' And he jumped up and walked about, looking in every corner.

" Just then, Tricksey-Wee and Buffy-Bob came out of the hole in the tree-root, and through the cat-hole in the door, and walked boldly towards the giant. Both kept their eyes busy watching him. Led by the love of his own heart, the giant soon spied them, and staggered furiously towards them.

" ' I will eat you, you vermin ! ' he cried. ' Give me my heart.'

" Tricksey gave the heart a sharp pinch ; when down fell the giant on his knees, blubbering, and crying, and begging for his heart.

" ' You shall have it if you behave yourself properly,' said Tricksey.

" ' What do you want me to do ? ' asked he, whimpering.

" ' To take all those boys and girls, and carry them home at once.'

" ' I'm not able ; I'm too ill.'

" ' Take them up directly.'

" ' I can't till you give me my heart.'

" ' Very well ! ' said Tricksey ; and she gave the heart another pinch.

" The giant jumped to his feet, and, catching up all the children, thrust some into his waistcoat-pockets, some into his breast-pocket, put two or three into his hat, and took a bundle of them under each arm. Then he staggered to the door. All this time poor Doodlem was sitting in her arm-chair, crying, and mending a white stocking.

" The giant led the way to the borders. He could not go fast, so that Buffy and Tricksey managed to keep up with him. When they reached the borders, they thought it would be safer to let the children find their own way home. So they told him to set them down. He obeyed.

"'Have you put them all down, Mr. Thunderthump?' asked Tricksey-Wee.

"'Yes,' said the giant.

"'That's a lie!' squeaked a little voice; and out came a head from his waistcoat-pocket.

"Tricksey-Wee pinched the heart till the giant roared with pain.

"'You're not a gentleman. You tell stories,' she said.

"'He was the thinnest of the lot,' said Thunderthump, crying.

"'Are you all there now, children?' asked Tricksey.

"'Yes, ma'am,' said they, after counting themselves very carefully, and with some difficulty; for they were all stupid children.

"'Now,' said Tricksey-Wee to the giant, 'will you promise to carry off no more children, and never to eat a child again all your life?'

"'Yes! yes! I promise,' answered Thunderthump, sobbing.

"'And you will never cross the borders of Giantland?'

"'Never.'

"'And you shall never again wear white stockings on a Sunday, all your life long. — Do you promise?'

"The giant hesitated at this, and began to expostulate; but Tricksey-Wee, believing it would be good for his morals, insisted; and the giant promised.

"Then she required of him, that, when she gave him back his heart, he should give it to his wife to take care of for him forever after. The poor giant fell on his knees and began again to beg. But Tricksey-Wee giving the heart a slight pinch, he bawled out : —

"'Yes, yes! Doodlem shall have it, I swear. Only she must not put it in the flour-barrel, or in the dust-hole.'

"'Certainly not. Make your own bargain with her. — And you promise not to interfere with my brother and me, or to take any revenge for what we have done?'

"'Yes, yes, my dear children; I promise everything. Do, pray, make haste and give me back my poor heart.'

"'Wait there, then, till I bring it to you.'

"'Yes, yes. Only make haste, for I feel very faint.'

"Tricksey-Wee began to undo the mouth of the bag. But

Buffy-Bob, who had got very knowing on his travels, took out his knife with the pretence of cutting the string; but, in reality, to be prepared for any emergency.

"No sooner was the heart out of the bag than it expanded to the size of a bullock; and the giant, with a yell of rage and vengeance, rushed on the two children, who had stepped sideways from the terrible heart. But Buffy-Bob was too quick for Thunderthump. He sprang to the heart, and buried his knife in it up to the hilt. A fountain of blood spouted from it; and, with a dreadful groan, the giant fell dead at the feet of little Tricksey-Wee, who could not help being sorry for him, after all."

"Silly thing!" said a little wisehead.

"What a horrid story!" said one small girl with great eyes, who sat staring into the fire.

"I don't think it at all a nice story for supper, with those horrid spiders, too," said an older girl.

"Well, let us have a game and forget it," I said.

"No; that we shan't, I am sure," said one.

"I will tell our Amy. Won't it be fun?"

"She'll scream," said another.

"I'll tell her all the more."

"No, no; you mustn't be unkind," said I; "else you will never help little children against wicked giants. The giants will eat you too, then."

"Oh! I know what you mean. You can't frighten me." .

This was said by one of the elder girls, who promised fair to reach before long the summit of uncompromising womanhood. She made me feel very small with my moralizing; so I dropped it. On the whole I was rather disappointed with the effect of my story. Perhaps the disappointment was no more than I deserved; but I did not like to think I had failed with children.

Nor did I think so any longer after a darling little blue-eyed girl, who had sat next me at tea, came to me to say good-night, and, reaching up, put her arms round my neck and kissed me, and then whispered very gently: —

"Thank you, dear Mr. Smith. I will be good. It was a very nice story. If I was a man, I would kill all the wicked people in the world. But I am only a little girl, you know; so I can only be good."

The darling did not know how much more one good woman can do to kill evil than all the swords of the world in the hands of righteous heroes.

———

CHAPTER XVII.

A CHILD'S HOLIDAY.

WHEN the next evening of our assembly came, I could see on Adela's face a look of subdued expectation, and I knew now to what to attribute it: Harry was going to read. There was a restlessness in her eyelids, — they were always rising, and falling as suddenly. But when the time drew near, they grew more still; only her color went and came a little. By the time we were all seated, she was as quiet as death. Harry pulled out a manuscript.

"Have you any objection to a ballad story?" he asked of the company generally.

"Certainly not," was the common reply; though Ralph stared a little, and his wife looked at him. I believe the reason was, that they had never known Harry write poetry before. But as soon as he had uttered the title — "*The Two Gordons*" —

"You young rascal!" cried his brother. "Am I to keep you in material forever? Are you going to pluck my wings till they are as bare as an egg? Really, ladies and gentlemen," he continued, in pretended anger, while Harry was keeping down a laugh of keen enjoyment, "it is too bad of that scapegrace brother of mine! Of course you are all welcome to anything I have got; but he has no right to escape from his responsibilities on that account. It is rude to us all. I know he can write if he likes."

"Why, Ralph, you would be glad of such a brother to steal your sermons from, if you had been up all night as I was. Of course I did not mean to claim any more credit than that of

unearthing some of your shy verses. May I read them or
not ? "

"Oh ! of course. But it is lucky I came prepared for some
escapade of the sort, and brought a manuscript of proper weight
and length in my pocket."

Suddenly Harry's face changed from a laughing to a grave
one. I saw how it was. He had glanced at Adela, and her
look of unmistakable disappointment was reflected in his face.
But there was a glimmer of pleasure in his eyes, notwithstanding ; and I fancied I could see that the pleasure would
have been more marked, had he not feared that he had placed
himself at a disadvantage with her, namely, that she would
suppose him incapable of producing a story. However, it was
only for a moment that this change of feeling stopped him.
With a gesture of some haste he reopened the manuscript,
which he had rolled up as if to protect it from the indignation
of his brother, and read the following ballad : —

"THE TWO GORDONS.

I.

"There was John Gordon, and Archibold,
    And an earl's twin sons were they.
When they were one and twenty years old,
    They fell out on their birthday.

"'Turn,' said Archibold, 'brother sly !
    Turn now, false and fell ;
Or down thou goest, as black as a lie,
    To the father of lies in hell.'

"'Why this to me, brother Archie, I pray ?
    What ill have I done to thee ? ' —
'Smooth-faced hound, thou shalt rue the day
    Thou gettest an answer of me.

"'For mine will be louder than Lady Janet's,
    And spoken in broad daylight ;
And the wall to scale is my iron mail,
    Not her castle wall at night.'

"'I clomb the wall of her castle tall,
    In the moon and the roaring wind ;
It was dark and still in her bower until
    The morning looked in behind.'

" ' Turn, therefore, John Gordon, false brother;
　　For either thou or I,
　On a hard, wet bed — wet, cold, and red,
　　For evermore shall lie.' '

" ' O Archibold, Janet is my true love;
　　Would I had told it thee ! ' —
　' I hate thee the worse.　Turn, or I'll curse
　　The night that got thee and me.'

" Their swords they drew, and the sparks they flew,
　　As if hammers did anvils beat;
　And the red blood ran. till the ground began
　　To plash beneath their feet.

" ' O Archie ! thou hast given me a cold supper,
　　A supper of steel, I trow;
　But reach me one grasp of a brother's hand,
　　And turn me, before you go.'

" But he turned himself on his gold-spurred heel,
　　And away. with a speechless frown;
　And up in the oak, with a greedy cronk,
　　The carrion-crow claimed his own.

II.

" The sun looked over a cloud of gold;
　　Lady Margaret looked over the wall.
　Over the bridge rode Archibold;
　　Behind him his merry men all.

" He leads his band to the holy land.
　　They follow with merry din.
　A white Christ's cross is on his back;
　　In his breast a darksome sin.

" And the white cross burned him like the fire
　　That he could nor eat nor rest;
　It burned in and in, to get at the sin
　　That lay cowering in his breast.

" A mile from the shore of the Dead Sea
　　The army lay one night.
　Lord Archibold rose; and out he goes,
　　Walking in the moonlight.

" He came to the shore of the old salt sea,
　　Yellow sands with frost-like tinge;
　The bones of the dead, on the edge of its bed,
　　Lay lapped in its oozy fringe.

" He sat him down on a half-sunk stone,
    And he sighed so dreary and deep:
  ' The devil may take my soul when I wake,
    If he'd only let me sleep! '

" Out from the bones and the slime and the stones,
    Came a voice like a raven's croak:
  ' Was it thou, Lord Archibold Gordon?' it said,
    Was it thou those words that spoke?'

" ' I'll say them again,' quoth Archibold,
    ' Be thou ghost or fiend of the deep.'
  ' Lord Archibold, heed how thou mayst speed,
    If thou sell me thy soul for sleep.'

" Lord Archibold laughed with a loud *ha! ha!*—
    The Dead Sea curdled to hear;
  ' Thou wouldst have the worst of the bargain curst;
    It has every fault but fear.'

" ' Done, Lord Archibold?' — ' Lord Belzebub, done!'
    His laugh came back in a moan.
  The salt glittered on, and the white moon shone,
    And Lord Archibold was alone.

" And back he went to his glimmering tent;
    And down in his cloak he lay;
  And sound he slept; and a pale-faced man
    Watched by his bed till day.

" And if ever he turned or moaned in his sleep,
    Or his brow began to lower,
  Oh! gentle and clear, in the sleeper's ear,
    He would whisper words of power;

" Till his lips would quiver, and sighs of bliss
    From sorrow's bosom would break;
  And the tear, soft and slow, would gather and flow;
    And yet he would not wake.

" Every night the pale-faced man
    Sat by his bed, I say;
  And in mail rust-brown, with his visor down,
    Rode beside him in battle-fray.

" But well I wot that it was not
    The devil that took his part;
  But his twin-brother John, he thought dead and gone,
    Who followed to ease his heart.

III.

"Home came Lord Archibold, weary wight,
Home to his own countree;
And he cried, when his castle came in sight,
'Now Christ me save and see!'

"And the man in rust-brown, with his visor down,
Had gone, he knew not where.
And he lighted down, and into the hall,
And his mother met him there.

"But dull was her eye, though her mien was high:
And she spoke like Eve to Cain:
'Lord Archibold Gordon, answer me true,
Or I'll never speak again.

"'Where is thy brother, Lord Archibold?
He was flesh and blood of thine.
Has thy brother's keeper laid him cold,
Where the warm sun cannot shine?'

"Lord Archibold could not speak a word,
For his heart was almost broke.
He turned to go. The carrion-crow
At the window gave a croak.

"'Now where art thou going, Lord Archie?' she said,
With thy lips so white and thin?'—
'Mother, good-by; I am going to lie
In the earth with my brother-twin.'

"Lady Margaret sank on her couch. 'Alas!
I shall lose them both to-day.'
Lord Archibold strode along the road,
To the field of the Brothers' Fray.

"He came to the spot where they had fought,
'My God!' he cried in fright,
'They have left him there, till his bones are bare;
Through the plates they glimmer white.'

"For his brother's armor lay there, dank,
And worn with frost and dew.
Had the long, long grass, that grew so rank,
Grown the very armor through?

"'O brother, brother!' cried the Earl,
With a loud, heart-broken wail,
'I would put my soul into thy bones,
To see thee alive and hale.'

" ' Ha! ha!' said a voice from out the helm,—
   'Twas the voice of the Dead Sea shore;
And the joints did close, and the armor rose,
   And clattered, and grass uptore.

" ' Thou canst put no soul into his bones,
   Thy brother alive to set;
For the sleep was thine, and thy soul is mine,
   And, Lord Archibold, well-met!'

" ' Two words to that!' said the fearless Earl;
   'The sleep was none of thine;
For I dreamed of my brother all the night,—
   His soul brought the sleep to mine.

" ' But I care not a crack for a soul so black,
   And thou mayst have it yet
I would let it burn to eternity,
   My brother alive to set.'

" The demon lifted his beaver up,
   Crusted with blood and mould;
And lo! John Gordon looked out of the helm,
   And smiled upon Archibold.

" ' Thy soul is mine, brother Archie,' he said,
   ' And I yield it thee none the worse;
No devil came near thee, Archie, lad,
   But a brother to be thy nurse.'

" Lord Archibold fell upon his knee,
   On the blood-fed, bright green sod:
' The soul that my brother gives back to me
   Is thine forever, O God!' "

" Now for a piece of good, honest prose!" said the curate, the moment Harry had finished, without allowing room for any remarks. "That is, if the ladies and gentlemen will allow me to read once more."

Of course, all assented heartily.

" It is nothing of a story, but I think it is something of a picture, drawn principally from experiences of my own child-hood, which I told you was spent chiefly in the north of Scotland. The one great joy of the year, although some years went without it altogether, was the summer visit paid to the shores of the Moray Firth. My story is merely a record of some of the impressions left on myself by such a visit, although the boy is certainly not a portrait of myself; and if it has no result, no end, reaching beyond childhood into what is commonly called life, I presume it is not of a peculiar or solitary character in that respect; for surely many that we count finished stories — life-histories — must look very different to the angels; and if they haven't to be written over again, at least they have to be carried on a few æons further.

"A CHILD'S HOLIDAY.

" Before the door of a substantial farm-house in the north of Scotland stands a vehicle of somewhat singular construction. When analyzed, however, its composition proves to be simple enough. It is a common agricultural cart, over which, by means of a few iron rods bent across, a semi-cylindrical covering of white canvas has been stretched. It is thus transformed from a hay or harvest cart into a family carriage, of comfortable dimensions, though somewhat slow of progress. The lack of springs is supplied by thick layers of straw, while sacks stuffed with the same material are placed around for seats. Various articles are being stowed away under the bags, and in the corners among the straw, by children with bright, expectant faces; the said articles having been in process of collection and arrangement for a month or six weeks previous, in anticipation of the journey which now lies, in all its length and brightness, — the length and brightness of a long northern summer's day, — before them.

" At last, all their private mysteries of provisions, playthings, and books having found places of safety more or less accessible on demand, every motion of the horse, every shake and rattle of the covered cart, makes them only more impatient to proceed; which desire is at length gratified by their moving on at a funeral pace through the open gate. They are followed by another cart loaded with the luggage necessary for a six-weeks' sojourn at one of the fishing-villages on the coast, about twenty miles distant from their home. Their father and mother are to follow in the gig, at a later hour in the day, expecting to overtake them about half-way on the road. Through the neighboring village they pass, out upon the lonely highway.

" Some seeds are borne to the place of their destiny by their own wings and the wings of the wind, some by the wings of birds, some by simple gravitation. The seed of my story, namely, the covered cart, sent forth to find the soil for its coming growth, is dragged by a stout horse to the sea-shore ; and as it oscillates from side to side like a balloon trying to walk, I shall say something of its internal constitution, and principally of its germ ; for, regarded as the seed of my story, a pale boy of thirteen is the germ of the cart. First, though he will be of little use to us afterwards, comes a great strong boy of sixteen, who considerably despises this mode of locomotion, believing himself quite capable of driving his mother in the gig, whereas he is only destined to occupy her place in the evening, and return. with his father. Then comes the said germ, a boy whom repeated attacks of illness have blanched, and who looks as if the thinness of its earthly garment made his soul tremble with the proximity of the ungenial world. Then follows a pretty blonde, with smooth hair, and smooth cheeks, and bright blue eyes, — the embodiment of home pleasures and love ; whose chief enjoyment, and earthly destiny indeed, so far as yet revealed, consist in administering to the cupidities of her younger brother, a very ogre of gingerbread men, and Silenus of bottled milk. This milk, by the way, is expected, from former experience, to afford considerable pleasure at the close of the journey, in the shape of one or two pellets of butter in each bottle ; the novelty of the phenomenon, and not any scarcity of the article, constituting the ground of interest. A baby on the lap of a rosy country-girl, and the servant in his blue Sunday coat, who sits outside the cover on the edge of the cart, but looks in occasionally to show some attention to the young woman, complete the contents of the vehicle.

" Herbert Netherby, though, as I have said, only thirteen years of age, had already attained a degree of mental development sufficient for characterization. Disease had favored the almost unhealthy predominance of the mental over the bodily powers of the child ; so that, although the constitution which at one time was supposed to have entirely given way, had for the last few years been gradually gaining strength, he was still to be seen far oftener walking about with his hands in his pockets, and his gaze bent on the ground, or turned up to the clouds, than joining in any of the boyish sports of those of his own age. A nervous dread of ridicule would deter him from taking his part, even when for a moment the fountain of youthfulness gushed forth, and impelled him to find rest in activity. So the impulse would pass away, and he would relapse into his former quiescence. But this partial isolation ministered to the growth of a love of Nature which, although its roots were coeval with his being, might not have so soon appeared above ground but for this lack of human companionship. Thus the boy became one of Nature's favorites, and enjoyed more than a common share of her teaching.

"But he loved her most in her stranger moods. The gathering of a blue cloud, on a sultry summer afternoon, he watched with intense hope, in expectation of a thunder-storm: and a windy night, after harvest, when the trees moaned and tossed their arms about, and the wind ran hither and thither over the desolate fields of stubble, made the child's heart dance within him, and sent him out careering through the deepening darkness. To meet him then, you would not have known him for the sedate, actionless boy, whom you had seen in the morning looking listlessly on while his school-fellows played. But, of all his loves for the shows of Nature, none was so strong as his love for water, — common to childhood, with its mills of rushes, its dams, its bridges, its aqueducts; only in Herbert it was more a quiet, delighted contemplation. Weakness prevented his joining his companions in the river; but the sight of their motions in the mystery of the water, as they floated half idealized in the clear depth, or glided along by graceful propulsion, gave him as much real enjoyment as they received themselves. For it was water itself that delighted him, whether in rest or motion; whether rippling over many stones, like the first half-articulate sounds of a child's speech, mingled with a strange musical tremble and cadence which the heart only, and not the ear, could detect; or lying in deep, still pools, from the bottom of which gleamed up bright green stones, or yet brighter water-plants, cool in their little grotto, with water for an atmosphere and a firmament, through which the sun-rays came, washed of their burning heat, but undimmed of their splendor. He would lie for an hour by the side of a hillstreamlet; he would stand gazing into a muddy pool, left on the road by last night's rain. Once, in such a brown-yellow pool, he beheld a glory, — the sun, encircled with a halo vast and wide, varied like the ring of opal colors seen about the moon when she floats through white clouds, only larger and brighter than that. Looking up, he could see nothing but a chaos of black clouds, brilliant towards the sun; the colors he could not see, except in the muddy water.

"In autumn the rains would come down for days, and the river grow stormy, forget its clearness, and spread out like a lake over the meadows; and that was delightful indeed. But greater yet was the delight when the foot-bridge was carried away; for then they had to cross the stream in a boat. He longed for water where it could not be; would fain have seen it running through the grass in front of his father's house; and had a waking vision of a stream with wooden shores that babbled through his bedroom. So it may be fancied with what delight he overheard the parental decision that they should spend some weeks by the shores of the great world-water, the father and the grave of rivers.

"After many vain outlooks and fruitless inquiries of their driver, a sudden turn in the road brought them in sight of the sea between the hills; itself resembling a low blue hill, covered with white stones. Indeed, the little girl only doubted whether those were white stones or sheep scattered all over it. They lost sight of it; saw it again; and hailed it with greater rapture than at first.

"The sun was more than half-way down when they arrived. They had secured a little cottage, almost on the brow of the high shore, which in most places went down perpendicularly to the beach or sands, and in some right into deep water; but opposite the cottage declined with a sloping, grassy descent. A winding track led down to the village, which nestled in a hollow, with steep footpaths radiating from it. In front of it, lower still, lay the narrow beach, narrow even at low water, for the steep, rocky shore went steep and rocky down into the abyss. A thousand fantastic rocks stood between land and water; amidst which, at half-tide, were many little rocky arbors, with floors of sunny sand, and three or four feet of water. Here you might bathe, or sit on the ledges with your feet in the water, medicated with the restless glitter and bewilderment of a half-dissolved sunbeam.

"A promontory, curving out into the sea, on the right, formed a bay and natural harbor, from which, towards the setting sun, many fishing-boats were diverging into the wide sea, as the children, stiff and weary, were getting out of the cart. Herbert's fatigue was soon forgotten in watching their brown-dyed sails, glowing almost red in the sunset, as they went out far into the dark, hunters of the deep, to spend the night on the waters.

"From the windows the children could not see the shore, with all its burst of beauties struck out from the meeting of things unlike; for it lay far down, and the brow of the hill rose between it and them; only they knew that below the waves were breaking on the rocks, and they heard the gush and roar filling all the air. The room in which Herbert slept was a little attic, with a window towards the sea. After gazing with unutterable delight on the boundless water, which lay like a condensed sky in the gray light of the sleeping day (for there is no night at this season in the North), till he saw it even when his eyelids closed from weariness, he lay down, and the monotonous lullaby of the sea mingled with his dreams.

"Next morning he was wakened by the challenging and replying of the sentinel-cocks, whose crowing sounded to him more clear and musical than that of any of the cocks at home. He jumped out of bed. It was a sunny morning, and his soul felt like a flake of sunshine, as he looked out of his window on the radiant sea, green and flashing, its clear surface here and there torn by the wind into spots of opaque white. So happy did he feel, that he might have been one who had slept through death and the judgment, and had awaked, a child, still in the kingdom of God, under the new heavens and upon the new earth.

"After breakfast they all went down with their mother to the sea-shore. As they went, the last of the boats which had gone out the night before were returning laden, like bees. The sea had been bountiful. Everything shone with gladness. But, as Herbert drew nearer, he felt a kind of dread at the recklessness of the waves. On they hurried, assailed the rocks, devoured the sands, cast themselves in wild abandonment on

whatever opposed them.   He feared at first to go near, for they
were unsympathizing, caring not for his love or his joy, and
would sweep him away like one of those floating sea-weeds.
'If they are such in their play,' thought he, 'what must they
be in their anger!'   But ere long he was playing with the
sea as with a tame tiger, chasing the retreating waters till they
rallied and he, in his turn, had to flee from their pursuit.
Wearied at length, he left his brother and sister building
castles of wet sand, and wandered alone along the shore.

" Everywhere about lay shallow lakes of salt water, so shallow that they were invisible, except when a puff of wind blew a
thousand ripples into the sun; whereupon they flashed as if a
precipitous rain of stormy light had rushed down upon them.
Lifting his eyes from one of these films of water, Herbert saw
on the opposite side, stooping to pick up some treasure of the
sea, a little girl, apparently about nine years of age.   When
she raised herself and saw Herbert, she moved slowly away
with a quiet grace, that strangely contrasted with her tattered
garments.   She was ragged like the sea-shore, or the bunch
of dripping sea-weed that she carried in her hand; she was
bare from foot to knee, and passed over the wet sand with a
gleam; the wind had been at more trouble with her hair than
any loving hand; it was black, lustreless, and tangled.   The
sight of rags was always enough to move Herbert's sympathies, and he wished to speak to the little girl, and give her
something.   But when he had followed her a short distance,
all at once, and without having looked round, she began to
glide away from him with a wave-like motion, dancing and
leaping; till a clear pool in the hollow of a tabular rock im-
bedded in the sand arrested her progress.   Here she stood
like a statue, gazing into its depth; then, with a dart like a
kingfisher, plunged half into it, caught something, at which
her head and curved neck showed that she looked with satisfaction, and again, before Herbert could come near her, was
skimming along the uneven shore.   He followed, as a boy
follows a lapwing; but she, like the lapwing, gradually
increased the distance between them, till he gave up the pursuit with some disappointment, and returned to his brother
and sister.   More ambitious than they, he proceeded to
construct — chiefly for the sake of the moat he intended to

draw around it — a sand-castle of considerable pretensions; but the advancing tide drove him from his stronghold before he had begun to dig the projected fosse.

" As they returned home, they passed a group of fishermen in their long boots and flapped sou'-westers, looking somewhat anxiously seaward. Much to Herbert's delight, they predicted a stiff gale, and probably a storm. A low bank of cloud had gathered along the horizon, and the wind had already freshened ; the white spots were thicker on the waves, and the sound of their trampling on the shore grew louder.

" After dinner, they sat at the window of their little parlor, looking out over the sea, which grew darker and more sullen, ever as the afternoon declined. The cloudy bank had risen and walled out the sun ; but a narrow space of blue on the horizon looked like the rent whence the wind rushed forth on the sea, and with the feet of its stormy horses tore up the blue surface, and scattered the ocean-dust in clouds. As evening drew on, Herbert could keep in the house no longer. He wandered away on the heights, keeping from the brow of the cliffs ; now and then stooping and struggling with a stormier eddy ; till, descending into a little hollow, he sunk below the plane of the tempest, and stood in the glow of a sudden calm, hearing the tumult all round him, but himself in peace. Looking up, he could see nothing but the sides of the hollow with the sky resting on them, till, turning towards the sea, he saw, at some distance, a point of the cliff rising abruptly into the air. At the same moment, the sun looked out from a crack in the clouds, on the very horizon ; and as Herbert could not see the sunset, the peculiar radiance illuminated the more strangely the dark vault of earth and cloudy sky. Suddenly, to his astonishment, it was concentrated on the form of the little ragged girl. She stood on the summit of the peak before him. The light was a crown, not to her head only, but to her whole person ; as if she herself were the crown set on the brows of the majestic shore. Disappearing as suddenly, it left her standing on the peak, dark and stormy ; every tress, if tresses they could be called, of her windy hair, every tatter of her scanty garments, seeming individually to protest, ' The wind is my playmate ; let me go ! ' If Aphrodite was born of the sunny sea, this child was the offspring of the windy shore ;

as if the mind of the place had developed for itself a consciousness, and this was its embodiment. She bore a strange affinity to the rocks, and the sea-weed, and the pools, and the wide, wild ocean; and Herbert would scarcely have been shocked to see her cast herself from the cliff into the waves, which now dashed half-way up its height. By the time he had got out of the hollow, she had vanished, and where she had gone he could not conjecture. He half feared she had fallen over the precipice; and several times that night, as the vapor of dreams gathered around him, he started from his half-sleep in terror at seeing the little genius of the storm fall from her rock-pedestal into the thundering waves at its foot.

"Next day the wind continuing off the sea, with vapor and rain, the children were compelled to remain within doors, and betake themselves to books and playthings. But Herbert's chief resource lay in watching the sea and the low gray sky, between which was no distinguishable horizon. The wind still increased, and before the afternoon it blew a thorough storm, winds and waves raging together on the rocky shore. The fishermen had secured their boats, drawing them up high on the land; but what vessels might be laboring under the low misty pall no one could tell. Many anxious fears were expressed for some known to be at sea; and many tales of shipwreck were told that night in the storm-shaken cottages.

"The day was closing in, darkened the sooner by the mist, when Herbert, standing at the window, now rather weary, saw the little girl dart past like a petrel. He snatched up his cap and rushed from the house, buttoning his jacket to defend him from the weather. The little fellow, though so quiet among other boys, was a lover of the storm as much as the girl was, and would have preferred its buffeting, so long as his strength lasted, to the warmest nook by the fireside; and now he could not resist the temptation to follow her. As soon as he was clear of the garden, he saw her stopping to gaze down on the sea — starting again along the heights — blown out of her course — and regaining it by struggling up in the teeth of the storm. He at once hastened in pursuit, trying as much as possible to keep out of her sight, and was gradually lessening the distance between them, when, on crossing the hollow already mentioned, he saw her on the edge of the cliff, close to the pinnacle on which she had stood the night before; where, after standing for a moment, she sank downwards and vanished, but whether into earth or air he could not tell. He approached the place. A blast of more than ordinary violence fought against him, as if determined to preserve the secret of its favorite's refuge. But he persisted, and gained the spot.

"He then found that the real edge of the precipice was several yards farther off, the ground sloping away from where he stood. At his feet, in the slope, was an almost perpendicular opening. He hesitated a little; but, sure that the child was a real human child and no phantom, he did not hesitate long. He entered and found it lead spirally downwards. Descending with some difficulty, for the passage was narrow, he arrived at a small chamber, into one corner of which the stone shaft, containing the stair, projected half its round. The chamber looked as if it had been hollowed out of the rock. A narrow window, little more than a loop-hole through the thick wall, admitted the roar of the waves and a dim gray light. This light was just sufficient to show him the child in the farthest corner of the chamber, bending forward with her hands between her knees, in a posture that indicated fear. The little playfellow of the winds was not sure of him. At the first word he spoke, a sea-bird, which had made its home in the apartment, startled by the sound of his voice, dashed through the window, with a sudden clang of wings, into the great misty void without; and Herbert, looking out after it, almost forgot the presence of the little girl in the awe and delight of the spectacle before him. It was now much darker, and the fog had settled down more closely on the face of the deep; but just below him he could see the surface of the ocean, whose mad waves appeared to rush bellowing out of the unseen on to the shore of the visible. When, after some effort, he succeeded in leaning out of the window, he could see the shore beneath him; for he was on its extreme verge, and the spray now and then dashed through the loop-hole into the chamber. He was still gazing and absorbed, when a sweet, timid voice, that yet partook undefinably of the wildness of a sea-breeze, startled him out of his contemplation.

"'Did my mother send you to me?' said the voice.

"He looked down. Close beside him stood the child, gazing

earnestly up into his face through the twilight from the window.

"'Where does your mother live?' asked Herbert.

"'All out there,' the child answered, pointing to the window.

"While he was thinking what she could mean, she continued:—

"'Mother is angry to-night; but when the sun comes out, and those nasty clouds are driven away, she will laugh again. Mother does not like black clouds and fogs; they spoil her house.'

"Still perplexed as to the child's meaning, Herbert asked:—

"'Does your mother love you?'

"'Yes, except when she is angry. She does not love me to-night; but to-morrow, perhaps, she will be all over laughs to me; and that makes me run to her; and she will smile to me all day, till night comes and she goes to sleep, and leaves me alone; for I hear her sleeping, but I cannot go to sleep with her.'"

Here the curate interrupted his reading to remark, that he feared he had spoiled the pathos of the child's words, by translating them into English; but that they must gain more, for the occasion, by being made intelligible to his audience, than they could lose by the change from their original form.

"Herbert's sympathies had by this time made him suspect that the child must be talking of the sea, which somehow she had come to regard as her mother. He asked:—

"'Where does your father live, then?'

"'I have not any father,' she answered. 'I had one, but mother took him.'

"Several other questions Herbert put; but still the child's notions ran in the same channel. They were wild notions, but uttered with confidence, as if they were the most ordinary facts. It seemed that whatever her imagination suggested, bore to her the impress of self-evident truth; and that she knew no higher reality.

"By this time it was almost dark.

"'I must go home,' said Herbert.

"'I will go with you,' responded the girl.

"She ran along beside him, but in the discursive manner natural to her, till, coming to one of the paths descending towards the shore, she darted down, without saying good-night even.

"Next day, the storm having abated, and the sun shining out, they were standing on the beach, near a fisherman, who like them was gazing seawards, when the child went skimming past along the shore. Mrs. Netherby asked the fisherman about her, and learned the secret of the sea's motherhood. She had been washed ashore from the wreck of a vessel, and was found on the beach tied to a spar. All besides had perished. From the fragment they judged it to have been a Dutch vessel. Some one had said in her hearing, 'Poor child! the sea is her mother;' and her imagination had cherished the idea. A fisherman, who had no family, had taken her to his house and loved her dearly. But he lost his wife shortly after; and a year or two ago the sea had taken him, the only father she knew. All, however, were kind to her. She was welcome wherever she chose to go and share with the family. But no one knew to-day where she would be to-morrow, where she would have her next meal, or where she would sleep. She was wild, impulsive, affectionate. The simple people of the village believed her to be of foreign birth and high descent, while reverence for her lonely condition made them treat her with affection as well as deference; so that the forsaken child, regarded as subject to no law, was as happy in her freedom and confidence as any wild winged thing of the land or sea. The summer loved her; the winter strengthened her. Her first baptism in the salt waters had made her a free creature of the earth and skies; had fortified her, Achilles-like, against all hardship, cold, and nakedness to come; had delivered her from the bonds of habit and custom, and shown in her what earth and air of themselves can do, to make the lowest, most undeveloped life, a divine gift.

"The following morning the sea was smooth and clear. So was the sky. Looking down from their cottage, the sea appeared to Herbert to slope steeply up to the horizon, so that the shore lay like a deep narrow valley between him and it. Far down, at the low pier, he saw a little boat belonging to a retired ship-captain. The oars were on board; and the owner and some one with him were walking towards the boat. Now the captain had promised to take him with him some day.

He was half-way down the road a moment after the words of permission had left his mother's lips, and was waiting at the boat when the two men came up. They readily agreed to let him go with them. They were going to row to a village on the opposite side of the bay, and return in the evening. Herbert was speechless with delight. They got in, the boat heaving beneath them, unmoored, and pushed off. This suspension between sea and sky was a new sensation to Herbert; for when he looked down, his eye did not repose on the surface, but penetrated far into a clear green abyss, where the power of vision seemed rather to vanish than be arrested. When he looked up, the shore was behind them; and he knew, for the first time, what it was to look at the land, as he had looked at the sea; to regard the land, in its turn, as a *phenomenon*, — observing it apart from himself.

" Running along the shore like a little bird, he saw the child of the sea; and further to the right, the peak on which she had stood in the sunset, and into whose mysterious chamber she had led him. The captain here put a pocket-telescope into his hand; and with this annihilator of space he made new discoveries. He saw a little window in the cliff, doubtless the same from which he had looked out on the dim sea; and then perceived that the front of the cliff, in that part, was no rock, but a wall, regularly and strongly built. It was evidently the remains of an old fortress. The front foundation had been laid in the rocks of the shore; the cliff had then been faced up with masonry; and behind chambers had been cut in the rock; into one of which Herbert had descended a ruined spiral stair. The castle itself, which had stood on the top, had mouldered away, leaving only a rugged and broken surface.

" By this time they were near the opposite shore, and Herbert looked up with dread at the great cliffs that rose perpendicularly out of the water, which heaved slowly and heavily, with an appearance of immense depth, against them. Their black jagged sides had huge holes, into which the sea rushed, — far into the dark, — with a muffled roar; and large protuberances of rock, bare and threatening. Numberless shadows lay on their faces; and here and there from their tops trickled little streams, plashing into the waves at their feet. Passing through a natural arch in a rock, lofty and narrow, called the Devil's Bridge, and turning a little promontory, they were soon aground on the beach.

"When the captain had finished his business, they had some dinner at the inn; and while the two men drank their grog, Herbert was a delighted listener to many a sea story, old and new. How the boy longed to be a sailor, and live always on the great waters! The blocks and cordage of the fast-rooted flagstaff before the inn assumed an almost magic interest to him, as the two sailors went on with their tales of winds and rocks, and narrow escapes and shipwrecks. And how proud he was of the friendship of these old seafarers!

"At length it was time to return home. As they rowed slowly along, the sun was going down in the west, and their shadows were flung far on the waves which gleamed and glistened in the rich, calm light. Land and sea were bathed in the blessing of heaven; its glory was on the rocks, and on the shore, and in the depth of the heaving sea. Under the boat, wherever it went, shone a paler green. The only sounds were of the oars in the rowlocks, of the drip from their blades as they rose and made curves in the air, and the low plash with which they dipped again into the sea; while the water in the wake of the boat hastened to compose itself again to that sleep from which it had been unwillingly aroused by the passing keel. The boy's heart was full. Often in after years he longed for the wings of a dove, that he might fly to that boat (still floating in the calm sea of his memory), and there lie until his spirit had had rest enough.

"The next time that Herbert approached the little girl, she waited his coming; and while they talked Mrs. Netherby joined them with her Effie. Presently the gaze of the sea-child was fixed upon little Effie, to the all but total neglect of the others. The result of this contemplation was visible the next day. Mrs. Netherby having invited her to come and see them, the following morning, as they were seated at breakfast, the door of the room opened, without any prefatory tap, and in peeped with wild confidence the smiling face of the untamed Undine. It was at once evident that civilization had laid a finger upon her, and that a new, womanly impulse had been

awakened.   For there she stood, gazing at Effie, and with both
hands smoothing down her own hair, which she had managed,
after a fashion, to part in the middle, and had plentifully
wetted with sea-water.   In her run up the height it had begun
to dry, and little spangles of salt were visible all over it.   She
could not alter her dress, whose many slashes showed little
lining except her skin; but she had done all she could to
approximate her appearance to that of Effie, whom she seemed
to regard as a little divinity.

Mrs. Netherby's heart was drawn towards the motherless
child, and she clothed her from head to foot; though how far
this was a benefit, as regarded cold and heat, is a question.
Herbert began to teach her to read; in which her progress was
just like her bodily movements over the earth's surface, — now
a dead pause, and now the flight of a bird.   Now and then she
would suddenly start up, heedless where her book might happen
to fall, and rush out along the heights; returning next day, or
the same afternoon, and, without any apology, resuming her
studies.

" This holiday was to Herbert one of those seasons which
tinge the whole of the future life.   It was a storehouse of
sights and sounds and images of thought; a tiring-room,
wherein to clothe the ideas that came forth to act their parts
upon the stage of reason.   Often at night, just ere the sleep
that wipes out the day from the overfilled and blotted tab-
lets of the brain, enwrapped him in its cool, grave-like garments, a vision of the darkened sea, spotted and spangled with
pools of unutterable light, would rise before him unbidden, in
that infinite space for creation which lies dark and waiting under
the closed eyelids.   The darkened sea might be but the out-
thrown image of his own overshadowed soul; and the spots of
light the visual form of his hopes.   So clearly would these
be present to him sometimes, that when he opened his eyes and
gazed into the darkness of his room he would see the bright
spaces shining before him still.   Then he would fall asleep and
dream on about the sea, — watching a little cutter perhaps, as
'she leaned to the lee, and girdled the wave,' flinging the
frolicsome waters from her bows, and parting a path for herself
between.   Or he would be seated with the helm in his hand,
and all the force and the joy wherewith she dashed headlong

on the rising waves, and half pierced them and half drove them under her triumphant keel, would be issuing from his will and his triumph.

"Surely even for the sad, despairing waves there is some hope, out in that boundless room which borders on the sky, and upon which, even in the gloomiest hour of tempest, falls sometimes from heaven a glory intense.

"So when the time came that the lover of waters must return, he went back enriched with new visions of them in their great home and motherland. He had seen them still and silent as a soul in holy trance; he had seen them raving in a fury of livid green, swarming with 'white-mouthed waves;' he had seen them lying in one narrow ridge of unbroken blue, where the eye, finding no marks to measure the distance withal, saw miles as furlongs; and he had seen sweeps and shadows innumerable stretched along its calm expanse, so dividing it into regions, and graduating the distance, that the eye seemed to wander on and on from sea to sea, and the ships to float in oceans beyond oceans of infinite reach. O lonely space! awful indeed wert thou, did no one love us! But he had yet to receive one more vision of the waters, and that was to be in a dream. With this dream I will close the story of his holiday; for it went with him ever after, breaking forth from the dream-home, and encompassing his waking thoughts with an atmosphere of courage and hope, when his heart was ready to sink in a world which was not the world the boy had thought to enter, when he ran to welcome his fate.

"On their last Sunday, Herbert went with his mother to the evening service in a little chapel in the midst of the fishermen's cottages. It was a curious little place, with galleries round, that nearly met in the middle, and a high pulpit, with a great sounding-board over it, from which came the voice of an earnest little Methodist, magnified by his position into a mighty prophet. The good man was preaching on the parable of *the sheep and the goats;* and, in his earnestness for his own theology and the souls of his hearers, was not content that the Lord should say these things in his own way, but he must say them in his too. And a terrible utterance it was! Looking about, unconsciously seeking some relief from the accumulation of horrors with which the preacher was threatening the goats of his congregation, Herbert spied, in the very front of one of the side galleries, his little pupil, white with terror, and staring with round, unwinking eyes full in the face of the prophet of fear. Never after could he read the parable without seeing the blanched face of the child, and feeling a renewal of that evening's sadness over the fate of the poor goats, which afterwards grew into the question, 'Doth God care for oxen, and not for goats?' He never saw the child again; for they left the next day, and she did not come to bid them good-by.

"As he went home from the chapel, her face of terror haunted him.

"That night he fell asleep, as usual, with the sound of the waves in his soul. And as he slept he dreamed. He stood, as he thought, upon the cliff, within which lay the remnants of the old castle. The sun was slowly sinking down the western sky, and a great glory lay upon the sea. Close to the shore beneath, by the side of some low rocks, floated a little boat. He thought how delightful it would be to lie in the boat in the sunlight, and let it die away upon his bosom. He scrambled down the rocks, stepped on board, and laid himself in the boat, with his face turned towards the sinking sun. Lower and lower the sun sank, seeming to draw the heavens after him, like a net. At length he plunged beneath the waves; but as his last rays disappeared on the horizon, lo! a new splendor burst upon the astonished boy. The whole waters were illuminated from beneath with the permeating glories of the buried radiance. In rainbow circles, and intermingling, fluctuating sweeps of colors, the sea lay like an intense opal, molten with the fire of its own hues. The sky gave back the effulgence with a less deep but more heavenly loveliness.

"But betwixt the sea and the sky, just over the grave of the down-gone sun, a dark spot appeared, parting the earth and the heaven where they had mingled in embraces of light. And the dark spot grew and spread, and a cold breath came softly over the face of the shining waters; and the colors paled away; and as the blossom-sea withered and grew gray below, the clouds withered and darkened above. The sea began to swell and moan and look up, like the soul of a man whose joy is going down in darkness; and a horror came over the heart of the sleeper, and in his dream he lifted up his head, meaning to rise and hasten to his home. But, behold, the shore was far away, and the great castle-cliff had sunk to a low ridge! With a cry, he sank back on the bosom of the careless sea.

"The boat began to rise and fall on the waking waves. Then a great blast of wind laid hold of it, and whirled it about. Once more he looked up, and saw that the tops of the waves were torn away, and that 'the white water was coming out of the black.' Higher and higher rose the billows; louder and louder roared the wind across their jagged furrows, tearing awful descants from their bursting chords, and tossing the little boat like a leaf in the lone desert of storms; now holding it perched on the very crest of a wave, in the mad eye of the tempest, while the chaotic waters danced, raving about, in hopeless confusion; now letting it sink in the hollow of the waves, and lifting above it cold, glittering walls of water, that becalmed it as in a sheltered vale, while the hurricane, roaring above, flung arches of writhing waters across from billow to billow overhead, and threatened to close, as in a transparent tomb, boat and boy. At length, when the boat rose once more, unwilling, to the awful ridge, jagged and white, a yet fiercer blast tore it from the top of the wave. The dreamer found himself choking in the waters, and soon lost all consciousness of the buffeting waves or the shrieking winds.

"When the dreamer again awoke, he felt that he was carried along through the storm above the waves; for they reached him only in bursts of spray, though the wind raged around him more fiercely than ever. He opened his eyes and looked downwards. Beneath him seethed and boiled the tumultuous billows, their wreathy tops torn from them, and shot, in long vanishing sheets of spray, over the distracted wilderness. Such was the turmoil beneath that he had to close his eyes again to feel that he was moving onwards.

"The next time he opened them, it was to look up. And lo! a shadowy face bent over him, whence love unutterable was falling in floods, from eyes deep, and dark, and still, as the heavens that are above the clouds. Great waves of hair streamed back from a noble head, and floated on the tides of the tempest. The face was like his mother's and like his father's, and like a face that he had seen somewhere in a picture, but far more beautiful and strong and loving than all. With a sudden glory of gladness, in which the spouting pinnacles of the fathomless pyramids of wandering waters dwindled into the confusion of a few troubled water-drops, he knew, he knew that the Lord was carrying his lamb in his bosom. Around him were the everlasting arms, and above him the lamps that light heaven and earth, the eyes that watch and are not weary. And now he felt the arms in which he lay, and he nestled close to that true, wise bosom, which has room in it for all, and where none will strive.

"Over the waters went the Master, now crossing the calm hollows, now climbing the rising wave, now shrouded in the upper ocean of drifting spray, that wrapped him around with whirling force, and anon calmly descending the gliding slope into the grassy trough below. Sometimes, when he looked up, the dreamer could see nothing but the clouds driving across the heavens, whence now and then a star, in a little well of blue, looked down upon him; but anon he knew that the driving clouds were his drifting hair, and that the stars in the blue wells of heaven were his love-lighted eyes. Over the sea he strode, and the floods lifted up their heads in vain. The billows would gather and burst around and over them; but a moment more, and the billows were beneath his feet, and on they were going, safe and sure.

"Long time the journey endured; and the dream faded and again revived. It was as if he had slept, and again awaked; for he lay in soft grass on a mountain-side, and the form of a mighty man lay outstretched beside him, who was weary with a great weariness. Below, the sea howled and beat against the base of the mountain; but it was far below. Again the Lord arose, and lifted him up, and bore him onwards. Up to the mountain-top they went, through the keen, cold air, and over the fields of snow and ice. On the peak the Master paused and looked down.

"In a vast amphitheatre below was gathered a multitude that no man could number. They crowded on all sides beyond the reach of the sight, rising up the slopes of the surrounding mountains till they could no longer be distinguished; grouped and massed upon height above height; filling the hollows, and plains, and platforms all about. But every eye looked towards the lowest centre of the mountain-amphitheatre, where a little vacant spot awaited the presence of some form, which should be the heart of all the throng. Down towards this centre the Lord bore him. Entering the holy circle, he set him gently down, and then looked all around, as if searching earnestly for some one he could not see.

"And not finding whom he sought, he walked across the open space. A path was instantly divided for him through the dense multitude surrounding it. Along this lane of men and women and children, he went; and Herbert ran, following close at his feet; for now all the universe seemed empty save where he was. And he was not rebuked, but suffered to follow. And although the Lord walked fast and far, the feet following him were not weary, but grew in speed and in power. Through the great crowd and beyond it, never looking back, up and over the brow of the mountain they went, and, leaving behind them the gathered universe of men, descended into a pale night. Hither and thither went the Master, searching up and down the gloomy valley; now looking behind a great rock, and now through a thicket of brushwood; now entering a dark cave, and now ascending a height and gazing all around; till at last, on a bare plain, seated on a gray stone, with her hands in her lap, they found the little orphan child who had called the sea her mother.

"As he drew near to her, the Lord called out, 'My poor little lamb, I have found you at last!' But she did not seem to hear or understand what he said; for she fell on her knees, and held up her clasped hands, and cried, 'Do not be angry with me. I am a goat; and I ran away because I was afraid. Do not burn me.' But all the answer the Lord made was to stoop, and lift her, and hold her to his breast. And she was an orphan no more.

"So he turned and went back over hill and over dale, and Herbert followed, rejoicing that the lost lamb was found.

"As he followed, he spied in a crevice of a rock, close by his path, a lovely primrose. He stooped to pluck it. And ere he began to follow, a cock crew shrill and loud; and he knew that it was the cock that rebuked Peter; and he trembled and stood up. The Master had vanished. He, too, fell a-weeping bitterly. And again the cock crew; and he opened his eyes and knew that he had dreamed. His mother stood by his bedside, comforting the weeper with kisses. And he cried to her :—

"'O mother! surely he would not come over the sea to find me in the storm, and then leave me because I stopped to pluck a flower!'"

"Too long, I am afraid," said the curate, the moment he had finished his paper, looking at his watch.

"We have not thought so, I am sure," said Adela, courteously.

The ladies rose to go.

"Who is to read next?" said the school-master.

"Why, of course," said the curate, indignantly, "it ought to be my brother; but there is no depending on him."

"If this frost lasts, I will positively read next time," said the doctor. "But, you know, Ralph, it will be better for you to bring something else with you, lest I should fail again."

"Cool!" said the curate. "I think it is time we dropped it."

"No, please don't," said Harry, with a little anxiety in his tone. "I really want to read my story."

"It looks like it, doesn't it?"

"Now, Ralph, a clergyman should never be sarcastic. Be as indignant as you please, — but — sarcastic — never. It is very easy for you, who, know just what you have to do, and have besides whole volumes in that rickety old desk of yours, to keep such an appointment as this. Mine is produced for the occasion, *bond fide;* and I cannot tell what may be required of me from one hour to another."

He went up to Adela.

"I am very sorry to have failed again," he said.

"But you won't next time, will you?"

"I will not, if I can help it."

CHAPTER XVIII.

INTERRUPTION.

But it was Adela herself who failed next time. I had seen her during the reading draw her shawl about her as if she were cold. She seemed quite well when the friends left, but she had caught a chill; and before the morning she was quite feverish, and unable to leave her bed.

"You see, colonel," said Mrs. Cathcart at breakfast, "that this doctor of yours is doing the child harm instead of good. He has been suppressing instead of curing the complaint; and now she is worse than ever."

"When the devil—" I began to remark in reply.

"Mr. Smith!" exclaimed Mrs. Cathcart.

"Allow me, madam, to finish my sentence before you make up your mind to be shocked.—When the devil goes out of a man, or a woman either, he gives a terrible wrench by the way of farewell. Now, as the prophet Job teaches us, all disease is from the devil; and—"

"The prophet Job!—Mr. Smith?"

"Well, the old Arab scheik, if you like that epithet better."

"Really, Mr. Smith!"

"Well, I don't mind what you call him. I only mean to say that a disease sometimes goes out with a kind of flare, like a candle,—or like the poor life itself. I believe, if this is an intermittent fever,—as, from your description, I expect it will prove to be,—it will be the best thing for her."

"Well, we shall see what Dr. Wade will say."

"Dr. Wade?" I exclaimed.

"Of course my brother will not think of trusting such a serious case to an inexperienced young man like Mr. Armstrong."

"It seems to me," I replied, "that for some time the case has ceased to be a serious one. You must allow that Adela is better."

"Seemed to be better, Mr. Smith. But it was all excitement, and here is the consequence. I, as far as I have any

influence, decidedly object to Mr. Armstrong having anything
more to do with the case."

"Perhaps you are right, Jane," said the colonel. "I fear
you are. But how can I ask Dr. Wade to resume his attendance?"

Always nervous about Adela, his sister-in-law had at length
succeeded in frightening him.

"Leave that to me," she said; "I will manage him."

"Pooh!" said I, rudely. "He will jump at it. It will
be a grand triumph for him. I only want you to mind what
you are about. You know Adela does not like Dr. Wade."

"And she does like *Doctor* Armstrong?" said Mrs. Cathcart, stuffing each word with significance.

"Yes," I answered, boldly. "Who would not prefer the
one to the other?"

But her arrow had struck. The colonel rose, and saying
only, "Well, Jane, I leave the affair in your hands," walked
out of the room. I was coward enough to follow him. Had
it been of any use, coward as I was, I would have remained.

But Mrs. Cathcart, if she had not reckoned without her
host, had, at least, reckoned without her hostess. She wrote
instantly to Dr. Wade, in terms of which it is enough to say
that they were successful, for they brought the doctor at once.
I saw him pass through the hall, looking awfully stiff, important, and condescending. Beeves, who had opened the door to
him, gave me a very queer look as he showed him into the
drawing-room, ringing, at the same time, for Adela's maid.

Now Mrs. Cathcart had not expected that the doctor would
arrive so soon, and had, as yet, been unable to make up her
mind how to communicate to the patient the news of the change
in the physical ministry. So, when the maid brought the message, all that her cunning could provide her with at the moment was the pretence that he had called so opportunely by
chance.

"Ask him to walk up," she said, after just one moment's
hesitation.

"Adela heard the direction her aunt gave, through the cold
shiver which was then obliterating rather than engrossing her
attention, and concluded that they had sent for Mr. Armstrong.
But Mrs. Cathcart, turning towards her, said : —

"Adela, my love, Dr. Wade has just called; and I have asked him to step upstairs."

The patient started up.

"Aunt, what do you mean? If that old wife comes into this room, I will make him glad to go out of it!"

You see she was feverish, poor child, else I am sure she could not have been so rude to her aunt. But before Mrs. Cathcart could reply, in came Dr. Wade. He walked right up to the bed, after a stately obeisance to the lady attendant.

"I am sorry to find you so ill, Miss Cathcart."

"I am perfectly well, Dr. Wade. I am sorry you have had the trouble of walking upstairs."

As she said this, she rung the bell at the head of her bed. Her maid, who had been listening at the door, entered at once. I had all this from Adela herself afterwards.

"Emma, bring me my desk. Dr. Wade, there must be some mistake. It was my aunt, Mrs. Cathcart, who sent for you. Had she given me the opportunity, I would have begged that the interview might take place in her room instead of mine."

Dr. Wade retreated towards the fireplace, where Mrs. Cathcart stood, quite aware that she had got herself into a mess of no ordinary complication. Yet she persisted in her cunning. She lifted her finger to her forehead.

"Ah?" said Dr. Wade.

"Yes," said Mrs. Cathcart.

"Wandering?"

"Dreadfully."

After some more whispering, the doctor sat down to write a prescription. But, meantime, Adela was busy writing another. What she wrote was precisely to this effect:—

"DEAR MR. ARMSTRONG:— I have caught a bad cold, and my aunt has let loose Dr. Wade upon me. Please come directly, if you will save me from ever so much nasty medicine, at the least. My aunt is not my mother, thank Heaven! though she would gladly usurp that relationship.

"Yours most truly,

"ADELA CATHCART."

She folded and sealed the note, — sealed it carefully, — and gave it to Emma, who vanished with it, followed instantly by Mrs. Cathcart. As to what took place outside the door — shall I confess it? — Beeves is my informant.

"Where are you going, Emma? Emma, come here directly," said Mrs. Cathcart.

Emma obeyed.

"I am going a message for mis'ess."

"Who is that note for?"

"I didn't ask. John can read well enough."

"Show it me."

Emma, I presume, closed both lips and hand very tight.

"I command you."

"Miss Cathcart pays me my wages, ma'am," said Emma, and, turning, sped downstairs like a carrier-pigeon.

In the hall she met Beeves, and told him the story.

"There she comes!" cried he. "Give me the letter. I'll take it myself."

"You're not going without your hat, surely, Mr. Beeves," said Emma.

"Bless me! It's downstairs. There's master's old one! He'll never want it again. And if he does, it'll be none the worse."

And he was out of the door in a moment. Beeves' alarm, however, as to Mrs. Cathcart's approach, was a false one. She returned into the sick-chamber, with a face fiery red, and found Dr. Wade just finishing an elaborate prescription.

"There!" said he, rising. "Send for that at once, and let it be taken directly. Good-morning."

He left the room instantly, making signs that he was afraid of exciting his patient, as she did not appear to approve of his presence.

"What is the prescription?" said Adela, quite quietly, as Mrs. Cathcart approached the bed, apparently trying to decipher it.

"I am glad to see you so much calmer, my dear. You must not excite yourself. The prescription? I cannot make it out. Doctors do write so badly. I suppose they consider it professional."

"They consider a good many things professional which are only stupid. Let me see it."

Mrs. Cathcart, thrown off her guard, gave it to her. Adela tore it in fragments, and threw it in a little storm on the floor.

"Adela!" screamed Mrs. Cathcart. "What *is* to be done?"

"Pay Dr. Wade his fee, and tell him I shall never be too ill to refuse his medicines. Now, aunt! You find I am determined. I declare you make me behave so ill that I am ashamed of myself."

Here the poor impertinent child crept under the clothes, and fell a-weeping bitterly. Mrs. Cathcart had sense enough to see that nothing could be done, and retired to her room. Getting weary of her own society after a few moments of solitude, she proceeded to go downstairs. But half-way down she was met full in the face by Henry Armstrong ascending two steps at a time. He had already met Dr. Wade, as he came out of the dining-room, where he had been having an interview with the colonel. Harry had turned, and held out his hand with a "How do you do, Dr. Wade?" But that gentleman had bowed with the utmost stiffness, and kept his hand at home.

"So it is to be open war and mutual slander, is it, Dr. Wade?" said Harry. "In that case, I want to know how you come to interfere with my patient. I have had no dismissal, which punctilio I took care to know was observed in your case."

"Sir, I was sent for," said Dr. Wade, haughtily.

"I have in my pocket a note from the lady of this house, requesting my immediate attendance. If you have received a request to the same purport from a visitor, you obey it at your own risk. Good-morning."

Then Harry walked quietly up the first half of the stair, while Beeves hastened to open the door to the crestfallen Dr. Wade; but by the time he met Mrs. Cathcart his rate of ascent had considerably increased. As soon as she saw him, however, without paying any attention to the usual formality of a greeting, she turned and re-entered her niece's room. Her eyes were flashing, and her face spotted red and white with helpless rage. But she would not abandon the field. Harry bowed to her, and passed on to the bed, where he was greeted with a smile.

"There's not much the matter, I hope?" he said, returning the smile.

"It may suit you to make light of my niece's illness, Mr. Armstrong; but I beg to inform you that her father thought it serious enough to send for Dr. Wade. He has been here already, and your attendance is quite superfluous."

"No doubt; no doubt. But, as I am here, I may as well prescribe."

"Dr. Wade has already prescribed."

"And I have taken his prescription, have I not, aunt? — and destroyed it, Mr. Armstrong, instead of my own chance."

"Of what?" said Mrs. Cathcart, with vulgar significance.

"Of getting rid of two officious old women at once," said Adela, — in a rage, I fear I must confess, as the only excuse for impertinence.

"Come, come," said Harry, "this won't do. I cannot have my patient excited in this way. Miss Cathcart, may I ring for your maid?"

For answer, Adela rang the bell herself. Her aunt was pretending to look out of the window.

"Will you go and ask your master," said Harry, when Emma made her appearance, "to be so kind as to come here for a moment?"

The poor colonel — an excellent soldier, a severe master, with the highest notions of authority and obedience — found himself degraded by his own conduct, as other autocrats have proved before, into a temporizing incapable. It was the more humiliating that he was quite aware in his own honest heart that it was jealousy of Harry that had brought him into this painful position. But he obeyed the summons at once; for wherever there was anything unpleasant to be done, there, with him, duty assumed the sterner command. As soon as he entered the room, Harry, without giving time for any one else to determine the course of the conference, said: —

"There has been some mistake, Colonel Cathcart, between Dr. Wade and myself, which has already done Miss Cathcart no good. As I find her very feverish, though not by any means alarmingly ill, I must, as her medical attendant, insist that *no* one come into her room but yourself or her maid."

Every one present perfectly understood this; and however, in other circumstances, the colonel might have resented the tone of authority with which Harry spoke, he was compelled, for his daughter's sake, to yield; and he afterwards justified Harry entirely. Mrs. Cathcart walked out of the room with her neck invisible from behind. The colonel sat down by the fire. Harry wrote his prescription on the half sheet from which Dr. Wade had torn his; and then saying that he would call in the evening, took his leave of the colonel, and bowed to his patient, receiving a glance of acknowledgment which could not fail to generate the feeling that there was a secret understanding between them, and that he had done just what she wanted. He mounted his roan horse, called Rhubarb, with a certain elation of being, which he tried to hide from every one but himself.

When doctors forget that their patients are more like musical instruments than machines, they will soon need to be reminded that they are men and women, and not dogs or horses. Yet, alas for the poor dogs and horses that fall into the hands of a man without a human sympathy even with them ! I, John Smith bless you, my doctor-friends, that ye are not doctors merely, but good and loving men ; and, in virtue thereof, so much the more — so exceedingly the more — *Therapeutæ.*

I need not follow the course of the fever. Each day the arrival of the cold fit was longer delayed, and the violence of both diminished, until they disappeared altogether. But a day or two before this happy result was completed, Adela had been allowed to go down to the drawing-room, and had delighted her father with her cheerfulness and hopefulness. It really seemed as if the ague had carried off the last remnants of the illness under which she had been so long laboring. But then, you can never put anything to the *experimentum crucis;* and there were other causes at work for Adela's cure, which were perhaps more powerful than even the ague. However this may have been, she got almost quite well in a very short space of time ; and, with her father's consent, issued invitations to another meeting of the story-club. They were at once satisfactorily responded to.

CHAPTER XIX.

PERCY.

By this time Percy had returned to London. His mother remained; but the terms understood between her niece and herself were those of icy politeness and reserve. I learned afterwards that something of an understanding had also been arrived at between Percy and Harry; ever since learning the particulars of which, I have liked the young rascal a great deal better. So I will trouble my reader to take an interest in my report of the affair.

Percy met Harry at the gate, after one of his professional visits, and accosted him thus: —

"Mr. Armstrong, my mother says you have been rude to her."

"I am not in the least aware of it, Mr. Percy."

"Oh! I don't care much. She *is* provoking. Besides, she can take care of herself. That's not it."

"What is it, then?"

"What do you mean about Adela?"

"I have said nothing more than that she has had a sharp attack of intermittent fever, which is going off."

"Come, come, — you know what I mean."

"I may suspect, but I don't choose to answer hints, the meaning of which I *only* suspect. I might make a fool of myself."

"Well, I'll be plain. Are you in love with her?"

"Suppose I were, you are not the first to whom I should think it necessary to confess."

"Well, are you paying your addresses to her?"

"I am sorry I cannot consent to make my answers as frank as your questions. You have the advantage of me in straightforwardness, I confess. Only you have got sun and wind of me both."

"Come, come, — I hate dodging."

"I dare say you do. But just let me shift round a bit, and see what you will do then. Are *you* in love with Miss Cathcart?"

" Yes."

" Upon my word, I shouldn't have thought it. Here have
we been all positively conspiring to do her good, and you have
been paying ten times the attention to the dogs and horses that
you have paid to her."

" By Jove ! it's quite true. But I couldn't somehow."

" Then she hasn't encouraged you ? "

" By Jupiter ! you are frank enough now. No, damn it,
— not a bit. But she used to like me, and she would again,
if you would let her alone."

" Now, Mr. Percy, I'll tell you what. I don't believe
you are a bit in love with her."

" She's devilish pretty."

" Well ? "

" And I declare I think she got prettier and prettier every
day till this cursed ague took her. Your fault, too, my mother
says."

" We'll leave your mother out of the question now, if you
please. Do you know what made her look prettier and prettier, — for you are quite right about that ? "

" No. I suppose you were giving her arsenic."

" No. I was giving her the true *elixir vitæ*, unknown even
to the Rosicrucians."

Percy stared.

" I will explain myself. Her friend, Mr. Smith — "

" Old fogie ! "

" Old bachelor, — yes. Mr. Smith and I agreed that she
was dying of ennui ; and so we got up this story-club, and got
my brother and the rest to bear a hand in it. It did her all
the good the most sanguine of us could have hoped for."

" I thought it horrid slow."

" I am surprised at that, for you were generally asleep."

" I was forced, in self-defence. I couldn't smoke."

" It gave her something to think about."

" So it seems."

" Now, Mr. Percy, how could you think you had the
smallest chance with her, when here was first one and then
another turning each the flash of his own mental prism upon
her weary eyes, and healing them with light ; while you would
not take the smallest trouble to gratify her, or even to show

yourself to anything like advantage? My dear fellow, what a fool you are!"

"Mr. Armstrong!"

"Come, come, — you began with frankness, and I've only gone on with it. You are a good-hearted fellow, and ought to be made something of."

"At all events, you make something of yourself, to talk of your own productions as the *elixir vitæ*."

"You forget that I am in disgrace as well as yourself on that score; for I have not read a word of my own since the club began."

"Then how the devil should I be worse off than you?"

"I didn't say you were. I only said you did your best to place yourself at a disadvantage. I at least took a part in the affair, although a very humble one. But depend upon it, a girl like Miss Cathcart thinks more of mental gifts than of any outward advantages which a man may possess; and in the company of those who *think*, a fellow's good looks don't go for much. She could not help measuring you by those other men — and women too. But you may console yourself with the reflection that there are plenty of girls, and pretty ones too, of a very different way of judging; and for my part you are welcome to the pick of them."

"You mean to say that I shan't have Addie?"

"Not in the least, But, come now — do you think yourself worthy of a girl like that?"

"No. Do you?"

"No. But I should not feel such a hypocrite, if she thought me worthy, as to give her up on that ground."

"Then what *do* you mean?"

"To win her, if I can."

"Whew!"

"But, if you are a gentleman, you will let me say so myself, and not betray my secret."

"Damned if I do! Good luck to you! There's my hand. I believe you are a good fellow after all. I wish I had seen you ride to hounds. They tell me it's a sight."

"Thank you heartily. But what are you going to do?'

"Go back to the sweet-flowing Thames, and the dreams of the desk."

"Well — be a man as well as a gentleman. Don't be a fool."

"Hang it all! I believe it was her money, after all, I was in love with. Good-by!"

But the poor fellow looked grave enough as he went away. And I trust that, before long, he, too, began to reap some of the good corn that grows on the wintry fields of disappointment. I have my eye upon him; but it is little an *old fogie* like me can do with a fellow like Percy.

———

CHAPTER XX

THE CRUEL PAINTER.

Now to return to the Story-Club.

On the night appointed, we met. And, to the delight of all the rest of us, Harry arrived with a look that satisfied us that he was to be no defaulter this time. The look was one of almost nervous uneasiness. Of course this sprung from anxiety to please Adela, — at least, so I interpreted it. She occupied her old place on the couch; we all arranged ourselves nearly as before; and the fire was burning very bright. Before he began, however, Harry, turning to our host, said: —

"May I arrange the scene as I please, for the right effect of my story?"

"Certainly," answered the colonel.

Harry rose, and extinguished the lamp.

"But, my dear sir," said the colonel, "how can you read now?"

"Perfectly, by the firelight," answered Harry.

He then went to the windows, and, drawing aside the curtains, drew up the blinds.

It was full high moon, and the light so clear that, notwithstanding the brightness of the fire, each window seemed to lie in ghostly shimmer on the floor. Not a breath of wind was abroad. The whole country being covered with snow, the air was filled with a snowy light. On one side rose the high roof of another part of the house, on which the snow was lying thick and smooth, undisturbed save by the footprints, visible in the moon, of a large black cat, which had now paused in the middle of it, and was looking round suspiciously towards the source of the light which had surprised him in his midnight walk.

"Now," said Harry, returning to his seat, and putting on an air of confidence to conceal the lack of it, "let any one who has nerves retire at once, both for his own sake and that of the company! This is just such a night as I wanted to read my story in, — snow — stillness — moonlight outside, and nothing but firelight inside. Mind, Ralph, you keep up the fire, for the room will be more ready to get cold now the coverings are off the windows. You will say at once if you feel it cold, Miss Cathcart?"

Adela promised; and Harry, who had his manuscript gummed together in a continuous roll, so that he might not have to turn over any leaves, began at once :—

"THE CRUEL PAINTER.

"Among the young men assembled at the University of Prague, in the year 159–, was one called Karl von Walkenlicht. A somewhat careless student, he yet held a fair position in the estimation of both professors and men, because he could hardly look at a proposition without understanding it. Where such proposition, however, had to do with anything relating to the deeper insights of the nature, he was quite content that, for him, it should remain a proposition; which, however, he laid up in one of his mental cabinets, and was ready to reproduce at a moment's notice. This mental agility was more than matched by the corresponding corporeal excellence, and both aided in producing results in which his remarkable strength was equally apparent. In all games depending upon the combination of muscle and skill, he had scarce rivalry enough to keep him in practice. His strength, however, was embodied in such a softness of muscular outline, such a rare Greek-like style of beauty, and associated with such a gentleness of manner and behavior, that, partly from

the truth of the resemblance, partly from the absurdity of
the contrast, he was known throughout the university by the
diminutive of the feminine form of his name, and was always
called Lottchen.

" ' I say, Lottchen,' said one of his fellow-students, called
Richter, across the table in a wine-cellar they were in the
habit of frequenting, ' do you know, Heinrich Höllenrachen
here says that he saw this morning, with mortal eyes, — whom
do you think ? — Lilith.'

" ' Adam's first wife ? ' asked Lottchen, with an attempt at
carelessness while his face flushed like a maiden's.

" ' None of your chaff ! ' said Richter. ' Your face is
honester than your tongue, and confesses what you cannot
deny, that you would give your chance of salvation — a small
one to be sure, but all you've got — for one peep at Lilith.
Wouldn't you now, Lottchen ? '

" ' Go to the devil ! ' was all Lottchen's answer to his
tormentor ; but he turned to Heinrich, to whom the students
had given the surname above mentioned, because of the
enormous width of his jaws, and said with eagerness and
envy, disguising them, as well as he could, under the appearance of curiosity : —

" ' You don't mean it, Heinrich ? You've been taking the
beggar in ! Confess now.'

" ' Not I. I saw her with my two eyes.'

" ' Notwithstanding the different planes of their orbits,'
suggested Richter.

" ' Yes, notwithstanding the fact that I can get a parallax to
any of the fixed stars in a moment, with only the breadth of
my nose for the base,' answered Heinrich, responding at once
to the fun, and careless of the personal defect insinuated.
' She was near enough for even me to see her perfectly.'

" ' When ? Where ? How ? ' asked Lottchen.

" ' Two hours ago. In the church-yard of St. Stephen's.
By a lucky chance. Any more little questions, my child ? '
answered Höllenrachen.

" ' What could have taken her there, who is seen nowhere ? '
said Richter.

" ' She was seated on a grave. After she left, I went to the
place ; but it was a new-made grave. There was no stone up.

I asked the sexton about her. He said he supposed she was the daughter of the woman buried there last Thursday week. I knew it was Lilith.'

"'Her mother dead!' said Lottchen, musingly. Then he thought with himself, 'She will be going there again, then!' But he took care that the ghost-thought should wander unembodied. 'But how did you know her, Heinrich? You never saw her before.'

"'How do you come to be over head and ears in love with her, Lottchen, and you haven't seen her at all?' interposed Richter.

"'Will you, or will you not, go to the devil?' rejoined Lottchen, with a comic *crescendo;* to which the other replied with a laugh.

"'No one could miss knowing her,' said Heinrich.

"'Is she so very like, then?'

"'It is always herself, her very self.'

"A fresh flask of wine, turning out to be not up to the mark, brought the current of conversation against itself; not much to the dissatisfaction of Lottchen, who had already resolved to be in the church-yard of St. Stephen's at sundown the following day, in the hope that he, too, might be favored with a vision of Lilith.

"This resolution he carried out. Seated in a porch of the church, not knowing in what direction to look for the apparition he hoped to see, and desirous as well of not seeming to be on the watch for one, he was gazing at the fallen rose-leaves of the sunset, withering away upon the sky, when, glancing aside by an involuntary movement, he saw a woman seated upon a new-made grave, not many yards from where he sat, with her face buried in her hands, and apparently weeping bitterly. Karl was in the shadow of the porch, and could see her perfectly, without much danger of being discovered by her; so he sat and watched her. She raised her head for a moment, and the rose-flush of the west fell over it, shining on the tears with which it was wet, and giving the whole a bloom which did not belong to it, for it was always pale, and now pale as death. It was indeed the face of Lilith, the most celebrated beauty of Prague.

"Again she buried her face in her hands; and Karl sat with a strange feeling of helpnessness, which grew as he sat; and the longing to help her whom he could not help drew his heart towards her with a trembling reverence which was quite new to him. She wept on. The western roses withered slowly away, and the clouds blended with the sky, and the stars gathered like drops of glory sinking through the vault of night, and the trees about the church-yard grew black, and Lilith almost vanished in the wide darkness. At length she lifted her head, and, seeing the night around her, gave a little broken cry of dismay. The minutes had swept over her head, not through her mind, and she did not know that the dark had come.

"Hearing her cry, Karl rose and approached her. She heard his footsteps, and started to her feet. Karl spoke : —

" 'Do not be frightened,' he said. 'Let me see you home. I will walk behind you.'

" 'Who are you ?' she rejoined.

" 'Karl Wolkenlicht.'

" 'I have heard of you. Thank you. I can go home alone.'

" Yet, as if in a half-dreamy, half-unconscious mood, she accepted his offered hand to lead her through the graves, and allowed him to walk beside her, till, reaching the corner of a narrow street, she suddenly bade him good-night and vanished. He thought it better not to follow her, so he returned her good-night and went home.

" How to see her again was his first thought the next day ; as, in fact, how to see her at all had been his first thought for many days. She went nowhere that he ever heard of ; she knew nobody that he knew ; she was never seen at church, or at market ; never seen in the street. Her home had a dreary, desolate aspect. It looked as if no one ever went out or in. It was like a place on which decay had fallen because there was no indwelling spirit. The mud of years was baked upon its door, and no faces looked out of its dusty windows.

" How, then, could she be the most celebrated beauty of Prague? How, then, was it that Heinrich Höllenrachen knew her the moment he saw her? Above all, how was it that Karl Wolkenlicht had, in fact, fallen in love with her before ever he saw her? It was thus : —

"Her father was a painter. Belonging thus to the public, it had taken the liberty of re-naming him. Every one called him Teufelsbürst, or Devilsbrush. It was a name with which, to judge from the nature of his representations, he could hardly fail to be pleased. For, not as a nightmare-dream, which may alternate with the loveliest visions, but as his ordinary every-day work, he delighted to represent human suffering.

"Not an aspect of human woe or torture, as expressed in countenance or limb, came before his willing imagination, but he bore it straightway to his easel. In the moments that precede sleep, when the black space before the eyes of the poet teems with lovely faces, or dawns into a spirit-landscape, face after face of suffering, in all varieties of expression, would crowd, as if compelled, by the accompanying fiends, to present themselves, in awful levee, before the inner eye of the expect-ant master. Then he would rise, light his lamp, and, with rapid hand, make notes of his visions; recording, with swift, successive sweeps of his pencil, every individual face which had rejoiced his evil fancy. Then he would return to his couch, and, well satisfied, fall asleep, to dream yet further embodiments of human ill.

"What wrong could man or mankind have done him, to be thus fearfully pursued by the vengeance of the artist's hate?

"Another characteristic of the faces and forms which he drew was, that they were all beautiful in the original idea. The lines of each face, however distorted by pain, would have been, in rest, absolutely beautiful; and the whole of the exe-cution bore witness to the fact that upon this original beauty the painter had directed the artillery of anguish, to bring down the sky-soaring heights of its divinity to the level of a hated existence. To do this, he worked in perfect accordance with artistic law, falsifying no line of the original forms. It was the suffering, rather than his pencil, that wrought the change. The latter was the willing instrument to record what the imagi-nation conceived with a cruelty composed enough to be correct.

"To enhance the beauty he had thus distorted, and so to enhance yet further the suffering that produced the distortion, he would often represent attendant demons, whom he made as ugly as his imagination could compass; avoiding, however, all grotesqueness beyond what was sufficient to indicate that they were demons, and not men. Their ugliness rose .from hate, envy, and all evil passions; amongst which he especially delighted to represent a gloating exultation over human distress. And often in the midst of his clouds of demon faces, would some one who knew him recognize the painter's own likeness, such as the mirror might have presented it to him when he was busiest over the incarnation of some exquisite torture.

"But, apparently with the wish to avoid being supposed to choose such representations for their own sakes, he always found a story, often in the histories of the church, whose name he gave to the painting, and which he pretended to have inspired the pictorial conception. No one, however, who looked upon his suffering martyrs, could suppose for a moment that he honored their martyrdom. They were but the vehicles for his hate of humanity. He was the torturer, and not Diocletian or Nero.

"But, stranger yet to tell, there was no picture, whatever its subject, into which he did not introduce one form of placid and harmonious loveliness. In this, however, his fierceness was only more fully displayed. For in no case did this form manifest any relation either to the actors or the endurers in the picture. Hence its very loveliness became almost hateful to those who beheld it. Not a shade crossed the still sky of that brow, not a ripple disturbed the still sea of that cheek. She did not hate, she did not love the sufferers; the painter would not have her hate, for that would be to the injury of her loveliness; would not have her love, for he hated. Sometimes she floated above, as a still, unobservant angel, her gaze turned upward, dreaming along, careless as a white summer cloud, across the blue. If she looked down on the scene below, it was only that the beholder might see that she saw and did not care; that not a feather of her outspread pinions would quiver at the sight. Sometimes she would stand in the crowd, as if she had been copied there from another picture, and had nothing to do with this one, nor any right to be in it at all. Or when the red blood was trickling drop by drop from the crushed limb, she might be seen standing nearest, smiling over a primrose or the bloom on a peach. Some had said that she was the painter's wife; that she had been false to him; that he had killed her; and, finding that that was no sufficing revenge, thus, half in love, and half in deepest hate, immortalized his vengeance. But it was now universally understood that it was his daughter, of whose loveliness extravagant reports went abroad; though all said, doubtless reading this from her father's pictures, that she was a beauty without a heart. Strange theories of something else supplying its place were rife among the anatomical students. With the girl in the pictures, the wild imagination of Lottchen, probably in part from her apparently absolute unattainableness and her undisputed heartlessness, had fallen in love, as far as the mere imagination can fall in love.

"But again, how was he to see her? He haunted the house, night after night. Those blue eyes never met his. No step responsive to his came from that door. It seemed to have been so long unopened that it had grown as fixed and hard as the stones that held its bolts in their passive clasp. He dared not watch in the daytime, and with all his watching at night, he never saw father or daughter or domestic cross the threshold. Little he thought that, from a shot-window near the door, a pair of blue eyes, like Lilith's, but paler and colder, were watching him, just as a spider watches the fly that is likely ere long to fall into his toils. And into those toils Karl soon fell. For her form darkened the page; her form stood on the threshold of sleep; and when, overcome with watching, he did enter its precincts, her form entered with him, and walked by his side. He must find her; or the world might go to the bottomless pit for him. But how?

"Yes. He would be a painter. Teufelsbürst would receive him as a humble apprentice. He would grind his colors, and Teufelsbürst would teach him the mysteries of the science which is the handmaiden of art. Then he might see *her*, and that was all his ambition.

"In the clear morning light of a day in autumn, when the leaves were beginning to fall scared from the hand of that Death which has his dance in the chapels of nature as well as in the cathedral aisles of men, — he walked up and knocked at the dingy door. The spider painter opened it himself. He was a little man, meagre and pallid, with those faded blue eyes, a low nose, in three distinct divisions, and thin, curveless, cruel lips. He wore no hair on his face; but long gray locks, long

as a woman's, were scattered over his shoulders, and hung
down on his breast. When Wolkenlicht had explained his
errand, he smiled a smile in which hypocrisy could not hide
the cunning, and, after many difficulties, consented to receive
him as a pupil, on condition that he would become an inmate
of his house. Wolkenlicht's heart bounded with delight, which
he tried to hide; the second smile of Teufelsbürst might have
shown him that he had ill·succeeded. The fact that he was
not a native of Prague, but, coming from a distant part of the
country, was entirely his own master in the city, rendered this
condition perfectly easy to fulfil; and that very afternoon he
entered the studio of Teufelsbürst as his scholar and servant.

" It was a great room, filled with the appliances and results
of art. Many pictures, festooned with cobwebs, were hung
carelessly on the dirty walls. Others, half finished, leaned
against them, on the floor. Several, in different stages of
progress, stood upon easels. But all spoke the cruel bent of the
artist's genius. In one corner a lay-figure was extended on a
couch, covered with a pall of black velvet. Through its folds
the form beneath was easily discernible; and one hand and
fore-arm protruded from beneath it, at right angles to the rest
of the frame. Lottchen could not help shuddering when he
saw it. Although he overcame the feeling in a moment, he
felt a great repugnance to seating himself with his back towards it, as the arrangement of an easel, at which Teufelsbürst wished him to draw, rendered necessary. He contrived
to edge himself round, so that when he lifted his eyes he
should see the figure, and be sure that it could not rise without his being aware of it. But his master saw and understood
his altered position, and, under some pretence about the light,
compelled him to resume the position in which he had placed
him at first; after which he sat watching, over the top of his
picture, the expression of his countenance as he tried to draw;
reading in it the horrid fancy that the figure under the pall
had risen, and was stealthily approaching to look over his
shoulder. But Lottchen resisted the feeling, and, being already
no contemptible draughtsman, was soon interested enough to
forget it. And then, any moment, *she* might enter.

" Now began a system of slow torture, for the chance of
which the painter had been long on the watch, — especially

since he had first seen Karl lingering about the house. His opportunities of seeing physical suffering were nearly enough even for the diseased necessities of his art; but now he had one in his power, on whom, his own will fettering him, he could try any experiments he pleased for the production of a kind of suffering, in the observation of which he did not consider that he had yet had sufficient experience. He would hold the very heart of the youth in his hand, and wring it and torture it to his own content. And lest Karl should be strong enough to prevent those expressions of pain for which he lay on the watch, he would make use of further means, known to himself, and known to few besides.

"All that day Karl saw nothing of Lilith; but he heard her voice once, — and that was enough for one day. The next, she was sitting to her father the greater part of the day, and he could see her as often as he dared glance up from his drawing. She had looked at him when she entered, but had shown no sign of recognition; and all day long she took no further notice of him. He hoped, at first, that this came of the intelligence of love: but he soon began to doubt it. For he saw that, with the holy shadow of sorrow, all that distinguished the expression of her countenance from that which the painter so constantly reproduced, had vanished likewise. It was the very face of the unheeding angel whom, as often as he lifted his eyes higher than hers, he saw on the wall above her, playing on a psaltery in the smoke of the torment ascending forever from burning Babylon. The power of the painter had not merely wrought for the representation of the woman of his imagination: it had had scope as well in realizing her.

"Karl soon began to see that communication, other than of the eyes, was all but hopeless; and to any attempt in that way she seemed altogether indisposed to respond. Nor, if she had wished it, would it have been safe; for as often as he glanced towards her, instead of hers, he met the blue eyes of the painter, gleaming upon him like winter-lightning. His tones, his gestures, his words, seemed kind; his glance and his smile refused to be disguised.

"The first day he dined alone in the studio, waited upon by an old woman; the next he was admitted to the family table, with Teufelsbürst and Lilith. The room offered a strange contrast to the study. As far as handicraft, directed by a sumptuous taste, could construct a house-paradise, this was one. But it seemed rather a paradise of demons; for the walls were covered with Tuefelsbürst's paintings. During the dinner, Lilith's gaze scarcely met that of Wolkenlicht; and once or twice, when their eyes did meet, her glance was so perfectly unconcerned, that Karl wished he might look at her forever without the fear of her looking at him again. She seemed like one whose love had rushed out, glowing with seraphic fire, to be frozen to death in a more than wintry cold: she now walked lonely without her love. In the evenings, he was expected to continue his drawing by lamp-light; and at night he was conducted by Teufelsbürst to his chamber. Not once did he allow him to proceed thither alone, and not once did he leave him there without locking and bolting the door on the outside. But he felt nothing except the coldness of Lilith.

"Day after day she sat to her father, in every variety of costume that could best show the variety of her beauty. How much greater that beauty might be, if it ever blossomed into a beauty of soul, Wolkenlicht never imagined; for he soon loved her enough to attribute to her all the possibilities of her face as actual possessions of her being. To account for everything that seemed to contradict this perfection, his brain was prolific in inventions; till he was compelled at last to see that she was in the condition of a rose-bud, which, on the point of blossoming, has been chilled into a changeless bud by the cold of an untimely frost. For one day, after the father and daughter had become a little more accustomed to his silent presence, a conversation began between them, which went on until he saw that Teufelsbürst believed in nothing except his art. How much of his feeling for that could be dignified by the name of belief, seeing its objects were such as they were, might have been questioned. It seemed to Wolkenlicht to amount only to this: that, amidst a thousand distastes, it was a pleasant thing to reproduce on the canvas the forms he beheld around him, modifying them to express the prevailing feelings of his own mind.

"A more desolate communication between souls than that which then passed between father and daughter could hardly be imagined. The father spoke of humanity and all its experiences in a tone of the bitterest scorn. He despised men, and himself amongst them; and rejoiced to think that the generations rose and vanished, brood after brood, as the crops of corn grew and disappeared. Lilith, who listened to it all unmoved, taking only an intellectual interest in the question, remarked that even the corn had more life than that; for, after its death, it rose again in the new crop. Whether she meant that the corn was therefore superior to man, forgetting that the superior can produce being without losing its own, or only advanced an objection to her father's argument, Wolkenlicht could not tell. But Teufelsbürst laughed like the sound of a saw, and said, 'Follow out the analogy, my Lilith, and you will see that man is like the corn that springs again after it is buried; but unfortunately the only result we know of is a vampire.'

"Wolkenlicht looked up, and saw a shudder pass through the frame, and over the pale, thin face of the painter. This he could not account for. But Teufelsbürst could have explained it, for there were strange whispers abroad, and they had reached his ear; and his philosophy was not quite enough for them. But the laugh with which Lilith met this frightful attempt at wit grated dreadfully on Wolkenlicht's feeling. With her, too, however, a reaction seemed to follow. For, turning round a moment after, and looking at the picture on which her father was working, the tears rose in her eyes, and she said, 'O father, how like my mother you have made me this time!'—'Child!' retorted the painter, with a cold fierceness, 'you have no mother. That which is gone out is gone out. Put no name in my hearing on that which is not. Where no substance is, how can there be a name?'

"Lilith rose and left the room. Wolkenlicht now understood that Lilith was a frozen bud, and could not blossom into a rose. But pure love lives by faith. It loves the vaguely beheld and unrealized ideal. It dares believe that the loved is not all that she ever seemed. It is in virtue of this that love loves on. And it was in virtue of this, that Wolkenlicht loved Lilith yet more after he discovered what a grave of misery her unbelief was digging for her within her own soul. For her sake he would bear anything,—bear even with calmness the torments of his own love; he would stay on, hoping and hoping. The text, that we know not what a day may bring forth, is just as true of good things as of evil things; and out of Time's womb the facts must come.

"But with the birth of this resolution to endure, his suffering abated; his face grew more calm; his love, no less earnest, was less imperious; and he did not look up so often from his work when Lilith was present. The master could see that his pupil was more at ease, and that he was making rapid progress in his art. This did not suit his designs, and he would betake himself to his further schemes.

"For this purpose he proceeded first to simulate a friendship for Wolkenlicht the manifestations of which he gradually increased, until, after a day or two, he asked him to drink wine with him in the evening. Karl readily agreed. The painter produced some of his best, but took care not to allow Lilith to taste it; for he had cunningly prepared and mingled with it a decoction of certain herbs and other ingredients, exercising specific actions upon the brain, and tending to the inordinate excitement of those portions of it which are principally under the rule of the imagination. By the reaction of the brain, during the operation of these stimulants, the imagination is filled with suggestions and images. The nature of these is determined by the prevailing mood of the time. They are such as the imagination would produce of itself; but increased in number and intensity. Teufelsbürst, without philosophizing about it, called his preparation a simple love-philter — a concoction well known by name, but the composition of which was the secret of only a few. Wolkenlicht had, of course, not the least suspicion of the treatment to which he was subjected.

"Teufelsbürst was, however, doomed to fresh disappointment. Not that his potion failed in the anticipated effect; for now Karl's real sufferings began; but that such was the strength of Karl's will, and his fear of doing anything that might give a pretext for banishing him from the presence of Lilith, that he was able to conceal his feelings far too successfully for the satisfaction of Teufelsbürst's art. Yet he had to fetter himself with all the restraints that self-exhortation could load him with, to refrain from falling at the feet of Lilith and kissing the hem of her garment; for that, as the lowliest part of all that surrounded her, itself kissing the earth, seemed to come nearest within the reach of his ambition, and therefore to draw him the most.

"No doubt the painter had experience and penetration enough to perceive that he was suffering intensely; but he wanted to see the suffering embodied in outward signs, bringing it within the region over which his pencil held sway. He kept on, therefore, trying one thing after another, and rousing the poor youth to agony, till to his other sufferings were added, at length, those of failing health, — a fact which notified itself evidently enough even for Teufelsbürst, though its signs were not of the sort he chiefly desired. But Karl endured all bravely.

"Meantime, for various reasons, he scarcely ever left the house.

"I must now interrupt the course of my story to introduce another clement.

"A few years before the period of my tale, a certain shoemaker of the city had died under circumstances more than suggestive of suicide. He was buried, however, with such precautions, that six weeks elapsed before the rumor of the facts broke out; upon which rumor, not before, the most fearful reports began to be circulated, supported by what seemed to the people of Prague incontestable evidence. A *spectrum* of the deceased appeared to multitudes of persons, playing horrible pranks, and occasioning indescribable consternation throughout the whole town. This went on till at last, about eight months after his burial, the magistrates caused his body to be dug up; when it was found in just the condition of the bodies of those who in the eastern countries of Europe are called *vampires*. They buried the corpse under the gallows; but neither the digging up nor the reburying were of avail to banish the spectre. Again the spade and pickaxe were set to work, and the dead man, being found considerably improved in *condition* since his last interment, was, with various horrible indignities, burnt to ashes, 'after which the *spectrum* was never seen more.'

"And a second epidemic of the same nature had broken out a little before the period to which I have brought my story.

"About midnight, after a calm, frosty day, for it was now

winter, a terrible storm of wind and snow came on. The
tempest howled frightfully about the house of the painter, and
Wolkenlicht found some solace in listening to the uproar, for
his troubled thoughts would not allow him to sleep. It raged
on all the next three days, till about noon on the fourth day,
when it suddenly fell, and all was calm. The following night,
Wolkenlicht, lying awake, heard unaccountable noises in the
next house, as of things thrown about, of kicking and fighting
horses, and of opening and shutting gates. Flinging wide his
lattice and looking out, the noise of howling dogs came to
him from every quarter of the town. The moon was bright
and the air was still. In a little while he heard the sounds of
a horse going at full gallop round the house, so that it shook
as if it would fall; and flashes of light shone into his room.
How much of this may have been owing to the effect of the
drugs on poor Lottchen's brain, I leave my readers to determine. But when the family met at breakfast in the morning,
Teufelsbürst, who had been already out of doors, reported that
he had found the marks of strange feet in the snow, all about
the house and through the garden at the back; stating, as his
belief, that the tracks must be continued over the roofs, for
there was no passage otherwise. There was a wicked gleam
in his eye as he spoke; and Lilith believed that he was only
trying an experiment on Karl's nerves. He persisted that he
had never seen any footprints of the sort before. Karl informed him of his experiences during the night; upon which
Teufelsburst looked a little graver still, and proceeded to tell
them that the storm, whose snow was still covering the ground,
had arisen the very moment that their next-door neighbor died,
and had ceased as suddenly the moment he was buried, though
it had raved furiously all the time of the funeral, so that 'it
made men's bodies quake and their teeth chatter in their
heads.' Karl had heard that the man, whose name was
John Kuntz, was dead and buried. He knew that he had been
a very wealthy, and therefore most respectable, alderman of
the town; that he had been very fond of horses; and that he
had died in consequence of a kick received from one of his
own, as he was looking at his hoof. But he had not heard
that, just before he died, a black cat 'opened the casement
with her nails, ran to his bed, and violently scratched his face

and the bolster, as if she endeavored by force to remove him out of the place where he lay. But the cat afterwards was suddenly gone, and she was no sooner gone, but he breathed his last.

"So said Teufelsbürst, as the reporter of the town-talk. Lilith looked very pale and terrified; and it was perhaps owing to this that the painter brought no more tales home with him. There were plenty to bring, but he heard them all, and said nothing. The fact was that the philosopher himself could not resist the infection of the fear that was literally raging in the city; and perhaps the reports that he himself had sold himself to the devil had sufficient response from his own evil conscience to add to the influence of the epidemic upon him. The whole place was infested with the presence of the dead Kuntz, till scarce a man or woman would dare to be alone. He strangled old men, insulted women; squeezed children to death; knocked out the brains of dogs against the ground; pulled up posts; turned milk into blood; nearly killed a worthy clergy-man, by breathing upon him the intolerable airs of the grave, cold and malignant and noisome; and, in short, filled the city with a perfect madness of fear, so that every report was believed without the smallest doubt or investigation.

"Though Teufelsbürst brought home no more of the town-talk, the old servant was a faithful purveyor, and frequented the news-mart assiduously. Indeed she had some nightmare experiences of her own that she was proud to add to the stock of horrors which the city enjoyed with such a hearty community of goods. For those regions were not far removed from the very birthplace and home of the vampire. The belief in vampires is the quintessential concentration and embodiment of all the passion of fear in Hungary and the adjacent regions. Nor of all the other inventions of the human imagination has there ever been one so perfect in crawling terror as this. Lilith and Karl were quite familiar with the popular ideas on the subject. It did not require to be explained to them that a vampire was a body retaining a kind of animal life after the soul had departed. If any relation continued between it and the vanished ghost, it was only sufficient to make it restless in its grave. Possessed of vitality enough to keep it uncorrupted and pliant, its only instinct was a blind hunger for the solo food, which could keep its awful life persistent, — living human blood. Hence it, or if not it, a sort of semi-material exhalation or essence of it, retaining its form and material relations, crept from its tomb, and went roaming about till it found some one asleep, towards whom it had an attraction founded on old affection. It sucked the blood of this unhappy being, transferring so much of its life to itself as a vampire could assimilate. Death was the certain consequence. If suspicion conjectured aright, and they opened the proper grave, the body of the vampire would be found perfectly fresh and plump, sometimes indeed of rather florid complexion; with grown hair, eyes half open, and the stains of recent blood about its greedy, leech-like lips. Nothing remained but to consume the corpse to ashes, upon which the vampire would show itself no more. But what added infinitely to the horror was the certainty that whoever died by the mouth of the vampire, wrinkled grandsire, or delicate maiden, must in turn rise from the grave, and go forth a vampire, to suck the blood of the dearest left behind. This was the generation of the vampire brood. Lilith trembled at the very name of the creature. Karl was too much in love to be afraid of anything. Yet the evident fear of the unbelieving painter took a hold of his imagination; and under the influence of the potions of which he still partook unwittingly, when he was not thinking about Lilith, he was thinking about the vampire.

"Meantime, the condition of things in the painter's household continued much the same for Wolkenlicht, — work all day; no communication between the young people; the dinner and the wine; silent reading when work was done, with stolen glances, many over the top of the book, — glances that were never returned; the cold good-night; the locking of the door; the wakeful night, and the drowsy morning. But at length a change came, and sooner than any of the party had expected. For, whether it was that the impatience of Teufelsbürst had urged him to yet more dangerous experiments, or that the continuance of those he had been so long employing had overcome at length the vitality of Wolkenlicht, one afternoon, as he was sitting at his work, he suddenly dropped from his chair and his master, hurrying to him in some alarm, found him rigid and apparently lifeless. Lilith was not in the study when

this took place. In justice to Teufelsbürst, it must be confessed that he employed all the skill he was master of, which
for beneficent purposes was not very great, to restore the youth;
but without avail. At last, hearing the footsteps of Lilith, he
desisted, in some consternation; and that she might escape being
shocked by the sight of a dead body where she had been accustomed to see a living one, he removed the lay figure from the
couch, and laid Karl in its place, covering him with the black
velvet pall. He was just in time. She started at seeing no
one in Karl's place, and said : —

" ' Where is your pupil, father ? '

" ' Gone home,' he answered, with a kind of convulsive grin.

" She glanced round the room; caught sight of the lay figure
where it had not been before; looked at the couch, and saw the
pall yet heaved up from beneath; opened her eyes till the entire
white sweep around the iris suggested a new expression of consternation to Teufelsbürst, though from a quarter whence he
did not desire or look for it; and then, without a word, sat
down to a drawing she had been busy upon the day before.
But her father, glancing at her now, as Wolkenlicht had used
to do, could not help seeing that she was frightfully pale. She
showed no other sign of uneasiness. As soon as he released
her, she withdrew, with one more glance, as she passed, at the
couch and the figure blocked out in black upon it. She hastened to her chamber, shut and locked the door, sat down on
the side of the couch, and fell, not a-weeping, but a-thinking.
Was he dead ? What did it matter ? They would all be dead
soon. Her mother was dead already. It was only that the
earth could not bear more children, except she devoured those
to whom she had already given birth. But what if they had
to come back in another form, and live another sad, hopeless,
loveless life over again ? And so she went on questioning,
and receiving no replies; while through all her thoughts
passed and repassed the eyes of Wolkenlicht, which she had
often felt to be upon her when she did not see them, wild with
repressed longing, the light of their love shining through the
veil of diffused tears, ever gathering and never overflowing.
Then came the pale face, so worshipping, so distant in its self-
withdrawn devotion, slowly dawning out of the vapors of her
reverie. When it vanished, she tried to see it again. It would

not come when she called it; but when her thoughts left knocking at the door of the lost and wandered away, out came the pale, troubled, silent face again, gathering itself up from some unknown in her world of fantasy, and once more, when she tried to steady it by the fixedness of her own regard, fading back into the mist. So the phantasm of the dead drew near and wooed, as the living had never dared. What if there were any good in loving? What if men and women did not die all out, but some dim shade of each, like that pale, mind-ghost of Wolkenlicht, floated through the eternal vapors of chaos? And what if they might sometimes cross each other's path, meet, know that they met, love on? Would not that revive the withered memory, fix the fleeting ghost, give a new habitation, a body even, to the poor, unhoused wanderers, frozen by the eternal frosts, no longer thinking beings but thoughts wandering through the brain of the 'Melancholy Mass'? Back with the thought came the face of the dead Karl, and the maiden threw herself on her bed in a flood of bitter tears. She could have loved him if he had only lived; she did love him, for he was dead. But even in the midst of the remorse that followed, — for had she not killed him? — life seemed a less hard and hopeless thing than before. For it is love itself, and not its responses or results, that is the soul of life and its pleasures.

"Two hours passed ere she could again show herself to her father, from whom she seemed in some new way divided by the new feeling in which he did not, and could not, share. But at last, lest he should seek her, and, finding her, should suspect her thoughts, she descended and sought him; for there is a maidenliness in sorrow, that wraps her garments close around her. But he was not to be seen; the door of the study was locked. A shudder passed through her as she thought of what her father, who lost no opportunity of furthering his all but perfect acquaintance with the human form and structure, might be about with the figure which she knew lay dead beneath that velvet pall, but which had arisen to haunt the hollow caves and cells of her living brain. She rushed away, and up once more to her silent room, through the darkness which had now settled down in the house; threw herself again on her bed, and lay almost paralyzed with horror and distress.

"But Teufelsbürst was not about anything so frightful as

she supposed, though something frightful enough. I have already implied that Wolkenlicht was, in form, as fine an embodiment of youthful manhood as any old Greek republic could have provided one of its sculptors with as model for an Apollo. It is true that to the eye of a Greek artist he would not have been more acceptable in consequence of the regimen he had been going through for the last few weeks; but the emaciation of Wolkenlicht's frame, and the consequent prominence of the muscles, indicating the pain he had gone through, were peculiarly attractive to Teufelsbürst. He was busy preparing to take a cast of the body of his dead pupil, that it might aid in the perfection of his future labors.

"He was deep in the artistic enjoyment of a form, at the same time so beautiful and strong, yet with the lines of suffering in every limb and feature, when his daughter's hand was laid on the latch. He started, flung the velvet drapery over the body, and went to the door. But Lilith had vanished. He returned to his labors. The operation took a long time, for he performed it very carefully. Towards midnight, he had finished encasing the body in a close-clinging shell of plaster, which, when broken off, and fitted together, would be the matrix to the form of the dead Wolkenlicht. Before leaving it to harden till the morning, he was just proceeding to strengthen it with an additional layer all over, when a flash of lightning, reflected in all its dazzle from the snow without, almost blinded him. A peal of long-drawn thunder followed; the wind rose; and just such a storm came on as had risen some time before at the death of Kuntz, whose spectre was still tormenting the city. The gnomes of terror, deep hidden in the caverns of Teufelsbürst's nature, broke out jubilant. With trembling hands he tried to cast the pall over the awful white chrysalis, — failed, and fled to his chamber. And there lay the studio naked to the eyes of the lightning, with its tortured forms throbbing out of the dark, and quivering, as with life, in the almost continuous palpitations of the light; while on the couch lay the motionless mass of whiteness, gleaming blue in the lightning, almost more terrible in its crude indications of the human form, than that which it enclosed. It lay there as if dropped from some tree of chaos, haggard with the snows of eternity, — a huge misshapen nut, with a corpse for its kernel.

"But the lightning would soon have revealed a more terrible sight still, had there been any eyes to behold it. At midnight, while a peal of thunder was just dying away in the distance, the crust of death flew asunder, rending in all directions; and, pale as his investiture, staring with ghastly eyes, the form of Karl started up, sitting on the couch. Had he not been far beyond ordinary men in strength, he could not thus have rent his sepulchre. Indeed, had Teufelsbürst been able to finish his task by the additional layer of gypsum which he contemplated, he must have died the moment life revived; although, so long as the trance lasted, neither the exclusion from the air, nor the practical solidification of the walls of his chest, could do him any injury. He had lain unconscious throughout the operations of Teufelsbürst; but now the catalepsy had passed away, possibly under the influence of the electric condition of the atmosphere. Very likely the strength he now put forth was intensified by a convulsive reaction of all the powers of life, as is not unfrequently the case in sudden awakenings from similar interruptions of vital activity. The coming to himself and the bursting of his case were simultaneous. He sat staring about him, with, of all his mental faculties, only his imagination awake, from which the thoughts that occupied it when he fell senseless had not yet faded. These thoughts had been compounded of feelings about Lilith, and speculations about the vampire that haunted the neighborhood; and the fumes of the last drug of which he had partaken, still hovering in his brain, combined with these thoughts and fancies to generate the delusion that he had just broken from the embrace of his coffin, and risen, the last-born of the vampire-race. The sense of unavoidable obligation to fulfil his doom was yet mingled with a faint flutter of joy, for he knew that he must go to Lilith. With a deep sigh, he rose, gathered up the pall of black velvet, flung it around him, stepped from the couch, and left the study to find her.

"Meant me, Teufelsburst had sufficiently recovered to remember that he had left the door of the studio unfastened, and that any one entering would discover in what he had been engaged, which, in the case of his getting into any difficulty about the death of Karl, would tell powerfully against him. He was at the further end of a long passage, leading from the

house to the studio, on his way to make all secure, when Karl
appeared at the door, and advanced towards him. The painter,
seized with invincible terror, turned and fled. He reached his
room, and fell senseless on the floor. The phantom held on
its way heedless.

"Lilith, on gaining her room the second time, had thrown
herself on her bed as before, and had wept herself into a
troubled slumber. She lay dreaming, and dreadful dreams.
Suddenly she awoke in one of those peals of thunder which
tormented the high regions of the air, as a storm billows the
surface of the ocean. She lay awake and listened. As it
died away, she thought she heard, mingling with its last muffled
murmurs, the sound of moaning. She turned her face towards
the room in keen terror. But she saw nothing. Another
light, long-drawn sigh reached her ear, and at the same moment a flash of lightning illumined the room. In the corner
farthest from her bed she spied a white face, nothing more.
She was dumb and motionless with fear. Utter darkness followed, a darkness that seemed to enter into her very brain.
Yet she felt that the face was slowly crossing the black gulf
of the room, and drawing near to where she lay. The next
flash revealed, as it bended over her, the ghastly face of Karl,
down which flowed fresh tears. The rest of his form was lost
in blackness. Lilith did not faint, but it was the very force
of her fear that seemed to keep her alive. It became for the
moment the atmosphere of her life. She lay trembling and
staring at the spot in the darkness where she supposed the face
of Karl still to be. But the next flash showed her the face
far off, looking through the panes of her lattice-window.

"For Lottchen, as soon as he saw Lilith, seemed to himself
to go through a second stage of awaking. Her face made him
doubt whether he could be a vampire after all; for, instead of
wanting to bite her arm and suck the blood, he all but fell down
at her feet in a passion of speechless love. The next moment he
became aware that his presence must be at least very undesirable
to her; and in an instant he had reached her window, which
he knew looked upon a lower roof that extended between two
different parts of the house, and before the next flash came
he had stepped through the lattice and closed it behind him.

"Believing his own room to be attainable from this quarter,

he proceeded along the roof in the direction he judged best. The cold winter air by degrees restored him entirely to his right mind, and he soon comprehended the whole of the circumstances in which he found himself. Peeping through a window he was passing, to see whether it belonged to his room, he spied Teufelsbürst, who at the very moment was lifting his head from the faint into which he had fallen at the first sight of Lottchen. The moon was shining clear, and in its light the painter saw, to his horror, the pale face staring in at his window. He thought it had been there ever since he had fainted, and dropped again in a deeper swoon than before. Karl saw him fall, and the truth flashed upon him that the wicked artist took him for what he had believed himself to be when first he recovered from his trance, namely, the vampire of the former Karl Wolkenlicht. The moment he comprehended it, he resolved to keep up the delusion if possible. Meantime he was innocently preparing a new ingredient for the popular dish of horrors to be served at the ordinary of the city the next day. For the old servant's were not the only eyes that had seen him besides those of Teufelsbürst. What could be more like a vampire, dragging his pall after him, than this apparition of poor, half-frozen Lottchen, crawling across the roof? Karl remembered afterwards that he had heard the dogs howling awfully in every direction, as he crept along; but this was hardly necessary to make those who saw him conclude that it was the same phantasm of John Kuntz, which had been infesting the whole city, and especially the house next door to the painter's, which had been the dwelling of the respectable alderman who had degenerated into this most disreputable of moneyless vagabonds. What added to the consternation of all who heard of it, was the sickening conviction that the extreme measures which they had resorted to in order to free the city from the ghoul, beyond which nothing could be done, had been utterly unavailing, successful as they had proved in every other known case of the kind. For, urged as well by various horrid signs about his grave, which not even its close proximity to the altar could render a place of repose, they had opened it, had found in the body every peculiarity belonging to a vampire, had pulled it out with the greatest difficulty, on account of a

quite supernatural ponderosity; which rendered the horse
which had killed him — a strong animal — all but unable to
drag it along, and had at last, after cutting it in pieces, and
expending on the fire two hundred and sixteen great billets,
succeeded in conquering its incombustibleness, and reducing it
to ashes.   Such, at least, was the story which had reached
the painter's household, and was believed by many; and if
all this did not compel the perturbed corpse to rest, what
more could be done?

" When Karl had reached his room, and was dressing
himself, the thought struck him that something might be made
of the report of the extreme weight of the body of old Kuntz,
to favor the continuance of the delusion of Teufelsbürst,
although he hardly knew yet to what use he could turn this
delusion.   He was convinced that he would have made no
progress however long he might have remained in his house;
and that he would have more chance of favor with Lilith if
he were to meet her in any other circumstances whatever
than those in which he invariably saw her, namely, surrounded by her father's influences, and watched by her father's
cold blue eyes.

" As soon as he was dressed, he crept down to the studio,
which was now quiet enough, the storm being over, and the
moon filling it with her steady shine.   In the corner lay in all
directions the fragments of the mould which his own body had
formed and filled.   The bag of plaster and the bucket of
water which the painter had been using stood beside.   Lottchen
gathered all the pieces together, and then making his way to
an outhouse where he had seen various odds and ends of
rubbish lying, chose from the heap as many pieces of old
iron and other metal as he could find.   To these he added a
few large stones from the garden.   When he had got all into
the studio, he locked the door, and proceeded to fit together the
parts of the mould, filling up the hollow as he went on with
the heaviest things he could get into it, and solidifying the
whole by pouring in plaster; till, having at length completed it, and obliterated, as much as possible, the marks of
joining, he left it to harden, with the conviction that now it
would make a considerable impression on Teufelsbürst's imagination. as well as on his muscular sense.   He then left every-

thing else as nearly undisturbed as he could; and, knowing all the ways of the house, was soon in the street, without leaving any signs of his exit.

"Karl soon found himself before the house in which his friend Höllenrachen resided. Knowing his studious habits he had hoped to see his light still burning, nor was he disappointed. He contrived to bring him to his window, and, a moment after, the door was cautiously opened.

"'Why, Lottchen, where do you come from?'

"'From the grave, Heinrich, or next door to it.'

"'Come in, and tell me all about it. We thought the old painter had made a model of you, and tortured you to death.'

"'Perhaps you were not far wrong. But get me a horn of ale, for even a vampire is thirsty, you know.'

"'A vampire!' exclaimed Heinrich, retreating a pace, and involuntarily putting himself upon his guard.

"Karl laughed.

"'My hand was warm was it not, old fellow?' he said. 'Vampires are cold, all but the blood.'

"'What a fool I am!' rejoined Heinrich. 'But you know we have been hearing such horrors lately that a fellow may be excused for shuddering a little when a pale-faced apparition tells him at two o'clock in the morning that he is a vampire, and thirsty too.'

"Karl told him the whole story; and the mental process of regarding it, for the sake of telling it, revealed to him pretty clearly some of the treatment of which he had been unconscious at the time. Heinrich was quite sure that his suspicions were correct. And now the question was, what was to be done next.

"'At all events,' said Heinrich, 'we must keep you out of the way for some time. I will represent to my landlady that you are in hiding from enemies, and her heart will rule her tongue. She can let you have a garret room, I know; and I will do as well as I can to bear you company. We shall have time then to invent some plan of operation.'

"To this proposal Karl agreed with hearty thanks, and soon all was arranged. The only conclusion they could yet arrive at was, that somehow or other the old demon-painter must be tamed.

"Meantime, how fared it with Lilith? She, too, had no doubt that she had seen the body-ghost of poor Karl, and that the vampire had, according to rule, paid her the first visit, because he loved her best. This was horrible enough if the vampire were not really the person he represented; but if in any sense it were Karl himself, at least it gave some expectation of a more prolonged existence than her father had taught her to look for; and if love, anything like her mother's, still lasted, even along with the habits of a vampire, there was something to hope for in the future. And then, though he had visited her, he had not, as far as she was aware, deprived her of a drop of blood. She could not be certain that he had not bitten her, for she had been in such a strange condition of mind that she might not have felt it; but she believed that he had restrained the impulses of his vampire nature, and had left her, lest he should yet yield to them. She fell fast asleep; and when morning came, there was not, as far as she could judge, one of those triangular, leech-like perforations to be found upon her whole body. Will it be believed that the moment she was satisfied of this, she was seized by a terrible jealousy, lest Karl should have gone and bitten some one else? Most people will wonder that she should not have gone out of her senses at once; but there was all the difference between a visit from a real vampire and a visit from a man she had begun to love, even although she took him for a vampire. All the difference does *not* lie in a name. They were very different causes, and the effects must be very different.

"When Teufelsbürst came down in the morning, he crept into the studio like a murderer. There lay the awful white block, seeming to his eyes just the same as he had left it. What was to be done with it? He dared not open it. Mould and model must go together. But whither? If inquiry should be made after Wolkenlicht, and this were discovered anywhere on his premises, would it not be enough to bring him at once to the gallows? Therefore it would be dangerous to bury it in the garden, or in the cellar.

"'Besides,' thought he, with a shudder, 'that would be to fix the vampire as a guest forever.' And the horrors of the past night rushed back upon his imagination with renewed intensity. What would it be to have the dead Karl crawling abcut his house forever, now inside, now out, now sitting on the stairs, now staring in at the windows?

" He would have dragged it to the bottom of his garden past which the Moldau flowed, and plunged it into the stream ; but then, should the spectre continue to prove troublesome, it would be almost impossible to reach the body so as to destroy it by fire ; besides which, he could not do it without assistance, and the probability of discovery. If, however, the apparition should turn out to be no vampire, but only a respectable ghost, they might manage to endure its presence, till it should be weary of haunting them.

" He resolved at last to convey the body for the mean time into a concealed cellar in the house, seeing something must be done before his daughter came down. Proceeding to remove it, his consternation was greatly increased when he discovered how the body had grown in weight since he had thus disposed of it, leaving on his mind scarcely a hope that it could turn out not to be a vampire, after all. He could scarcely stir it, and there was but one whom he could call to his assistance, — the old woman who acted as his housekeeper and servant.

" He went to her room, roused her, and told her the whole story. Devoted to her master for many years, and not quite so sensitive to fearful influences as when less experienced in horrors, she showed immediate readiness to render him assistance. Utterly unable, however, to lift the mass between them, they could only drag and push it along ; and such a slow toil was it that there was no time to remove the traces of its track, before Lilith came down and saw a broad white line leading from the door of the studio down the cellar-stairs. She knew in a moment what it meant ; but not a word was uttered about the matter, and the name of Karl Wolkenlicht seemed to be entirely forgotten.

" But how could the affairs of a house go on all the same when every one of the household knew that a dead body lay in the cellar? — nay, more, that, although it lay still and dead enough all day, it would come half alive at nightfall, and, turning the whole house into a sepulchre by its presence, go creeping about, like a cat, all over it in the dark, — perhaps with phosphorescent eyes? So it was not surprising that the painter abandoned his studio early, and that the three found themselves together in the gorgeous room formerly described, as soon as twilight began to fall.

"Already Teufelsbürst had begun to experience a kind of shrinking from the horrid faces in his own pictures, and to feel disgusted at the abortions of his own mind. But all that he and the old woman now felt was an increasing fear as the night drew on, a kind of sickening and paralyzing terror. The thing down there would not lie quiet, — at least its phantom in the cellars of their imagination would not. As much as possible, however, they avoided alarming Lilith, who, knowing all they knew, was as silent as they. But her mind was in a strange state of excitement, partly from the presence of a new sense of love, the pleasure of which all the atmosphere of grief into which it grew could not totally quench. It comforted her somehow, as a child may comfort when his father is away.

"Bedtime came, and no one made a move to go. Without a word spoken on the subject, the three remained together all night; the elders nodding and slumbering occasionally, and Lilith getting some share of repose on a couch. All night the shape of death might be somewhere about the house; but it did not disturb them. They heard no sound, saw no sight; and when the morning dawned, they separated, chilled and stupid, and for the time beyond fear, to seek repose in their private chambers. There they remained equally undisturbed.

"But when the painter approached his easel a few hours after, looking more pale and haggard still than he was wont, from the fears of the night, a new bewilderment took possession of him. He had been busy with a fresh embodiment of his favorite subject, into which he had sketched the form of the student as the sufferer. He had represented poor Wolkenlicht as just beginning to recover from a trance, while a group of surgeons, unaware of the signs of returning life, were absorbed in a minute dissection of one of the limbs. At an open door he had painted Lilith passing, with her face buried in a bunch of sweet peas. But when he came to the picture, he found, to his astonishment and terror, that the face of one of the group was now turned towards that of the victim, regarding his revival with demoniac satisfaction, and taking pains to prevent the others from discovering it. The face of this prince of torturers was that of Teufelsbürst himself. Lilith had altogether vanished, and in her place stood the dim vampire reiteration of the body that lay extended on the table. staring greedily at the assembled company. With trembling hands the painter removed the picture from the easel, and turned its face to the wall.

"Of course this was the work of Lottchen. When he left the house, he took with him the key of a small private door, which was so seldom used that, while it remained closed, the key would not be missed, perhaps for many months. Watching the windows, he had chosen a safe time to enter, and had been hard at work all night on these alterations. Teufelsbürst attributed them to the vampire, and left the picture as he found it, not daring to put brush to it again.

"The next night was passed much after the same fashion. But the fear had begun to die away a little in the hearts of the women, who did not know what had taken place in the study on the previous night. It burrowed, however, with gathered force in the vitals of Teufelsbürst. But this night likewise passed in peace; and before it was over, the old woman had taken to speculating in her own mind as to the best way of disposing of the body, seeing it was not at all likely to be troublesome. But when the painter entered his study in trepidation the next morning, he found that the form of the lovely Lilith was painted out of every picture in the room. This could not be concealed; and Lilith and the servant became aware that the studio was the portion of the house in haunting which the vampire left the rest in peace.

"Karl recounted all the tricks he had played to his friend Heinrich, who begged to be allowed to bear him company the following night. To this Karl consented, thinking it would be considerably more agreeable to have a companion. So they took a couple of bottles of wine and some provisions with them, and before midnight found themselves snug in the study. They sat very quiet for some time, for they knew that if they were seen, two vampires would not be so terrible as one, and might occasion discovery. But at length Heinrich could bear it no longer.

"'I say, Lottchen, let's go and look for your dead body. What has the old beggar done with it?'

" 'I think I know. Stop; let me peep out. All right! Come along.'

" With a lamp in his hand, he led the way to the cellars, and, after searching about a little, they discovered it.

" 'It looks horrid enough,' said Heinrich; 'but I think a drop or two of wine would brighten it up a little.'

" So he took a bottle from his pocket, and, after they had had a glass apiece, he dropped a third in blots all over the plaster. Being red wine, it had the effect Höllenrachen desired.

" 'When they visit it next they will know that the vampire can find the food he prefers,' said he.

" In a corner close by the plaster, they found the clothes Karl had worn.

" 'Hillo!' said Heinrich, 'we'll make something of this find.'

" So he carried them with him to the study. There he got hold of the lay-figure.

" 'What are you about, Heinrich?'

" 'Going to make a scarecrow to keep the ravens off old Teufel's pictures,' answered Heinrich, as he went on dressing the lay-figure in Karl's clothes. He next seated the creature at an easel, with its back to the door, so that it should be the first thing the painter should see when he entered. Karl meant to remove this before he went, for it was too comical to fall in with the rest of his proceedings. But the two sat down to their supper, and by the time they had finished the wine they thought they should like to go to bed. So they got up and went home, and Karl forgot the lay-figure, leaving it in busy motionlessness all night before the easel.

" When Teufelsbürst saw it, he turned and fled with a cry that brought his daughter to his help. He rushed past her, able only to articulate : —

" 'The vampire! The vampire! Painting!'

" Far more courageous than he, because her conscience was more peaceful, Lilith passed on to the study. She, too, recoiled a step or two when she saw the figure; but with the sight of the back of Karl, as she supposed it to be, came the longing to see the face that was on the other side. So she crept round and round by the wall, as far off as she could. The figure remained motionless. It was a strange kind of shock that she experienced when she saw the face, disgusting from its inanity. The absurdity next struck her; and with the absurdity flashed into her mind the conviction that this was not the doing of a vampire; for of all creatures under the moon he could not be expected to be a humorist. A wild hope sprang up in her mind that Karl was not dead. Of this she soon resolved to make herself sure.

She closed the door of the study; in the strength of her new hope, undressed the figure, put it in its place, concealed the garments, — all the work of a few minutes; and then, finding her father just recovering from the worst of his fear, told him there was nothing in the study but what ought to be there, and persuaded him to go and see. He not only saw no one, but found that no further liberties had been taken with his pictures. Reassured, he soon persuaded himself that the spectre in this case had been the offspring of his own terror-haunted brain. But he had no spirit for painting now. He wandered about the house, himself haunting it like a restless ghost.

"When night came, Lilith retired to her own room. The waters of fear had begun to subside in the house; but the painter and his old attendant did not yet follow her example.

"As soon, however, as the house was quite still, Lilith glided noiselessly down the stairs, went into the study, where as yet there assuredly was no vampire, and concealed herself in a corner.

"As it would not do for an earnest student like Heinrich to be away from his work very often, he had not asked to accompany Lottchen this time. And indeed Karl himself, a little anxious about the result of the scarecrow, greatly preferred going alone.

"While she was waiting for what might happen, the conviction grew upon Lilith, as she reviewed all the past of the story, that these phenomena were the work of the real Karl, and of no vampire. In a few moments she was still more sure of this. Behind the screen where she had taken refuge hung one of the pictures out of which her portrait had been painted the night before last. She had taken a lamp with her into the study, with the intention of extinguishing it the moment she heard any sign of approach; but, as the vampire lingered, she began to occupy herself with examining the picture beside her. She had not looked at it long, before she wetted the tip of her forefinger, and begun to rub away at the obliteration. Her suspicions were instantly confirmed: the substance employed was only a gummy· wash over the paint. The delight she experienced at the discovery threw her into a mischievous humor.

" ' I will see,' she said to herself, ' whether I cannot match Karl Wolkenlicht at this game.'

" In a closet in the room hung a number of costumes, which Lilith had at different times worn for her father. Among them was a large white drapery, which she easily disposed as a shroud. With the help of some chalk, she soon made herself ghastly enough, and then placing her lamp on the floor behind the screen, and setting a chair over it so that it should throw no light in any direction, she waited once more for the vampire. Nor had she much longer to wait. She soon heard a door move, the sound of which she hardly knew, and then the study door opened. Her heart beat dreadfully, not with fear lest it should be a vampire after all, but with hope that it was Karl. To see him once more was too great joy. Would she not make up to him for all her coldness! But would he care for her now? Perhaps he had been quite cured of his longing for a hard heart like hers. · She peeped. It was he, sure enough, looking as handsome as ever. He was holding his light to look at her· last work, and the expression of his face, even in regarding her handiwork, was enough to let her know that he loved her still. If she had not seen this, she. dared not have shown herself from her hiding-place. Taking the lamp in her hand, she got upon the chair, and looked over the screen, letting the light shine from below upon her face. She then made a slight noise to attract Karl's attention. He looked up, evidently rather startled, and saw the face of Lilith in the air. He gave a stifled cry, threw himself on his knees, with his arms stretched towards her, and moaned: —

" ' I have killed her! I have killed her! '

" Lilith descended, and approached him noiselessly. He did not move. She came close to him and said: —

" ' Are you Karl Wolkenlicht? '

" His lips moved, but no sound came.

" ' If you are a vampire, and I am a ghost,' she said — but a low, happy laugh alone concluded the sentence.

" Karl sprang to his feet. Lilith's laugh changed into a burst of sobbing and weeping, and in another moment the ghost was in the arms of the vampire.

" Lilith had no idea how far her father had wronged Karl, and though, from thinking over the past, he had no doubt that the painter had drugged him, he did not wish to pain her by imparting this conviction. But Lilith was afraid of a reaction of rage and hatred in her father after the terror was removed; and Karl saw that he might thus be deprived of all further intercourse with Lilith, and all chance of softening the old man's heart towards him; while Lilith would not hear of forsaking him who had banished all the human race but herself. They managed at length to agree upon a plan of operation.

" The first thing they did was to go to the cellar where the plaster mass lay, Karl carrying with him a great axe used for cleaving wood. Lilith shuddered when she saw it, stained as it was with the wine Heinrich had spilt over it, and almost believed herself the midnight companion of a vampire after all, visiting with him the terrible corpse in which he lived all day. But Karl soon reassured her; and a few good blows of the axe revealed a very different core to that which Teufelsbürst supposed to be in it. Karl broke it into pieces, and with Lilith's help, who insisted on carrying her share, the whole was soon at the bottom of the Moldau, and every trace of its ever having existed removed. Before morning, too, the form of Lilith had dawned anew in every picture. There was no time to restore to its former condition the one Karl had first altered; for in it the changes were all that they seemed; nor indeed was he capable of restoring it in the master's style; but they put it quite out of the way, and hoped that sufficient time might elapse before the painter thought of it again.

" When they had done, and Lilith, for all his entreaties, would remain with him no longer, Karl took his former clothes with him, and, having spent the rest of the night in his old room, dressed in them in the morning. When Teufelsbürst entered his study next day, there sat Karl, as if nothing had happened, finishing the drawing on which he had been at work when the fit of insensibility came upon him. The painter started, stared, rubbed his eyes, thought it was another spectral illusion, but was on the point of yielding to his terror, when Karl rose, and approached him with a smile. The healthy, sunshiny countenance of Karl, let him be ghost or goblin, could not fail to produce somewhat of a tranquillizing effect on Teufelsbürst. He took his offered hand mechanically, his countenance utterly vacant with idiotic bewilderment. Karl said : —

"'I was not well, and thought it better to pay a visit to a friend for a few days; but I shall soon make up for lost time, for I am all right now.'

"He sat down at once, taking no notice of his master's behavior, and went on with his drawing. Teufelsbürst stood staring at him for some minutes without moving, then suddenly turned and left the room. Karl heard him hurrying down the cellar stairs. In a few moments he came up again. Karl stole a glance at him. There he stood in the same spot, no doubt more full of bewilderment than ever; but it was not possible that his face should express more. At last he went to his easel, and sat down with a long-drawn sigh as if of relief. But though he sat at his easel, he painted none that day; and as often as Karl ventured a glance he saw him still staring at him. The discovery that his pictures were restored to their former condition aided, no doubt, in leading him to the same conclusion as the other facts, whatever that conclusion might be, — probably that he had been the sport of some evil power, and had been for the greater part of the week utterly bewitched. Lilith had taken care to instruct the old woman, with whom she was all powerful; and as neither of them showed the smallest traces of the astonishment which seemed to be slowly vitrifying his own brain, he was at last perfectly satisfied that things had been going on all right everywhere but in his inner man; and in this conclusion he certainly was not far wrong in more senses than one. But when all was restored again to the old routine, it became evident that the peculiar direction of his art in which he had hitherto indulged had ceased to interest him. The shock had acted chiefly upon that part of his mental being which had been so absorbed. He would sit for hours without doing anything, apparently plunged in meditation. Several weeks elapsed without any change, and both Lilith and Karl were getting dreadfully anxious about him. Karl paid him every attention; and the old man, for he now looked much older than before, submitted to receive his services as well as those of Lilith. At length, one morning, he said in a slow, thoughtful tone : —

"'Karl Wolkenlicht, I should like to paint you.'

"'Certainly, sir,' answered Karl, jumping up; 'where would you like me to sit?'

"So the ice of silence and inactivity was broken, and the painter drew and painted; and the spring of his art flowed once more; and he made a beautiful portrait of Karl, — a portrait without evil or suffering. And as soon as he had finished Karl, he began once more to paint Lilith; and when he had painted her, he composed a picture for the very purpose of introducing them together; and in this picture there was neither ugliness nor torture, but human feeling and human hope instead. Then Karl knew that he might speak to him of Lilith; and he spoke, and was heard with a smile. But he did not dare to tell him the truth of the vampire story till one day that Teufelsbürst was lying on the floor of a room in Karl's ancestral castle, half-smothered in grand-children; when the only answer it drew from the old man was a kind of shuddering laugh, and the words, 'Don't speak of it, Karl, my boy!'"

No one had interrupted Harry. His brother had put a shovelful of coals on the fire, to keep up the flame; but not a word had been spoken. The cold moon had shone in at the windows all the time, her light made yet colder by the snowy sheen from the face of the earth; and any horror that the story could generate had had full freedom to operate on the minds of the listeners.

"Well, I'm glad it's over, for my part," said Mrs. Bloomfield. "It made my flesh creep."

"I do not see any good in founding a story upon a superstition. One knows it is false, all the time," said Mrs. Cathcart.

"But," said Harry, "all that I have related might have taken place; for the story is not founded on the superstition itself, but on the belief of the people of the time in the super-

stition. I have merely used this belief to give the general
tone to the story, and sometimes the particular occasion for
events in it, the vampire being a terrible fact to those
times."

"You write," said the curate, "as if you quoted occasionally from some authority."

"The story of John Kuntz, as well as that of the shoemaker,
is told by Henry More in his "Antidote against Atheism." He
believed the whole affair. His authority is Martin Weinrich,
a Silesian doctor. I have only taken the liberty of shifting
the scene of the *post-mortem* exploits of Kuntz from a town
of Silesia to Prague."

"Well, Harry," said his sister-in-law, "if your object was
to frighten us, I confess that I for one was tolerably uncomfortable. But I don't know that that is a very high aim in
story-telling."

"If that were all, certainly not," replied Harry, glancing
towards Adela, who had not spoken. Nor did she speak yet.
But her expression showed plainly enough that it was not the
horror of the story that had taken chief hold of her mind.
Her face was full of suppressed light, and she was evidently
satisfied — or shall I call it *gratified?* — as well as delighted
with the tale. Something or other in it had touched her not
only deeply, but nearly.

Nothing was said about another meeting, — perhaps because,
from Adela's illness, the order had been interrupted, and the
present had required a special summons.

The ladies had gone upstairs to put on their bonnets. I had
crossed into the library, which was on the same floor with the
drawing-room, to find out if I was right in supposing I had
seen some volumes of Henry More's works on the shelves;
certainly the colonel could never have bought them. Our
host, the curate, and the school-master had followed me. Harry
had remained behind in the drawing-room. Thinking of
something I wanted to say to him before he went, I left the
gentlemen looking over the book-shelves, and went to cross
again to the drawing-room. But when I reached the door,
there stood, at the top of the stair, Adela and Harry. She had
evidently just said something warm about the story. I could
almost read what she had said still lingering on her face, which

was turned up a good deal to look into his, so near each other were they standing. Hers had a rosy flush, as of sunset, over it, while his glowed like the sun rising in a mist. Evidently the pleasures of giving and receiving were in this case nearly equal. But they were not of long duration; for the moment I appeared they bade each other a hurried good-night, and parted. I, thinking it better to pretermit my speech to Harry, retreated into the library, and was glad to think that no one had seen that conference but myself. Such a conjunction of planets prefigured, however, not merely warm spring weather, but sultry gloom, and thunderous clouds to follow; and, although I was delighted with my astronomical observation, I could not help growing anxious about the omen.

CHAPTER XXI.

THE CASTLE.

THE next day, as I passed the school-house on my way to call on the curate, I heard such an uproar that I stopped involuntarily to listen. I soon satisfied myself that it was only the usual water-spout occasioned on the ocean of boyhood by the vacuum of the master. As soon as I entered the curate's study, there stood the missing master, hat in hand. He had not sat down, and would not, hearing all the time, no doubt, in his soul, the far confusion of his forsaken realm. He had but that moment entered.

"You come just in the right time, Smith," said the curate. — We had already dropped unnecessary prefixes. — "Here is Mr. Bloomfield come to ask us to spend a final evening with him and Mrs. Bloomfield. And in the name of the whole company, I have taken upon me to assure him that it will give us pleasure. Am I not right?"

"Undoubtedly," I replied. "What evening have you fixed upon, Mr. Bloomfield?"

"This day week," he answered. "Shall I tell you why I put it off so long?"

"If you please."

"I heard your brother, Mr. Armstrong, say that you were very fond of parables. Now, I have always had a leaning that way myself; and for years I have had one in particular glimmering before my mental sight. The ambition seized me to write it out for one of our meetings, and to submit it to your judgment; for, Mr. Armstrong, I am so delighted with your sermons and opinions generally, that I long to let you know that I am not only friendly, but capable of sympathizing with you. But it is only in the rough yet, and I want to have plenty of time to act the dutiful bear to my offspring, and lick it into thorough shape. So if you will come this day week, Mrs. Bloomfield and I will be delighted to entertain you in our humble fashion. But, bless me! the boys will be all in a heap of confusion worse confounded before I get back to them. I have no business to be away from them at this hour. Good-morning, gentlemen."

And off ran the worthy Neptune, to quell, by the vision of his returning head, the rebellious waves of boyish impulse.

"That man will be a great comfort to you, Armstrong," I said.

"I know he will. He is a far-seeing and, what is better, a far-feeling man."

"There is true wealth in him, it seems to me, although it may be of narrow reach in expression," said I.

"I think so, quite. He seems to me to be one of those who have never grown robust, because they have labored in-doors instead of going out to work in the open air. There is a shrinking delicacy about him, when with those whom he doesn't feel to be of his own kind, which makes him show to a disadvantage. But you should see him amongst his boys to do him justice."

We were interrupted by the entrance of Mrs. Armstrong, who came, after their simple fashion, to tell her husband that dinner was ready. I took my leave.

In the evening Mrs. Bloomfield called to invite Adela and the colonel; and the affair was settled for that day week.

"You're much better, my dear, are you not?" said the worthy woman to my niece.

"Indeed I am, Mrs. Bloomfield. I could not have be-

lieved it possible that I should be so much better in so short a
time, — and at this season of the year too."

"Mr. Armstrong is a very clever young man, I think;
though I can't say I quite relished that extraordinary story of
his."

"I suppose he is clever," replied Adela, something demurely
as I thought "I must say I liked the story."

"Ah, well! Young people, you know, Mr. Smith — But,
bless me! I'm sure I beg your pardon. I had forgotten you
weren't a married man. Of course you're one of the young
people too, Mr. Smith."

"I don't think there's much of youth to choose between you
and me, Mrs. Bloomfield," said I, "if I may venture to say so.
But I fear I do belong to the young people, if a liking for
extravagant stories — so long as they mean well, you know —
is to be the test of the classification. I fear I have a depraved
taste that way. I don't mean in this particular instance,
though, Adela."

"I hope not," answered Adela, with a blushing smile,
which I, at least, could read, having had not merely the key
to it, but the open door and window as well, ever since I had
seen the two standing together at the top of the stair.

That night the weather broke. A slow thaw set in; and,
before many days were over, islands of green began to appear
amid the "wan water" of the snow, — to use a phrase
common in Scotch ballads, though with a different application.
The graves in the church-yard lifted up their green altars of
earth, as the first whereon to return thanks for the prophecy
of spring; which, surely, if it has force and truth anywhere,
speaks loudest to us in the church-yard. And on Sunday the
sun broke out and shone on the green hillocks, just as good
old Mr. Venables was reading the words, "I will not leave
you comfortless — I will come to you."

And the ice vanished from the river, and the dark stream
flowed, somewhat sullen, but yet glad at heart, on through the
low meadows bordered with pollards, which, poor things, mal-
treated and mutilated, yet did the best they could, and went
on growing wildly in all insane shapes, — pitifully mingling
formality and grotesqueness.

And the next day the hounds met at Castle Irksham. **And** that day Colonel Cathcart would ride with them.

For the good man had gathered spirit just as the light grew upon his daughter's face. And he was merry like a boy now that the first breath of spring — for so it seemed, although no doubt plenty of wintriness remained and would yet show itself — had loosened the hard hold of the frost, which is the death of Nature. The frost is hard upon old people; and the spring is so much the more genial and blessed in its sweet influences on them. Do we grow old that, in our weakness and loss of physical self-assertion, we may learn the benignities of the universe, — only to be learned first through the feeling of their want? I do not envy the man who laughs the east wind to scorn. He can never know the balmy power of its sister of the west, which is the breath of the Lord, the symbol of the one *genial* strength at the root of all life, resurrection, and growth, — commonly called the Spirit of God. Who has not seen, as the infirmities of age grow upon old men, the haughty, self-reliant spirit that had neglected, if not despised, the gentle ministration of love, grow as it were a little scared, and begin to look about for some kindness; begin to return the warm pressure of the hand, and to submit to be waited upon by the anxiety of love? Not in weakness alone comes the second childhood upon men, but often in childlikeness; for in old age, as in nature, to quote the song of the curate, —

> " Old Autumn's fingers
> Paint in hues of Spring."

The necessities of the old man prefigure and forerun the dawn of the immortal childhood. For is not our necessity towards God our highest blessedness, — the fair cloud that hangs over the summit of existence? Thank God, he has made his children so noble and high that they cannot do without him ! I believe we are sent into this world just to find this out.

But to leave my reflections and return to my story, — such as it is. The colonel mounted me on an old horse of his, " whom," to quote from Sir Philip Sidney's "Arcadia," "though he was near twenty years old, he preferred, for a piece of sure service, before a great number of younger." Now the piece of sure service, in the present instance, was to take care of old

John Smith, who was only a middling horseman, though his friend, the colonel, would say that he rode pretty well for a lad. The old horse, in fact, knew not only what he could do, but what I could do, for our powers were about equal. He looked well about for the gaps and the narrow places. From weakness in his forelegs, he had become a capital buck-jumper, as I think Cathcart called him, always alighting over a hedge on his hind legs, instead of his fore ones, which was as much easier for John Smith as for Hop o' my Thumb,—that was the name of the old horse,—he being sixteen hands, at least. But I beg my reader's pardon for troubling him with all this about my horse, for, assuredly, neither he nor I will perform any deed of prowess in his presence. But I have the weakness of garrulity in regard to a predilection from the indulgence of which circumstances have debarred me.

At nine o'clock my friend and I started upon hacks for the meet. Now, I am not going to describe the "harrow and weal away!" with which the soul of poor Reynard is hunted out of the world, — if, indeed, such a clever wretch can have a soul. I dare say, I hope, at least, that the argument of the fox-hunter is analogically just, who, being expostulated with on the cruelty of fox-hunting, replied, "Well, you know the hounds like it; and the horses like it; and there's no doubt the men like it, — and who knows whether the fox doesn't like it too?" But I would not have introduced the subject, except for the sake of what my reader will find in a course of a page or two, and which assuredly is not fox-hunting.

We soon found. But just before, a sudden heavy noise, coming apparently from a considerable distance, made one or two of the company say, with passing curiosity, "What is that?" It was instantly forgotten, however, as soon as the fox broke cover. He pointed towards Purley-bridge. We had followed for some distance, circumstances permitting Hop o' my Thumb to keep in the wake of his master, when the colonel, drawing rein, allowed me — I ought to say *us*, for the old horse had quite as much voice in the matter as I had — to come up with him.

"The cunning old dog!" said he. "He has run straight for the deepest cutting in the railway. They'll all be pounded presently! They don't know this part so well as I do. I know every field and gate in it. I used to go larking over it all when I was only a cub myself. Confound it! I'm not up to much to-day. I suppose I'm getting old, you know; or I'd strike off here at right angles to the left, and make for the bridge at Crumple's Corner. I should lose the hounds though, I fear. I wonder what his lordship will do."

All the time my old friend was talking we were following the rest of the field, whom, sure enough, as soon as we got into the next inclosure, we saw drawing up one after another on top of the railway cutting, which ran like the river of death between them and the fox-hunter's paradise. But at the moment we entered this field, whom should we see approaching us at right angles, from the direction of Purley-bridge, but Harry Armstrong, mounted on *the* mare! I rode towards him.

"Trapped, you see," said I. "Are you after the fox — or some nobler game?"

"I was going my rounds," answered Harry, "when I caught sight of the hounds. I have no very pressing case to-day, so I turned a few yards out of the road to see a bit of the sport. Confound these railways!"

At the moment, — and all this passed, as the story-teller is so often compelled to remind his reader, in far less time than it takes to tell, — over the hedge on the opposite side from where Harry had entered the field, blundered a country fellow, on a great, heavy, but spirited horse, and ploughed his way up the soft furrow to where we stood.

"Doctor!" he cried, half-breathless with haste and exertion. — "Doctor!"

"Well?" answered Henry, alert.

"There's a awful accident at Grubblebon Quarry, sir. Powder blowed up. Legs and arms! Good God! sir, make haste.'

"Well," said Harry, whose compressed lips alone gave sign of his being ready for action, "ride to the town, and tell my house-keeper to give you bandages, and wadding, and oil, and splints, and whatever she knows to be needful. Are there many hurt?"

"Half a dozen alive, sir."

"Then you'd better let the other doctors know as well. And just tell my man to saddle Jilter, and take him to my brother, the curate. He had better come out at once. Ride now."

" I *will*, sir," said the man, and was over the hedge in another minute.

But not before Harry was over the railway. For he rode gently towards it, as if nothing particular was to be done, and chose as the best spot one close to where several of the gentlemen stood, disputing for a moment as to which was the best way to get across. Now, on the top of the cutting there was a rail, and between the rail and the edge of the cutting a space of about four feet. Harry trotted his mare gently up to the rail, and went over. Nor was the mutual confidence of mare and master misplaced from either side. She lighted and stood stock still within a foot of the slope, so powerful was she to stop herself. An uproar of cries arose among the men. I heard the old soldier's voice above them all.

" Damn you, Armstrong, you fool ! " he cried ; " you'll break your neck, and serve you right too ! "

I don't know a stronger proof that the classical hell has little hold on the faith of the Saxons, than that good-hearted and true men will not unfrequently damn their friends when they are most anxious to save them. But before the words were half out of the colonel's mouth, Harry was half-way down the cutting. He had gone straight at it, like a cat, and it was of course the only way. I had galloped to the edge after him, and now saw him, or rather her, descending by a succession of rebounds, — not bounds, — a succession, in fact, of short falls upon the fore-legs, while Harry's head was nearly touching her rump. Arrived at the bottom, she gave two bounds across the rails, and the same moment was straining right up the opposite bank in a fierce agony of effort, Harry hanging upon her neck. Now the mighty play of her magnificent hind quarters came into operation. I could see, plainly enough across the gulf, the alternate knotting and loosening of the thick muscles as, step by step, she tore her way up the grassy slope ; it was a terrible trial of muscle and wind, and very few horses could have stood it. As she neared the top, her pace grew slower and slower, and the exertion more and more severe. If she had given in, she would have rolled to the bottom ; but nothing was less in her thoughts. Her master never spurred or urged her, except it may have been by whispering in her ear, to which his mouth was near. enough ; he knew she needed no excitement to that effort. At length the final heave of her rump, as it came up to a level with her withers, told the breathless spectators that the attempt was a success, when a loud "Hurrah for the doctor and his mare!" burst from their lips. The doctor, however, only waved his hand in acknowledgment, for he had all to do yet. Fortunately there was space enough between the edge and the fence on that side to allow of his giving his mare a quarter of a circle of a gallop before bringing her up to the rail, else in her fatigue she might have failed to top it. Over she went and away, with her tail streaming out behind her, as if she had done nothing worth thinking about, once it was done. One more cheer for the doctor; but no one dared to follow him. They scattered in different directions to find a less perilous crossing. I stuck by my leader.

"By Jove! Cathcart," said Lord Irksham, as they parted, "that doctor of yours is a hero. He ought to have been bred a soldier."

"He's better employed, my lord," bawled the old colonel; for they were now a good many yards asunder, making for different points in the hedge. From this answer, I hoped well for the doctor. At all events, the colonel admired his manliness more than ever, and that was a great thing. For me, I could hardly keep down the expression of an excitement which I did not wish to show. It was a great relief to me when the *hurrah!* arose, and I could let myself off in that way. I told you, kind reader, I was only an old boy. But, as the Arabs always give God thanks when they see a beautiful woman, and quite right too, so, in my heart, I praised God who had made a mare with such muscles, and a man with such a heart. And I said to myself, "A fine muscle is a fine thing; but the finest muscle of all, keeping the others going too, is the heart itself. That is the true Christian muscle. And the real muscular Christianity is that which pours in a life-giving torrent from the devotion of the heart, receiving only that it may give."

But I fancy I hear my reader saying:—

"Mr. Smith, you've forgotten the fox. What a sportsman you make!"

Well, I had forgotten the fox. But then we didn't kill him

or find another that day. So you won't care for the rest of the run.

I was tired enough by the time we got back to Purley-bridge. I went early to bed.

The next morning, the colonel, the moment we met at the breakfast table, said to me : —

"You did not hear, Smith, what that young rascal of a doctor said to Lord Irksham last night?"

"No, what was it?"

"It seems they met again towards evening, and his lordship said to him, 'You hare-brained young devil!' — you know his lordship's rough way," interposed the colonel, forgetting how roundly he had sworn at Harry himself, — "'by the time you're my age, you'll be more careful of the few brains you'll have left.' To which expostulation Master Harry replied· 'If your lordship had been my age, you would have done it yourself to kill a fox; when I am your lordship's age, I hope I shall have the grace left to do as much to save a man.' Whereupon his lordship rejoined, holding out his hand, 'By Jove! sir, you are an honor to your profession. Come and dine with me on Monday.' And what do you think the idiot did? — Backed out of it, and wouldn't go, because he thought his lordship condescending, and he didn't want his patronage. But his lordship's not a bit like that, you know."

"Then, if he isn't, he'll like Harry all the better for declining, and will probably send him a proper invitation."

And, sure enough, I was right; and Harry did dine at Castle Irksham on Monday.

Adela's eyes showed clearly enough that her ears were devouring every word we had said; and the glow on her face could not be mistaken by me at least, though to another it might well appear only the sign of such an enthusiasm as one would like every girl to feel in the presence of noble conduct of any kind. She had heard the whole story last night, you may be sure; and I do not doubt that the unrestrained admiration shown by her father for the doctor's conduct was a light in her heart which sleep itself could not extinguish, and which went shining on in her dreams. Admiration of the beloved is dear to a woman. You see I like to show that, although I am an old bachelor, I know something about *them*.

I met Harry that morning; that is, I contrived to meet him.

"Well, how are you to-day, Harry?" I said.

"All right, thank you."

"Were there many hurt at the quarry?"

"Oh! it wasn't so very bad, I'm happy to say."

"You did splendidly yesterday."

"Oh, nonsense! It was my mare. It wasn't me. I had nothing to do with it."

"Well! well! you have my full permission to say so, and to think so too."

"Well! well! say no more about it."

So it was long before the subject was again alluded to by me. But it will be long, too, before it is forgotten in that county.

And so the evening came when we were to meet — for the last time as the Story-telling Club — at the school-master's house. It was now past the time I had set myself for returning to London, and, although my plans were never of a very unalterable complexion, seeing I had the faculty of being able to write wherever I was, and never admitted chairs and tables, and certain rows of bookshelves, to form part of my mental organism, without which the rest of the mechanism would be thrown out of gear, I had yet reasons wishing to be in London; and I intended to take my departure on the day but one after the final meeting. I may just remark, that before this time one or two families had returned to Purley-bridge, and others were free from their Christmas engagements, who would have been much pleased to join our club; but, considering its ephemeral nature, and seeing it had been formed only for what we hoped was a passing necessity, we felt that the introduction of new blood, although essential for the long life of anything constituted for long life, would only hasten the decay of its butterfly constitution. So we had kept our meetings entirely to ourselves.

We all arrived about the same time, and found our host and hostess full of quiet cordiality, to which their homeliness lent an additional charm. The relation of host and guest is weakened by every addition to a company, and in a large assembly all but disappears. Indeed, the tendency of the present age is to blot from the story of every-day life all reminders of the ordinary human relations, as commonplace and insignificant, and to mingle all society in one concourse of atoms, in which the only distinctions shall be those of *rank ;* whereas the sole power to keep social intercourse from growing stale is the recognition of the immortal and true in all the simple human relations. Then we look upon all men with reverence, and find ourselves safe and at home in the midst of divine intents, which may be violated and striven with, but can never be escaped, because the will of God is the very life and well-being of his creatures.

Mrs. Bloomfield looked very nice in her black silk dress, and collar and cuffs of old lace, as she presided at the tea-table, and made us all feel that it was a pleasure to her to serve us.

After repeated apologies, and confessions of failure, our host then read the following *parable,* as he called it, though I dare say it would be more correct to call it an *allegory.* But as that word has so many wearisome associations, I, too, intend, whether right or wrong, to call it a parable. So, then, it shall be

"THE CASTLE: A PARABLE.

" On the top of a high cliff, forming part of the base of a great mountain, stood a lofty castle. When or how it was built, no man knew; nor could any one pretend to understand its architecture. Every one who looked upon it felt that it was lordly and noble ; and where one part seemed not to agree with another, the wise and modest dared not to call them incongruous, but presumed that the whole might be constructed on some higher principle of architecture than they yet understood. What helped them to this conclusion was, that no one had ever seen the whole of the edifice; that, even of the portion best known, some part or other was always wrapped in thick folds of mist from the mountain; and that, when the sun shone upon this mist, the parts of the building that appeared through the vaporous veil were strangely glorified in their indistinctness, so that they seemed to belong to some aerial abode in the land of the sunset; and the beholders could hardly tell whether they had ever seen them before, or whether they were now for the first time partially revealed.

"Nor, although it was inhabited, could certain information be procured as to its internal construction. Those who dwelt in it often discovered rooms they had never entered before; yea, once or twice, whole suites of apartments, of which only dim legends had been handed down from former times. Some of them expected to find, one day, secret places, filled with treasures of wondrous jewels; amongst which they hoped to light upon Solomon's ring, which had for ages disappeared from the earth, but which had controlled the spirits, and the possession of which made a man simply what a man should be, the king of the world. Now and then, a narrow, winding stair, hitherto untrodden, would bring them forth on a new turret, whence new prospects of the circumjacent country were spread out before them. How many more of these there might be, or how much loftier, no one could tell. Nor could the foundations of the castle in the rock on which it was built be determined with the smallest approach to precision. Those of the family who had given themselves to exploring in that direction found such a labyrinth of vaults and passages, and endless successions of down-going stairs, out of one underground space into a yet lower, that they came to the conclusion that at least the whole mountain was perforated and honeycombed in this fashion. They had a dim consciousness, too, of the presence, in those awful regions, of beings whom they could not comprehend. Once, they came upon the brink of a great black gulf, in which the eye could see nothing but darkness; they recoiled with horror; for the conviction flashed upon them that that gulf went down into the very central spaces of the earth, of which they had hitherto been wandering only in the upper crust; nay, that the seething blackness before them had relations mysterious, and beyond human comprehension, with the far-off voids of space, into which the stars dare not enter.

"At the foot of the cliff whereon the castle stood lay a deep lake, inaccessible save by a few avenues, being surrounded on all sides with precipices, which made the water look very black, although it was pure as the night sky. From a door in the castle, which was not to be otherwise entered, a broad flight of steps, cut in the rock, went down to the lake, and disappeared below its surface. Some thought the steps went to the very bottom of the water.

"Now in this castle there dwelt a large family of brothers and sisters. They had never seen their father or mother. The younger had been educated by the elder, and these by an unseen care and ministration, about the sources of which they had, somehow or other, troubled themselves very little, for what people are accustomed to they regard as coming from nobody; as if help and progress and joy and love were the natural crops of Chaos or old Night. But Tradition said that one day — it was utterly uncertain *when* — their father would come, and leave them no more; for he was still alive, though where he lived nobody knew. In the mean time all the rest had to obey their eldest brother, and listen to his counsels.

"But almost all the family was very fond of liberty, as they called it, and liked to run up and down, hither and thither, roving about, with neither law nor order, just as they pleased. So they could not endure their brother's tyranny, as they called it. At one time they said that he was only one of themselves, and therefore they would not obey him; at another, that he was not like them, and could not understand them, and *therefore* they would not obey him. Yet, sometimes, when he came and looked them full in the face, they were terrified, and dared not disobey, for he was stately, and stern, and strong. Not one of them loved him heartily, except the eldest sister, who was very beautiful and silent, and whose eyes shone as if light lay somewhere deep behind them. Even she, although she loved him, thought him very hard sometimes, for when he had once said a thing plainly, he could not be persuaded to think it over again. So even she forgot him sometimes, and went her own ways, and enjoyed herself without him. Most of them regarded him as a sort of watchman, whose business it was to keep them in order; and so they were indignant, and disliked him. Yet they all had a secret feeling that they ought to be subject to him; and after any particular act of disregard, none of them could think, with any peace, of the old story about the return of their father to his house. But, indeed, they never thought much about it, or about their father at all; for how could those who cared so little for their brother, whom they saw every day, care for their father, whom they had never seen? One chief cause of complaint against him was, that he interfered with their favorite studies and pursuits; whereas he only sought to make them give up trifling with earnest things, and seek for truth, and not for amusement, from the many wonders around them. He did not want them to turn to other studies, or to eschew pleasures; but in those studies to seek the highest things most, and other things in proportion to their true worth and nobleness. This could not fail to be distasteful to those who did not care for what was higher than they. And so matters went on for a time. They thought they could do better without their brother, and their brother knew they could not do at all without him, and tried to fulfil the charge committed into his hands.

"At length, one day, for the thought seemed to strike them simultaneously, they conferred together about giving a great entertainment in their grandest rooms to any of their neighbors who chose to come, or indeed to any inhabitants of the earth or air who would visit them. They were too proud to reflect that some company might defile even the dwellers in what was undoubtedly the finest palace on the face of the earth. But what made the thing worse was, that the old tradition said that these rooms were to be kept entirely for the use of the owner of the castle. And, indeed, whenever they entered them such was the effect of their loftiness and grandeur upon their minds, that they always thought of the old story, and could not help believing it. Nor would the brother permit them to forget it now; but, appearing suddenly amongst them, when they had no expectation of being interrupted by him, he rebuked them, both for the indiscriminate nature of their invitation, and for the intention of introducing any one, not to speak of some who would doubtless make their appearance on the evening in question, into the rooms kept sacred for the use of the unknown father. But by this time their talk with each other had so excited their expectations of enjoyment, which had previously been strong enough, that anger sprung up within them at the thought of being deprived of their hopes, and they looked each other in the eyes; and the look said, 'We are many, and he is one; let us get rid of him, for he is always finding fault, and thwarting us in the most innocent pleasures; as if we would wish to do anything wrong!' So, without a word spoken, they rushed upon him; and although he was stronger than any of them, and struggled hard at first, yet they overcame him at last. Indeed, some of them thought he yielded to their violence long before they had the mastery of him; and this very submission terrified the more tender-hearted among them. However, they bound him, carried him down many stairs, and, having remembered an iron staple in the wall of a certain vault, with a thick rusty chain attached to it, they bore him thither, and made the chain fast around him. There they left him, shutting the great gnarring brazen door of the vault, as they departed for the upper regions of the castle.

"Now all was in a tumult of preparation. Every one was talking of the coming festivity; but no one spoke of the deed they had done. A sudden paleness overspread the face, now of one, and now of another; but it passed away, and no one took any notice of it; they only plied the task of the moment the more energetically. Messengers were sent far and near, not to individuals or families, but publishing in all places of concourse a general invitation to any who chose to come on a certain day, and partake, for certain succeeding days, of the hospitality of the dwellers in the castle. Many were the preparations immediately begun for complying with the invitation. But the noblest of their neighbors refused to appear; not from pride, but because of the unsuitableness and carelessness of such a mode. With some of them it was an old condition in the tenure of their estates, that they should go to no one's dwelling except visited in person, and expressly solicited. Others, knowing what sort of persons would be there, and that, from a certain physical antipathy, they could scarcely breathe in their company, made up their minds at once not to go. Yet multitudes, many of them beautiful and innocent as well as gay, resolved to appear.

"Meanwhile the great rooms of the castle were got in readiness, — that is, they proceeded to deface them with decorations; for there was a solemnity and stateliness about them in their ordinary condition which was at once felt to be unsuitable for the light-hearted company so soon to move about in them with the self-same carelessness with which men walk abroad within the great heavens and hills and clouds. One day, while the workmen were busy, the eldest sister, of whom I have already spoken, happened to enter, she knew not why. Suddenly the great idea of the mighty halls dawned upon her, and filled her soul. The so-called decorations vanished from her view, and she felt as if she stood in her father's presence. She was at once elevated and humbled. As suddenly the idea faded and fled, and she beheld but the gaudy festoons and draperies and paintings which disfigured the grandeur. She wept, and sped away. Now it was too late to interfere, and things must take their course. She would have been but a Cassandra-prophetess to those who saw but the pleasure before them. She had not been present when her brother was imprisoned; and indeed for some days had been so wrapped in her own business, that she had taken but little heed of anything that was going on. But they all expected her to show herself when the company was gathered; and they had applied to her for advice at various times during their operations.

"At length the expected hour arrived, and the company assembled. It was a warm summer evening. The dark lake reflected the rose-colored clouds in the west, and through the flush rowed many gayly painted boats, with various colored flags, towards the massy rock on which the castle stood. The trees and flowers seemed already asleep, and breathing forth their sweet dream-breath. Laughter and low voices rose from the breast of the lake to the ears of the youths and maidens looking forth expectant from the lofty windows. They went down to the broad platform, at the top of the stairs in front of the door, to receive their visitors. By degrees the festivities of the evening commenced. The same smiles flew forth, both at eyes and lips, darting like beams through the gathering crowd. Music, from unseen sources, now rolled in billows, now crept in ripples through the sea of air that filled the lofty rooms. And in the dancing halls, when hand took hand, and form and motion were moulded and swayed by the indwelling music, it governed not these alone, but, as the ruling spirit of the place, every new burst of music for a new dance swept before it a new and accordant odor, and dyed the flames that glowed in the lofty lamps with a new and accordant stain. The floors bent beneath the feet of time-keeping dancers. But twice in the evening some of the inmates started, and the pallor occasionally common to the household overspread their faces, for they felt underneath them a counter-motion to the dance, as if the floor rose slightly to answer their feet. And all the time their brother lay below in the dungeon, like John the Baptist in the castle of Herod, when the lords and captains sat around, and the daughter of Herodias danced before them. Outside, all around the castle, brooded the dark night unheeded; for the clouds had come up from all sides, and were crowding together overhead. In the unfrequent pauses of the music, they might have heard, now and then, the gusty rush of a lonely wind, coming and going no one could know whence or whither, born and dying unexpected and unregarded.

"But when the festivities were at their height, when the external and passing confidence which is produced between superficial natures by a common pleasure, was at the full, a sudden crash of thunder quelled the music, as the thunder quells the noise of the uplifted sea. The windows were driven in, and torrents of rain, carried in the folds of a rushing wind, poured into the halls. The lights were swept away; and the great rooms, now dark within, were darkened yet more by the dazzling shoots of flame from the vault of blackness overhead. Those that ventured to look out of the windows saw, in the blue brilliancy of the quick-following jets of lightning, the lake at the foot of the rock, ordinarily so still and so dark, lighted up, not on the surface only, but down to half its depth ; so that, as it tossed in the wind, like a tortured sea of writhing flames, or incandescent, half-molten serpents of brass, they could not tell whether a strong phosphorescence did not issue from the transparent body of the waters, as if earth and sky lightened together, one consenting source of flaming utterance.

"Sad was the condition of the late plastic mass of living form that had flowed into shape at the will and law of the music. Broken into individuals, the common transfusing spirit withdrawn, they stood drenched, cold, and benumbed, with clinging garments; light, order, harmony, purpose, departed and chaos restored ; the issuings of life turned back on their sources, chilly and dead. And in every heart returned that falsest of despairing convictions that this was the only reality, and that was but a dream. The eldest sister stood with clasped hands and down-bent head, shivering and speechless, as if waiting for something to follow. Nor did she wait long. A terrible flash and thunder-peal made the castle rock; and in the pausing silence that followed, her quick sense heard the rattling of a chain far off, deep down; and soon the sound of heavy footsteps, accompanied with the clanking of iron, reached her ear. She felt that her brother was at hand. Even in the darkness, and amidst the bellowing of another deep-bosomed cloud-monster, she knew that he had entered the room. A moment after, a continuous pulsation of angry blue light began, which, lasting for some moments, revealed him standing amidst them, gaunt, haggard, and motionless; his hair and beard untrimmed, his face ghastly, his eyes large and hollow. The light seemed to gather around him as a centre. Indeed, some believed that it throbbed and radiated from his person, and not from the stormy heavens above them. The lightning had rent the wall of his prison, and released the iron staple of his chain, which he had wound about him like a girdle. In his hand he carried an iron fetter-bar, which he had found on the floor of the vault. More terrified at his aspect than at all the violence of the storm, the visitors, with many a shriek and cry, rushed out into the tempestuous night. By degrees, the storm died away. Its last flash revealed the forms of the brothers and sisters lying prostrate, with their faces on the floor, and that fearful shape standing motionless amidst them still.

" Morning dawned, and there they lay, and there he stood. But at a word from him, they arose and went about their various duties, though listlessly enough. The eldest sister was the last to rise; and when she did, it was only by a terrible effort that she was able to reach her room, where she fell again on the floor. There she remained lying for days. The brother caused the doors of the great suite of rooms to be closed, leaving them just as they were, with all the childish adornment scattered about, and the rain still falling in through the shattered windows. 'Thus let them lie,' said he, 'till the rain and frost have cleansed them of paint and drapery; no storm can hurt the pillars and arches of these halls.'

"The hours of this day went heavily. The storm was gone, but the rain was left; the passion had departed, but the tears remained behind. Dull and dark the low, misty clouds brooded over the castle and the lake, and shut out all the neighborhood. Even if they had climbed to the loftiest known turret, they would have found it swathed in a garment of clinging vapor, affording no refreshment to the eye, and no hope to the heart. There was one lofty tower that rose sheer a hundred feet above the rest, and from which the fog could have been seen lying in a gray mass beneath; but that tower they had not yet discovered, nor another close beside it, the top of which was never seen, nor could be, for the highest clouds of heaven clustered continually around it. The rain fell continuously, though not heavily, without; and within, too, there were clouds from which dropped the tears which are the rain of the spirit. All the good of life seemed for the time departed, and their souls lived but as leafless trees that had forgotten the joy of the summer, and whom no wind prophetic of spring had yet visited. They moved about mechanically, and had not strength enough left to wish to die.

"The next day the clouds were higher, and a little wind blew through such loopholes in the turrets as the false improvements of the inmates had not yet filled with glass, shutting out, as the storm, so the serene visitings of the heavens. Throughout the day, the brother took various opportunities of addressing a gentle command, now to one, and now to another of his family. It was obeyed in silence. The wind blew fresher through the loopholes and the shattered windows of the great rooms, and found its way, by unknown passages, to faces and eyes hot with weeping. It cooled and blessed them. When the sun arose the next day, it was in a clear sky.

"By degrees, everything fell into the regularity of subordination. With the subordination came increase of freedom. The steps of the more youthful of the family were heard on the stairs and in the corridors more light and quick than ever before. Their brother had lost the terrors of aspect produced by his confinement, and his commands were issued more gently, and oftener with a smile, than in all their previous history. By degrees, his presence was universally felt through the house. It was no surprise to any one at his studies, to see him by his side, when he lifted up his eyes, though he had not before known that he was in the room. And although some dread still remained, it was rapidly vanishing before the advances of

a firm friendship. Without immediately ordering their labors,
he always influenced them, and often altered their direction
and objects. The change soon evident in the household was
remarkable. A simpler, nobler expression was visible on all
the countenances. The voices of the men were deeper, and
yet seemed by their very depth more feminine than before;
while the voices of the women were softer and sweeter, and at
the same time more full and decided. Now the eyes had often
an expression as if their sight was absorbed in the gaze of the
inward eyes; and when the eyes of two met, there passed between those eyes the utterance of a conviction that both meant
the same thing. But the change was, of course, to be seen
more clearly, though not more evidently, in individuals.

"One of the brothers, for instance, was very fond of
astronomy. He had his observatory on a lofty tower, which
stood pretty clear of the others, towards the north and east.
But, hitherto, his astronomy, as he had called it, had been more
of the character of astrology. Often, too, he might have
been seen directing a heaven-searching telescope to catch the
rapid transit of a fiery shooting-star, belonging altogether to
the earthly atmosphere, and not to the serene heavens. He
had to learn that the signs of the air are not the signs of the
skies. Nay, once his brother surprised him in the act of
examining through his longest tube a patch of burning heath
upon a distant hill. But now he was diligent from morning
till night in the study of the laws of the truth that has to do
with stars; and when the curtain of the sunlight was about to
rise from before the heavenly worlds which it had hidden all
day long, he might be seen preparing his instruments with
that solemn countenance with which it becometh one to look
into the mysterious harmonies of Nature. Now he learned
what law and order and truth are, what consent and harmony
mean; how the individual may find his own end in a higher
end, where law and freedom mean the same thing, and the
purest certainty exists without the slightest constraint. Thus
he stood on the earth, and looked to the heavens.

"Another, who had been much given to searching out the
hollow places and recesses in the foundations of the castle, and
who was often to be found with compass and ruler working
away at a chart of the same which he had been in process of

constructing, now came to the conclusion, that only by ascending the upper regions of his abode could he become capable of understanding what lay beneath; and that, in all probability, one clear prospect, from the top of the highest attainable turret, over the castle as it lay below, would reveal more of the idea of its internal construction than a year spent in wandering through its subterranean vaults. But the fact was, that the desire to ascend wakening within him had made him forget what was beneath; and, having laid aside his chart for a time at least, he was now to be met in every quarter of the upper parts, searching and striving upward, now in one direction, now in another; and seeking, as he went, the best outlooks into the clear air of outer realities.

"And they began to discover that they were all meditating different aspects of the same thing; and they brought together their various discoveries, and recognized the likeness between them; and the one thing often explained the other, and combining with it helped to a third. They grew in consequence more and more friendly and loving; so that every now and then one turned to another and said, as in surprise, 'Why, you are my brother!' — 'Why, you are my sister!' And yet they had always known it.

"The change reached to all. One, who lived on the air of sweet sounds, and who was almost always to be found seated by her harp or some other instrument, had, till the late storm, been generally merry and playful, though sometimes sad. But for a long time after that she was often found weeping, and playing little, simple airs which she had heard in childhood, — backward longings, followed by fresh tears. Before long, however, a new element manifested itself in her music. It became yet more wild, and sometimes retained all its sadness, but it was mingled with anticipation and hope. The past and the future merged in one; and while memory yet brought the rain-cloud, expectation threw the rainbow across its bosom; and all was uttered in her music, which rose and swelled, now to defiance, now to victory, then died in a torrent of weeping.

"As to the eldest sister, it was many days before she recovered from the shock. At length, one day, her brother came to her, took her by the hand, led her to an open window, and told her to seat herself by it, and look out. She did so; but at first saw nothing more than an unsympathizing blaze of sunlight. But as she looked, the horizon widened out, and the dome of the sky ascended, till the grandeur seized upon her soul, and she fell on her knees and wept. Now the heavens seemed to bend lovingly over her, and to stretch out wide cloud-arms to embrace her; the earth lay like the bosom of an infinite love beneath her, and the wind kissed her cheek with an odor of roses. She sprang to her feet, and turned, in an agony of hope, expecting to behold the face of the father; but there stood only her brother, looking calmly, though lovingly, on her emotion. She turned again to the window. On the hill-tops rested the sky: heaven and earth were one; and the prophecy awoke in her soul, that from betwixt them would the steps of the father approach.

"Hitherto she had seen but Beauty; now she beheld truth. Often had she looked on such clouds as these, and loved the strange ethereal curves into which the winds moulded them; and had smiled as her little pet sister told her what curious animals she saw in them, and tried to point them out to her. Now they were as troops of angels, jubilant over her new birth, for they sang, in her soul, of beauty, and truth, and love. She looked down, and her little sister knelt beside her.

"She was a curious child, with black, glittering eyes and dark hair, at the mercy of every wandering wind; a frolicsome, daring girl, who laughed more than she smiled She was generally in attendance on her sister, and was always finding and bringing her strange things. She never pulled a primrose, but she knew the haunts of all the orchis tribe, and brought from them bees and butterflies innumerable, as offerings to her sister. Curious moths and glow-worms were her greatest delight; and she loved the stars, because they were like the glow-worms. But the change had affected her too; for her sister saw that her eyes had lost their glittering look, and had become more liquid and transparent. And from that time she often observed that her gayety was more gentle, her smile more frequent, her laugh less bell-like; and although she was as wild as ever, there was more elegance in her motions, and more music in her voice. And she clung to her sister with far greater fondness than before.

"The land reposed in the embrace of the warm summer days. The clouds of heaven nestled around the towers of the castle, and the hearts of its inmates became conscious of a warm atmosphere, — of a presence of love. They began to feel like the children of a household, when the mother is at home. Their faces and forms grew daily more and more beautiful, till they wondered as they gazed on each other. As they walked in the gardens of the castle, or in the country around, they were often visited, especially the eldest sister, by sounds that no one heard but themselves, issuing from woods and waters; and by forms of love that lightened out of flowers, and grass, and great rocks. Now and then the young children would come in with a slow, stately step, and, with great eyes that looked as if they would devour all the creation, say that they had met the father amongst the trees, and that he had kissed them; 'and,' added one of them once, 'I grew so big!' and when others went out to look they could see no one. And some said it must have been the brother, who grew more and more beautiful, and loving, and reverend, and who had lost all traces of hardness, so that they wondered they could ever have thought him stern and harsh. But the eldest sister held her peace, and looked up, and her eyes filled with tears. 'Who can tell,' thought she, 'but the little children know more about it than we?'

"Often, at sunrise, might be heard their hymn of praise to their unseen father, whom they felt to be near, though they saw him not. Some words thereof once reached my ear through the folds of the music in which they floated, as in an upward snow-storm of sweet sounds. And these are some of the words I heard; but there was much I seemed to hear, which I could not understand, and some things which I understood, but cannot utter again: —

"'We thank thee that we have a father, and not a maker; that thou hast begotten us, and not moulded us as images of clay; that we have come forth of thy heart, and have not been fashioned by thy hands. It *must* be so. Only the heart of a father is able to create. We rejoice in it, and bless thee that we know it. We thank thee for thyself. Be what thou art, — our root and life, our beginning and end, our all in all. Come home to us. Thou livest; therefore we live. In thy light we see. Thou art, — that is all our song.'

"Thus they worship, and love, and wait. Their hope and expectation grow ever stronger and brighter, that one day, ere long, the Father will show himself amongst them, and thenceforth dwell in his own house for evermore. What was once but an old legend has become the one desire of their hearts.

"And the loftiest hope is the surest of being fulfilled."

"Thank you, heartily," said the curate. "I will choose another time to tell you how much I have enjoyed your parable, which is altogether to my mind, and far beyond anything I could do."

Mr. Bloomfield returned no answer, but his countenance showed that he was far from hearing this praise unmoved. The faces of the rest showed that they, too, had listened with pleasure; and Adela's face shone as if she had received more than delight, — hope, namely, and onward impulse. The colonel alone — I forgot to say that Mrs. Cathcart had a headache, and did not come — seemed to have been left behind.

"I am a stupid old fellow, I believe," said he; "but, to tell the truth, I did not know what to make of it. It seemed all the time to be telling me in one breath something I knew, and something I didn't and couldn't know. I wish I could express what I mean, but it puzzled me too much for that; although every now and then it sounded very beautiful indeed."

"I will try and tell you what it said to me, some time, papa," said Adela.

"Thank you, my child; I should much like to understand it. I believe I have done my duty by my king and country, but a man has to learn a good deal after all that is over and done with; and I suppose it is never too late to begin, Mr. Armstrong?"

"On the contrary, I not merely believe that no future time can be so good as the present, but I am inclined to assert that no past time could have been so good as the present. This seems to be a paradox, but I think I could explain it very easily. I find, however, that the ladies are looking as if they wanted to go home, and I am quite ready, Mrs. Armstrong.

But while the ladies put their bonnets on, just let Smith see your school-room, Mr. Bloomfield. As an inhabitant of Purley-bridge, I already begin to be proud of it."

The ladies did go to put on their bonnets. I followed Mr. Bloomfield and the colonel into the school-room, and the curate followed me. But after we had looked about us and remarked on the things about for five minutes, finding I had left my handkerchief in the drawing-room, I went back to fetch it. The door was open, and I saw Adela — no bonnet on her head yet — standing face to face with Harry. They were alone. I hesitated for a moment what I should do, and while I hesitated I could not help seeing the arm of the doctor curved and half-outstretched, as if it would gladly have folded about her, and his face droop and droop, till it could not have been more than half a foot from hers. Now, as far as *my* seeing this was con-cerned, there was no harm done. But behind me came the curate and the school-master, and they had eyes in their heads, at least equal to mine. Well, no great harm yet. And just far enough down the stair to see into the drawing-room, ap-peared their wives, who could not fail to see the unconscious pair, at least as well as we men below. Still there was no great harm done, for Mrs. Cathcart was at home, as I have said. But, *horresco referens !*— excuse the recondite quotation — at the same moment the form of the colonel appeared, looking over the heads of all before him right in at the drawing-room door, and full at the young sinners, who had heard no sound along the matted passage.

"Here's a go !" said I to myself, — not aloud, observe, for it was slang.

For just think of a man like Harry caught thus in a perfect trap of converging looks.

As if from a sudden feeling of hostile presence, he glanced round — and stood erect. The poor fellow's face at once flushed as red as shame could make it; but he neither lost his self-possession, nor sought to escape under cover of a useless pre-tence. He turned to the colonel.

"Colonel Cathcart," he said, "I will choose a more suit-able time to make my apology. I wish you good-night."

He bowed to us all, not choosing to risk a refusal of his hand by the colonel, and went quickly out of the house.

The colonel stood for some seconds, which felt to me like minutes, as if he had just mounted guard at the drawing-room door. His face was perfectly expressionless. We men felt very much like stale oysters, and would rather have skipped that same portion of our inevitable existence. What the ladies felt, I do not pretend, being an old bachelor, to divine.

Adela, pale as death, fled up the stair. The only thing left for the rest of us was to act as much as possible as if nothing were the matter, and get out of the way before the poor girl came down again. As soon as I got home, I went to my own room, and thus avoided the *tête-à-tête* with my host which generally closed our evenings.

The colonel went up to his daughter's room, and remained there for nearly an hour. Adela was not at the breakfast-table the next morning. Her father looked very gloomy, and Mrs. Cathcart grimly satisfied, with *I told you so* written on her face as plainly as I have now written it on the paper. How she came to know anything about it, I can only conjecture.

CHAPTER XXII.

WHAT NEXT?

HARRY called early, and was informed that the colonel was not at home.

"Something's the matter, Mr. Armstrong," said Beeves. "Master's not at home to you to-day, he says, nor any other day till he countermands the order, — that was the word, sir. I'm sure I am very sorry, sir."

"So am I," said Harry. "How's your mistress?"

"Haven't seen her to-day, sir. Emma says she's poorly. But she is down. Emma looks as if she knew something and wouldn't tell it. I'll get it out of her though, sir. We'll be having that old Wade coming about the house again, I'm afeard, sir. *He's* no good."

"At all events you will let your master know that I have

called," said Harry, as he turned, disconsolately, to take his departure.

"That I will, sir. And I'll be sure he hears me. He's rather deaf, sometimes, you know, sir."

"Thank you, Beeves. Good-morning.

Now what could have been Harry's intention in calling upon the colonel? Why, as he had said himself, to make an apology. But what kind of apology could he make? Clearly there was only one that would satisfy all parties; and that must be in the form of a request to be allowed to pay his addresses — (that used to be the phrase in my time; I don't know the young ladies' slang for it nowadays) — to Adela. Did I say — *satisfy all parties?* This was just the one form affairs might take, which would least of all satisfy the colonel. I believe, with all his rigid proprieties, he would have preferred the confession that the doctor had so far forgotten himself as to attempt to snatch a kiss, — a theft of which I cannot imagine a gentleman guilty, least of all a doctor from his patient; which relation no doubt the colonel persisted in regarding as the sole possible and everlastingly permanent one between Adela and Harry. The former was, however, the only apology Harry could make; and evidently the colonel expected it when he refused to see him.

But why should he refuse to see him? The doctor was not on an equality with the colonel. Well, to borrow a form from the Shorter Catechism: Wherein consisted the difference between the colonel and the doctor? The difference between the colonel and the doctor consisted chiefly in this, that whereas the colonel lived by the wits of his ancestors, Harry lived by his own, and therefore was not so respectable as the colonel. Or, in other words: the colonel inherited a good estate, with the ordinary quantity of brains; while Harry inherited a good education, and an extraordinary quantity of brains. So of course it was very presumptuous in Harry to aspire to the hand of Miss Cathcart.

In the forenoon the curate called upon me, and was shown into the library where I was.

"What's that scapegrace brother of mine been doing, Smith?" he asked, the moment he entered.

"Wanting to marry Adela," I replied.

"What has he done?"

" Called this morning."

" And-seen Colonel Cathcart? "

" No."

" Not at home? "

" In a social sense, not at home; in a moral sense, very far from at home; in a natural sense, seated in his own arm-chair, with his own work, on the Peninsular War, open on the table before him."

" Wouldn't see him? "

" No."

" What's he to do, then? "

" I think we had better leave that to him. Harry is not the man I take him for if he doesn't know his own way better than you or I can tell him."

" You're right, Smith.   How's Miss Cathcart? "

" I have never seen her so well.   Certainly she did not come down to breakfast; but I believe that was merely from shyness. She appeared in the dining-room directly after, and, although it was evident she had been crying, her step was as light, and her color as fresh, as her lover even could wish to see them."

" Then she is not without hope in the matter? "

" If she loves him, and I think she does, she is not without hope.   But I do not think the fact of her looking well would be sufficient to prove that.   For some mental troubles will favor the return of bodily health.   They will at least give one an interest in life."

" Then you think her father has given in a little about it? "

" I don't believe it.   If her illness and she were both of an ordinary kind, she would gain her point now by taking to her bed.   But, from what I know of Adela, she would scorn and resist that."

" Well, we must let matters take their course.   Harry is worthy of the best wife in Christendom."

" I believe it.   And more, if Adela will make that best wife, I think he will have the best wife.   But we must have patience."

Next morning, a letter arrived from Harry to the colonel. I have seen it, and it was to this effect: —

" My dear Sir: — As you will not see me, I am forced to

write to you. Let my earnest entreaty to be allowed to address your daughter cover, if it cannot make up for, my inadvertence of the other evening. I am very sorry I have offended you. If you will receive me, I trust you will not find it hard to forget. Yours, etc."

To this the colonel replied: —

" SIR: — It is at least useless, if not worse, to apply for an *ex post facto* permission. What I might have answered, had the courtesies of society been observed, it may be easy for me to determine, but it is useless now to repeat. Allow me to say, that I consider such behavior of a medical practitioner towards a young lady, his patient, altogether unworthy of a gentleman, as every member of a learned profession is supposed to be. I have the honor, etc."

I returned the curate's call, and while we were sitting in his study, in walked Harry with a rather rueful countenance.

" What do you say to that, Ralph?" said he, handing his brother the letter.

" Cool," replied Ralph. " But Harry, my boy, you have given him quite the upper hand of you. How could you be so foolish as kiss the girl there and then?"

" I didn't," said Harry.

" But you did just as bad. You were going to do it."

" I don't think I was. But somehow those great eyes of hers kept pulling and pulling my head, so that I don't know what I was going to do. I remember nothing but her eyes. Suddenly a scared look in them startled me, and I saw it all. Mr. Smith, was it so very dishonorable of me?"

" You are the best judge of that yourself, Harry," I answered. " Just let me look at the note."

I read it, folded it up carefully, and, returning it, said: —

" He's given you a good hold of him there. It is really too bad of Cathcart, being a downright good fellow, to forget that he ran away with Miss Selby, old Sir George, the baronet's daughter. Neither of them ever repented it; though he was only Captain Cathcart then, in a regiment of foot too, and was not even next heir to the property he has now."

"Hurrah!" cried Harry.

"Stop, stop. That doesn't make it a bit better," said his brother. "I suppose you mean to argue with him on that ground, do you?"

"No, I don't. I'm not such a fool. But if I *should* be forced to run away with her, *he* can't complain, you know."

"No, no, Harry, my boy," said I. "That won't do. It would break the old man's heart. You must have patience for a while."

"Yes, yes. I know what I mean to do."

"What?"

"When I've made up my mind, I never ask advice. It only bewilders a fellow."

"Quite right, Hal," said his brother. "Only don't do anything foolish."

"I won't do anything she doesn't like."

"No, nor anything you won't like yourself afterwards," I ventured to say.

"I hope not," returned he, gravely, as he walked out, too much absorbed to bid either of us *good-morning*.

It was now more than time that I should return to town; but I could not leave affairs in this unsatisfactory state. I therefore lingered on to see what would come next.

CHAPTER XXIII.

GENERALSHIP.

THE next day Harry called again.

"Master 'aint countermanded the order, doctor. He aint at home, — not a bit of it. He 'aint been out of the house since that night."

"Well, is Miss Cathcart at home?"

"She's said nothing to the contrairy, sir. I believe she *is* at home. I know she's out in the garding, — on the terridge."

And old Beeves held the door wide open, as if to say, "Don't stop to ask any questions, but step into the garden." Which Harry did.

There was a high gravel terrace along one end of it, always dry and sunny when there was any sun going; and there she was, overlooked by the windows of her papa's room.

Now I do not know anything that passed upon that terrace. How should I know? Neither of them was likely to tell old Smith. And I wonder at the clumsiness of novelists in pretending to reveal all that *he* said, and all that *she* answered. But if I were such a clumsy novelist, I should like to invent it all, and see if I couldn't make you believe every word of it.

This is what I would invent: —

The moment Adela caught sight of Harry, she cast one frightened glance up to her father's windows, and stood waiting. He lifted his hat, and held out his hand. She took it. Neither spoke. They turned together and walked along the terrace.

" I am very sorry," said Harry at last.

" Are you? What for? "

" Because I got you into a scrape."

" Oh! I don't care."

" Don't you? "

" No; not a bit."

" I didn't mean it."

" What didn't you mean? "

" It did look like it, I know."

" Look like what? "

" Adela, you'll drive me crazy. It was all your fault."

" So I told papa, and he was angrier than ever."

" You angel! It wasn't your fault. It was your eyes. I couldn't help it. Adela, I love you dreadfully."

" I'm *so* glad."

She gave a sigh as of relief.

" Why? "

" Because I wished you would. But I don't deserve it. A great clever man like you, love a useless girl like me! I *am* so glad! "

" But your papa? "

" I'm so happy I can't think about him steadily just yet."

" Adela, I love you — so dearly! Only I am too old for you."

" Old! How old are you? "

" Nearly thirty."

" And I'm only one-and-twenty. You're worth one and a half of me, — yes, twenty of me."

And so their lips played with the ripples of love, while their hearts were heaving with the ground swell of its tempest.

Now what I do know about is this : —

The colonel came downstairs in his dressing-gown and slippers, and found Beeves flattening his nose against the glass of the garden-door.

" Beeves ! " said the colonel.

" Sir ! " said Beeves, darting round and confronting his master with a face purple and pale from the sense of utter unpreparedness.

" Beeves, where is your mistress ? "

" My mistress, sir ? I beg your pardon, sir, I'm sure, sir ! How should I know, sir ? I 'aint let her out. Shall I run upstairs and see if she is in her room ? "

" Open the door."

Beeves laid violent hold upon the handle of the door, and pulled and twisted, but always took care to pull before he twisted.

" I declare if that stupid Ann 'aint been and locked it. It aint nice in the garden to day, sir, — leastways without goloshes," added he, looking down at his master's slippers.

Now the colonel understood Beeves, and Beeves knew that he understood him. But Beeves knew likewise that the colonel would not give in to the possibility of his servant's taking such liberties with him.

" Never mind," said the colonel; " I will go the other way."

The moment he was out of sight, Beeves opened the garden-door, and began gesticulating like a madman, fully persuaded that the doctor would make his escape. But so far from being prepared to run away, Harry had come there with the express intention of forcing a conference. So that when the colonel made his appearance on the terrace, the culprits walked slowly towards him. He went to meet them with long military strides, and was the first to speak.

" Mr. Armstrong, to what am I to attribute this intrusion ? "

" Chiefly to the desire of seeing you, Colonel Cathcart."

" And I find you with my daughter ! — Adela, go in-doors."

Adela withdrew at once.

"You denied yourself, and I inquired for Miss Cathcart."

"You will oblige me by not calling again."

"Surely I have committed no fault beyond forgiveness."

"You have taken advantage of your admission into my family to entrap the affections of my daughter."

"Colonel Cathcart, as far as my conscience tells me, I have not behaved unworthily."

"Sir, is it not unworthy of a gentleman to use such professional advantages to gain the favor of one who — you will excuse me for reminding you of what you will not allow me to forget — is as much above him in social position as inferior to him in years and experience."

"Is it always unworthy in a gentleman to aspire to a lady above him in social position, Colonel Cathcart?"

The honesty of the colonel checked all reply to this home-thrust.

Harry resumed : —

"At least I am able to maintain my wife in what may be considered comfort."

"Your wife!" exclaimed the colonel, his anger blazing out at the word. "If you use that expression with any prospective reference to Miss Cathcart, I am master enough in my own family to insure you full possession of the presumption. I wish you good morning."

The angry man of war turned on his slippered heel, and was striding away.

"One word, I beg," said Harry.

The colonel had too much courtesy in his nature not to stop and turn half towards the speaker.

"I beg to assure you," said Harry, "that I shall continue to cherish the hope that after-thoughts will present my conduct, as well as myself, in a more favorable light to Colonel Cathcart."

And he lifted his hat, and walked away by the gate.

"By Jove!" said the colonel to himself, notwithstanding the rage he was in, "the fellow can express himself like a gentleman, anyhow."

And so he went back to his room, where I heard him pacing about for hours. I believe he found that his better self was not to be so easily put down as he had supposed; and that that better self sided with Adela and Harry.

CHAPTER XXIV.

AN UNFORESEEN FORESIGHT.

WHAT else is a Providence?

Harry went about his work as usual, only with a graver face.

Adela looked very sad, but without any of her old helpless and hopeless air. Her health was quite established; and she now returned all the attention her father had paid to her. Fortunately Mrs. Cathcart had gone home.

"Cunning puss!" some of my readers may say; "she was trying to coax the old man out of his resolution." But such a notion would be quite unjust to my niece. She was more in danger of going to the other extreme, to avoid hypocrisy. But she had the divine gift of knowing what any one she loved was feeling and thinking; and she knew that her father was suffering, and all about it. The old man's pace grew heavier; the lines about his mouth grew deeper; he sat at table without speaking; he ate very little, and drank more wine. Adela's eyes followed his every action. I could see that sometimes she was ready to rise and throw her arms about him. Often I saw in her lovely eyes that peculiar clearness of the atmosphere which indicates the nearness of rain. And once or twice she rose and left the room, as if to save her from an otherwise unavoidable exposure of her feelings.

The gloom fell upon the servants too. Beeves waited in a leaden-handed way, that showed he was determined to do his duty, although it should bring small pleasure with it. He took every opportunity of unburdening his bosom to me.

"It's just like when mis'ess died," said he. "The very cocks walk about the yard as if they had hearse-plumes in their tails. Everybody looks ready to hang hisself, except you, Mr. Smith. And that's a comfort."

The fact was, that I had very little doubt as to how it would all end. But I would not interfere; for I saw that it would be much better for the colonel's heart and conscience to right themselves, than that he should be persuaded to anything. It was very hard for him. He had led his regiment to victory and glory; he had charged and captured many a gun; he had driven the enemy out of many a boldly defended entrenchment; and was it not hard that he could not drive the *eidolon* of a country surgeon out of the bosom of his little girl? (It was hard that he could not; but it would have been a deal harder if he could.) He had nursed and loved, and petted and spoiled her. And she *would* care for a man whom he disliked !

But here the old man was mistaken. He did not dislike Harry Armstrong. He admired and honored him. He almost loved him for his gallant devotion to his duty. He would have been proud of him for a son — but not for a son-in-law. He would not have minded adopting him, or doing anything *but* giving him Adela. There was a great deal of pride left in the old soldier, and that must be taken out of him. We shall all have to thank God for the whip of scorpions which, if needful, will do its part to drive us into the kingdom of heaven.

"How happy the dear old man will be," I said to myself, " when he just yields this last castle of selfishness, and walks unhoused into the new childhood of which God takes care ! "

And this end came sooner than I had looked for it.

I had made up my mind that it would be better for me to go.

When I told Adela that I must go, she gave me a look in which lay the whole story in light and in tears. I answered with a pressure of her hand and an old uncle's kiss. But no word was spoken on the subject.

I had a final cigar with the curate, and another with the school-master; bade them and their wives good-by; told them all would come right if we only had patience, and then went to Harry. But he was in the country, and I thought I should not see him again.

With the assistance of good Beeves, I got my portmanteau packed that night. I was going to start about ten o'clock next morning. It was long before I got to sleep, and I heard the step of the colonel, whose room was below mine on the drawing-room floor, going up and down, up and down, all the time, till slumber came at last, and muffled me up. We met at breakfast, a party lugubrious enough. Beeves waited like a mute; the colonel ate his breakfast like an offended parent; Adela trifled with hers like one who had other things to think about; and I ate mine like a parting guest who was being anything but sped. When the post-bag was brought in, the colonel unlocked it mechanically; distributed the letters; opened one with indifference, read a few lines, and with a groan fell back in his chair. We started up, and laid him on the sofa. With the privilege of an old friend, I glanced at the letter, and found that a certain speculation in which the colonel had ventured largely had utterly failed. I told Adela enough to satisfy her as to the nature of the misfortune. We feared apoplexy, but before we could send for any medical man he opened his eyes and called Adela. He clasped her to his bosom, and then tried to rise, but fell back helpless.

"Shall we send for Dr. Wade?" said Adela, trembling and pale as death.

"Dr. Wade!" faltered the old man, with a perceptible accent of scorn.

"Which shall we send for?" I said.

"How can you ask?" he answered, feebly. "Harry Armstrong, of course."

The blood rushed into Adela's white face, and Beeves rushed out of the room. In a quarter of an hour, Harry was with us. Adela had retired. He made a few inquiries, administered some medicine he had brought with him, and, giving orders that he should not be disturbed for a couple of hours, left him with the injunction to keep perfectly quiet.

"Take my traps up to my room again, Beeves; and tell the coachman he won't be wanted this morning."

"Thank you, sir," said Beeves. "I don't know what we should do without you, sir."

When Harry returned, we carried the colonel up to his own room, and Beeves got him to bed. I said something about a nurse, but Harry said there was no one so fit to nurse him as Adela. The poor man had never been ill before; and I dare say he would have been very rebellious, had he not had a great trouble at his heart to quiet him. He was as submissive as could be desired.

I felt sure he would be better as soon as he had told Adela. I gave Harry a hint of the matter, and he looked very much as if he would shout "Oh, jolly!" but he did not.

Towards the evening, the còlonel called his daughter to his bedside, and said : —

"Addie, darling, I have hurt you dreadfully."

"Oh, no, dear papa; you have not. And it is so easy to put it all right, you know," she added, turning her head away a little.

"No, my child," he said, in a tone full of self-reproach, "nobody can put it right. I have made us both beggars, Addie, my love."

"Well, dearest papa, you can bear a little poverty surely?"

"It's not of myself I am thinking, my darling. Don't do me that injustice, or I shall behave like a fool. It's only you I am thinking of."

"Oh, is that all, papa? Do you know that, if it were not for your sake, I could sing a song about it?"

"Ah! you don't know what you make so light of. Poverty is not so easy to endure."

"Papa," said Adela, solemnly, "if you knew how awful things looked to me a little while ago, — but it's all gone now! — the whole earth black and frozen to the heart, with no God in it, and nothing worth living for, — you would not wonder that I take the prospect of poverty with absolute indifference, — yes, if you will believe me, with something of a strange excitement. There will be something to battle with and beat."

And she stretched out a strong, beautiful white arm, from which the loose open sleeve fell back, as if with that weapon of might she would strike poverty to the earth; but it was only to adjust the pillow which had slipped sideways from the loved head.

"But Mr. Armstrong will not want to marry you now, Addie."

"Oh, won't he?" thought Adela; or at least I think she thought so. But she said, rather demurely, and very shyly : —

"But that won't be any worse than it was before; for you would never have let me marry him anyhow."

"Oh, yes, I would, in time, Adela. I am not such a brute as you take me for."

"O you dear, darling papa!" cried the poor child, and burst into tears, with her head on her father's bosom. And he began comforting her so sweetly, that you would have thought she had lost everything, and he was going to give her all back again.

"Papa! papa!" she cried, "I will work for you; I will be your servant; I will love you and love you to all eternity. I won't leave you. I won't indeed. What *does* it matter for the money?"

At this moment the doctor entered.

"Ah!" he said, "this won't do at all. I thought you would have made a better nurse, Miss Adela. There you are, both crying together!"

"Indeed, Mr. Henry," said Adela, rather comically, "it's not my fault. He would cry."

And as she spoke she wiped away her own tears.

"But he's looking much better, after all," said Harry. "Allow me to feel your pulse."

The patient was pronounced much better; fresh orders were given, and Harry took his leave.

But Adela felt vexed. She did not consider that he knew nothing of what had passed between her father and her. To the warm fireside of her knowledge he came in wintry and cold. Of course it would never do for the doctor to aggravate his patient's symptoms by making love to his daughter; but ought he not to have seen that it was all right between them now? How often we feel and act as if our mood where the atmosphere of the world! It may be a cold frost within us when our friend is in the glow of a summer sunset; and we call him unsympathetic and unfeeling. If we let him know the state of our world, we should see the rose-hues fade from his, and our friend put off his singing robes, and sit down with us in sackcloth and ashes, to share our temptation and grief.

"You see I cannot offer you to him now, Adela," said her father.

"No, papa."

But I knew that all had come right, although I saw from Adela's manner that she was not happy about it.

So things went on for a week, during which the colonel was slowly mending. I used to read him to sleep. Adela would sit by the fire, or by the bedside, and go and come while I was reading.

One afternoon, in the twilight, Harry entered. We greeted, and then, turning to the bed, I discovered that my friend was asleep. We drew towards the fire, and sat down. Adela had gone out of the room a few minutes before.

"He is such a manageable patient!" I said.

"Noble old fellow!" returned the doctor. "I wish he would like me, and then all would be well."

"He doesn't dislike you personally," I said.

"I hope not. I can understand his displeasure perfectly, and repugnance too. But I assure you, Mr. Smith, I did not lay myself out to gain her affections. I was caught myself before I knew. And I believe she liked me, too, before she knew."

"I fear their means will be very limited after this."

"For his sake I am very sorry to hear it; but, for my own, I cannot help thinking it the luckiest thing that could have happened."

"I am not so sure of that. It might increase the difficulty."

At this moment I thought I heard the handle of the door move, but there was a screen between us and it. I went on.

"That is, if you still want to marry her, you know."

"Marry her!" he said. "If she were a beggar-maid, I would be proud as King Cophetua, to marry her to-morrow."

There was a rustle in the twilight, and a motion of its gloom. With a quick gliding, Adela drew near, knelt beside Harry, and hid her eyes on his knee. I thought it better to go.

Was this unmaidenly of her?

I say "No, for she knew that he loved her."

As I left the room, I heard the colonel call:—

"Adela."

And when I returned, I found them both standing by the bedside, and the old man holding a hand of each.

"Now, John Smith," I said to myself, "you may go when you please."

Before we, that is, I and my reader, part, however, my reader may be inclined to address me thus : —

"Pray, Mr. Smith, do you think it was your wonderful prescription of story-telling that wrought Miss Cathcart's cure ?"

"How can I tell ?" I answer. "Probably it had its share. But there were other things to take into the account. If you went on to ask me whether it was not Harry's prescriptions ; or whether it was not the curate's sermons ; or whether it was not her falling in love with the doctor ; or whether even her father's illness and the loss of their property had not something to do with it ; or whether it was not the doctor's falling in love with her ; or that the cold weather suited her, — I should reply in the same way to every one of the interrogatories."

But I retort another question : —

"Did you ever know anything whatever resulting from the operation of one separable cause ?"

In regard to any good attempt I have ever made in my life, I am content to know that the end has been gained. Whether *I* have succeeded or not is of no consequence, if I have tried well. In the present case, Adela recovered ; and my own conviction is that the cure was effected mainly from within. Except in physics, we can put nothing to the *experimentum crucis*, and must be content with conjecture and probability.

The night before I left I had a strange dream. I stood in a lonely cemetery in a pine forest. Dark trees, that never shed their foliage, rose all around, — strange trees that mourn forever, because they never die. The dreamlight that has no visible source, because it is in the soul that dreams, showed all in a dim blue-gray dawn, that never grew clearer. The night wind was the only power abroad save myself. It went with slow, intermitting, sigh-like gusts, through the tops of the dreaming trees ; for the trees seemed, in the midst of my dream, to have dreams of their own.

Now this burial-place was mine. I had tended it for years. In it lay all the men and women whom I had honored and loved.

And I was a great sculptor. And over every grave I had

placed a marble altar, and upon every altar the marble bust of the man or woman who lay beneath; each in the supreme beauty which all the defects of birth, and of time, and of incompleteness could not hide from the eye of the prophetic sculptor. Each was like a half-risen glorified form of the being who had there descended into the realms of Hades. And through these glimmering rows of the dead I walked in the dreamlight; and from one to another I went in the glory of having known and loved them; now weeping sad tears over the loss of the beautiful; now rejoicing in the strength of the mighty; now exulting in the love and truth which would yet dawn upon me when I, too, should go down beneath the visible, and emerge in the realms of the actual and the unseen. All the time I was sensible of a wondrous elevation of being, a glory of life and feeling hitherto unknown to me.

I had entered the secret places of my own hidden world by the gate of sleep, and walked about them in my dream.

Gradually I became aware that a foreign sound was mingling with the sighing of the tree-tops overhead. It grew and grew, till I recognized the sound of wheels, — not of heavenly chariots, but of earthly motion and business. I heard them stop at the lofty gates of my holy place, and by twos and threes, or in solitary singleness, came people into my garden of the dead. And who should they be but the buried ones? — all those whose marble busts stood in ghostly silence, within the shadows of the everlasting pines. And they talked, and laughed, and jested. And my city of the dead melted away. And lo! we stood in the midst of a great market-place; and I knew it to be the market-place in which the children had sat, who said to the other children : —

"We have piped unto you, and ye have not danced; we have mourned unto you, and ye have not lamented."

And to my misery, I saw that the faces of my fathers and brothers, my mothers and sisters, had not grown nobler in the country of the dead, in which I had thought them safe and shining. Cares, as of this world, had so settled upon them, that I could hardly recognize the old likeness; and the dim forms of the ideal glory, which I had reproduced in my marble busts, had vanished altogether. Ah me! my world of the

dead! my city of treasures, hid away under the locks and bars
of the unchangeable! Was there then no world of realities?
— only a Vanity Fair, after all? The glorious women went
sweeping about, smiling and talking, and buying and adorning,
but they were glorious no longer; for they had common thoughts,
and common beauties, and common language, and aims, and
hopes; and everything was common about them. And ever
and anon, with a kind of shiver, as if to keep alive my misery
by the sight of my own dreams, the marble busts would glimmer out, faintly visible amidst the fair, as if about to reap-
pear, and, dispossessing the vacuity of folly, assert the noble
and the true, and give me back my dead to love and worship
once more, in the loneliness of the pine-forest. Side by side
with a greedy human face would shimmer out for a moment the
ghostly marble face; and the contrast all but drove me mad
with perplexity and misery.

"Alas!" I cried, "where is my future? Where is my
beautiful death?"

All at once I saw the face of a man who went round and
round the skirts of the market, and looked earnestly in amongst
the busy idlers. He was head and shoulders taller than any
there; and his face was a pale face, with an infinite future in
it, visible in all its grief. I made my way through the crowd,
which regarded me with a look which I could not understand,
and came to the stranger. I threw myself at his feet and
sobbed: "I have lost them all. I will follow thee." He
took me by the hand, and led me back. We walked up and
down the fair together. And as we walked, the tumult lessened
and lessened. They made a path for us to go, and all eyes
were turned upon my guide. The tumult sank, and all was
still. Men and women stood in silent rows. My guide looked
upon them all, on the right and on the left. And they all
looked on him till their eyes filled with tears. And the old
faces of my friends grew slowly out of the worldly faces, until
at length they were such as I had known of yore.

Suddenly they all fell upon their knees, and their faces
changed into the likeness of my marble faces. Then my guide
waved his hand — and lo! we were in the midst of my garden
of the dead; and the wind was like the sound of a going in

the tops of the pine trees; and my white marbles glimmered, glorified on the altars of the tombs. And the dream vanished, and I came awake.

And I will not say here, whose face the face of my guide was like

THE END.